COURTING DEATH AND DESTRUCTION

EMILY SHORE

COURTING DEATH AND DESTRUCTION

Book One of the *Death and Destruction Series*

Copyright © 2023 Emily Shore
emilybethshore.info

All rights reserved. No part of this publication may be reproduced, distributed, or transmitted in any form or by any means, including photocopying, recording, or other electronic or mechanical methods, without the prior written permission of the publisher, except in the case of brief quotations embodied in critical reviews and certain other noncommercial uses permitted by copyright law.

This book is a work of fiction. Names, characters, places, and incidents are either products of the author's imagination or are used fictitiously. Any resemblance to actual persons, living, dead or otherwise, events, or locales is entirely coincidental.

Cover Design by
Molly Phipps of We've Got You Covered Design
Interior Design by
Kate Seger

OTHER WORKS BY EMILY SHORE

POST 2020 AUTHOR JOURNEY:
Kidnapped by the Krampus (**#1 Amazon Bestseller/Top 100**) – **Roars and Romances Series Standalone**
Captured by the Cupid – **January/2024** – **Roars and Romances Series #2 Standalone**
Bride of the Corpse King – Book One (Kindle Vella Bestseller – Now on KU)

Hell's Angel Series
Bride of Lucifer: Hell on Earth – Book One (Kindle Vella Bestseller – Now on KU)
Bride of Lucifer: The Bride Trials – Book Two (Kindle Vella Bestseller – Now on KU)
Bride of Lucifer: Mate of Destruction – Book Three (Kindle Vella Bestseller – Now on KU))

Her Monstrous Boys Series
The Sacrifice (Kindle Vella Bestseller/Trending on KU Kindle Top 100 New Release/Dragons)
The Surrender (Kindle Vella Bestseller/Trending on KU/Kindle Top 100 New Release/Dragons)

The Death and Destruction Series (Emily's Baby)
Courting Death and Destruction (Kindle Vella bestseller/Vella Grand Prize Contest Winner – Now on KU)
Tempting Death and Destruction (Brand new to KU)
Hunting Death and Destruction (Coming to KU 4/24)
Redeeming Death and Destruction (Coming to KU 7/24)

Kindle Vella Original Works
Bride of the Shifter King – (Kindle Vella Bestseller), *The Grymm Beauty* (Kindle Vella Bestseller)
Find all of Emily's Kindle Vella works where she rebranded after finding her voice* * *

PRE 2020 AUTHOR JOURNEY:
The Uncaged Series – temporarily unavailable
The Roseblood Series - Shifting to KU in 2024
The Flesh and Ash Series
Flesher – Book One, *Flesher: Resurrection* – Book Two (WIP)

To the person I was before I wrote these books. I'm learning to be kind to you when you were suppressed and validating your journey to your calling: writing dark romantasy.

Sidenote: *For anyone who must hide their true identity but feels it deep inside, my empath heart goes out to you. I hope you will find your safe space, your support system, and your beautiful voice as I did. This book brought me healing, my author voice, and the courage to show my identity. I hope you may find healing on this journey as I did...*

PLAYLIST

(I wrote this 3 years ago, so cut me some slack for giving you the YouTube playlist vs. Spotify)

ELYSIA'S THEME:
"I'm Not An Angel" by Halestorm
NEO'S THEME:
"Angel" by Theory of a Deadman
BOTH:
"You Raise Me Up" by Josh Groban
GENERAL:
"My Heart is Broken" by Evanescence
"October" by Evanescence (Trauma aka Noralice chapter song)
"Halo" by Beyonce
"My Immortal" by Evanescence
"Imaginary" by Evanescence (For Elysia's lair)
"Take me to Church" by Hozier
"Drops of Jupiter" by Train
"Lips of an Angel" by Hinder

"Broken" by Seether/Amy Lee
"U + Ur Hand" by Pink
"Inside Out" by Emmy Rossum
"Stay" by Emmy Rossum
"Listen to Your Heart" Roxette Cover
"Evermore" (Disney's *Beauty and the Beast*) Jonathan Young rock cover
"What Hurts the Most" by State of Mine (Rascal Flatts Rock Cover)

Once upon a time, the Princess went to the tower to kill the Dragon. She saved him instead.

WANT TO SEE MORE SPECIAL ART?
SUPPORT ON KINDLE VELLA *KICKSTARTER*:

Art by Clever Crow on IG

While I originally wrote Courting Death and Destruction before Kindle Vella, I brought it to the platform where it joined the bestseller rank next to *The Sacrifice* and *Bride of Lucifer*. It also won the championship round for the Kindle Vella Summer Madness!

What is Kindle Vella? Amazon's new serialized fiction platform.

Why? It helped me rebrand myself and kept our family afloat through 2021 and 2022 with my husband's cancer and all my chronic health issues.

How? Please consider voting for any of my books on Kindle Vella and supporting me as an author. The minimum to vote aka **Top Fave** is less than $2.00 a month via tokens. Consider it like a Kickstarter since it enables me to bring my books to paperback!

PERKS: ALL my Vella supporters get exclusive super fan group perks like the art above and **UNCENSORED NSFW art**, voting rights, spicy bonus scenes, and even advanced chapters! If you Top Fave, message me, so I can show you how and so you can get the perks. I'd love to send you an art postcard as a thank you, too!

PROs: NO signup. NO subscription. NO app download.

CONs: Only for USA. (It's OK! Radish or Ream supporters still get the perks!

Learn more at Emily Shore's Reader Court on Facebook: a public group where I share fun memes, teasers, games, and giveaways.

Please follow my TikTok: @authoremilybshore and my IG: @emilybshore.

MAP OF THE COURT O' NINES

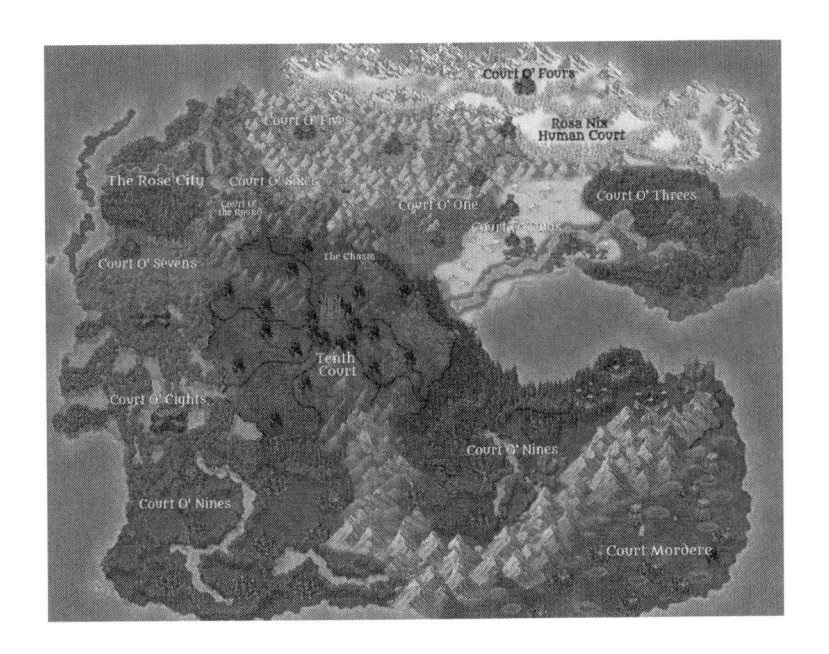

Author's Note: Mental Health/Content Warning
PLEASE READ

Courting Death and Destruction was birthed from a dark place, but it turned into the most beautiful book. I channeled *my* trauma into the main healing scene. I did this *symbolically*, with non-graphic details. I hope you will respect my raw and beautiful journey that brought healing to my heart and my sisterhood community. Dark trauma scenes are related by the protagonist but written with emotion and intimacy. There is a light beyond the darkness, I promise you this.

It's NOT your typical fantasy book. This book is character-driven, focusing on the heart and soul and relationships—namely the romance.

Elysia does NOT pick up a sword or go to war, conquer some big trial, or lead a rebellion—not in this book. She wears dresses more than leggings. She fights for those she loves, but she is not a warrior. If I summed up Elysia in one word, it would be a *healer*. She is also a princess, a smuggler, a witty feminist, a proud bisexual, and a friend.

All LGBTQIA+ identities are normalized and accepted.

P.S. I did a little F U to purity culture in one chapter. I stayed true to my voice and background and how the social construct of "virginity" has no bearing on one's sexual empowerment or physical confidence. All women and their stories should be validated.

DID NOTE:

One significant character, not the protagonist, has the mental health condition of Dissociative Identity Disorder. What is known as a DID systems. This used to be called Multiple Personality Disorder. It is negatively stereotyped in society. As someone who has DID friends, including sensitivity readers, they are worthy of profound respect. And their alters.

This may be difficult to understand, but one must accept the alters as separate identities from the original known as the Host. Alters are not manifestations of the Host's imagination. They are not spirits or ghosts. They are their own entities, who rise, for many, during extreme trauma periods. They exist to help the Host cope with the trauma. Examples of alters include the Internal Systems Helper, the sexual alter, the protector, the trauma alter, child alters, and more.

DID systems individuals are not broken. Their alters are not broken. You will meet multiple alters over the series. For the sake of this book and inspired by a DID systems friend, I feature the hypersexual alter most as she was the first I met in real life. And full of life herself!

I ask people to keep an open mind, to separate the alters from their Host, and to respect the beauty of these survivors. And to research if you want to learn more. Extreme trauma is referenced in this book but not shown while accompanied by overcoming and healing.

Thank you for reading these valuable notes! I appreciate it!

PROLOGUE
REINA

Ninety-Six Years Ago

This series was "technically" a spin-off of my *Roseblood* Series. You do **NOT** need to read *Roseblood* to understand *Courting Death and Destruction*. The Prologue simply offers a *foundation* through the eyes of the protagonist's mother, the origins of this world, and how the Halo came to be. **Please read the MENTAL HEALTH NOTE before this.**

"I will make you a deal, Your Highness," the Father of Vampires crooned while circling me.

Hunger dilated his pupils as his power prickled the hairs on the back of my neck.

On each side of him stood his sons: Thanatos, Prince of Death, and Neoptolemus, the Prince of Destruction. With the Father of Vampires, they comprised an omnipotent force responsible for the greatest wars and genocides. If I didn't stop him, he would unleash another Dark Age upon the world.

I stiffened from Neoptolemus, Prince of Destruction, the

youngest son, who licked his lips, fangs coated in the blood of my *people*. Under the eager eye of his damned Father, the destructive warlord had made my city his personal playground, waging war against my people because we protected bitten vampires as well as born. Not to mention werewolves. And I'd played with him for too long.

Ever since that fateful night of my 18th birthday when my powers awoke following my blood sacrifice, I was considered the Father's greatest challenger. My blood didn't turn to ice at the memory. Not when it was the most redemptive moment of my past.

Not when it saved the man I loved.

Tears burned in my throat as the Father meandered toward Raoul. No matter how I'd woven a telekinetic shield around my fiancé, it wouldn't stop the Father. Like me, he was a Creator. The ancestor of my blood, he could bring forth any power he desired, but he had centuries of experience.

In moments, he annihilated the shield. My heart slammed against my chest, but I could barely lurch. Thanatos gripped my wrist, drew me to himself, so my back crashed against his chest while his destructive brother smirked to one side and stalked toward the two of us.

Seething, I brandished my flames—hot enough to match the younger Prince while his fiendish shades curled around my body. Enough to give me an inch.

"I won't tell you again, Father..." I spat out the word, approaching him and hissing, "No deals. No bargains. Get the hell out of my city. As long as I still hold breath, I will never become your weapon."

I'd had enough. Enough of the Prince of Destruction's games. Enough of Thanatos breathing down my neck. Enough of the Father forcing my people to battle in gladiator games for his pleasure.

What the Father did next stole all the breath from my lungs. He drew his palm to his mouth and sliced a clean line with his fang, spilling his blood. A sign, a precursor to a blood oath. "I vow to you, Reina Caraway, Queen of Le Couvènte, I will leave your city with my sons and never return. I will spare all within it from wolf to bitten vampire. You will never need to see my face again, though I'm certain our paths will certainly cross."

"What do you fucking want?" I demanded, stepping toward him, prepared to unleash any of my Creator powers. If it took a cataclysmic battle, I'd release the energy of the earth itself. I'd form craters, I'd bring forth a volcanic eruption, I'd shift the tide and the gravity of the moon itself if it meant he'd leave my city and the rest of my family, the man I loved, who needed to be spared above all, alone.

"All I desire is your blood," the Father declared, extending his palm to me. "To show my generosity, I will even spare your self-sacrificial paramour," he added with a chuckle, throwing his chin toward Raoul.

My heart faltered at the sight of the bitten vampire on his knees. I gazed at his dark eyes, dark skin, and the dark locks I loved that eclipsed his cheeks. My most loyal and faithful of all guardians. The man who loved and cherished me above all. The man who had shed his blood for me would lay his soul down upon an altar if it allowed me to draw one more breath. The first thing he did was shake his head. Because of what this meant.

Giving up my life force, my essence, my roseblood of my own free will meant the Father would have all-consuming control over me, body, mind, heart, and soul. I would sign my own death warrant. It would be my soul upon an altar. My sacrifice.

I took one step forward.

I closed the distance between the Father and myself, slit a line in my palm, and crashed it against his.

In that single moment of the blood bond, of this otherworldly and almighty oath, a blade pierced my heart with the pain of ten thousand burning suns. A blade to end all blades. A blade to silence the stars themselves.

Not a scythe of Destruction. A sickle...of Death.

As Thanatos whispered his cold-as-death words into my ear, I smiled at Raoul with nothing but warmth growing inside me, "Long live the Queen!"

He gripped the hilt of the blade and wrenched it from my body. My smile grew when Raoul caught me. It wasn't the first time my blood had soaked his hands. But it was the first time my heart stopped beating. It was the first time my soul shook loose from my body.

Angels gathered me into their arms. And the one who gave me this Creator power, this Mother Goddess, gazed down at me and proclaimed, "Queen Reyna Rose, Creator-gifted, your time has not ended. You will return to the City of the Rose." I shuddered from the prophetic voice with the power to rewrite the stars. "You will bear a child. A child who will carry the gift of the Halo inside her heart."

I knelt before the heavenly host and boldly gazed into their eyes, as fathomless and blinding as a hundred solar eclipses. An earthquake seized my soul.

The Goddess echoed, "You will call her Elysia, for she will walk the realms of the dead. Her Haloed heart will end the Father of Vampires. She will be known as the Everblood."

Yes, my heart and soul ignited with the vow. A new child of prophecy, of destiny, far more powerful than I ever could be.

With the message of what I would do next like a Goddess-whisper within my being, I obeyed.

I returned. My soul escaped the bonds of the Prince of Death.

I rose. With the light of ten thousand dawns, I stood, spun around, stole the blade coated in my own blood from his hands. Instead, I swung it in the most supreme arc. The Father's scream was enough to rattle the moon and snuff the light of the stars when I cut off the head of Thanatos, of Death itself.

I dropped the sword as the head tumbled to the ground and landed before the very boots of the Prince of Destruction. I braced myself, waiting for the wrath of the youngest Prince's flames and shades to consume me. Instead, his eyes darkened... and widened in shock, in awe at the demise of his older brother.

The Triumvirate was broken. The Father's power was broken.

"Now...Father," I addressed the origin of all vampires. With the image of my future daughter emblazoned like a sign and seal within me, I forged a new path of rebirth and resurrection and proclaimed, "It is time for a *new* deal."

I
"THE LANNISTERS SEND THEIR REGARDS."

A BONE-DEEP CHILL HOWLS UP MY SPINE AS I SHUFFLE OVER GRIT AND broken glass, press against the stone wall ruins, and peer through the cracks at the Sevens blood farm two hundred yards away. This is my fifth night. By now, I've memorized the overseers' patterns and guard shifts, and I've stolen the schedule for any visiting blood masters.

Nervous energy rattles the very blood in my veins.

A small human skull brushes my boot.

My chest spasms. The empath in me nearly shatters the delicate armor protecting my three-sizes-too-big heart.

Refusing to fall apart, I fall to my knees and say a prayer for mercy over the lost soul. The ruins are echoes, remnants of the early days when vampires rose to power under the all-powerful rule of their *Father* and established their courts and *farms*.

The world isn't too different. It's simply darker with more blood magic and technology that...well *seems* like magic. And the geography, of course. We had no choice but to adjust to the supernatural when that spawn of Satan and his followers emerged.

Sucking a deep inhale, I steel myself, clenching my muscles.

Still-breathing children are waiting for me.

It's my last chance to get two little ones out before they're shipped to a court for a blood banquet. The kind where tots are considered a delicacy and served live on silver platters to elite vampires who pay a higher price to feed.

Some survive.

Some don't.

Scooting aside the skull, I dip my fingers into layers of bone powder, remind myself to breathe, and try not to imagine the souls this skeletal dust once belonged to. I coat my skin and cape, spreading the powder along my face, my neck...even my curls to help cover my scent.

After, I thank the lost souls.

Bless the living, Elysia. Lament the dead. I hear Mom's voice inside my head.

The Phoenix Queen is the only monarch who has survived the last ninety-five years of the Father's reign. Infinite and boundless, Mom's Creator magic keeps our borders strong, and our city hidden. It's the only kingdom that hasn't fallen to the Father's continental-wide realm: the Court O' Nines.

A deep ache throbs in my chest as I remember reading about the violence and bloodshed that followed. Especially when he opened the gateway to the Underworld, the Chasm as we call it now.

It was a stroke of dictatorial genius when the Father shifted the tectonic plates, returning Earth to a Pangea-like state. He then instituted his "Court" realms, transforming the world into his personal playground, alongside his son, Neoptolemus, the Prince of Destruction. Thanks to the Prince's power rendering once-sprawling cities into ruins like this, the Father built his empire.

Now, he sends Neoptolemus to execute whomever he desires—rebels, traitors, or the Prince's failed brides.

One person, alone, is prophesied to end his reign. The Everblood. Lucky me.

The web of emotions inside me tangles more. My heart teeters on the edge of lament from the ghosts of those brides haunting it. I don't know any of their names, but the weight of their corpses burdens me nonetheless. My blood congeals at the memory of the Prince's countless wedding announcement reels. A prompt execution for each bride follows not long after.

What I wouldn't give to stake him...or his prick tick of a son.

The Father and his Prince want nothing more than to see the Phoenix Queen's daughter enter the Bridal Path. One reason I wear a hood and have a sexy renegade of an alter ego.

A cold wind murmurs along my back, interrupting my thoughts just in time to make out the vampire overseers combing the nearby woods a hundred feet away.

Shit!

They should be back at the farm by now, not suspending more bones from trees to spread warnings to escapees...or smugglers. One approaches my hiding place, and I cover my quivering breath, hoping Echo won't ping my earpiece.

Soft breaths of wind rattle the bones, transforming them into ominous, organic windchimes as if warning me.

Fear clots my stomach.

I bite my tongue while raking my gloved fingers into the gritty stone until they hurt.

No fangs will get close to your throat again.

My hands long to rub the invisible marks on my skin. They

may be three-year-old scars, but healing the mind takes far longer than the body.

The overseer flares his nostrils, scenting the air, scenting *me*.

Cursing my "heaven-scented" blood, as my father dubs it, I lower my trembling fingers to my belt of weapons. Maybe Echo will arrive in time to see me tasing the overseer like last time.

Barbecued vampire balls, I chuckle at our inside joke.

Instead, my fingertips settle on one of the iron stakes.

I smirk. It may be a felony punishable by death, but staking a vampire would be a birthday treat to add to my long list of outlaw crimes.

At least the waning moon bows to the shadows, permitting them to hide me.

The overseer crosses the border into the ruins, and my racing pulse stumbles when my heart skips a beat.

He sniffs the air a second time.

I retrieve the stake, mentally preparing myself when he snaps his head back to the farm entrance. Mumbling incoherent words, he returns with the others, their thin wings skittering behind them.

Relief rushes through me.

I turn back to the farm as they release the 'prisoners'.

Prisoners.

I spit out the term and correct myself.

Blood slaves.

"Lys Spirit to Echo," I signal my girlfriend through my earpiece.

"Echo to Spirit."

I can almost picture Echo's sharp emerald eyes and obsidian black hair bound in a sleek ponytail to keep it out of her piercing gaze.

"Any sightings?" Her lilting voice stops my wandering thoughts.

"I'm about to head out. Be ready"

Pain bursts in my finger as I push off the wall. I gasp at the rusty nail piercing my glove. A tiny teardrop of gold blood oozes down my finger.

Guess I spoke too soon.

I cringe at the anomaly of my gold 'holier than thou' blood. A sign of my heavenly heritage, the 'oh, so blessed' birth gift from the Goddess. And the reason for that corpse-host weight upon my heart.

"Spirit, you gasped. Are you hurt?" Asks my protector.

"I'm fine." I scramble to remove the glove and dip the wound in bone powder stemming the scent.

Can't have any slick ticks coming for my pure gold blood.

At least I'm not shedding glittery stardust or glowing...

Yet.

"Tell me the truth. The last thing we need is you glowing like last week."

Of course, she would bring that up. It wasn't my fault the damned Halo sparked giving away my location. I was on a high after smuggling two tots and three older children from the Court O' Eights farm.

I roll my eyes. "I'm *not* glowing. That was a glitch."

"And the week before when you shed stardust?"

Caging a groan, I wrinkle my nose.

"That treasonous cheerio will *not* betray me tonight, Echo. I won't fail these kids."

Up until the past week, I'd managed to suppress that bitch of a destiny bangle in my chest. The Halo as Mom calls it: a one-way Goddess telegram. The Goddess made me her mortal "angel" and didn't even have the decency to give me wings.

As if overhearing, the sentient device around my heart spits embers from my ungloved palm.

"Stick it where the sun don't shine," I hiss, shoving my hand into the glove, smothering the sparks.

"Hurry, Lys," Echo urges. "If you don't make it to your birthday party on time, your mother's going to kill me."

I snort. "She'd light me on fire first."

I can almost hear Echo rolling her eyes.

Exhaling frustration, I break into a steady run, using the trees bordering the farm as cover. Pausing, I see overseers usher humans from the underbelly hollows; men, women...*children*.

A trauma-born pang invades the spaces behind my ribs.

I'm quietest when I'm in pain. Echo has memorized every shade of my silence...and softly brings me back. "Steady, Spirit."

"Yes, steady. Because Goddess forbid the few humans *not* brainwashed by the Father's courts don't wish to be a bloody appetizer."

I substitute humor to help with my empath, not an imaginary friend but more of a mental manifestation of a deep part of my psyche. It helps me cope on these missions. The last thing I need is to curl into a shuddering fetal position clutching skulls to my chest like some mad bone collector.

"Good girl. You're the best damn smuggler in the Underground, Lys Spirit," she cites my false identity on reward posters throughout the Courts.

Rescuing child blood slaves would guarantee me life in a Court prison.

I smirk, lifting my chin in pride.

All the vampires have is a name and a blurry image of a young woman in a cape and hood. I can't resist a 'flair for the dramatic'.

Slowly and carefully, I move around the fallen trees.

With each step, I murmur breath prayers and the names of my heavenly foremothers.

"Deborah...Hadassah...Jael...Rahab."

Keep going, Elysia.

I swear I hear their whispers, feel their strength within my blood.

The holographic ad parading the Father's profile on the farm gates stops me, clotting my throat.

Pernicious patriarch.

I seethe from behind a tree.

"May the feminist force be with you." Echo pauses. "And remember, if you're caught and they blood-type you, you can look forward to the—"

"—grandest shotgun wedding of all time, I know."

My body trembles with rage and terror at the thought of the Prince of Destruction. The man who once tortured my mother and wreaked havoc on our city...before the treaty.

A treaty I break on these missions, missions that carry a sentence of death by slow matrimony.

He would love to sink his fangs into my blood *and* take me as his latest bride. If only the damn demon weren't so unlawfully alluring.

Probably airbrushed tech.

Wrinkling my nose, I tiptoe along, staying low to the ground as I make for the gates.

I imagine Echo steeling her jaw. "Your smart mouth won't get you anywhere with the Prince when you're halfway down the aisle."

"Aww, don't worry, Echo. You know you have first claim on my smart mouth."

"One more wisecrack *Elysia*, and I swear the next time you

glow will be because I'm lighting you on fire—destiny or no destiny."

The heat flushing my skin from our familiar banter fades as I tense. I had no quarrel with destiny...until that bitch took the night off. I rub my neck, count to eight, and block out memories of when the Halo abandoned me.

No more marks. No more fangs. No more...*touching*.

I nearly lurch when I spot the target families.

"Moses' in sight. I repeat, Moses in sight."

I make out the families I've spent the past week speaking to. I can only take the willing little ones...the absolute quietest.

Not all can part with their children; not all can put their hope in humans. I don't blame them. With what vampires do to those who are caught and Chasm monsters and demons roaming the night, many have little hope left.

Regret twists my stomach. I wish I could take more than two.

With bated breath, I wait for Echo's response while biting my lip, pulling out my retro tech.

I raise my camera and snap a few quick shots, zooming in on their neck brands.

Every human is blood-typed and logged into the Court O' Nines database; ranked for purity. Purer bloods are sent to the blood bishops for genetic testing. More valuable ones are given to one of nine Rooks who are charged with a realm.

Even simple memory boxes like these are banned in the Father's Court O' Nines. A slow process of stripping human rights over the past century—unless they reside in a privileged Court O' Nines' city, humans have no access to technology.

Thankfully, the Underground has its ways.

Any information I provide is valuable.

"Diversion set to time. You have six minutes." Echo

acknowledges from her position on the opposite side of the farm.

My breath hitches.

I just have to get to the tunnel. The Underground does the hard work.

"Lys. You good?"

With a deep breath, I muster my strength.

"Six minutes," I confirm. No sass.

Best not to mess with my lightning-wielding *vampire* girlfriend when she's in High Guardian mode.

Teetering on my heels, I wipe beads of sweat from my brow. I blow an annoyed breath at the shimmering droplets coating my palm.

*It's time, Elysia...*the Halo whispers in my mind.

Please. I plead. *These kids need me.*

"Echo to Lys, The Prince is on scene! Abort! I repeat, the Prince is on scene," Echo commands, voice insistent and domineering.

My blood curdles in my veins.

Why on earth is the Prince visiting a lowly blood farm?

Retrieving my binoculars, I examine the farm entrance where a troop of vampire knights with black wings unleashed like shields escort the formidable Prince in all his Court finery.

Blood bludgeons my eardrums.

I ball my hands into fists, curling my upper lip, disgusted by his history of destruction. All the injustices. The dead brides.

Everything he touches, he destroys.

A deep warmth rouses my blood feeding on my righteous rage. That golden ghost of a Halo awakens, haunting me with memories so bitter. My mouth turns cinder dry.

Jaw clenched, I will the Goddess' birth gift down.

I'm no match for the vampire, especially if the urban legend of his other title, The Dragon, is true.

There is no way in hell I will let Neoptolemus spoil my night.

"Abort now, Lys. Do you copy?" Echo repeats.

I wonder if she suspects what I'm about to do.

"*Elysia...*" Echo's voice thunders in my ear. "Don't even think about it."

I pause and purse my lips, muscles spasming.

I shouldn't. Mom has risked too much to enforce the treaty, to protect me.

If the Prince of Destruction discovers famed smuggler Lys Spirit is really *Princess Elysia Rose...*

"Noralice," I whisper the name from my past to grant me strength.

After that night three years ago, I vowed there would be no more left behind. This is my unfulfilled penance. My purgatory.

The crackling of the bone fires haunts me, and I shudder. I still pretend the embers were fireflies, and my blood soaking the ground was a shallow golden lake. My heart weeps at the memory of the baby's cry...

I open my teary eyes to the present.

A spark flees my chest.

Fuck the Prince!

Armed with two iron stakes, I take off into a run.

"I'm going, Echo."

"Damn it all to hell, Lys!"

Yes. Hell. I'm sure all the monsters in the Chasm would throw me a grand birthday party.

○

GRITTING MY TEETH, I PUSH TOWARDS THE FENCE.

I'll have less than three minutes to get the children to the ruins' tunnel.

My skin tingles, chest warming from the Halo bound to my emotions. Hot tears glisten in my eyes.

I reach the fence line, damming my bursting breath as I dismantle this section of the fence with a high-tech taser. And silently thank all the vampires in my city for donating their silver blood, the most advanced commodity, and giving me the tool to nullify the fence with the otherworldly technology. Echo's diversion will take any security's eyes off the sensors.

With hearts breaking and eyes swollen from tears, the parents slip two tots to me.

I swallow a remorseful lump.

My empath longs to wrap around the parents, to offer them some comfort. I growl at Empath Elysia. Whimpering, she curls into the fetal position in the corner of my mind.

Apologies will come later. The parents need my arms, swift feet, and strength.

"I'll get them to safety," I assure them, securing the children in my prepared sling—equipped with front and back carriers. The tots are fast asleep thanks to the melatonin drops I buried here last night.

A young teen scurries towards us cradling a dark bundle.

My breath stalls.

Don't run!

At the end of the farm, a vampire overseer turns, suspicious of the girl's movements.

Panic bolts up my spine when she crashes to her knees before me and thrusts the bundle into my arms.

"Please!" She begs, breathless, eyes wide with fear. "Save my baby."

Goddess, no!

Terror paralyzes me as I survey the sleeping infant. A

battleground rampages inside me while distress signals clamor in my mind.

Noralice. Noralice. Noralice.

My spine prickles with a familiar pain, traveling upward like invisible thorns feeding on the back of my neck.

I *never* take babies! Not anymore. And my limit is two.

Tonight, this package will be heavier than millstones.

I look to the mothers and fathers echoing her pleas. Granting me their blessing to take the risk.

"She's a good girl." The teen whimpers. "She won't cry."

The vampire at the end of the farm disappears.

Time's up. Diversion set.

My heart howls in my ears as my breathing surges.

I bite my tongue, hard, and all my fear dissolves into raw willpower.

I make a split-second choice and take off with the two tots secured in the sling—and the babe in my arms.

She feels like death. She feels like murder. Like sin and *suffering*.

My muscles burn from the effort, but I do not curse my human limbs. I bless them. I speak a power blessing on the pain because it means I am alive. I can suffer, bleed, grow, and thrive. My father may not have blessed me with his vampire immortality, but he did give me quicker reflexes and faster speed, which is why I'm the best damn smuggler.

I am no half-blood. Still more human than anything. I'm thankful for my humanity.

I head back to the ruins beyond the trees, avoiding the tangles of barbed wire.

A familiar gurgling makes me freeze a few hundred feet from the tunnel. Dread trundles my stomach and I slip into the shadow of a dilapidated tower. Through the chink in the wall, decrepit fingers, skin scraps hanging off its bones like damp wallpaper, creep along the stone.

A ghoul.

A pity I don't have fangs to bare a snarl like my father—another oversight of my unfortunate anatomy. I press myself to the wall, then quietly lower the tots. One wakes. Thank the foremothers, he's the oldest: a three-year-old little warrior prince. The one on my chest. A chill skitters along my spine as I hush a finger to my mouth and whisper, "Shh…"

I hold my breath as the ghoul snaps its deformed neck in our direction.

Keeping my cape's hood over my ripples of dark hair, I clench one of many iron stakes embedded in my belt.

Blind and mindless, ghouls roam the wilds, circling the human farms, drawn to the scent. They were once vampires who incurred the Father's fury. Their fangs and tongues were ripped out and their throats branded. Left to wither, they survive off the thinnest amounts of blood.

I narrow my eyes as the ghoul sniffs the air and inches toward the tower's corner.

"Close your eyes," I whisper to the little prince.

It appears, mouth open to roar, shaking its membranous, translucent tattered wings.

Freeing my quaking breath, I cage a scream and drive my stake hard and fast into its jutting ribcage, shattering bones as I bury the weapon in its heart.

Squelching, the ghoul droops.

I circle my chest, making the eternity sign. Because I pray over ones I kill—whether they have souls or not. *May the blood of the Angels welcome and restore you to the land of the light…*

I kiss the air, sensing my chest warming more before I tell the boy he may open his eyes. I wink at him. "They get smellier every time." Mission accomplished when he smiles. "Time to get you home." I take his hand, and he yawns, nestling close to my side.

My earpiece beeps an alarm, and I snap my head toward the farm.

We're out of time.

Desperation ricochets inside me, but I smuggle the children deeper into the ruins—and don't let go of my stake for anything.

The farm horn blares its omen. By now, the overseers have discovered the missing children. They will search the forest, then the ruins.

At best, I have one minute.

The baby cries, and nausea swirls my stomach, but I resist the urge to dry heave.

Noralice

Clinging to adrenaline, I drive my aching limbs onward.

Sliding across layers of bone dust and fragments, I find the camouflaged hatch and knock twice. It opens, and I pass the children without any words to the Underground transporters. I nod to them and close it.

I never go inside.

Vampires inside the ruins gnash their teeth, hissing, their powerful bodies thundering against one another from their blood craze. For my blood. Speed and sharper reflexes are my greatest advantages, allowing me to lure the overseers away.

I take off and zig zag in the ruins.

My scent will confuse them for days. They will never locate the tunnel.

The worst is over, but my shoulders don't sink with relief. I'm too well trained.

Echo's melodious voice haunts me. *"Never let down your guard. Come home to me, Lightning Rod."*

I smile at the thought of her cold arms surrounding me, her

scent of spices and sensual pomegranates. Her warm lips welcoming mine every time. Years ago, when the Halo and I were still on speaking terms, I'd conjure star fire whips and use them on her during our training sessions.

I'll always come home.

A vampire's shadow draws near my spine, but I don't stop running. More join him, encroaching. No wonder! My finger gash is open, trickling gold blood from my palm. I ball my hands into a fist.

Damn that rusty nail!

A rabble of vampires charge at me, feasting on my blood scent permeating the air. Closing in on me.

Harnessing my breaths, welcoming the adrenaline, I push my worn body further into the woods. Further to my city—to my home.

"My blood shake brings all the ticks to the yard!" I sing song my modernized taunt.

When every vampire retreats, I stop dead in my tracks. Dumbfounded, I gape as they return to the farm.

The taunt wasn't that good!

Laughing off the stroke of luck, I spin, prepared to run again, but a cold hand seizes my wrist. Dark, umber, and lustrous.

Holy foremothers!

My stomach somersaults. No wonder the others retreated.

Wreathed in pure black flames and clothed in velvety dusk robes with iron armor epaulettes spiked with stakes; the vampire's massive form towers over me.

My breath grows heavier in his wake.

Oh, shit, shit, shit!

No advanced tech. He *is* that unlawfully alluring. Especially with his shimmering tattoos. It's as if he swallowed star flames to embellish his deep yet warm skin, a shade darker than my autumnal gold.

The Prince of Destruction sends every nerve ending in my body haywire. If he wasn't a sick, demented torturer, executioner, bride killer, etc., he'd be just my type.

My inner Halo glows as a fever thickens in my chest. Violent and insatiable, it spreads, flushing all of me and pooling liquid heat in my belly. I internally chastise the infernal hula hoop.

His black flames curl up on my legs, warm and lascivious, and I hiss at the invasion. No worse than his gaze roving across my throat, migrating to my elevated pulse. I flare my nostrils, gritting my teeth.

"Well, now...what have we here?" croons Neoptolemus.

His silvery locks fall down his chest as he dips his head to me and parts his lips to exhibit his fang tips like keen pearls.

Stunned to paralysis, my very pores drink in his deeply hooded eyes, icy winter mist surrounding midnight pupils.

Is he wearing...silver eyeliner? Fuuuuuck.

"If it isn't Lys Spirit in the *flesh*. And blood..." He purrs. His eyes narrow, one brow arching, far too curious of my golden blood. "My Father is most eager to meet you."

Chest warmer than a kiln, I tilt my neck to the side and leer at the most powerful vampire in the Court O' Nines. "Wish I could stay and chat, but it's my birthday, and I have a party to get to."

Brows threading, he hums, "Why settle for a birthday when you could have a wedding?"

Gripping the stake I've concealed behind my back, I pit my eyes to the Prince's and equally hum with the perfect *vintage* quote, "The Lannisters send their regards."

I hardly realize what I'm doing until I've stabbed the stake deep in his chest. Targeting all vampires' weak spot: the heart.

It sticks there, jutting out.

Neoptolemus scrutinizes my failed weapon, then eyes me, and grins—wicked and predatory.

Pure scarlet hatred clouds my eyesight from my wounded pride. But I shouldn't be surprised the Prince of Destruction has no heart.

My gut tightens as he releases my wrist to yank out the stake, grinning malevolently.

Before he can reach for me again, I run.

Driving myself harder through the trees, I scramble for the odorant at my belt, like bug repellant for vampires. Before I get the chance to apply it, a familiar figure tears beyond the next tree, plucks my body from the ground, and whips into vampire speed.

Relief gushes through me. Echo, my High Guardian, holds me in her arms.

It doesn't take long before we plunge through the protected border of the Rose City.

She stops to put me down.

"Elysia!" she exclaims as my knees buckle, adrenaline nose-diving.

Breathless, I cling to my girlfriend, my protector cupping my face. I blurt out, "I just beat the Prince of Destruction in a battle of wits, Verena!"

I fucking staked him!

"We've got far bigger problems, Princess." She announces. "You're *glowing*."

Following her eyes, I gaze at my chest where pure light beams radiate through my clothes, shimmering with an otherworldly incandescence. Far brighter than any time in my idealistic and emotional childhood.

Hairs on my arms prick to static life.

The light mushrooms, and Verena leaps away from the

vampire-searing flaming shafts. An undercurrent thrums, resonating in my blood, thrashing heat in my chest.

It's time, Elysia, the Halo whispers again, an echo of destiny's supreme Goddess bitch.

My heart twists painfully.

I can't suppress it anymore.

I can't control the mad, wild glow that confirms what I've feared.

The Halo is awake.

And...it left a glowing trail to the Rose City.

2
"He'll never catch me."

"Your mom's going to kill me," Verena groans, thrusting out her wings. I nearly gush but refrain from touching them. The gleaming silver-blooded network of veins inside the black membrane of her elite vampire wings reminds me of thin comet streaks against a moonless night.

If I ever get wings, I'd want them to resemble Verena's. Or peacock feathers. Or dragon scales. It depends on the day. And my aesthetic mood.

"Not a chance. She likes you way more than me." I giggle and stick out my tongue. Years ago, Mom fell in love with Verena's amethyst energy and dedicated months to mastering it and personally trained my vampire girlfriend.

Thanks to her Creator abilities, she's a feared and respected Queen despite her humanity. I'm just the sweet Princess who smiles at court meetings, rocks babies, and smuggles. Much to Mom's chagrin since she's spent years trying to train me. But unlike her, I'll always be a runner, a smuggler—never a warrior. Or a Queen since Mom's immortal, and I'm not. Another convenient Goddess exemption.

"I have to alert the other Guardians. The Prince almost caught you, you're bleeding, and you left a shining trail straight for the Rose City. Oh, and you're late for your 22nd birthday party. Pretty sure I'm dead." Verena's static electricity purrs along my still-glowing skin, rousing goosebumps right before she collects me and launches us into the air until we arrive on my bedroom balcony—thanks to my home located near the border.

"Undead," I correct with a manic laugh and glance at the Rose City beyond the trees. If I don't keep up my humor, the adrenaline crash will do me in, and I'll never make it to my party.

"Don't worry, V," I assure her, squeezing her shoulder. "I doubt the Prince will break the treaty tonight." Yes, the treat Mom arranged with the Father after she came back to life. One that guaranteed he could have the world—but leave the Rose City alone. It's lasted nearly 95 years.

Verena still relays a message to the border guard to be wary and increase the patrols. It will have to suffice until Mom can deal with it *after* my party.

Unamused, Verena curls her lip to reveal one keen fang. Pulsing her energy into my body and prickling my curls, she prompts me into the bedroom.

Swiping at her annoying tendrils of static electricity, I stab a finger at her. "You zap me one more time, V, and I'll show you the meaning of lightning in a bottle!"

"Oh, I like that one. How long were you waiting to use it?" She hauls me away from the window, drags me to my dresser, and kisses my cheek.

I blush, forgetting how long I've been practicing that as I eye Verena's figure clad in a scarlet leather mini-dress. She wears what she wants as my High Guardian, and no one contests her. Not when she's the youngest and one of the most powerful Guardians with her amethyst lightning.

I lift my still-bleeding finger and suck it—until a microscopic lightning bolt pricks me. "Ow!" I yelp, glowering at Verena.

"Cut that out," she reprimands. "You'll give yourself a disease."

"Yes, because the Goddess has fated me to destroy the most powerful being on earth with "diseased" blood."

Baring her fangs, Verena opens my dresser drawer, tugs on the false bottom, and retrieves an emergency silver blood vial. Her pupils dilate upon my wound, flushing with bloodlust. But I don't flinch. Not when Verena only drinks synthetic blood. My vegan Verena.

"Here..." she uncorks the vial, handing it to me, "silver blood will stem the wound. Unless you want to use your healing power since the "light of your life" has returned."

I cringe. The Halo gave me healing, but I haven't used *that* power in years. "You're my only light," I guffaw and take the vial. Rubbing the silver blood in the wound, I hiss at the sting fading to a tingle as it repairs the flesh and seals the wound. Silver blood is a marvel with its multitude of uses—from healing to digital decoration to powering all forms of technology. Thankfully, some of the elite vampire blood powers our city.

Verena crosses her arms and studies me. "Cute. Just so you remember yours is the P that I want most on *this* V...P for Princess, of course," she slyly remarks, sliding her hands all over her body, making me smile. "But I'll never be monogamous. Or marriage material, much to the chagrin of your more *traditional* sensibilities."

I throw her a begrudging look and giggle, a squall of heat reddening my cheeks. Yes, Verena knows I want the grandest wedding to end all weddings. A perfect honeymoon. The happily ever after. And at least two children. *In a perfect world*...I sigh internally because such a world can never exist with the Father of Vampires in power.

"But if you ever find that special she or *he*, since you so lamentably swing both ways, I'll still bust out the fireworks for your wedding. And be your twice-a-year fling as long as they're good with it." She grins.

The Halo responds to my emotions until the glow engulfs my face and flows from my strands.

I grin. "Thrice-a-year."

○

AFTER ALERTING MOM WE WOULD BE LATE, VERENA HELPS ME PICK MY outfit. A black, lacy mini dress with fondant-like ruffles that cascade from each of the hips. Parted in a wide and high inverted V, it will showcase my long, lithe legs.

"Oh, yes! Like hell and high lightning, Princess. You pair this with your fierce eye-wing," she kisses her fingertips, "absolute perfection."

"Only if I get your Medusa heels," I demand, bobbing my brows, eager for the seductive strappy heels with the criss-crossing pattern tangling like serpents.

Verena blinks, then groans, tossing her head so her long, black hair falls past her waist. "Okay." She snaps her head to me, glittery green eyes narrowing in a warning. "One night. And only because it's your special night."

"And because you won't be able to take your eyes off my gorgeous stems." I chuff a laugh, but my cheeks burn as I take the dress.

"Admiring my bit of crackling, Elysia?" Verena twirls her

lightning in spiral patterns along her hand. She puckers her lips.

"Oh, I've always taken a *shine* to you," I quip and bite my lower lip, impure thoughts abundant. No, an angel would definitely not have my dirty mind.

"You certainly did a lot of shining after your little run-in with Neoptolemus," Verena points out, causing me to arch an incredulous brow.

My Halo sparks, and I blow a raspberry at my chest, scowling at it.

"You need to stop smuggling," urges Verena. "You're far too high profile for the Underground. And now, the Prince has seen your face."

"Come hell and high water, V, nothing will ever keep me from the Underground," I proclaim.

"Right…" Verena dances across the floor which is like the bottom of a hamster cage but with fabric. "Should've figured a brush with Destruction wouldn't stop you."

My flesh crawls at the image of me walking down the aisle to belong to him. The last thing I ever will be is Destruction's bride.

"He'll never catch me." I wink, but my smile fades. Neither of us mentions the night my Halo shut down almost four years ago.

I'll never get caught again. Least of all by the Prince of Destruction.

3
HOLY FOREMOTHERS! THE PRINCE OF DESTRUCTION FOLLOWED MY TRAIL

After doing my makeup, I slip into the lacy black number and face my reflection. Hmm...not bad. The gold rings surrounding my irises and the highlights in my hair glimmer brighter. My Halo signatures.

Tossing back my wild curls, I turn to leave until the golden rays return with tiny beams curling into the air from my chest.

"Stop!" I slam my frenzied hand on them, forbidding them to rise. "I don't know why you've come back, but you are four years past your expiration date. If the Goddess ever shows herself, I'm returning you, you bloody blazing ring."

A few flickers spit from my chest. Vexed, I scrunch my nose as I consider how the Goddess brought Mom back to life like a phoenix rising from the ashes. Turning her future child into the "Halo-Bearer" with the "blessing of the stars" was just a convenient bonus.

Compared to Mom, I am a dim morning star bowing before her sunrise.

My heritage is a fiercely guarded secret to anyone *outside* the Rose City, but Mom throws a celebration inside at every opportunity. She believed I would surpass her legacy, and I'd bask in the glow. Now, the parties rub salt in the wound—a hundred wounds—all from my past.

Anxiety twitches my fingers and prickles the back of my neck. But I banish the trauma memories, shoving them deep into an island in my mind. But my body always remembers.

The beams dim.

Taking a deep breath, I open my bedroom door to head out.

Verena waits in front of my house with the heels and wings already primed.

I'd kill for her wings. And her stronger vampire skin and elite silver blood. If I ever have wings, I'm certain they will be fragile and skeletal—delicate as sparrow bones.

"Ready, Princess?"

"Almost." I accept the heels. "Guardians doubled at the border?"

Verena nods, but I know we're battling apprehension.

As predicted, her eyes linger on my legs after I strap on the heels. The mini dress hugging my lower thighs also entices my girlfriend's eye. My favorite part is how the black fabric attachments ripple like dark, ruffled waves on each side of me. I grin, appreciating my long stems, my ample ass, and my hips that Verena calls downright *deadly*.

All my skin tingles as I coil my arms around her neck and murmur low and sultry in her ear, "Let's fly!"

Windswept curls are so sexy.

As I print my lips to her throat, memorizing her pomegranate scent, I imagine her fangs brushing along mine. When we first met, she dubbed me "tinsel teeth" thanks to my braces.

I fell in love with her the same day I trussed her with my Halo whips. Guilt throbs inside me when I consider our background. As my faithful High Guardian, Verena has seen me through more scrapes than anyone. She grounds me and leads me home from the Underground. But despite our mutual attraction and history, my trauma has kept her mouth away from my skin.

Tonight, newfound desire heats my blood and swells between my thighs. Maybe after the party, we can rekindle some flames.

"What?" Verena snarls, tapping her earpiece, signaling her words aren't for me. Somehow, she can still fly straight while multitasking. And after another pause, she says, "I'll be there momentarily. Dropping off Glitter Bomb first."

I wince. I really wish she and the Guardians had a different code name for me.

"What's going on?" I ask, suspicious of her edgy body language.

Verena presses her lips into a tight seam. "Nothing for your pretty head to worry about. Just a few ghouls on the outskirts. I'll char them to cinders and be back in time for cake. Your party awaits..."

"Holy foremothers!" I exclaim after Verena lowers me before the Main Square gates. Big plans indeed.

An instinctive thrill of delight pulses through me. People might respect my mom, but they *love* me. My smile fades because I don't deserve this. The trauma wounds threaten to reopen. I turn, prepared to run.

"Not a chance." Verena blocks my path and wags a finger before pointing at the cobblestone entryway with the wrought-iron gates parted.

I stick out my tongue. "You are so dead."

"Undead, but why quibble? Go." Verena shoves me lightly.

COURTING DEATH AND DESTRUCTION

Gulping a knot of anxiety, I face the hundreds of masked vampires and humans—potentially the entire Rose City gathered in the town square—waiting to greet their Princess. Canopies of hundreds of thousands of roses and fiery orbs float above everyone's head, casting a glow upon all. Mom's handiwork.

The moment I proceed beyond the gates, the audience erupts into applause, cheers, and whistles. A bitter taste invades my mouth, and I prepare to flee again...until the two most important vampires and men in my life arrive to each take an arm and steady me. Despite their simple leather masks, I'd recognize them anywhere.

Shoulders relaxing, I smile at my father first. Love shines through his bronze come-hither eyes. So similar to mine, apart from the sultry eye-wing. Dad's hand is as warm and brown as his eyes as he holds mine and greets me, "Happy Birthday, Elysia. You're glowing like you did when you were born. My heaven-*scent* angel." Smiling, I shake my head and turn to my uncle.

I wag my uncle's rainbow bowtie that compliments his modern pin-stripe suit and vest. "You're so fancy, Uncle Heath." I admire him and giggle because if the gates of hell broke open, my uncle would still wear his best vest and bowtie as he does now.

Striding down the main path, I murmur, "Maybe you'll meet your special beau tonight." I tease my uncle. We joke about how I must have inherited my bisexuality from him.

"I'll do no such thing, Lyssi. It's *your* special night," Uncle Heath insists, indigo eyes sparkling. When I open my mouth, he cuts me off, "I wish I could stay the whole night, but I must leave soon thanks to my spy exploits." He winks.

As the Underground's top spy for the Court O' Nines, Uncle

Heath often supplies me with tech. On his next visit, I'll ask him about the latest in court politics...and gossip.

For now, I follow Dad and Uncle Heath past the applauding partygoers and banquet tables laden with hors d'oeuvres, along with chocolate and blood fountains. My mouth waters at the chocolate ones. Human blood is not forbidden in the Rose City, but we have anti-hunting laws and strict limits for familiars—as well as a steady supply of synthetic blood for the vegan vamps like Verena.

Finally, we arrive at the head table draped in white linen, erected onto a makeshift stage where my mother waits in a form-fitting amaranthine gown to match her eyes—cinnamon waves swept into an elegant chignon.

Oh, I gush...she looks so beautiful!

My shoulders lift with affection. I reflect my parents' lovely blend: autumnal gold skin, sultry eyes, pronounced cheekbones like subtle apples, but my curls are far more chaotic than Mom's luscious waves. Her pale arms open to embrace me as I ascend the staircase to more applause. I kiss her flushed cheeks —one of few things we have in common.

"Leave it to you to go all Pomp and Circumstance," I say while Mom guides me right to her very throne of velvet and gold. Naturally, she relocated it from our town hall.

"You're the Everblood, Elysia," she reminds me. "You can't run from your destiny."

No, but I'll sure as hell go kicking and screaming, I want to say but don't bother. It's not the time, nor the place for the repetitive conversation. Destiny will have to hunt me down before I accept this Halo. Not like I've ever managed to control the salty thing.

Still, my stomach flutters as I lower myself onto the throne and beam at the audience. At this point, I wouldn't be surprised if my mother conjures some fireworks with her elemental powers. Just like on my sixteenth birthday, Mom crowns my head with the same gold-winged diadem. She always insists I wear it, especially after I've returned from the Underground. I wince, swearing the gold shocks me every time.

Mom applies her mask: royal purple feathered with peacock plumage with tiny, encrusted diamonds trimming it. I am the only unmasked one.

While Mom commences my party, I lift my hand, acknowledging the citizens. Many I recognize from our city hall for routine court matters. My chest expands, appreciating the attention, the admiration. This is my home. These are my people—vampires and humans alike. This is what the world *should* be.

"People of the Rose City..." Mom begins, "We gather to celebrate my daughter's twenty-second birthday. But we have another cause for celebration. In exactly five years, it will be the Centennial Eclipse and the Everblood's time to shine."

Heat clots my ears, and I squeeze my knees because I could give the speech. The legend of the Everblood prophecy. For nearly a century, human parents have tucked their children in at night and sing to them about the Everblood. Most vampires liken her to a monster. Yes, as Verena tells me: I am downright *monstrous*.

"We have lived in peace and protection for ninety-five years," the Queen proclaims, and I'm grateful she doesn't launch into the long history of the Rose City, or her triumph of killing the Prince of Death. How she destroyed the Father's most powerful blood magic: the Triumvirate. The act that led to the peace treaty.

"In five years," continues Mom, reaching for her champagne glass, "the Everblood will rise on the Blood Moon's Centennial Eclipse."

On my sixteenth birthday, Mom showed me a piece of the prophecy. How stars embraced her, gold showers clothed her, and angels surrounded her—thousands of hosts kissing—granting her the future blessing of the Halo.

The memory burns a path straight through my blood. I touch my chest, that rising warmth of my heritage effusing my body. Mom shared with me the vision of my birth, how my Halo light emanated from my chest to her first kiss upon my cheek. My father always says: on the day of my birth, I *glowed*.

Mom raises her glass and eyes me from the side. "With the power of the Halo inside her heart, she will break the Father's throne and seal the Chasm."

Right. Because I am some "warrior of light" destined to destroy the Father of Vampires. Lucky me. My throat constricts, and I turn to my citizens, smiling at them.

"Tonight," Mom concludes, "we honor my daughter and celebrate the future, of when all our races, born and bitten vampires and humans will be free and live as equals!"

Neck and shoulders tightening, I raise my glass alongside them. Everyone drinks to my mother's toast. My treasonous lips sample, too.

Dad rescues me when he takes my other hand, clears his throat, and announces, "I have a little gift, too. Come..." He nods to the dance floor. *Aww!* Warmth floods my face, grateful for Dad's rescue.

I recognize the opening melody and beam, joyful tears glistening in my eyes. Dad winks, slides a hand to my waist, and jokes, "They're playing our song, Lyssi."

Eyes soft, I lean into my father and sing with him to Rosie and the Originals, "Angel Baby". Dad's teasing Everblood hints and puns are far more preferable than Mom's speeches...and training.

Under projection lights scintillating a pirouetting constellation on the floor, I dance, resting my head against my father's stalwart shoulder. With how flushed my cheeks are, I wonder if I'll glow. Featherlight, I imagine gold wings to match my diadem. It's the closest I've come to dreaming in the past three years, to forgetting what happened on that long dark night.

After I dance to "Rainbow Connection" with Uncle Heath, I whisper my birthday request in his ear. Chuckling, he kisses my cheek and responds, "You can paint my wings whenever you desire...when I return, of course."

After I say farewell to my uncle, who departs for spy work, I laugh and twirl, prepared to meet the next request, but my hand collapses into an all-too-familiar umber velvet one.

The vampire wears a black diamond mask, but his face is still the most recognizable in all the Court O' Nines. That infernal silver *eyeliner*. With his black flames and shades of destructive power. And the formidable chest I staked earlier.

Holy foremothers! The Prince of Destruction followed my trail.

I've endangered everyone—My people. My family. Verena.

I part my lips and search for my voice through my dry throat. Horror drains all the color from my cheeks as one question preys on me.

How long before the Father of Vampires arrives?

4
"THE PRINCESS AND I HAVE SOME UNFINISHED BUSINESS..."

Before Neoptolemus can address me, Dad shadows to my side and snarls while Mom marches toward us. With fire wreathing her figure, the Queen rises on an invisible throne to confront the Prince. "You are not welcome here, Neoptolemus. Unhand my daughter now. I have held up my end of the bargain," Mom confronts him, eyes not once departing from his, prepared for any trickery. Is she referring to the treaty?

Violent heat overthrows my insides when the Prince lifts my hand to rub his lips along my knuckles. I breathe fury through my nostrils as he responds, "True...please accept my deepest apologies."

Terror in my veins quickens my pulse. The Prince of Destruction *never* apologizes. It's a ruse, a trick, some destructive machination. That beguiling twisted smirk confirms it. The glint in his eyes brightens as he gazes at me.

"I merely came to wish the Princess a happy birthday," he expresses, voice deep and silky. His pupils center on me, dilating.

What? My heart springs into my throat.

He's here alone. He hasn't brought his Father. But there is no way in hell I will let my mother's archenemy, *my* archenemy tug my strings with his dragon smile and a threat wrapped in honeyed words.

I bite the inside of my trembling lip, reclaim my hand, and stab out one deadly hip to retort, "Send a card next time."

The Prince purrs, reminding me of an eager dragon. "The Princess and I have some unfinished business..." Chills invade my spine. *Does he know I'm the...Everblood?* If nothing else, he suspects.

With hardly a thought, I glare at his fangs and seethe, "Perhaps you should mind your own."

"Oh, I *like* her, Reyna," Neoptolemus croons, lips pressing into a carnal grin.

"Enough!" Mom cups my shoulders and urges me to my father. Thankfully, Verena stands next to him and gathers me into her arms.

"Out of time," are the last words I overhear as Verena whisks me beyond the rose canopies. I bury my face into her shoulder as she carries me beyond the tents, past blurring buildings, and to a side street alley behind a bakery.

"Damned dragon must've followed your trail," Verena huffs as I catch my breath. "Oh, hell, you're shining again, Princess."

I raise my hands, annoyed by the starlight incandescence illuminating my body. "Why is this happening?" I gasp and shake off the light, but glittery stardust sheds from my skin, growing stronger. This is the second time I've glowed following an encounter with Neoptolemus. It can't be a coincidence. What does the Halo know?

Sighing, Verena pauses against the bakery wall, pulls out a small bottle, and uncorks it. "Not my department. But this might help. I was saving it for your birthday." She beckons.

I sniff the contents, then thrill, hands clawing at the bottle.

Giggling, Verena holds it out of my reach, toying with me. "Care for a bit of venom *spirit*, Lys Spirit?" She teases and touches her lips in a light kiss to mine.

"V, give it now!" I demand, licking my lips. My parents only let me sample a drop or two of venom, but Verena sneaks me doses. After my rather lascivious brush with Destruction, it's the perfect treatment. "Now!" I go for Verena's weak spot.

"Don't you dare do the pouty lip and puppy dog eyes! Okay, fine," she surrenders and hands it to me. I waste no time in downing it.

Unlike liquor, the venom's effects penetrate my digestive system and bloodstream immediately. Venom has no negative side effects: no hangover, no prolonged liver damage. Best of all, it gives me a warmer and tipsier sensation. Flesh tingling, practically ready to burst into a firefly shimmer, I sweep Verena into a back-alley dance.

"Remember, Lys, your spirit is beautiful," she whispers, then arches a brow. "Are you humming 'Lips of an Angel'?" She asks as I sing-song and hiccup. "Holy shit!"

"Well, would you look at that?"

The tiny star I hiccupped dances into the night like a glittery ember. Something like angel wings flutters heat in my belly. I hiccup a stream of little stars this time... and a tiny gold kite tail. A silly smile curls the corners of my lips. The first time I hiccupped a star was with Verena.

"What the—"

Before she can wonder what's going on, I pin her against the warm alley wall and kiss her long and full. My throat grows thick with desire. Verena was my first kiss, my first *touch*.

Ever since the Halo shut down, I've never been so forward. Desires suppressed for far too long, now, all of me feels like I'm waking up! The auto-pilot exterior of smuggler Lys Spirit crumbles to unleash some new entity of gold dust and star flame.

Strong fingers snap me out of my daze. Eyes deep and lustful, Verena thrusts me against the wall while her lightning tendrils spark my body. *Oh, Saints!* She kisses me back. Her pelvis crushes mine, stirring the heat between my thighs. But it's too triggering. So, I stop her before it goes beyond kissing—before I lose all control.

"V, I'm—"

"Save it." My protector raises a hand. "You know I'll never cross your 'no touchies' boundary, Elysia. Not after I found you in your bedroom three years ago. You're not comfortable sharing what happened, I get it. If your *Lair* and kissing are all it can be for now, I'm good with that. We're getting there."

A distant scream alerts us, chilling my blood.

"V, watch out!"

Panic rockets my adrenaline. But it's too late. Verena spins around in time for the ghoul to lunge for her, charging at her chest, claws raking at her face.

On instinct, I lunge and ram my stake into the ghoul's bony chest, burying the iron in its chest. With a gurgle and a squelch, the ghoul droops, falling onto my spike.

Verena blows a black strand off of her face. Thankfully, her cheek has only a few cuts. Relieved, I lower my shoulders.

"Seriously?" Verena distracts me as I grip the weapon at the ghoul's back and tug. "Wherever did you manage to store a stake in that getup?"

Once I free it, the ghoul squelches again. Ugh. Lifting the ends of my snug skirt, I slyly grin and showcase the leather stakeholder girding my inner thigh. After wiping off the stake, I tuck it inside.

"You've never been sexier, Princess," Verena compliments

but wags a finger. "But remember, I'm the protector. My responsibility."

"Of course, V for Verena." My sarcastic brat rises to the surface, and I offer a mocking bow. "High Guardian, girlfriend, protector...with all your titles, you're more royal than I am. Care to take the Halo while you're at it?" I point to my chest, knowing my humor is detracting from the thought of how a ghoul made it this far into the city.

At the sound of more screaming, Verena and I snap our heads to the east...close to our border. She turns to me, deadpanning. "Don't even think about it."

Too late. Before she can branch out her lightning to stop me, I grab the vampire pepper spray I always keep on me, target her eyes, and run.

Her pained shriek turns wrathful, and I jolt, knowing she'll punish me for that later.

About a hundred feet from the border, I stop in my tracks, a shriek hitching in my chest. Dozens of ghouls cross into our territory, overwhelming the guardians. With his graceful prowess and multiple lifetimes of experience in battle, Dad leads the guardian charge.

He jerks his chin toward me, then views the sky, and shouts, "Lyssi, get back!"

Flinging my head up, I gasp from the ghoul flying above me after it's breached the Guardian lines.

It angles its malformed chin toward me before plunging through the canopy at break-neck speed. My breath seizes. Before the ghoul can land, lightning strikes its chest, burning a hole right through its heart. Charred to a crisp, it tumbles at my feet.

Cringing, I step back, then smile at my High Guardian who does a little bow.

Never have so many ghouls trespassed into our city.

Guttural screeches overlap the bellowing voices of the charging vampires who tear into the ghouls with their bare hands and fangs.

"What's going on?" I ask Verena, my knees quivering as more guardians arrive and form ranks while she shields me.

Mom flies from the tree canopy thanks to her magnificent, swan-white vampire wings, the membrane thrumming with silver blood veins. She lands before the guardians.

Rushing behind the nearest tree, I grip the bark and thrill in her display. My throat thickens with pride for my mother. She hurtles the ghouls across our border, fracturing their bones.

They don't rise. Whatever is twitching burns once she unleashes her deadly phoenix flames, incinerating them until the scent of rancid blood and putrid flesh stains the air.

If I had Mom's power, we would be unstoppable. We could bring the Father of Vampires to his knees, rip his heart from his chest, and send him to hell where he belongs. We could free so many.

I slap the tree and curse my useless body, wondering if the Halo is good for anything, apart from hiccupping a star and glowing.

More ghouls break our borders, weakening the Queen's defenses. Never tiring, she rises—a force to be reckoned with.

Out of the corner of my eye, I make out Verena, firing lightning bolts. Too many ghouls press in on her because she's protecting me. They're always drawn to the one with the most potent blood. My chest lurches when a ghoul lands on a nearby guardian's chest, claws penetrating.

Verena leaps right onto its back and slashes the creature's wings with her wicked skills.

At the sound of sniffing far too close, I spin my head. Several creatures encroach upon me, scenting my pure blood through the heavy brush. Too vulnerable to act on the offensive, I back away, but it's too late. Two ghouls spring for me.

"Lys!" Verena screams and dives between us.

My heart spasms when their claws sink deep into her chest at the same time she unleashes her lightning, blazing through their bodies. All three forms roll together, then she shoves a ghoul off her and coughs. Silver blood bathes her chest. Terror swells, silent and thick, in my soul. I hurdle for Verena.

No, oh no, oh no, oh no!

Frenzied, I plant my hands on the lethal wounds.

"What are you doing?" she whimpers, coughs, and splatters more silver blood.

I grit my teeth and snarl at the Halo, "You want to come out?" For the first time, I pray for the healing I haven't used in over three years, dread chilling me. "Time to prove yourself."

Sucking hyperventilating breaths, I summon healing power into her body. Adrenaline surges through my nerve endings. Fog swirls in my vision, preparing to darken my mind, but I push through. Leaning into that long-lost power, I repair every deep gash and hole in my girlfriend's heart. I bind her arteries and veins and restore her blood.

Until my muscles weaken.

Tears form little wells behind my eyes while black dots fill my vision, and I crash to the ground.

5
"THE FATHER IS COMING."

"Elysia!" Mom's voice jumpstarts me. Her hands pressed to my chest.

Sharp and sudden, I inhale. Soil needles into my fingernails while the scent of charred ghoul flesh and smoke swarms my nostrils. Guardians surround the area while Mom holds me with Dad next to her—and Verena on my other side. In the past, if I used too much of the Halo, I'd pass out for seven hours. But when Mom channels her power into me bringing me to consciousness, it's murder on my system.

I breathe relief through my nostrils at the sight of Verena. She's alive. That's all that matters. Not her eyes storming against mine, promising lightning strikes for my audacity. I chew on my lower lip.

"I'm sorry, my Lady Queen," apologizes Verena, lowering her head. Her voice sharpens...keen as her fangs. "She sprayed me this time and ran."

I mouth 'I'm sorry', but my shrug isn't convincing. Or my smirk.

Mom cups my face in her hands while I inspect her royal

amethyst eyes. *Why is there fear inside their depths?* My stomach spasms.

I face Mom and press, "What's going on?"

"There's no time!" A foreign edge cuts into her voice, stinging me with the reminder of what the Prince said. *Out of time.* Mom collects the gold crown that slipped from my hair when I'd passed out. She places it in my hand, closing my fingers around it. "Whatever happens, Elysia, do not let go."

I open my mouth to ask why but more ghouls screech in the distance. Mom shoves me toward Verena and faces the border. Judging from her narrowed eyes and her hands clenching into fists, she's doing everything she can to reinforce her power.

"Reyna—" Dad begins.

"She's not ready, Raoul," she barks at him. "Even if it damns me, I'll protect her until her time comes."

Until my time comes...the Centennial Eclipse. Five years.

My chest strains as if my ribcage is preparing to splinter so it may carve out the Halo. But the Halo just helped me heal Verena, so I can't exactly complain.

*Ugh...*Mom's little jolt prompts a slow cyclone to swirl in my stomach, and I clamp my lips and eyes shut to fight the urge to retch.

"This isn't what we agreed," Dad says, pulling me to him, his fingers desperate. He lowers his head to my hair, taking a deep, unhindered breath of my heaven-scent.

What? I snap my eyes to his, brows soaring high. He *never* scents me this much! He tremors, wings close to erupting from bloodlust. *What the hell?*

Mom doesn't face us as she gathers fire and prepares for the next onslaught. "It's not about what we want. Or what she wants," she denies, "Take her now, Verena," she orders as more ghouls crash through the trees. "It's too late to evacuate the city. Get her somewhere safe."

She trains her eyes on me. "Elysia, hide and don't come out for anything. And do not let go of the crown."

Bewildered, I curl my fingers around the edge of the crown and plead, voice cracking as Verena collects me, "What's happening?"

"The Father is coming."

Hoisting herself into the air, Mom launches fire in targeted strikes of the oncoming ghouls while the guardians pick off the rest. "Take her now, Verena!"

Stomach rolling, I sag against my protector. Emotion wells up inside me, a raw ache constricting my chest. The last thing I want to do is leave my parents, but the nausea overloads my system.

Dad kisses my cheek and nods to Verena who charges into the air while his voice fades behind me, "Elysia! I love you!"

I cage a scream. Befuddled more at the crown tingling my palm, prompting the lines in my hand to flare.

I'm a little tired of being fucked by the fickle finger of fate.

Bitter frost assaults my flesh beyond my black dress, but Verena doesn't stop. Not till she reaches my shed I built with Dad as a child: it descends to my underground lair.

Vigilant, she scans the area. My limbs shake, chest pained from the sound of more distant ghouls. And my peoples' screams. I hold my rolling stomach, a whimper escaping my throat.

The Father is coming.

"Ninety-five years…" I practically sob to my girlfriend. "This was because of me…" I trail off.

Verena deadpans before lifting her eyes to the sky.

Neither of us regrets smuggling the children. But there are children here, too.

Will they get everyone out in time? And what about Verena?

My vision glazes over, stomach whirling. I stumble while Verena storms her lightning above my head, causing the hairs on the back of my neck to stand on end. A ghoul howls behind me—and drops right at my feet, cauterized. I taste bile in my throat.

Verena hauls me inside. "Come on. You can't do anything in your condition." She flips her endless high, sleek ponytail off her chest and onto her back. After closing the shed door, my High Guardian ushers me underground.

In the dark of my lair, Verena shifts into her lightning self of subtle amethyst ripples. Something she's perfected over the years. "You need your pick-me-up."

I lurch and hold my bile.

"Now," I demand because she's right. Without my restart, I'm useless.

"Your wish is my command."

ON MY KNEES CLOTHED IN NOTHING, I PREPARE FOR VERENA TO GIVE me my recharge. Shoulders low, relaxed because I feel safest here.

In the darkness, I shine like a golden, naked orb.

Verena brandishes her lightning, growing those sparks closer. "Hair up, Lightning Rod," she uses my lair name, reminding me that here, I am neither Princess nor the Halo-bearer.

According to my rules, my *needs*, Verena is sovereign. She will distract me, protect me. So, I welcome my empath and allow her full reign while I shift into auto-pilot mode.

The sound of my people screaming haunts me, deafening my ears. Mom said it was too late for evacuation. Above ground, a battle must be raging.

My chest lurches, breath heaving. *How can I hide when I have this healing power? If anyone is hurt, I can—*

"Hair up," commands Verena, voice firmer, and I dart my eyes to hers. Lightning stokes them, transforming her irises to amethyst flames.

No matter how much I want to rush the process I can't. Sighing, I obey and tighten my hair into a bun at my scalp.

"How many children did you rescue on your last mission?" She weaves her energy, surprising me with a current along my spine. I stiffen.

"Please, V, can't you—" When her lightning sparks the back of my neck, I yelp, "Hey!"

"Quiet!" she orders, and I drop my Princess, banning her from our lair, trusting my girlfriend. Verena's lightning, her energy will set my blood right. But she must be in absolute control, otherwise, she could easily stop my heart.

So, when Verena hums electricity again, sweeping tendrils to my shoulders, I answer her question. "Three. But one was...a baby."

Her lightning bristles, prickling to match her tone. "You know you never accept babies anymore, Lightning Rod. You need to stop taking risks."

I purse my lips, reflecting on the mission, on the teenager who scrambled to the fence and begged me to take the precious bundle. "She was sleeping so peacefully. And her mother was desperate. My heart—"

My girlfriend interrupts by chaining my throat with her lightning while she seethes, "Your heart is too big, my exasperating empath. You risked your life to heal me today. But I want my Lightning Rod safe. Do you understand?"

My voice rasps, but I nod which satisfies her. Enough for her to web her lightning along my chest.

Verena pirouettes her lightning in a wave to current from my head to my toes, transforming my curls to wild static. "Remind me how Father grew into such power, Lightning Rod," she urges, setting her teeth.

"Because he convinced humankind he was their savior, their *god*," I snarl, then swallow an anxious knot in my throat.

"What happened in the early days?" She circles around my back.

I lower my head and breathe. "Concentration camps throughout the country. Millions yielding their blood and bodies to him and his children. So, he built his empire on their corpses. With his Prince of Destruction at his side, the Father ushered in his masterpiece: a new Dark Age." Both horrific and fantastical.

Verena knits her lightning currents to lick my spine. I freeze, remembering what happened when I arched the first time—our trial-and-error practice ended with Verena branding my flesh by mistake before healing me with her silver blood.

She finishes rippling her currents to my neck. "But Father left the Rose City alone, didn't he, Lightning Rod?" Verena hisses and tightens the lightning, so it heats my flesh but doesn't burn.

"He did."

Verena wraps my chest in lightning, holding it there. It

hums. It *sings* into my veins! "Because of your mother's sacrifice."

"Right," I manage to wheeze. To protect me.

And I ruined it all. Neoptolemus caught me...learned my identity.

Sweat blooms on my neck and cheeks.

One last tighten—a lightning flicker to lash a warning into my skin. The pain centers me.

"Remind me, why are you number one on the Prince's "Most Wanted" bride list?"

I don't begrudge the tear tumbling down my cheek.

Her lightning collars my throat, its streams inching closer to my heart. "Because my lifespan is longer due to my father. My pure blood. And because I'm the Princess of the Rose City. The Phoenix Queen's daughter."

The Princess who's endangered everyone, I internally chastise myself.

Verena kneels before me. Neither dominant nor submissive. My equal. Her violet eyes deadpan with my gold-ringed irises. "And what does the Prince do with his brides, Elysia?"

Anger reddens my being. That crimson onslaught in my vision when I consider the Prince executing hundreds of brides.

I press my lips into a thin seam, hardening my voice. "He destroys them!"

How many has he reduced to ash? How many trophy corpses does he keep?

Verena rises, her leather boot digging into the ground. "But he would torture you first. And Father will rip the Halo right out of your chest and use its power to raise a Chasm army. So, whatever happens, you will hide like the Queen ordered. Promise, Lightning Rod?"

I gulp. "I promise, V for Verena."

Verena pulses her energy into my heart, freeing me to arch my back.

I scream from her worthy defibrillator. The network of lightning trailblazes through my veins and resets my blood and heart, my powers. Hyperventilating, I topple over, fingers curling into the cold dirt as I harness my breath, then rise, invigorated.

Verena hands me my gown and the diadem and nods.

What happens in my lair stays in my lair.

Verena narrows her eyes, testing me. "I'm going to keep a lookout. You stay here in your 'woe is me" pit of desolation."

"What if I can help? What if someone needs healing?" I touch my chest, considering the healing power I've embraced, wondering if I can heal more.

"You promised, Elysia. Be good. *Stay down!*" Verena reiterates, brandishing a finger, pulsing her lightning to spike my hair before she departs.

For her, I try my ultimate hardest.

After dressing, I light incense sticks to canvas my blood. Inhaling the woodsy fragrance, I touch the photographs on my wallboard. Little flickers of halo light in the children's eyes. Each became a beacon—one that fueled the flames of the next and the next until they became burning bridges lighting a fiery quest in the depths of my heart.

I consider the memory of the babe I lost. And the morning after my Halo went dark…

I wake on a bed of ash.

I spy my tunic lying nearby, then my tattered jeans, thankful they are not blood-stained. Everything aches as I tug on my clothes.

Charred bones and glowing embers are all that remains of last night's smoldering pyres. Guilt festers inside me because I am not among them, and I should be. The hundred-fang marks on my flesh testify to this. They will fade tomorrow, but I will remember every single bite.

I don't return to the Underground. I turn back to the bone-fires... back to her.

Dawn provides protection, so I move slower and wince at the dozens of human bodies, fang marks all over their flesh strewn like broken birds.

Some unconscious

Others dead.

My bare feet sweep along the cinders until I find her nearly buried under them. kneeling before her, I breathe a sigh of relief. She didn't end up in the fire. I wept an ocean of gold last night, but tears still flow. One tumbles onto her cheek—a glittering fleck.

I couldn't save her.

She reminds me of a porcelain snowdrop. She weighs little more than a daisy crown, but she is heavier than a tablet chiseled with the record of my sins.

Bearing her body, I return to the Underground so I may fulfill my mission...and go home.

Pushing aside the memory, I lose myself in all the children's eyes: the most beautiful sights I've ever captured. None came to the Rose City. All remained in the Underground. Sometimes, I imagine meeting the children, dancing with them in the moonlight, free and unburdened by the Father.

It's the only dream I have left. None of us should ever have to hide.

Damn it all to hell! I can't stay here.

When I open my hatch and slide open the barn door, a torrent of embers *and* ash besieges my throat. Everything outside is burning.

And...I smell blood on the air.

6
"HOW ABOUT YOU SHOVE THAT INVITE RIGHT UP YOUR ASS?"

Icy horror rips through me.

I grab a stake from my shed. Blood thunders in my eardrums, fueled by my howling heartbeat. Armed with the stake in one hand and the crown in my other, I step outside.

Cinders from burning trees clot the air around me. Thousands of tiny embers flicker into my hair and singe my cheeks. The ground is not cold anymore.

"Verena!" I cry, choking as cinders invade my throat.

She doesn't answer.

A few hundred feet away a pack of ghouls feasting on corpses...vampire and human alike.

But not Verena.

I bite back a scream as hundreds of ghouls howl and screech around my city.

How many more ravage my people's flesh? Where are the Guardians? Where is Mom? If Verena...no, I can't go there yet.

Vaulting into a run, I struggle past the burning forests of my home, but there is no escape from the conflagration.

COURTING DEATH AND DESTRUCTION

All of the Rose City burns. Not one building, not one home, not one *tree* is left untouched.

Stumbling across more bodies, some half-eaten, others scorched, I vomit all my stomach's contents. The grief and woe sink like heavy stones deep inside me. Great giant Redwoods that once soared to the sky are little more than burning husks barely passing my head. Our sprawling lake is nothing but a charred crater.

Blinding ash blemishes my vision as I hurry past burning stump after burning stump. It coats my gown. So much burns. It's like a dragon has unleashed the fires of its belly upon my city.

No, *the* Dragon.

Desolation of this kind in such a short time can only be from Neoptolemus. If he's done this, it must mean he returned with…

No!

Horror ricochets through every fiber of my being. Is the destruction of the Rose City payment for my rebellion?

"He's not here. He's not here. He's *not* here," I repeat and cough from the cinders invading my throat again.

I reach the tree line on the border of my home and take refuge behind what is left of the largest Redwood.

My home is gone!

Denying what I've witnessed, I press my back to the burnt tree, wincing from the heat lashing my bare skin. Every stone, brick, book, photograph, belonging, *memory*…is destroyed!

Mom has kept the Father back by almost a hundred years. And now, all that remains is charred rubble.

I dry heave onto the ground. Numb from the ash as if it's dressing me for a funeral. I cough again until low voices interrupt me. Caging the coughs, I peek beyond the Redwood's edge.

A cold sweat infects the back of my neck, but I force myself to stare at the Father and Prince Neoptolemus, standing before my parents.

My heart plummets. I shut my eyes, wishing it is all a nightmare. I pinch myself dozens of times and drag the edge of the stake across my skin, but it doesn't help.

This is no dream.

The Father and his son are a paradox.

On his neck, the Father bears the unholy mark of his maker along with cadaverous pale skin. Neoptolemus, in his dusky robes, wreathed in black flames, stands next to him.

"*Now*, Neoptolemus."

My mother raises her hand to strike, but the Father grips her wrists forcing her to the ground. To her knees! No one has ever brought the Phoenix Queen to her knees. His back is turned to me, and his laugh is sinister. He's savoring her pain.

My eyes move to Neoptolemus who steps forward. The Prince cocks his head, thrusts out a mighty hand, and seizes my father's throat. In less than a second, he reduces him to ashes.

My mother's piercing scream overlaps mine, suffocating it.

No, Goddess, no!

Mom crashes to the ground, hands diving for Dad's remains until his ash blankets her flesh.

Agony drowns me. My knees buckle, as I hurl myself against the tree, wishing it could steal me into her dying soul. Instead, I crumple to the ground, clutching the stake to my chest, my life preserver of a weapon.

No, no, no.

I urge my eyes back to the sight. It had to be a trick.

My father with his charming smile and patient heart. Our dark knight who danced with me earlier and called me his heaven-scent angel...he can't be gone.

But he is. He is nothing but dust floating on the wind, covering my mother.

Raking my nails into the tree, I prepare to leap. But Mom's voice resounds in my head.

No, Elysia. You must run. Get out of the Rose City. Don't let them catch you.

I lurch, struggling to breathe. *I can't! I. Can't. Leave. You.*

She must be mustering every army of ability so she can speak to me, protect me. The only reason the Father and his son haven't scented me...yet.

The Father kneels, hovering over Mom, and drags a finger across her cheek. "I'm going to enjoy breaking your throne tonight, Reyna. You will tell me all I want to know of the Everblood. But do share with me..." He grips her curls, exposing her throat. "Where is your precious little Princess? Perhaps my son will keep her longer than all his other brides."

No!

For a moment, the Prince's chin pivots in my direction as if he senses me. I hide behind the tree, praying he didn't notice.

Squeezing my eyes shut, I claw at the tree and listen to my mother seethe, "You will *never* find her!"

Elysia, the crown you are holding, it's the Halo.

What?

I hold my breath and open my eyes to the gold diadem in my hand. Beneath my skin, it warms, pulsating. If this is the Halo, then why have I still bled gold for years? How did I shine or use the healing power?

I wish I could explain everything, but there's no time. Protect the Halo, Elysia. Go. Her voice wanes, powers struggling beneath the Father's superiority. *Remember, you will never lose your value. Go!*

I war with myself. I am a coward. A useless, pathetic coward. Shame gnaws on me.

She says nothing else.

I run.

I barely make it to the edge of our property before cold shades and warm flames surround me holding me in place. A scream catches in my throat.

Familiar fiery tendrils tickle me, lurking across my skin, but thorny gooseflesh pricks my body. A heart-deep shiver shudders through me with the knowledge of what it means.

With fire in his wake, the vampire circles me, turning his head in my direction. Not once can I look away from the Prince wrapped in flames and shadows—the vampire who destroyed my father.

Neoptolemus.

Those twilight pupils dilate until they overwhelm his winter mist eyes.

I bite hard, drawing blood from my tongue. Anything to devour my screams. Though I'm not petite, Neoptolemus is beyond a head taller. Undaunted, the vampire who has destroyed my homeland and my father has come to finish his work.

Over my...hopefully...not dead body!

His shades and flames part before him as he closes the distance between us. Eyes feral and glinting, Neoptolemus' flames thrust me to the ground mooring me to the ashy earth.

The crown slips from my hand.

Frozen from fear and his indomitable force, all I can do is glare at him when he unleashes his wings, darker and more powerful than any vampire I've encountered, trimmed by his flames and shadows. They batter torrents against my face, against my body, pulling at my gown scraps.

Clothed in pure black flame, his massive form poises over me. I defy his vampiric beauty, his scythe-sharp cheekbones. His gleaming silver blood, his frost and sterling hair, and that infernal silver eyeliner. I defy the whirlpool of heat churning in my stomach.

"About my wedding invitation," he hints, returning to where we left off.

I open my mouth to scream, but his fire lances my throat, squeezing. Neck muscles straining, I thrash my head back and forth, wrestling with what little movement I can. I grapple for air.

The Prince tilts his head to me, eyes bloodthirsty, taking pleasure in my pain. Nostrils flaring as he scents my blood, he bows his head to inhale closer. A dam of tears unleashes from my eyes at knowing what he will do.

Neoptolemus leans in closer, tempting my flesh with his dark flames, and whispers, "Pretty, pretty Princess..." He pauses, tapers his substantial brows, and trails a finger along my arm, to the wound where I dragged my stake. He inspects my gold blood, rubbing it between his fingers, curious.

I choke when his grip loosens, tasting ash and dirt from the ground.

"How about you shove that invite right up your ass?" I hurl the words, side-eying him, causing him to arch a brow.

A wild cackle flees his throat.

Pursing my lips, I close my eyes to embrace death, praying in vain my foremothers will welcome me. I picture them as warrior queens. As saints bearing shields, forming endless rows on each side of me...right before they drag my unworthy ass to hell.

Neoptolemus drapes cold knuckles across my cheek and spreads his lips to exhibit his fangs.

No, he will not kill me.

He will mark me for his new bride, his blood whore.

Righteous indignation sears my insides when his fangs crawl across my neck.

No! I'll never be the Prince of Destruction's bride.

The crown, the *Halo* sparks fire latching onto my heart, swelling and shooting in celestial beams. Eyes open and burning, I seize the crown, rise to my knees, arch my back, and launch my arms in a wide stretch. The highlight of the rest of my life will be Neoptolemus battling this energy, this light.

His lips part. When his flames faint, overshadowed by my glow.

I laugh.

Like a drunken martyr, I laugh in the face of destruction.

He backs away. The Prince of Destruction backs away from...*me*!

A few moments ago, I felt powerless. Now, I stand, wrecked from the light coursing through me, spewing from my chest. Verena would laugh with me and battle with her lightning. She is the real reason I can do this...because of her jumpstart.

Wings brawling with the light, Neoptolemus gapes at me in awe; brows high, eyes vast as the Chasm. One more great burst of light assaults him, catapulting him to the ground.

To his knees!

In the midst of my Halo attack, the Prince cocks his head uttering, "This just got a lot more *interesting*."

I narrow my eyes to his, steel my voice, and dare. "Catch me if you can."

I turn with the crown and run.

And make it three steps before his flames and shades surround my waist, hook their dark fiery claws into me, and haul me back to him. He rips the crown from my grasp, growling as if in pain before he practically slams it down on my head and knocks me out with his shades.

7
A HUNDRED YEARS OF BRIDES FOR THE PRINCE OF DESTRUCTION

I wake to a rumbling beneath my body. At the touch of warm velvet hugging my cheek, I open my eyes to the window of a coach with a view of dark, sprawling forests.

Shades and flames spiral around the edges of my body as if hinting of my doomed fate.

"What the fuck is this?" I whisper, moaning a little from the throbbing pain in my head.

"What the fuck does it look like?"

Holy foremothers.

Heated flames erupt all over my body. Sitting directly across from me with his winter mist eyes preying on mine is Neoptolemus.

"You're my prisoner, Princess." He leans toward me. "And I long to know all about you."

I scramble as far into the corner of the coach as possible as the Prince's shades hem me in on both sides. That's when I realize I'm still clothed in my tattered dress. At least I still have the crown on my head. He may suspect, but he doesn't know it's the Halo. As far as he's concerned, it's a new weapon of my mother's. A second look at my skin confirms my wounds from our battle have healed into scratches instead of gashes.

"What did you do to me?"

"You're welcome." Neoptolemus gestures to my body. "You were quite spoiled after our encounter. Since I prefer my prisoners as healthy as possible, I destroyed the refuse on your flesh and used my shades to heal your wounds of any infection."

Ignited and incensed, I narrow my eyes. "Don't ever use your destructive power on my skin again!" I hiss, half-tempted to lunge and rake my nails across his face. But he would simply knock me out again, which is the last thing I need.

Destruction's sitting dark shadow is a fortress assaulting me. Still garbed in the same robes and iron-spiked epaulets.

Shaking out my dizzy thoughts, I wonder, "How long have I—"

"A couple of hours." He cuts me off, and I flinch when he traces a solitary finger down my cheek, scrawling a shade along my skin so I shiver. "Some business took me on the more scenic route toward my realm. But I thoroughly enjoyed watching you sleep."

Bet you did. I wince, waiting for him to react to that stray thought, but his face is stoic, apart from that smirk.

His dark energy puffs like a dragon at the doorway to my mind, but he doesn't enter. *Why? He can take whatever he wants.* Or destroy whatever he wants, including the mind.

I'm not sticking around to find out.

Without another word, I grab the crown from my head, charge for Neoptolemus, and slam a sharpened gold spike right above his collarbone. He howls in pain. Growls follow as silver blood spews from the wound. Jaw dropping at his fangs gnashing and the retribution in his eyes, I yank out the crown, pull on the coach door handle, and throw myself out of the moving vehicle. He swipes for me at the last second, but it's too late. I'm rolling and tumbling down the hill into the sprawling forest.

Bruises form on my side as I stagger through the trees, already second-guessing my rash choice. My impulsivity and desperation to get away from the Prince of Destruction has led me right into the forest's edge where white shapes shift like gruesome phantasms. They almost cross my path. Hoarfrost nips at my cheeks as the icy wind bites into my flesh, numbing me to my core.

This must be the Father's Spirit Woods. Rumored to be the playground for Chasm escapees.

Dozens of ghouls roam the woods, undaunted by the sunlight due to their blindness.

With my eyes peeled for the creatures, I head for the area where the woodlands clear and stumble over a root, body striking a tree. Moaning, I hit the ground, dry heaving.

Side wailing in pain, I blink my eyes open and come face to face with a human skull. I cover my mouth, stifling a shriek.

Shrill and torturous screams echo from those woods as I rush through the labyrinth of tangled trees, hoping my stabby moment was enough to slow the Prince down. A mystical fog billows around me, restricting my vision. I growl at the forest's deception.

The fabric of reality is thinner here—able to be shredded by the strongest claws.

Bearing scraps of skin, chunks of bone, and teeth, the trees act as portals of dark power. Deformed, twisted, and bent into unnatural and chaotic patterns from the Chasm monsters that travel through them. Any moment, one could emerge and sink its eager fangs into my flesh.

Gooseflesh gnaws on my skin as if a ghost has licked my spine. Waves of nausea overcome me, and my stomach reels until I pitch myself against the nearest tree and retch.

There is a reason the Father placed his fortress with the Chasm on one side and hundreds of miles of forests on the other. If any Tenth Court humans ever get beyond the walls, they will drive themselves mad in these woods—devoured by monsters or hunted by vampires.

I grasp onto the nearest tree, stand, and clamber up a thickly-netted hill, hoping to find some bearings. It slopes upward, turning steep. Apprehension thickens inside me as my bare feet sweep aside more bones fumbling behind me knocking against one another.

My last footsteps to reach the hill's peak are the heaviest.

At the top, I take a severe, deep gust of air and hold it, wishing I could deny the sight.

Thousands of skeletons and corpses engulf the canyon, shading decay over the air. All are female. A hundred years of brides for the Prince of Destruction.

The ones he scorned...and threw away as if they were more bags of desecrated flesh. Half-bloods or humans. A mass grave.

A dumping ground.

This is what happens to them after Neoptolemus is finished with them. He destroys them and moves on to the next...and the next... and the next.

I sink to my knees and drop the crown. Anguish consumes me, threatening to unravel my heart.

"Holy foremothers..." I cry striving to center myself, tracing the circle on my chest until my hand aches.

I twist my head, torturing myself by studying the fresher corpses. That's when I see *her*! Getting to my feet, I storm through the labyrinth of bodies, but all I can see is her.

"Verena..."

Kneeling, I gather my High Guardian's corpse into my arms.

My V.

Face ashen, eyes vacant not a single crackle of lightning to her name.

Tremors conquer me. Every last muscle and limb shudders.

Like blood rubies mixed with gold, sunlight spreads across the sky, its glow silencing the darkness. The sunrise empathizes with my people's deaths. It's why it bleeds.

Cradling Verena's head, I drip rivers of gold tears onto her, praying she didn't suffer. I should desire the most biblical of vengeance, but for some reason, I can't foster it. I just shut down, my body numbing. Woe pulls me lower.

Careless of whether or not the Prince captures me, I curl into the fetal position and nestle close to my girlfriend. I become part of the bones...the corpses. I am ready for the canyon to swallow me, to devour me as it has thousands of others.

Shades and flames, dark and feverish, whisper across my back and trace the curves of my body, sifting into my hair—as if trying to comfort me. Asshole. The moment Neoptolemus touches me, a hand cupping my shoulder, I thrust my head back, arch my neck, and scream my pain and fury and vow of vengeance against him. Shaking with violence and ruination, I bite and kick and claw at him, knowing but not caring how catatonic I am.

A subtle clicking is all I hear before everything shuts down.

Damn. I recognize the cold cuffs shackling my wrists, humming with dark energy. Fused with the Prince's elite silver blood and destruction, the power-dampening cuffs not only inhibit the Halo, but one wrong move, and I'll get a little zap—the perfect shock collar. My mother uses the same for her prisoners but with her blood and fire.

I won't escape anytime soon.

8
TIME TO ENTER YOUR NEW HOME, PRINCESS..."

"I'll admit this was not my original expectation when I first used cuffs on you—" he chuckles, "—but I'm flexible and more than willing to mix business with *pleasure*..."

Eyes burning from the heady implication, I deadpan, thrusting out my jaw. "Get me out of these cuffs, and you'll learn how *I* take care of business, Neoptolemus. And it won't be a pleasure for you. Only for me."

"Hmm, this pretty princess has a kinky side," he croons draping his knuckles along my jawline. "How delightful. A quality I appreciate."

Shaking off his knuckles, I peer outside the window, grateful for the silence that settles around us. After the adrenaline rush of stabbing the Prince and throwing myself out of the coach, I'm crashing. A nebulous haze takes over my mind, and I welcome sleep.

When I wake, it's to the rumbling of the coach as it travels along one sweeping arc of an upper highway, leading straight to the Tenth Court gates. I rub the sleep out of my eyes.

From what I can make out, this highway is reserved for

elite subjects such as rooks or the Prince. Cargo trains swarm networks of more highways below us. Homeless encampments budge close to the Walls.

Compassion tugs at my heart when I consider all those human and vampire souls: escapees from the warring Court Mordere to the south—bitten vampires. Most humans will sell their blood and flesh to smugglers to make it here.

I crane my neck to discover snow-dusted, jagged mountain peaks. My gut clenches at the sight of thousands of humans, some bound in chains, while vampire overseers corral and herd others.

A shadow darkens my heart because the majority are fated for blood farms.

My thoughts turn to my mother and our ruined homeland. Grief becomes a scythe carving into my heart. Everything is gone. I tip my head forward so my curls fall over my face, trading my woe for rage.

Neoptolemus cups my chin and tilts my face upward to greet his.

"Where's my mother, you blood-mongering bastard?"

The fingers cradling my chin curve. "You have a foul mouth...for one who smells so *pure*."

I brace my spine.

He's hunting, but I am no prey.

"Take the high road," the Prince's voice is low, but the driver hears the command. "The *scenic* route." He eases his lips into a smile, the points of his fangs winking at me. I crane my neck.

Spine-chilling horror overwhelms all my discomfort. Will he take me past the Chasm? I fade to my empath as the Chasm's dark energy preys on my blood. Closer than ever, the opposing force oppresses and lures my Haloed heart—billions of cursed souls, hellions, monsters of mayhem, demons, and damned.

The coach takes a sharp left. Outside, relentless horses snort, piqued. Smoke from their breath drifts along the coach's sides while they spit countless embers from their uphill effort. Chasm mares birthed from hellfire.

After the coach rolls to a stop, Neoptolemus climbs out, stretching a hand toward me, but I recoil. "Don't touch me!" I get out on my own and nearly lose my balance, pretending it wasn't the Prince's shades steadying me.

As he chuckles, deep and throaty, my bare feet sink into a layer of snow. It doesn't crunch but drifts away into a whirlwind of gray fluff.

It's *ash*!

I look up to an endless slate-gray sky filled with coal-black bruises for miles. The skies here rain ash.

My breath rasps. My lashes freeze...unable to blink.

"No sunlight shines here," Neoptolemus declares proudly, extending his hand toward a lookout point. "Unless Father wills it."

With the Prince's shadow escorting me, I follow him along the ascending path flanked by the same iron trees with their black spectral leaves eclipsing the mountains. At the lookout point, the trees clear.

I catch my breath, stemming the urge to lurch.

Media promotions don't do it justice. The Father's Court isn't one castle but nine circling the three Towers. Shrouded in smoke, the gothic cathedral Towers impale the night sky, disappearing to ferocious heights beyond the ashy expanse. A simultaneous symbolic, Babel-like "fuck off" to the heavens along with his chess-based court system based on the Nine Circles of Hell. All perched on the edge of the Chasm, but I can't view the monstrous opening from this vantage point.

"Father's Trinity Eye." Neoptolemus notes.

A network of bridges branches out from the Towers to the castle territories of small cities.

Red ribbons stream from arched openings in the Towers, feeding crisscrossing canals connecting to the various castles. I narrow my vision to confirm my horrific suspicion of thin crimson falls of...blood.

Panic triggers in my spine. All my muscles tighten.

Run! Run and hide, Elysia, Mom's voice chimes.

You are the perfect bait and weapon. The Goddess whispers back.

I steady my breath.

The Prince's shades curve along my upper back and my trembling wrists to pacify them. I hadn't realized I was shaking.

"Time to enter your new home, Princess," Neoptolemus murmurs taking my elbow, dragging me back to the coach.

This will never be my home.

The Prince masks the windows with his shades so I can't memorize the journey. He folds his hands in his lap and eyes me. "I must admit I owe you a debt of gratitude, considering you granted me a reprieve. Tonight is First Favor, and I loathe the sycophantic suck-up of rooks currying their favor at my festival. Not that I can expect a human girl to understand the affairs of state."

I rise, sitting straight with my spine pressed to the seat, and pronounce in a strong voice, "Pomp and circumstance is always a matter of state. After all, I would fully expect Rook Viktor Idrys of the Court O' Nines to easily surpass all others with his purer blood-bought and bred *trophies*." I don't hide my loathing.

The Prince arches a brow, surprised by my knowledge, but

he curves his lips into an impressed smirk. "Your mother taught you well, I see."

I roll my eyes and scoff, "Because it's inconceivable I taught myself." How many times did I sit through court proceedings and research the Father's laws? Only two rooks are permitted at the Tenth Court during tax season. On the Centennial Eclipse, all nine will be present...

He roots his gaze on me for the duration of the journey. I keep mine pinched and my posture stiff.

The coach finally jerks to a halt. Knots strangle my throat.

Neoptolemus opens the door to more shades and darkness and the demon mares snort upon my exit. The Prince poises his fingers above my waist, but I screw my brows low in a lethal warning. To my astonishment, he draws his fingers away, though they hover.

From beyond his shades, I survey the Tenth Court architecture. Fantastical, daring, and grandiose. From the forest of spires and pinnacles of decorative carved needles to the intricate sculpted flying buttresses. To soaring-stained glass arched windows to the winged statues and gargoyles.

The Prince steers me inside, leading me into a cell of undulating shades and flames masking the walls. I scurry into the furthest corner and sit as the vampire gestures. "This is my personal prison, Princess. I built it and bled my destructive energy into it." Neoptolemus shakes out his robe. "We have some unfinished business. And I assure you, escape attempts would simply waste your energy. Energy I intend to put to good use later."

"Oh, yes, I'm full of big dick energy." I splay my legs, careless of the tattered gown ends riding up my thighs. When he glimpses me, I throw him my iciest glare, but I'm sure I don't intimidate much in my current state.

"Oh, yes, do forgive me." Neoptolemus' eyes journey across

my ruined gown right before he excuses himself and shadows out of the cell.

At first, I'm concerned he won't return and leave me here to wither as his power radiates from the walls encasing my body. But he said we had *unfinished business*. So, I rest my head against the corner and avoid the shades and flames stalking me. Annoyed when they encroach, I pitch forward and hiss, giggling because they dart away.

The Prince returns, clutching a long, white dress that reminds me too much of a thin, silky bridal gown. With a grunt, Neoptolemus chucks it to the floor beside me and waves a hand and the cuffs clatter to the floor.

Tentative, I finger the gown and slowly stand. "A game, Prince?"

"Tell you what, Princess." He folds his hands behind his back, leaning toward me, and I can almost imagine him growing scales and talons. "I'm going to give you a *golden* opportunity. Tell me the truth now, and perhaps I won't destroy you."

"What's the matter? A little *blocked*?" I detect the slight flaring of his nostrils, eyeliner wrinkling from his furrowed brows while a vein throbs in his neck. By now, I've assumed he can't access my mind, and I'm beyond thankful for the Halo's protection.

"We can do this the easy way or the hard way. Now..." He stabs a finger to the gown. "Put it on. You'll be spending quite some time with me, and I won't have you catching a cold. I'll give you two minutes. After, I'll enter regardless of your state of dress."

He winks, and I fully believe him.

When Neoptolemus enters two minutes later, I stand before him, crossing my arms—white dress still on the floor.

Eyes sparkling, I shrug, tapping the side of my arm. "Guess you'll have to learn some nursing skills."

I flinch when the Prince growls and curls his upper lip to showcase a gleaming, pearly fang.

"Guess we're choosing the hard way."

9
I WILL TAKE THE WAR TO THE PRINCE OF DESTRUCTION

I SAVOR THE SIGHT OF THE PRINCE GROWLING AND DRIVING HIS FIST into the wall. Whole stones shatter, raining grit and pebbles onto my head. Apathetic, I draw my knees to my chest and yawn at his latest failure to drag the truth out of me. "Temper, temper, Neo." When I'd first used the nickname, about an hour ago, he'd roared, and I'd sworn the tips of horns had thrust from his head.

Neo removes his robe and faces me. I clutch my knees, hoping to ignore the dark fortress of a chest. He's not merely a seasoned warrior, his entire being was created to be a weapon—a mighty war hammer of a vampire.

"Seriously, Princess, aren't you bored?"

I posture, chest lighter than a blossom to mirror my crooked smile. I imagine he hasn't had much experience with anyone he couldn't mentally break. He won't bring me to Daddy...not until he confirms my Everblood heritage.

"Or do you delight in testing my finite patience? Perhaps I should try a more *unpleasant* tactic?" he hints, brandishing flames from his fist.

"Huh? Oh, sorry...I wasn't listening."

Neo crouches, gathering shades and flames to consume his body, and leans closer.

I wince. He grins, relishing my fear, my thunderstruck heartbeat, but I'm not ashamed. Caped in his destructive force, he squats before me and leans closer because personal space matters little to him.

"Are you the *Everblood*, Princess?"

Finally, he uses the direct approach! After all the dancing around for hours, I don't know whether it's an insult or not.

"Elysia." I throw him a bone, diverting him.

He arches a brow. "What was that?"

"My name is Elysia," I clarify tightening my arms on my knees.

"Eh-lee-see-ah" he drags out every syllable, seductive, low, and dangerous.

I deny the urge to appreciate it. "You didn't answer my question."

"Funny, I thought you prefer destroy first, ask questions later."

"Answer me!" He slams his hand on the stone an inch from my body.

With a heavy sigh, I squeeze my knees, resting my cheek on one. Yes, I should cooperate. But by the Goddess, if there is one thing I enjoy almost as much as bringing the Prince of Destruction to his knees, it's seeing him sweat.

Besides, I'm damned anyway.

Utter loathing grows ice in my blood as I uncurl myself, narrow my eyes on him, and pour steel into my voice. "If I am some warrioress of light, Neo, then I'd suggest you say your prayers. Because if I ever get out of here, I'll hunt you. And I won't stop till I destroy you."

For the first time, Neo looks genuinely afraid. He parts his lips as if he's going to say something, but then he swallows and recovers—those thick, dark brows screwing low over the deadly hoods of his eyes.

"You'll never get out of here, Elysia," Neo shrugs into his robes. Bristling, he twists his head to mine. "I have a festival to get to."

I shrug. "Hmm...I love a good party."

"I'll return following First Favor. So, sit. Stay. And be a good Princess. No one has ever escaped my prison. So, if you do, it will confirm my suspicions. And I'll hunt you to the ends of the Court O' Nines if necessary."

I startle the moment his shade power locks the cuffs back on my wrists. When his eyes probe me at the last second, I wrinkle my nose, half-tempted to stick out my tongue as he leaves.

Worn out from all his interrogation, tremors prey on my body; threatening to rack me with an influx of sobs. Shutting my eyes, I nearly pass out...

Elysia...

A feminine smoky voice drifts into the prison cell—deep and dark like a breath of the cosmos. A heavenly melody.

When I open my eyes, my jaw drops.

"Elysia."

That voice! I've heard that voice! Deep and dark and beauteous. A voice I've heard in my mind and my dreams all my life.

Wings beat in the air. And I bask in the warmth of golden sunbeams shedding their grace upon me. My breath comes in waves until I'm ready to lift my head.

I spring back from the lightning-clad figure, wreathed in holy fire with several wings branching from her body. Dumbstruck, I curse a hundred different expletives, recognizing this otherworldly figure. My bones themselves are ready to liquefy.

The Goddess!

"Don't be afraid," she commands, her ethereal eyes housing galaxies without number. I fear they will render me blind.

Now...! She's coming to me now?

Flaming tendrils proliferate from her body, dark and full to bathe the cell with light. She extends her hand, and I let her guide me to my quivering knees. I don't dare get within an inch of her wings. Transfixed, I follow her beyond the mass grave, shrouded in her celestial warmth.

The Mother Goddess lowers her head to kiss my eyes.

"Elysia...you may return the Halo now."

The Goddess cups my cheeks with sun-kissed, dark hands. But my shoulders curl over my chest while I offer her nothing more than a pained stare and feeble eyes. I wear a tattered slip compared to her robed in sable black skin scribed with the constellations, voluminous hair like scrolls of twilight, and a gown more umbral than the dark side of the moon. "Your mother's boon is not your burden. This was not your choice."

A grief-born rage forges hellfire into my veins. "Damn right, it's not!" I wince, prepared for her holy smite but sigh because the Goddess only smiles. Burying my face in my hands, I free myself to ask, "Please tell me what in the hell is going on."

Lifting the crown from the ground, she raises it to me. "An ancient war exists between the Father and me. Whoever bears my Halo is the perfect bait and weapon."

My eyes rocket open wider than cathedral doors. "Why did you choose me when I was a baby? I'm the last one who..." I swallow, not wanting to return to that memory, to the darkness in my soul. "You should have chosen my mother." I claw my clothes, chastising myself for questioning the timeless being.

The Mother Goddess lowers one hand to palm my heart. "There is more than one way to be a warrior, Elysia."

I look to the golden diadem in her hand, my pulse thrumming harder with every second.

"But I will choose another, so you no longer carry this weight." The Mother slowly turns away, taking the crown.

"No!" I protest through tears while the Goddess smirks. I huff, rubbing my arms, marveling at the reverse psychology of this divine being...and her sense of humor. If she takes the Halo now, it will all be in vain. Mom's sacrifice. Killing the Prince of Death. Her bargain with the Father. Dad's death.

And my surest truth: I brought the Prince of Destruction to his knees. Mom started the work. I should damn well be able to finish it.

"I'm not a savior!" I scream, shaking my head, wild and fierce. Heat lashes my blood, a smoldering warning while the crown sparks in response.

When the Goddess impales my eyes with hers, burning me with her omnipotent knowledge, I still to her words.

"No. You are not."

The Highest Mother traces one finger across my cheek, granting me a whisper of a caress to tingle my skin, reminding me of V's lightning static. "But you still had faith, my daughter. I heard every time you prayed. And felt whenever you traced that circle upon your chest. But healing cannot come without a price."

"Was Verena the price?!" I scream, raking my nails into my scalp. "And my father?"

"Do you still have faith, Elysia? You may turn back now, return to the Underground as your mother desires, and spend the rest of your life smuggling as you have always wanted. Or..." She trails off, her eyes narrowing upon mine, and I struggle to swallow under the supreme black-hole gaze.

"Or?" I hold my breath.

"Perhaps this is not purgatory, my child. Consider it...limbo."

A trial. Unfulfilled penance. 'Healing cannot come without a price.'

It's why she took the Halo. But I never healed.

I slammed the door to it. Haunted by my past demons, I've spent all this time in the Underground, taunting them but never facing them.

And yet, the Halo never quit on me. Gold blood. My dreams. The Goddess never gave up on me.

Lips parting, I lick them flicking my eyes to the diadem.

"Yes, Elysia. You still carried some of its power in your bloodstream. I took the Halo after that night and gave it to your mother for safekeeping. Last night, the power you suppressed awoke when you faced the Prince. You are the Prince's equal."

Yes, an equal who ran from him, I almost snap. I'm always running...

But I don't have to. Not if I accept the Halo. I look around at the stone cold walls around me, alive with the Prince's energy. If I take the Halo's power back, use it against him, I will take mine back, too. And maybe that will be enough to get me out of this limbo, this purgatory.

This is why I have been truly drawn to the human blood farms. All my life, I've walked a thin tightrope between the human and the vampire world. Gifted or cursed with this Halo, I war between emotions threatening to destroy me. Loss, rage, hurt, abandonment, betrayal, guilt...*meaning*.

I'm on the edge of a great abyss, one I must cross to reveal the truest version of myself.

"Do you still have faith, daughter?"

I think of Verena, palms clammy, stomach ready to crumple from misery's rot.

"Will I—" I croak, then sob, breaking, knees buckling, daring to hope.

"Yes, Elysia..."

I crumble under the gravity of the gift she's just bestowed, but the Goddess combs her hands into my curls. "But you will not be the one to save Verena. Her spirit has a choice to make. Her own path to forge. A path that will cross with yours again."

Breathless from relief, a deluge of warmth strengthens my stomach, prompting me to rise...until raw thorns prickle the back of my neck, infecting me with pain.

"He's been hunting me, hasn't he...?" I breathe deep, my tears torrential.

All those girls in the canyon...their destruction is a mark upon *my* heart.

"Yes, the Father cannot recognize the Everblood. The Prince does his bidding and hunts her instead."

No more lives will be lost on my account. No more will be sent to that canyon.

All my life, this is what I have craved. I can't go back. This is why my light has been begging for more: I've been giving it a battle when it desires the war.

Neoptolemus will answer for his carnage. I will take the war to the Prince of Destruction.

"Do I get wings?" I ask, desperate brows lifting, but it sounds so idiotic coming from my mouth. Why on earth should I consider wings with all these corpses around me?

The Goddess lifts her chin and offers a hint of a smile. "No, you must earn your wings. The Halo merely grants you the capabilities of my angels. It is bound to you, your essence, and your emotions. You must learn to bond with it, accept its power and control. Consider yourself a *fallen* one. But understand this, Elysia. If you want those wings, they will not come without blood and fire, destruction, and...death."

I deadpan with the Mother, her words like a heavenly scroll impregnating my very soul with their promise. Whatever price I must pay, whatever penance I must fulfill, it will all be worth it to earn those wings.

To reunite with Verena.

I raise my royal chin, meet the Mother's eyes, and scream my acceptance, "Yes!"

The Goddess injects the crown deep into my chest cavity.

Billions of gold constellation particles shower my skin, dazzle my flesh, and engulf my blood. Radiating all over the cell walls, penetrating through the cracks. They voyage so deep until they lasso my heart and inject within my very essence, burning a divine trademark—a celestial seal. Warmth overflows, granting me a lifeforce, a power ten thousand times anything I've ever felt. The power of the brightest morning star to shine into dawn.

She leans down to kiss my brow. "From this moment on, you hold the power to heal—but not simply the body. To restore *souls* is within your kiss. But you must only bestow it on those who are worthy. Or your Halo will break," she warns, lowering her hands to her sides.

"My Halo can break..." I touch my lips. Desperate, I wring my fingers together and plead, "Can the Father break it?"

"Remember, the one with the most darkness inside his soul must never bite you." She continues. "First, you must seek the Altar hidden in the Tenth Court. It will tell you what to do. Your soul may only grow in the deepest of darkness. Though you will have trials and tribulations, you will never be alone." She touches my chest.

Am I strong enough to face such darkness?

"The Prince has a secret you must uncover. You know what you must do."

The Goddess evanesces, leaving me gasping in the wake of a whirlwind of holy fire. And the deafening silence of the prison with nothing but my breath thundering in my mind.

Gold dust wafts from my skin. My Haloed heart warms from the idea of facing Neoptolemus again, its beat quickening.

Maybe Destiny is a bitch, but I'm bringing her bigger sister, Karma, right to the Prince's door!

Seconds later, the infernal device, my beaming bangle, undulates from my chest in slow, bewitching tendrils. Fiery ribbons wander, congregating into the cuffs.

They break.

Shaking my head, I rub my wrists, peer at my chest, and bite my lower lip. "Well, that was...thank you." I pinch the bridge of my nose.

Why am I talking to the Halo?

Hmm...maybe...

"Don't suppose you can make me a door out of here, can you?" I exhale, imagining a golden arched door in the wall, exploring what else the magical entity can do.

I nearly topple over when the Halo beams vault from my chest and form the outline of a door. Breath staggering, I gawk at the spangled door, wondering how else the Halo will manage to surprise me infused with stardust but offering a shifting view of the outside. Before the gilded pineapple ring can change its mind, I ease onto the little overhanging ledge barely six inches in width. Gold dust showers my form, twinkling and tingling my skin.

My heart rate turns mad.

It's the perfect prison. Suspended in mid-air inside a

smaller stone tower, it doesn't connect to the Towers via bridges or roads. A canal of slow-rushing blood is the only opportunity of escape. I chew on my lower lip, repulsed.

But I can't back out now.

It's my turn to go hunting for a Prince.

Heaving a few gasps, I stare at the bloody river. Muscles taut, I brace myself. The metallic, rust-like stench overwhelms my nostrils.

A golden wagging tongue spews from my chest as if chastising me for my cowardice of a little blood.

"Did you stick your tongue out at me?" I chide the Halo.

Shaking my head, I take a deep breath and plunge into the stream.

Blood drenches my skin as the river carries me beyond the tower. Clenching my lips, I battle nausea, not wanting to imagine any number of diseases I could contract.

I duck low under the blood as the shadow of a bridge passes over me with knights standing sentry carrying bone armor swords. Breaking the surface, I gasp and empty all my stomach contents. A few yards ahead of me is a tunneled opening...Where it ends is a mystery, but I pray, *please not a bathing pool.*

Now, the thick, viscous fluid engulfs my shoulders, splashing droplets along my neck. The tunnel roof forms a shadow over my head, welcoming me into its dark embrace. Pitch blackness surrounds me. Preserving my energy, I harden my stomach muscles as the blood current strengthens, building in intensity and speed. The telltale downpour signals I'm approaching a drop. No turning back now. Could the Halo catch me with a net?

The current tips me over the edge, and I free-fall, counting the seconds. Before three my body hits solid marble. Shallow enough for me to stand.

"Well now, what do we have here?"
I snap my head toward the rich tenor of a voice.
Shit, shit, shit!
I'm kneeling in a blood bath!
With a naked vampire!

10
"I HOPE YOU ENJOY YOUR NIGHT, LYS SPIRIT...COURTING THE PRINCE OF DESTRUCTION."

"Seriously..." The vampire smirks shaking his head, dragging a hand through his close-cropped dark hair. "I told him I loathe the festivities, but will his pranks never end?" Baring his muscular pectorals with skin the color of burnished sienna, the vampire props his elbows onto the marble bath tiles.

I hold out my hands defensively, waiting for him to crouch. "My deepest apologies, sir, but it couldn't be helped."

He lowers one finger into the blood, circling it, surprising me with his disinterest. "What's your name?"

I rise and face the vampire, beyond grateful the blood conceals his lower regions. "Lys Spirit." I grin when he lifts his brows, surprised.

The vampire sucks on the dipped finger, then stares fixedly at me, judging, assessing with eyes so dark and warm, they remind me of rich hickory. "A rather unusual locale for a renowned smuggler."

He pokes his toes through the blood, wagging them back and forth. I sniff, perplexed. Apprehension pricks my spine like the tip of a stake. Is this some sort of ploy? A cat and mouse game? Or am I simply covered in so much other human cell matter he can't scent me?

"I just escaped from a prison, so forgive me for being in a *mood*." I plant my hands on the side of the tiled bath and pull myself out, keeping him to my side and not turning my back.

The vampire grumbles, "And are my," he reaches toward a wine glass, then clears his throat, "*bloodier* environs a better substitute that you had to disturb my private bath?"

My befuddled lashes blink quicker than hummingbird wings as I shake my arms—eager to rid myself of the rancid odor and sogginess. What is it with this bizarre vampire? A Tenth Court vampire should have no misgivings about devouring human blood.

My hair is slick with the pulpy human juice and I can't help it. I stomp my foot on the floor and unleash a shrill, disgusted shriek. Frenzied heat rampages through my veins as I struggle to wipe the fluid before finally crossing my arms over my chest. Now and then, the vampire flicks his eyes to their corners. Overall, I'm thankful for his apathy.

Finally, I jut my hip out, give him a mock, drippy bow, and spread my arms to explain, "I will take my leave, good sir. Disturbing your bath was not at all my intention."

He sips from his wine glass barely giving me a second glance, though his eyes flick to their corners every now and then. The vampire shifts his head toward me and asks, "Then, what was, fair bloodied maiden?"

I open my mouth and deadpan. "The Prince."

Eyeing me beneath heavy lids, the vampire licks the wine glass rim, and retorts, "Is that so?"

"I have unfinished business with Prince Neoptolemus." I keep my voice cool and even with the ungarnished, dark truth. Still, I have to refrain from laughing at my inside joke.

"Well then, best not keep the Prince waiting." The vampire sets his wine glass down, slowly rising. "He gets ever so cranky, especially when his future brides are not *punctual*. Especially for First Favor."

Without bothering to correct his assumption, I blush and spin away as he positions his foot on the tile. From the corner of my eye, I make out his well-muscled calf, but it's not the fleshy sinew that prompts my gasp. Countless scars riddle his legs—garish stripes as if a whip infused with UV torture balls flailed him.

"Thank you for respecting my modesty," the vampire chuckles, and I tilt my head over my shoulder to discover him in a black robe.

Sighing, I face him as he extends a hand.

"My name is Quillion. I am a Tenth Court bishop on the order of the Prince of Destruction."

Still wary, I accept the handshake but keep enough of a distance that I must fully stretch my arm. "Kill-ee-ahn." I admit how much I like the formal name. Not once does he move toward me. Nor does he flash his fangs. Quillion simply smiles, showing a full set of gleaming teeth with fangs retracted.

My breath stalls. Amazed by his control and how he inhales steadily, reminding me of...my father. Empath Elysia pokes my frontal lobe, but I drive her behind an invisible force field. She won't help me tonight.

"You'll need a change of garb." Quillion gestures to my ruined and bloodied gown.

Shrugging, I giggle spontaneously, dumbfounded by Quillion and his courtesy. At any point, the bishop could have called a host of knights to remove my pest presence and haul me off for questioning. Instead, he's offered to take me directly to the Prince.

"Come with me," he gestures. "My guest room is next door, and you may order whatever attire you prefer."

The bishop leads me through one of the bathhouse's four arched doorways fixed with marbled pillars laden with gold. He motions to the nearby shower, then introduces me to a digital bishop's tattoo on his wrist and summons a hologram database. Snickering, he opens a wardrobe app, and I can't help but match his grin at the irony.

"Mystic Princess: Fantasy Fashion for fans of the *Harem of Hades*."

The screen exhibits an appealing aerial view of the Tenth Court's tri-towers: the intro for the Prince's bachelor reality show. "Do you have what it takes to be the Prince's new rose?" The announcer holds a rose of passionate scarlet that erupts into a shower of petals before the screen pans to profiles of the latest *Harem* girls.

A sick pun directed at the Rose City.

Contemptuous heat roils in my belly, vying with a deep ache. Verena loved watching it, excusing it as "know thy enemy". I'd catch her on CourtTok for updates all the time.

Quillion drops his hands to his sides. "Hope it's not in too poor of taste."

"Not at all," I dissuade him and make my selection, thanking him for his generosity.

"Stunning pieces," he notes when I finish, prompting me to smile. "I'll give you some privacy."

It takes more time for me to shower than the fashion program does to announce the garb's arrival. Towel around my curls, I marvel at the pixelated wall that conveys a delivery system.

The gown is perfect. Silver filigree of intricate designs over the barest curve of my shoulders, twisting along my chest with a deep plunging neckline to expose the inner swell of my breasts and navel. The filigree coils and curls, sensuous, along my sides, ending in a V-shape at my pelvis. Dangerous hips exposed. Like a liquid halo, thin filigree curls around my thighs. And one single circlet of gold atop my head parades my Princess heritage and my Goddess-kissed status.

A braided cord of gold sits on my hips, with thin swaths of sparkling fabric covering my privates. Feathers adorn their lower half.

With matching silver filigree designs around my eyes and shimmering gold dust on my skin, I become my title: the Halo-Bearer.

Lastly, I armor myself with silver chain mail gloves—intricate and beautiful with claws as sharp as daggers donning my fingertips. Ensemble complete with my defined brow, subtle smoky eye, and bold, blood-red lip, I am ready.

The Halo hums inside me.

"Oh, you like?" I wink at myself in the mirror and blow a kiss to the Halo. But I remain apprehensive, tensing. I won't let it lure me into a false sense of security. Despite my newfound acceptance, it still betrayed me in the Spirit Woods.

If you want those wings, they will not come without blood and fire, destruction and...death...

I square my shoulders. I have no intention of dying tonight.

Once I step outside, Quillion lifts his brows, stunned eyes showing his approval. "Well, now. We best not keep the Prince waiting."

Grinning, I follow Quillion as he guides me beyond the bathhouse to a set of winding stone stairs. He cinches his bathrobe tighter.

"Do you need to change?" I inquire and gather the feathered swaths of my gown, so I may ascend with him.

"Whatever for?" Quillion angles his head at me. "I fully intend to finish my bath."

A tight knot forms in my stomach. "Are bishops not required to be present?"

A faint smile crosses his face as he ascends to the apex of the stairs. "Yes, but I am the exception."

I don't ask why. Something in his tone suggests he wouldn't share.

The path spills into an enclosed skyway; walls of arched stained glass, painting a colorful mural along the floor. Some blood still trickles from Quillion's calves, and I step over the smears, following him to the corner of a massive hall void of vampires.

"How long until we arrive?" I ask, glancing at the domed ceiling.

"Shortly. One mere elevator ride to the locale. Tonight is the grand reception," elaborates Quillion as we reach the halfway mark.

I pause when a shaft of crimson-red light spears the window, scooping me into its violent beam. I study the outside where the ashen expanse has shifted to reveal a blood moon.

The Father's doing. No doubt for the grand reception, vampires are far more *aggressive* on full-blood moons, their hunger more piqued.

At least it's not a harvest moon.

"Each night, nearly a hundred parties will be held at various Court sites. Confounding and grandiloquent." Quillion's nostrils flare from mocking derision. The seams of his mouth are etched, matching the tension in his shoulders.

*Huh...*he sounds annoyed.

The further we progress down the hall, the heavier my chest grows. As if all the bones of past brides have settled there. I banish any sense of guilt and stoke the fires of justice, of retribution.

None of this Tenth Court, this diabolical devilry finery will tempt me. Surrounded by demons, I am the vengeful angel who whispers among them.

Soon, I will roar.

At the great hall's end is an enormous, gilded cage with silver filigree doors in the design of chess pieces. The elevator.

Quillion presses his thumb to the knob on the outer door, grunts, revealing a dribble of silver blood.

Blood authentication code. A private elevator.

It carries us through a mostly enclosed tunnel. Every few seconds, the tunnel clears to arched gaps that offer an expanded view of the tower city. Countless levels spiral upward like a monstrous silvered serpent.

Pursing my lips, I regard Quillion, who crosses his legs while he casually folds his hands in his lap.

Déjà vu returns. Patience and an inner strength. My father's arms holding me, his peaceful heart.

The blood drains from my face.

"Is something wrong? The Prince's brides are normally far more eager and jubilant."

"Or terrified," I challenge. "Considering the Prince's reputation for not keeping one too long."

Quillion snickers and cinches his robe again. "Oh, trust me, they are not terrified for long. But it does beg the question, why are you playing such a dangerous game coming to Court unmarked, without any protection?"

"As I said, the Prince and I have unfinished business."

"A bit vague."

"As opposed to a blood bishop's willingness to help a Carrie-impersonating human who tumbled into his private bath?"

Quillion grins from ear to ear and says, "We both know you are no mere human, Lys Spirit. But trust me when I assure you. I hope you succeed in *keeping* the Prince longer than his other brides."

A fresh blush tethers my cheeks, but the elevator stops, diverting my attention.

Outside, a sweeping arc bows to an ascending staircase comprised of at least one hundred steps flanked by knights. One for each step.

My stomach churns fluttering as I war between anticipation and anxiety.

Quillion waits at the base of the stairs, his dark brows tapering low. No knights meet his eye. Chests still as cadavers, none breathe.

At the top of the staircase are two doors as large as castle arches. Quillion offers me his hand, and gratitude overwhelms my heart.

"I'm quite glad I did not accept your offer earlier. You deserve to be the gold star to my dark shade."

I grin at him from the side as we take the steps. My armored fingers curl on the backs of his palm. "I believe we both know you are no mere blood bishop, Quillion. Especially with your impressive shade." I tap his skin, a hint darker than mine. It reminds me of my father's, except Quillion's is warmer.

Monumental angel statues crying blood tears greet me at the staircase crest where we pause. One sharp glance from Quillion and the knights part. Beyond those doors thunders an orchestra laced with modern symphonic bass and digital renditions.

My heart pounds to the beats.

"I will announce you and take my leave." Quillion bows his

head to me at the same time that he raises my hand to kiss the silver armor. A stray lock of damp, dark hair lingers on his brow, casting a shadow over his right eye. "I hope you enjoy your night, Lys Spirit...courting the Prince of Destruction."

Another blood authentication prick and the doors crash open.

I hold my breath and pray to my spiritual foremothers while the pulsing music fades. *Pomp and circumstance indeed.*

This is no mere ballroom.

It's like stepping into a fairy tale stamped in blood and shadow, firelight, and lust. No chairs on the mezzanine level—only sumptuous floor beds for the frequent fucking.

Wisping gold fog corkscrews around the feet of hundreds of vampires and humans, but through the haze I see the floor... layered in blood. Its metallic scent taints the air, joining the dozens of angel statues embedded in the side walls—mouths open to gush blood arcs pirouetting in the air before diving to the floor. Private boxes rest on each end of the gargantuan theater for more elite Court members.

My eyes land on the stage backdrop, a blood fall cascades into a pool hollowed out into the floor. Several human girls frolic in the pool, naked and unashamed ignoring the collars on their necks. Others kneel before the Prince's throne—constructed of thousands of glimmering blood rubies, trimmed in skulls and bones.

And there sits the Prince on his throne, dark herculean chest exposed. Gold and iron armor gilds his boots and leathered legs, circling the shoulders and arms of his black velvet robe that pours to the ground.

The armor is for show.

The Prince himself is dragon armor and destructive fire. His flames and shadows decorate the throne's edges.

Though his harem girls occasionally fawn over him and kiss his robe and feet, Neo leans to the side, clearly bored.

Oh, he won't be bored for long.

I stand upon one massive sprawling staircase as steep as a cliff erected in the very center of the theater. Inescapable from attention. I side-eye Quillion, registering his wry grin.

His form of a joke for disturbing his bath. If I ever meet the bishop again, I will repay the favor.

Quillion raises his voice and proclaims in a thunderous tenor echoing throughout the theater.

"Lys Spirit, Courtier of the Court O' Nines."

He exits, massive doors closing behind him.

Bastard bishop. I smirk to one side.

Every single head sweeps to me. Hundreds of scarlet pupils dilate to my presence. The millions of diamonds from dozens of chandeliers seize the silver of my armor filigree, hailing my bearing from the heavens.

I take my first step, gown trailing behind me in a feathered bridal train.

Hundreds of bared fangs gleam. Tongues weep. Wings flare open wide.

Countless explode into vampire speed.

Unclaimed, my throat presents the most mouth-watering of vessels.

As soon as my chest hums its warmth, I chastise the Halo, *If you glow now, you'll get us both killed, you damned disco ball.* The salty Halo still tests its boundaries and offers a teasing glow to emanate from my chest.

The Prince does not look up.

The army of vampires crashing into each other does not fill me with dread. Nor rage. I wish I could rock the foundations of the theater, unleash the power of the Halo, and burn every vampire to a crisp, saving their ruler for last. Instead, my heartbeat hammers hysteria in my chest. My lungs slam together until breath thunders in my ears.

The Prince does not move.

Bold enough to meet the vampires' eyes, I descend, parting my tempting lips. One skull cracks against the bottom step. Each ominous step I take vibrates into my body like a precursor to my demise.

The Prince slowly sits up.

The filigree coating my feet echoes. Bodies gather as vampires overthrow one another, knocking each other unconscious.

The Prince raises the barest corner of his chin.

Wavering between elated breathlessness and terror-struck hyperventilation, I continue. In a few moments, I will step on one of many fallen heads piling up on the staircase.

Silver blood sprays everywhere, pooling along the staircase sides. All humans, pure blood courtiers, fang maids, and familiars alike stare at the Prince, baited breaths, watching...waiting.

He flicks his eyes to me.

My lips glide into an angelic smile.

Sucking in a deep breath, I take one more step, mere inches from the court vampires. Cracks fissure the staircase from their crashing bodies, but it holds. Fear sends my pulse into a tailspin. One more breath and a vampire will reach me.

Tempting fate with leaps of faith, I prepare to embark into the hoard of vampires.

Clothed in destructive flames and robed in shadows, *he* appears, captures my wrist, and purrs a low growl.

"*MINE!*"

Silence hangs in the air as every last vampire immediately retreats like squirming serpents with their heads chopped off.

My shoulders sink, relieved breath loosening, heat howling through my body.

"Welcome to my Court, Elysia Rose...Everblood," he whispers his confirmation.

Equal and sovereign, I raise my chin and prepare to court the Prince of Destruction.

II
"I. WILL. BE. YOUR. BRIDE."

My heart burns. My star-kissed soul weeps at Neo's deadly beauty and evil breath on my face, luring rebellious blood to my cheeks. I part my lips and slide my hand into his, captivating the vampire.

A slow, bewildering smile grows as Neo tilts his head and grips my jaw forcing my neck to arch.

Will the Prince of Destruction bite me here and now? *The one with the most darkness inside his soul must never bite you*, the Halo whispers the reminder.

His Father-fucking equal! I remind it.

I exhale long and slow. Damn it to hell, I should reduce him to ash for having the audacity to *touch* me!

Strike, Halo! The glow dims.

Oh, come on, not one little celestial shock?

Defeated, I sigh.

Neo inhales my scent rubbing his sensual lips upon my skin. The fire in my heart swells, enthralling my blood and tantalizing my senses.

Now, my Halo clusters along my chest like sunbeams, but Neo suffuses them in his destructive energy, preventing all from viewing.

Nothing and no one else exists in the Court but us.

He smells of chaos, of nightmares, of *ruination*.

When the Prince's other hand caresses the naked skin of my lower back, fingers curving onto my spine, I jerk my chin to command his winter mist eyes. Silver hair slicked away from his face only accents his dark skin, his powerful jaw, full and compelling mouth, and cheekbones as high as castle towers. And that diabolical eyeliner.

Caping us in shadow and flame, the Prince of Destruction raises my armored hand to his lips, kissing my skin through the gaps. "Dance with me, Princess."

Without releasing my hand, Neo leads me down the trail of vampire bodies. My eyes never stray from his. They smolder with a passion for justice, for his canyon of corpses, for what he did to my father.

He is a predator prince believing he can toy with this vengeful angel. How long until he alerts his Father? The memory of ash tickling my nostrils, of my ravaged homeland lingers in my mind. Somehow, I swallow it all, hold to the Halo, and remember my goal.

I'll be damned if I let Neoptolemus destroy my purpose.

I envision my future wings.

Flying with Verena.

Jaw hard and chin elevated, I refuse to cow as his eyes embark on an unholy crusade across every inch of me.

Neo snatches my waist, fingers digging into my naked flesh. Drawing me closer, he presses his body to mine. With his robe of undulating shadows parted, my filigreed breasts lean against the bottom edge of his powerhouse of a chest. Flames teeter along his form, but they do not burn me, they are warm. My skin tingles, heating with stardust.

His other hand glides into mine, dragging across the armored glove. Neo beams, waiting for me to accept the dance.

Heart pounding, fingers trembling, I raise my hand to his shoulder. Lifting my chin higher till my neck strains, I match his eyes. Those orbs may be windows to the soul, but if Neo has one, it was birthed in the ninth circle of hell.

Not one musician in the pit dares to miss a beat. Violins, filled with willpower and ego, commence the passionate song.

Scheherazade.

The beauteous music bleeds into me, alluring as a snake charmer, but it can't compete with Neo's eyes, nor his pretentious grin. Shadows cloak us while the lustful, intensifying music protects our conversation.

"Never in all my centuries have I met my match," he compliments me, breaking from my hand to momentarily skim his knuckles across my arm. "If your blinding light and blood purity in the woods weren't enough of a hint, you escaped my prison. Not to mention the beams from your fetching chest just now. Did you truly believe you could hide in my court?" He seizes my hand again and swings me around the room.

Thanks to the Rose City court festivals, I match the Prince's steps to perfection, but his body still commands mine.

"Who says I'm hiding?"

"Touché." his eyes travel down my scantily clad form.

"Is there something wrong with my body, Prince Neoptolemus?"

He smirks leaning to murmur against my ear, "Forbidden fruit, Princess."

Rolling my eyes, I glower. "Heaven forbid I deny the devil his due for his wicked thoughts on my goddess image. Perhaps you should gouge out your eyes," I pull away, entrapping him and causing him to pause. Like Scheherazade wooing her sultan.

A chuckle buds in the Prince's throat. "High and mighty. You are your mother's daughter."

On the next refrain, the Prince dips me at the waist. I am bold enough to scrape one claw along his knuckles, drawing blood. He pulls me forward, so I crash against him. Brows dancing, he flashes his fangs. *Supercilious ass.*

"What is your plan now?" I wonder as he sweeps me into the monarchial waltz.

He tilts his chin toward me. "I might ask you the same, but you already told me, didn't you? Humans are so predictable. Vengeance—"

"Do not compare me to another human, Destruction," my voice steady and merciless.

A muscle throbs in his jaw while his pupils dilate: a black swarm to cloak his silver moons.

"If you do so again, I will use my Halo to burn your tongue and force you to choke on its *ash*."

I cherish his fear.

How he pauses. How his eyes widen.

An ornamentation of notes swells into a lilting refrain to capture the sultan's imagination, as the Prince hovers close to my mouth. "My sincerest apologies, Princess."

His fingers creep an inch lower to thumb the tail end of my spine.

For one eerie moment, I imagine those fingers weaving to my front aiming beyond my pelvis. I shake off the sinful thought.

"As if the one who wears the heavens could entertain such an emotion as baseless and simple as *vengeance*," I scoff with my grand bluff.

COURTING DEATH AND DESTRUCTION

The Altar. His dark secret The Halo echoes barely above a whisper.

My jealous voice vies for attention. *Find Mom. Bring him to his knees!*

The Prince releases my waist so he may coax me into a series of twirls to mirror the exotic solo melodies of the second movement's woodwind instruments. His shadows frolic along my body, curling and eddying, charming me with their depravity. The moment his hand tiptoes along my spine again, he presses, "Then, *pray* tell, oh, blessed one…" he chortles at his ridiculous pun. "Why honor the demon's lair with your presence? You could have simply fled."

"One so corrupt and immoral as you could never hope to understand my motivations, much less my plans. And you *will* answer my question, Neo."

The Prince yanks me to him, voice deep and low and lovely, "As much as the idea of you flat on your back with me on top of you thrills me—"

"I recall *you* falling to your knees like a prostrate servant."

Neo hisses, exposing his fangs. He cradles my waist, wicked fingers dipping below the gold cord and fabric. "Did you know I have a dark blood oath with my Father?"

I hold my breath. Blood magic is the strongest power in the world of vampires.

"I am bound by oath to inform him if I ever find the Everblood."

The song lulls to an intimate sensuality. Upon the final notes, the Prince seizes me close, "Of course, he didn't stipulate *when*." His eyes flush with bloodlust. "Time to say *your* prayers, Elysia."

Before I can open my mouth, he erupts into a wraith of shadows. Within moments, Neo ushers me beyond the Tower, straight inside the mouth of…

The *Chasm*!

I can't help my screams. Or how I cling to his cold robes. I rake my armored claws at the shadowy fabric as he descends and throws his head back, chaotic laughter rocking his form.

Deeper he carries me until there is nothing but blackness and dozens of familiar dripping blood eyes.

The Fallen. Tremors rupture through me. Icy fear crept its fingers along my spine and lock up all my nerves, nearly paralyzing me.

"Take me out of here!" I cry, but the Prince edges me closer to the hoard, his laughter deepening.

Tempted by my scent, the creatures' decrepit hands extend.

Where is my Halo?

Hey, I'm sorry I called you a disco ball, all right? Please help!

Not one spark.

I bury myself in Neo's darkness to escape.

What was I thinking? I'm not strong enough to combat him. No matter how high the stakes, no matter how my heart burns with a zeal for justice, the Halo recognizes what an imposter I am.

Murderer, I remind myself of my chilling past I fight so hard never to relive even if it haunts me every day.

Flames cavort all over my body.

Neoptolemus toys with me again.

He'll deliver me broken and wounded to his Father.

I'm going to die in the Chasm!

As one claw creeps across the back of my neck, acid breath ready to singe my hair, the Prince shouts, "*Away!*"

At once, every creature skitters, disappearing into the darkness, talons scraping the rocks.

My breaths are nothing but gasps against his skin. His throaty chuckle vibrates into my flesh.

A game. Nothing but a game.

Seething, I lift my chin to meet his sterling eyes, "How dare yo—"

Neo chokes my words, gripping my throat. I'm helpless as he smashes me against the Chasm so the rocks bruise my flesh, cushioned only by his shades. He presses himself against me, and I claw at his chest while he wrenches my thigh to the side with his knee.

Beneath my dress swaths, his hand digs into my flesh before he anchors my leg on his hip and does the same with my other, spreading me, pinning me like I'm no more than a luna moth. I freeze, my scream catching in my constricting throat.

His flames showcase his dark features and those eyes—ghostly and effervescent in the pitch black. His dark desire wrecks the space between my thighs, igniting my own sinful craving—a carnal part I won't let win.

"Listen, *Elysia*," he whisper-purrs in my ear and nips the lower lobe, causing me to shiver. I moan when he fondles my inner thigh. The Prince chuckles. "You are right. A corrupt and immoral creature such as myself could never understand the purest of hearts. But perhaps we can pick up where we left off..."

"What are you waiting for?" I dare, snapping my head forward, only to realize my mistake when my mouth meets his.

Pain lances my chest—a Halo's warning—but I raise my chin to avoid him despite it granting him more access to my throat. "Will you destroy me or simply thrill in your Father torturing me as he did my mother?"

"I won't deny it was satisfying to watch the Rose Queen brought to her knees," he breathes savage ice against my mouth.

Pressing my cheek to the Chasm, I clench my eyes when his brazen fingers tiptoe higher along my thigh. I tense, flattening my spine against the rocks so they slice into my skin. The pain is a little relief from his delirious hand.

"You are nothing alike and yet so similar. You are so unexpected, Elysia. And I *love* the unexpected." He mouths my neck, sucking, trailing hot saliva on my skin.

I cringe.

"You were mad to come here. And I crave a little madness."

He flashes his fangs, ready to descend.

Don't let him bite you!

I scream the words before I hardly know they've left my throat, "I'll make you a deal!"

He pauses, his glittering eyes discovering mine, both brows arched. "What was that?"

"A solemn blood oath."

"Hmm…color me intrigued, Princess." Neo brushes a finger across my cheek, spreading skittery chills up my spine. I flinch when he asks, "What do I get out of this deal?"

I wait for the Halo to emerge. Instead, its warmth drifts from my chest, plummeting lower to heat my center. *Traitorous cheerio.*

"I. Will. Be. Your. Bride."

To buy me time, I agree to the one thing I vowed never to become. When he least expects, I will act. If I have to, I'll strangle him with the Halo itself.

His finger rubs my parted lips. "Beyond tempted. And what do you get?"

"Do not betray me to your Father."

"Your dowry is quite lofty. Exalted even," he chuckles, finger descending. "But despite such *rapture* as I can provide, I doubt you will want to pay the bride price."

I consider his deadly blood trail. Bride corpses in the dumping ground. The brainwashed minds of his harem, their vacant eyes as they swarmed his throne and played in his bloody pool.

I slam my eyes shut when his fingers sweep from my jawline to the space between my breasts.

"No more prison. I am a *Princess* bride. You will treat me with the sovereignty I deserve." *As he should with any girl.*

"I'm open to compromise." He rubs his knuckles against my inner breast swell. I gulp. He croons, breathing into my hair, "As my bride, you will sleep with only me in my bed."

"No!" I spit, a scarlet storm obstructing my vision.

When his lips drag along my neck, I slam my head against the rocks and bite my lower lip to keep from shrieking. A staggering heat plagues my core.

Damn my stupid, human urges. And the Halo!

The Prince's fangs tease out, but he bounces them along my throat. Another predatory move.

"Do you know what my Father will do to you, Elysia? He will have no qualms about stripping you bare and parading you before every last one of his Courts...before your own mother and anyone you hold dear."

"Stop," I plead in a mournful moan.

His lips pull back into a dangerous grin as he savors my dread. My fear.

"He will ransack your body. Again and again," he murmurs and prints his lips on my jawline.

Tears squeeze from my eyes.

"He will make it his mission to break you, to *shatter* you, the Mother Goddess's perfect, pure weapon."

Knowing it's futile, I raise my hand to strike him. Neo catches my wrist and shoves it against the rocks, breaking the armor. It falls to pieces. Will that be all that's left of my heart when this is over?

I may not be the perfect weapon. But I am his equal.

He will never break me. Somehow, I will break him first.

"He will reap all of your Halo power." Neo's words are fierce and graceful in my ear, eyes diamond-like. "What he fears most will be his greatest prize."

"I am no one's prize!" I whisper through tears.

The Prince leans in and kisses the glittery trail along my cheeks.

"Hmm..." he muses with a deep, throaty chuckle. "You weep sweet gold."

As soon as his tongue edges out of his mouth, I tense. "Don't."

His fingers at my thigh pause.

Heat breeds between my legs from his hesitation, how he regards me. I gaze into those eyes. They narrow upon mine with a silvery glimmer of...

Recognition. As if he remembers the Fallen's tongues on my skin. The last thing I want is Destruction's tongue now. Still, I recoil from this foreign hunger inside me.

Finally, the Prince licks his lips and cocks his head to the side. "So, what will it be, Elysia? Your nights with me in my bed or my Father's eternity of your public rape and torture until he reaps all your lovely heart's power?"

He truly is heartless. As long as he gets what he wants...but I can get what I want, too. I am not powerless, but I am *vulnerable*.

In spite of my dry throat, I plant one armored hand on his chest, dragging my claws along the skin between his robe. I smell his alluring silver blood and inhale a draught. "I have my own bride demands."

"Speak."

"My Halo power is *particular*." I sigh as I tightrope walk on a balance of give and take.

Neo snickers, "So, I've noticed."

"If I use too much at one time, I faint for seven hours."

"Charming." His cold fingers meet the hard bone of my pelvis.

So close...*boundaries.*

"You will protect me when that happens. You will *not* touch me when I am unconscious."

"It may be challenging to protect you if I am forbidden to touch you," he tests. Thumb so dangerously close, rubbing and rubbing.

"You will *not* touch me, Prince."

He breathes a sigh through his nostrils. "You wreck all the fun, but I agree. Unfortunately, such is too great a price for a mere bedmate."

"What *else*?" I hiss.

"What makes you come *alive*?" He rubs his other thumb in circles on the inside of my wrist, then urges it to his mouth to kiss my vein. "Do you sing? Dance?"

"No. I'm not fond of public performance, exploitation, or humiliation for that matter."

"Could have fooled me! At least for the first," he adds with a laugh and draws a line to my filigree.

"As if my sexual prowess is for yours or anyone's damn benefit!"

He laughs and I hate it, if only because I could wrap myself inside it like a deep, dark coverlet.

"I love photography," I announce to stop his laughter.

"Hmm...go on." His mouth prowls along my ear, his waves cascading across my cheek softer than swans-down and moonlight. I catch a scent on his hair, but I can't quite make it out. Nature-born. Nothing of the Tenth Court's ash, embers, or metallic blood.

"I photograph the night. Their revelries. Their farms."

"You tempt fate then," Neoptolemus hums. "The monsters emerge at night."

"I *capture* them, too."

He flicks my ear with his tongue, and I jerk to the side while he drawls, "You won't find anything more monstrous than me."

"You want me to photograph *you*?"

"Mmm...your lens will thank you."

"Share your bed every night and photograph you. That is all?"

"That is all," he concludes, facing me. "I will never tell a soul your secret. I will never betray you to my Father. And I will protect you after your fainting spells."

"And never touch me after I've fainted," I remind him, raising a finger.

He sighs again. "Your loss, but no touchies." His hand retreats from my thigh and I almost double over, melting. To my shock, I don't sink my shoulders in relief...or sigh.

"One last thing..." I stipulate.

He tips his index finger underneath my chin and beckons, "*Pray* continue."

"I can't ever kiss you. And you can never *bite* me." I hold my breath because it's a tall order. "My Halo will break."

The corners of his ravishing mouth tease upward. "Well, we can't have that now, can we?"

"Prince Neoptolemus," I proclaim the traitorous words—a poison in my blood.

"I, Elysia Rose, will be...your *last* bride."

He stares at me. Moments drift into seconds as he weighs the demand I've nailed to the wall of our deal.

No other brides will end up in that canyon. I will bear the weight of this cross. Of infinite crosses the whole world over.

Finally, the Prince thrusts himself toward me, gripping my

hands. "Granted. But here are my terms: I have the right to destroy you at any time if I so desire. And I am *very* demanding, sweet Princess. I have never met my match in battle or in the bedroom. So, please do not bore me."

"A battle in the bedroom?" I proffer the challenge, remembering there is more than one way to be a warrior.

His ravenous eyes gleam.

"I will bring every weapon in my armory. I expect you to do the same." He lowers my hand to his mouth. "My solemn blood oath. Are we agreed?"

"Agreed."

The Prince slices his fang into my palm, does the same to his, and unites our blood. The oath scribes a bond right into my cells, writes itself on my heart.

Evil demon darkness meeting pure angel light.

My Halo senses the connection, increasing my heart rate. A glow trims my fingertips, animating them. *Oh, sure, now you glow.*

Neo rubs a thumb across one of my eyelids and announces, "Glowing brighter for me, angel?"

"Don't call me an angel."

"You will wear this from now on." The Prince produces a digital tattoo marker similar to the one Quillion bore on his wrist. "It bears my signature and your status as Destruction's Bride. No vampire can touch you. And if one tries to bite you, they will pit their blood against mine thanks to our oath."

Remembering how I am a new entity, a true fallen angel with the undiluted power of the Halo, I nod and accept the tattoo of the horned crown. The permanent mark means nothing.

Its needle tech sinks into my flesh, binding. I wince, but the pain is short-lived.

Triggered, too afraid he will try more now that I've

accepted, I dig deep and channel a glow to rise, to roar. So, I savor it when I touch my blood-coated palm to the Prince's cheek. Sovereign and uncontrollable, I command, "Take me out of here...*now*."

I surge Halo flames from my chest to blind the Prince...right before I faint into his arms.

12
"I'LL WORSHIP YOU RIGHT OUT OF THAT GOWN IN THE BEDROOM TONIGHT…"

I wake in a private room somewhere in the Upper Tenth Court. The tattoo sparks a fresh holo-feed of a digital female of pixels.

"Bride-to-Be Spirit," her robotic feminine voice notifies me. Protecting my identity as he'd vowed. Neo will wed smuggler Lys Spirit—still a triumph, another trophy for him. Until this trophy wife wraps a star-fire noose around his throat. "Your escort has arrived for your bridal preparation. Please come immediately. Bring nothing. Everything you require will be provided for you."

At the tail end of the message, the Prince's silky dark voice coos, "I said I was demanding."

Slick tick.

Without bothering to change out of my filigree and feather gown from last night, I cross the floor of the ornate bedroom.

With bated breath, I prepare myself for a troop of vampire knights.

As soon as I open the door, I sigh in relief and shake my head, grinning at the familiar vampire.

"A pleasure to see you again, Lys Spirit." Quillion greets me with a hand to his chest before he extends it. Smiling, I accept, and he leads me down a main hall and beyond the grand doors of the castle. "The height of irony. You surprised me in my bath last night. Now, I will escort you to yours." He pecks the back of my hand before sliding my arm to loop through his.

Softening from the vampire's rare courtesy, I gratefully lean on him for support and wonder, "Is that where we're going? Another bathhouse?"

"Of a sort," he smirks.

A chill shivers my nerves as I wonder what the Prince has in store. For all I know, staff could prepare me and usher me into some honeymoon suite.

"You're looking far more clothed than the last time we met," I tease as the Court O' Nines gates part to welcome us onto the causeway leading to the Tenth Court tower. No blood authentication awaits him, of course.

Quillion's tailored blue overcoat fits snugly to his well-muscled chest and arms, parting at the waist to fall to his feet, exhibiting the inner silver lining. Simple black breeches, but the ascot compliments his spicy features.

Quillion strokes the bishop crest on his breast that glows from silver blood technology and sweeps his hand through his slick, dark waves. "My thanks. I do clean up rather nice."

"I hope your bath didn't get too cold." I glide my other hand along the side of the bridge that overlooks a smaller canyon layered deep in ash. Faded silver lines black and skeletal protrude from ash. Hundreds of vampire wings, stumped edges crusted with dried blood. I cringe, hoping my Halo doesn't explode from my overwhelmed emotions.

"It did, but it was worth it to witness your grand descent."

I can't help but throw my head back a little and giggle. "I'm going to get you back."

"Looking forward to it, my lady."

My chest lurches and I bite back a whimper.

Quillion stops in his tracks, midway across the bridge. He touches my shoulder, eyes creasing in concern. "Courtier Spirit, I apologize if I offended you in any way."

"No...it's not—" I shake my head, rubbing my lips and shoving my empath into her cage.

"My father. He called my mother his lady." Tears well in my eyes, but I hold the gold droplets back.

Quillion lowers his head, humble and listening.

"I always imagined he'd be here for my wedding day." I'd also never imagined my future husband would be his killer.

"If you wish, I could speak to the Prince—"

"No." I dig my nails into the bishop's jacket and face the Tenth Court, its spire mocking the sky.

"Right. Unfinished business." Quillion clears his throat and quickens his pace. "Give him hell tonight, Courtier Spirit."

"Princess Elysia *Rose*," I correct, marking the difference in his expression, the shock of his nearly freed irises, mouth puckering.

After Quillion gets over his initial surprise, I inspect the abrupt change in his demeanor. Now, I must lengthen my strides to match his pace. His posture is straight tipped as an arrow, all business. Mouth tight and thin as a bone needle. I wish I could read his mind.

We reach the tower's entrance. We are ushered inside, and I don't get the chance to fawn over the entryway with its domed, muraled ceilings. Or the archways with drapes of red velvet beckoning to several rooms, or the staircase on each side uniting at the second level.

A vampire approaches, her champagne blonde hair pulled into a bun, so flawless, it reminds me of a Christmas glass ball. Her form-fitting black gown bears the crest of a blood pawn.

"Courtier Spirit, my name is Pawn Amaris. If you will please follow me to the Preparatory. We only have till nightfall to ready you for the wedding ceremony."

My heart somersaults.

○

I'VE BEEN RELAXING HERE FOR TWO HOURS. NOT ONCE COMPLAINING.

Sinking into the steamy water, I drown in rose oil, ornamented by hundreds of rose petals that cling to my naked flesh. It's large enough for me to wade through, mirroring Quillion's, though this one is octagonal.

Pawn Amaris had stated the bath was blended with certain compounds and serums to soften my skin, eliminate any wrinkles—as if—detoxify my body, smooth any lines, and promote collagen growth. A waterproof mask on my neck and face does the same.

Every now and then, warm currents of lasers glide over my flesh from mirror technology above my head. The reflection makes for a rather *interesting* bath. Not that I mind the sight. Especially not with the Halo curling out and dancing before me in alluring filaments.

"Fine mess you've landed us in," I snigger at the filaments forming the image of a beating heart. I roll my eyes at the implication. "Not a chance. And don't get any ideas. We're here to kill him and the Father. Can you handle that?"

The Halo heart cracks.

I huff. "Deal with it, and I promise I'll stop calling you nicknames...most of the time."

"It's called a vampire facial," explains Pawn Amaris after she retrieves a vial of my blood in a single prick. "In the past, you'd have redness and bruising for a day or two. Thanks to our venom, we've improved the procedure. The effects of your increased blood flow will set in immediately. Our venom acts as a collagen and elastin-producing mechanism."

I recline against the facial bed and try to relax without considering the small needle on the metal table nearby. After mixing with the venom, Amaris injects the blood under my skin: an automatic regenerative facelift. I've heard of the countless beauty treatments in the Tenth Court. It's not unwelcome, though it reminds me of pins and needles prodding and tightening my flesh.

"It will also bring a youthful glow to your skin," Amaris adds as the venom-laced blood platelets firm my skin.

I rein in a giggle since I already have an *inner* glow. Uncle Heath would love all my new puns.

Amaris ignores me. "The Prince never orders such procedures for his brides. He must be planning to keep you for a long time."

"How long does the procedure last?" I dare to ask and nestle against the headrest.

"With our venom? Six months."

A long and slow exhale escapes my throat. Six months.

And five years till the Centennial Eclipse.

Another hour passes for the vampire facial to take effect. During that time, I am directed to remove all my clothes for a full-body massage. All the lights have been dimmed, but the dozens of candles on ledges circumnavigating the room romanticize the area. In the center is a massage bed and a transparent white sheet.

Apparently, my therapist is a world-famous vampire healer or something.

I wander to the arched glass windows and gape at the Court O' Sevens castles no bigger than children's toys. I hadn't realized we were so high. Ashy clouds curtain the sky betraying no stars. Only the pernicious blood moon.

Sighing, I stride to the massage bed, cast aside my white robe, and lower onto the bed. My thoughts wander to the ceremony, and I swallow a lump in my throat at the thought of after.

The battle in the bedroom.

The vampire therapist says nothing when she sweeps into the room. I'm pleased by her professionalism and simple questions.

Warming gel? Yes. Hot stones? Absolutely. Music? Definitely.

A world-famous vampire with an operatic voice on steroids fills the room. As soon as the therapist's hands settle, I sink deeper into the massage bed, curls blanketing one side of my face and tumbling to the floor.

Halfway through the massage, I nearly fall asleep. So relaxed, I barely registered the therapist pause.

Until the new and undefinably *manly* hands caress my skin.

I tense as his shades and flames lurk along the floor.

"I'd stay down if I were you," Neo coolly advises in a low purr, his cold fingers nestling deeper into my shoulders. "Unless you'd care to break tradition and truly allow the groom to see the bride before the wedding."

"Just keep your hands north of the spinal equator," I direct him, more than thankful for the silk sheet shielding my lower half. Sighing, I press my face into the circular gap of the headrest and add, "And between the arms."

He snickers. "I'll count it a *blessing* you do not revile my touch. Hmm...so much tension..." Neo burrows his fingers into my neck muscles, stirring his warm flames into my skin. "Carrying a weight, are you, Elysia?"

Groaning, I snap my head back so my curls scatter along the back of his hand. "What do you want, Prince?"

I still at the sight.

All he wears are plain black breeches and his robes, open to his chest. A single silver chain upon which dangles a cross of fangs.

Neo fingers one of my curls and smiles at me. I tip my head back as he strokes my skin. "Simply a precautionary measure to make sure you hold to your deal." He mines his fingers into the flesh of my shoulder blades.

I snort. "I brokered the deal. And I don't break my vows."

"I do hope you appreciate the dress. I spent a full hour weighing the options."

Dress...I battle a sob because it's another choice he's confiscated from me.

"Most bridal gowns get but a moment of my time," he boasts, knuckles skimming to the outer curve of my shoulder. "Or I delegate."

"Between," I remind him.

"I'll *worship* you right out of that gown in the bedroom tonight," he murmurs icy breath along my neck.

"Ugh, I don't know what's more annoying: you or your insufferable idioms."

"How old are you?" His thumb pressures a line down my spine. "I never did learn on my spontaneous visit."

"You royally fucked my twenty-second birthday."

His thumb pauses on its journey. Whether he's more surprised by my age or my colorful expletive, I can't tell, nor do I care.

"And you're centuries older than me, perv." I stick out my tongue.

His fingers trench deeper, and he leans in, breath casting to my ear, "I'll let you in on a little secret, my bride. My destruction is not limited to others. I've also used it on myself. I maintain certain necessary memories, and while I retain cursory knowledge of my centuries as everyone and some aspects of my language, I've destroyed so much of my consciousness and reduced my maturity. It makes life more...interesting. Even Destruction enjoys surprises."

Snapping my head to the side, I squeeze my shoulders but can't help my lips parting in curiosity, thirsty for more. "How old?"

He sniggers and taps my nose. "Let's just say you and I are closer in age than you believe. Especially considering that celestial trademark in your chest was *before* my time."

I lick my lips, considering the weight of the revelation, my naked body betraying a rush of stardust to infuse the gooseflesh on my skin.

No...none of it matters.

All of me turns cold again, glow dimming.

Neoptolemus is a demon, a monster bred in hell. However

close our maturity is due to supernatural forces, we are *universes* apart.

"By the way, I'm sorry for your birthday. But..." I stiffen, not accepting his apology, and recognizing the mischief in his voice as he leans in and concludes, "at least there will be cake at the reception." He casts my hair to the side. I glower and flip him the bird. "I'll chalk that up to pre-wedding jitters and allow you to finish preparing. After all, wouldn't want your feet to be cold in our bed."

I chuck a hot stone at him as he leaves and hear him chuckle when it breaks on the nearby wall. Leaning into the bed, I ignore the heat between my thighs and welcome the therapist again.

But something nags at me keeping relaxation at bay.

Why did Neo go along with my plan so easily? Why he didn't hand me to his Father who would have surely rewarded him?

What secret does he carry?

⸺

DAMN THAT VAMPIRE.

Damn that son of a demon spawn to *six feet under* the deepest circle of hell!

I gaze at myself in the mirror and gush. It's *everything* I've ever desired in a bridal gown. And more!

A perfect princess ballroom gown laden with stars...and lightning. A regal corset bodice of deep purple befitting my sovereign heritage along with off-the-shoulder transparent long sleeves— encrusted with tiny diamonds swirling to my wrists. The neckline showcases the barest tops of my breasts and a couple inches of pure cleavage. Hundreds of thousands of silver specks compliment the gold lightning filigree designs journeying halfway up the skirts. A hint of gold whorls edges out from the bodice to mirror the base ones. Back naked to the base of my spine...reminiscent of the previous night.

He took my idea and enhanced it. "Bloody bastard! I should sue for copyright."

The Halo coils out of my chest, glimmering into miniature hearts and I clench my hand to smother them.

I groan, pinching the bridge of my nose. Because he hasn't forced heels! The shoes he selected remind me of my armored gloves from last night. Except these silver pieces sweep from my mid-calf to curl between my second and third toe, leaving much of my feet bare. A gold halo of a rope for a garter.

He requested my curls loose and twisted to one side to exhibit my slender neck with only some swept and pinned to the back of my head.

He might be a prick of a tick, but I have to admit, Princey's got fine taste.

Amarys offers me a choker where a blood ruby dangles.

I shake my head. "No necklace." My throat will remain utterly bare to remind him of what is forbidden.

"Do you know where the ceremony is?"

"It's small. Up-tower. That's all I know."

Small is good.

SMALL AND YET SUBSTANTIAL AND NOT JUST UP-TOWER.

All the mirrored panel technology comprises uninhibited 360-degree views inside a tower sphere. As if there are no walls, no floor, no *room*.

It robs my breath.

There is Neo.

Like a dark god, he lingers in the middle of the ashy sky as the clouds roll behind him, casting hundreds of embers like whorls of fireflies.

Quillion stands next to him...on a much more *intimate* basis than I'd assumed. First, he regards me, then juts his jaw to Neo, pinching his lips, eyes sharp as a lance. The animosity he shows the Prince is not lost on me, perhaps he could be an ally.

Neo barely regards Quillion and steels his silvery eyes upon me.

My breath hitches. A flush feasts on my neck and cheeks from his unlawful allure. Right now, he can pass for a noble vampire lord dressed in black formal wear, his jacket mirroring Quillion's. Except, Neo's collar towers behind his ears, jacket open to his form-fitting vest—upper half donned in amethysts and silver filigree woven into his jacket. Plates of vampire bone armor arc over each of his shoulders with fang gauntlets for his arms. The fang necklace is gone, but he proudly wears a horned crown of black flames and a dragon crest in the center of his chest. Everything about him screams warrior of destruction.

Run and hide, Elysia, my fear warns.

No. I am a warrioress of light. Programmed within the walls, a haunting lyric plays. I almost tremble.

Scheherazade.

Our song, I guess.

Amaris hands me a bouquet of gold and silver-lacquered roses. For a moment, I remain rooted on the top step in the doorway before the sphere of cinders and clouds.

Closing my eyes, I reach deep for my Halo. Sense its inner Goddess presence to grant me peace, to grant me courage, and light. I warm my insides, free the Halo to grow into flickering ripple flames that erupt all over the curves of my body.

And take my first step.

"Neo, for heaven's sake!" Quillion lashes out at the Prince, but Neo only raises his hand to stay the bishop. Quillion lowers his head, shaking it, and mutters something incomprehensible under his breath.

A secret, the Halo coos.

Wary adrenaline feeds my blood, but I battle tremors of seismic proportion. I square my shoulders, chin raised royal-high. In Quillion's eyes, I identify an ironic blend of rage and commiseration. In the Prince's, I expect cold brutality or perhaps fiery lust.

What greets me shakes me to my core. Pupils so black and dilated—twilight surrounded by a thin ring of crystalized silver. While pupils dilate in darkness, it's not a necessity for vampires. It's as if Neo doesn't want to miss *one* nano-moment of my walk down this aisle. The culminating moment of my journey to belong to him.

No, *with* him.

My eyes mate with his through the journey to his side. I don't balk or cave. Nor do I stop breathing. We are two equal pieces on the board.

The Prince of Destruction opens his hand to mine.

I gaze at his open palm.

There is still time, some inner voice defies. *Run and hide, Elysia.*

Instead, I take the deepest breath ever, slide my fingertips onto the edge of his hand in acceptance, and sweep in to capture a Prince.

13

COULD HE...WILL HE EVER BE MINE?

Throughout the ceremony, Neo holds my hand. I entrench myself in his dilated eyes, searching for the windows to his soul, but I can't imagine anything beyond his twilight but broken glass.

Midway through the ceremony, the holographic priest addresses the ring. With Neo's eyes tethering mine, he gestures to the bishop. Quillion blows a frustrated breath but thrusts the ring into Neo's palm. The Prince holds the too-simple silver band and inches it toward my left hand. I pull back, but he captures the ends of my fingers, leans in, and pursues.

When he prepares to slip the ring onto my finger, I shake my head, test his eyes, and curl my fingers down. "I am *not* your property," I define, drawing this hard boundary to overlap the ancient tradition that signified a property transaction.

Neo shifts his weight and steps forward until his hips brush against my waist, possessive and predictive. Still, I do not submit but clench my hand into a fist so the unstoppable force of his ring budges against my immovable object of a knuckle. Apart from Quillion's piqued breath, we could hear a pin drop.

Locked in this moment of eternity on a battlefield, I breathe steadfastly, arching my neck while my stomach compacts. Finally, Neo's pupils contract into a snowfall, relenting, and the battle fades. He plucks a few strands of his moonlight hair, loops the ring through them, and tiptoes the makeshift necklace toward my throat. A test of a compromise. I nod my acceptance. Then tip my head so he may tie the necklace around my neck. His icy silk hands linger on my throat a few unnecessary moments, but his flames warm my skin.

When the priest calls for the vows, Quillion binds our wrists together with rope. Our palms flatten against each other's. Neo's shadow suffocates my body, his breath seductive against my face as he repeats the priest's traditional vows. I refrain from rolling my eyes at the patriarchal words. Can I ever expect him to keep those vows to love and honor?

My Halo radiates from my chest, currents treading so close to where Neo's heart *should* be. Does the Halo—the Goddess—want me to...win him? Win this ancient warrior's heart and turn him against the Father?

All I know is there is one thing he can never take from me. Something truer to my heart than my Halo. Something from tradition. No, from ancient tradition. From the original-sin rule-breaker, the first fallen one. So, after Neo finishes, I break the rules. I go *off-script*.

I push my hands against his and proclaim, "Prince Neoptolemus, I vow to be your *equal* partner in every respect as I was created to be."

His lips part, jaw lowering to my words, and curls his fingers into mine.

I continue, "I vow to be the bone of your bone and flesh of your flesh."

COURTING DEATH AND DESTRUCTION

With a deep inhale, I slowly raise our arms to a symbolic arch while bearing the weight of infinite dams to my tears. "I vow to be your Ezer Kenegdo. I vow to be your strong rescuer and warrior princess of light."

There is more than one way to be a warrior.

Neo does not move a muscle. His eyes remain black towers. He's laid claim to everything else, but this is *my* moment of reclaim. Whatever else he has done, he cannot take Ezer from me, for she is writ into my very blood and bone and the essence of my soul! Tonight, I will show the Prince of Destruction what a true bride is…and pray he will honor her beyond this moment.

The Halo quickens, pulsing more as if cheering me onward. All of me glows.

So, I muster my courage, muscles tightening, and continue, "I vow to be the power that will carry your burdens. I vow to be your shield, I vow to save you from danger, and I vow…" I pause at the last words, my breath cleaving and heaving.

The Halo bursts in staccato beams—powerful enough to erupt against Neo's chest.

What are you doing? I whisper as the beams burn a hole through his clothes and brand a perfect, unbroken circle into his chest. Neo grits his teeth. Why doesn't he destroy my beams? His nostrils flare, muscles flexing upon my hands until they whiten from the fiery pain. Still, he does not move. His shadows rake across my body—an equal contender because if I am to win him, I will settle for nothing less than *all* of him.

I take a leap of faith and pirouette my Halo light to trim his body, mimicking his shades cocooning mine, "And I vow to deliver you from…*death*."

When the priest announces Neo may kiss the bride, as if such an action should be one-sided, I hold my breath. Neo's mouth dips low toward my face but pauses at my forehead and rubs his lips dead center on my brow. I offer a faint smile.

Quillion untethers our hands, and I loose a deep breath as Neo guides me out of the sphere, down the stairs, and to the reception room. Under floating diamond chandeliers, we dance to our first song as bride and groom. As the chandeliers cast dancing prisms on the floor and the music plays, Neo carries me across the scintillating marble. So...romantic. The ring necklace reminds me of the tip of an iceberg. Neo's hand at the base of my spine is a soft, cold caress, contrasting his flames carousing my skin as he tips me lower, and confesses, "You are an angel tonight. *My* angel."

Mine, I remember his first word once I descended the Court staircase. Could he...will he ever be *mine*? That familiar sensation of fire and ice buds across my skin beneath his hand and strikes between my legs. No, I condemn myself. How could I make such a vow? How can the Halo want me to win him? He's a destroyer. A bride-slayer. A *murderer*.

And his title for me, however a pet name, is nothing more than a lie burning a hole in my stomach. The invisible marks on my skin ache. Their deep weight crushes me. Angels, saviors aren't murderers.

Something sharp pierces the fabric of my heart as if reminding me of how similar we are. No, I am different. I may have blood on my hands, but it's nothing compared to Destruction's. And besides, Neo took everything from me. If he desires forgiveness, it will only be after he's fallen to his *knees* before me and surrendered everything to my vengeful Goddess altar.

At least he made good on his promise of cake. Only once he's finished gently tucking the small piece into my mouth do I unleash a wicked grin and smash the cake against his face. First, he flinches, brows threading low. But I lift my shoulders in an innocent shrug and catch the corner of his lips curving into a smirk. At the corner of the table, Quillion chuckles and offers the Prince a cloth napkin.

After Neo wipes his face, he closes the distance between us and cups my chin. Mouth treading predatorily close. "It's time."

A tremor ripples through my entire body, seismic waves returning. My heart falters.

○

NEO HELPS ME GATHER THE CHAPEL TRAIN SO IT MAY COLLECT INSIDE the elevator. It is a brief ride, but my skin crawls as he regards me in silence. What could he possibly expect of this night? He said he'd worship me right out of the gown in the bedroom. Over my dead body. I shudder, close my eyes, and lean against the gilded elevator wall, thudding the back of my skull against the mirror.

I vowed to be Ezer. I will be...even if I defend myself.

Once the elevator stops, Neo shadows out, then opens his palm to me. I accept his support because this bridal gown is heavy. But after I stand, Neo settles his hands on my waist, a silent plea prompting a half-gasp. "If the bride would allow me to carry her across the threshold?"

I open my mouth, prepared to object, but I hesitate. Perhaps if his fingers had dug in, but they are light as paper petitions on my bodice while his flames tantalize the edges of my body. My Halo dust flirts with those flames. So, I swallow and offer him a weak nod. As if concerned I will change my mind, Neo sweeps me into his arms, bearing the full weight of me and the gown as if we are no more than a feather.

Oh, Saints...

My heart grows legs and springs into my throat. I close my eyes as he carries me to his wing while battling the urge to lean my head against his shoulder, to so much as wonder what it must feel like. His flames waltz with my fingers, wooing my palm to bed on his chest. I discern where the hole I'd charred into his tunic is. I inhale a sharp gust when I touch puckered flesh.

Neo kisses my brow again. "I'll never use my shadows to heal it, Elysia. Your destructive circle is my worthy wedding ring."

Fuuuuuuuck.

My empath nudges the bars of her cage, swooning a little, but I refuse to let her out. Yet.

I don't contemplate all the doors we pass, yet my breaths leave in gasps. Finally, he approaches two double-arched doors I believe are obsidian until they shift. Doors of shade, of impenetrable shadow wraiths that bend only to his will. Like his prison walls. Another prison then? I shut my mouth but don't hide the breathy whirlwind escaping my nose. He pauses at the doorway. I hold his gaze. Strengthening his arm on the underside of my legs, Neo frees his other hand in one brushing wave to part the shades and allow us entry.

It's not a prison. It's a *suite*. Slowly, Neo releases me, so I may stand and survey the surroundings. His hands center on my bodice at the waist—fingers lurking as much as his shades—as I peer at the floor of dark shadowy fog twisting and coiling in tempting curlicues along my bare feet and ankles. The same shadows form a backdrop on all the windows. My white bridal train is a ghost in comparison. Again, all shadows sweep aside like curtains to Neo's will. First, I behold the floor of transparent crystalline glass. Startle at the sight of the sheer cliff-high drop-off with the same glass walls bestowing an all-consuming expanse of night sky laden with the blood moon mimicking the sphere.

In the center of those walls is one massive arched door of fused bones. And skulls. I shiver for more reasons than one. I shiver at the evil draught whispering to me from the door—colder than snow-buried corpses. I take one step toward it, but Neo tugs me to him and tucks two fingers beneath my chin to tilt my face to his, curving me to his dark prowess. My skin blanches from the deadliness in his eyes, the silvery eyeliner disappearing beneath hooded shadows.

"Do not ever open the door," he commands, tone regal and authoritarian. In this moment, he is every inch the Prince of Destruction.

My eyes dart to their corners. From beyond the door, hundreds of thousands of souls scream, moan, shriek, and howl. Some human and most...not. Now, I understand where we are. The Chasm! Or at least on the verge.

Neo taps my cheek, summoning me, "And the room?"

Grateful for the diversion, I sweep my eyes to study and gape at the suite. Nudged against one glass wall is the largest and most luxurious bed the size of a small room—wreathed in shadows and flames that pirouette like lovers in a slow, sensual dance. A great fireplace to the right of the bed, a bed of ash clothing the marble hearth, a black diamond chandelier, archways leading to attached rooms. On the right side is an immense bath hollowed into the floor—canopied with an arced skylight and stabilized by four great pillars. Other than the blood moon casting its scarlet beams into the room, there is no light save for Neo's caressing flames.

"Lovely, dark, and deep..." I breathe the aged quote, my voice a reverent whisper. I don't know what I expected. Blood floors, weapons everywhere, a dungeon perhaps, but the suite leaves me awestruck.

An appreciative purr rumbles in his throat right before he brushes aside a few stray curls from one side of my neck, rubs his lips along its curve, and shrewdly adds, "And miles to go before we sleep."

I close my eyes and harness my gasps, imagine they are energized vapors to stoke my power. But his ring on my chest becomes a hot iron trickster. So, why is my skin still glowing?

"If you will pardon me while I retire to another room and change into something more comfortable." He jerks his head toward the arched doorways branching off from the main room to our right. Of course, he doesn't hesitate to cross his bulging arms over his chest and thread his brows to add, "Unless you'd prefer to undress me. I've been told many a time that it's quite a *thrilling* experience."

I give a soft shake of my head. But the Halo responds to my emotions, breeding from me in quick, thin flickers and imparts heat to my core. Neo chuckles at the sight, lingering, but after a moment of me steeling my eyes in a hard boundary, he drops his hands to his sides with a groaning sigh before he departs.

My heart thunders as soon as he leaves.

At first, I rush to the shadow door, but as predicted, the shades become hungry whorls to overwhelm me in nothing but a drowning darkness, thrusting me back.

A battle in the bedroom, I'd vowed. And he vowed to destroy me anytime.

"Goddess preserve me," I whisper, bracing myself and praying I will gain the upper hand. Neoptolemus is Destruction. And he has hundreds, no...thousands of years of training on me since his birth. Next to his Father and my mother, he's the most powerful being on earth. If he nullifies my power, I will be helpless!

Will I conquer the Prince of Destruction and make him my

warrior, or will I share the dark fate of his past murdered brides?

Ash and flames, echoes of his destruction, plague my vision of when he'd destroyed my city to smoldering ruins...when my father and my mother...I will *not* let him destroy me tonight.

To my left is one room, but inside is nothing but a hollowed-out area with three separate floors. I ascend a winding staircase, but each level circles without end. No exit. No doors. No windows. Why this barren room with no purpose?

I descend the stairs and into the main room, pulse barraging blood into my ears.

Then, I freeze before the bone door.

The curling hoarfrost from beyond tempts me again. I approach the doorway, its omen carving into my chest like a reaper armed with a scythe. From the windows on each side, I can make out a stone walkway that juts out over the sheer drop-off. No railings. No gate. Emptiness on each side. No more than a mile below is the cavernous canyon of the Chasm. This is the closest I've ever come. Breath quaking, I steady myself by stationing my hands on the glass and studying the entrance with its ever-roiling ash, chaotic fires, and deep thundering.

Touching my chest, my Halo grows colder as if sensing the millions of monsters, of lost souls. The Chasm's dark force tickles my blood, spreading affliction into my chest, reminding me of my own damnation. Those invisible trauma marks.

And then, Neo's shades, followed by warm flames, lurk across my back. I sigh because he's standing behind me. No more delays. No more opportunities for escape. Only my light against his darkness.

His shades and flames stroke my skin like dark, erotic poems, lulling me.

"I find the Chasm soothing," he utters behind me, removing the circlet from my head. Holding my breath, I keep my hands on the glass and purse my lips as he pulls the pins from my hair, dethroning all my curls. I touch my fingertips to the glass, wishing I could grip something.

His flame-swathed hands swallow my shoulders. He leans in to kiss the back of my head and applies pressure, luring me. "Prepared for our battle, Halo-Bearer? I am armored."

Shoulders tightening, chest heaving, gold dust thickening from my pores, I curve my fingers to my throat, garnering courage. Putting the Chasm behind me, I prepare my power and slowly turn to face him.

"Holy fuckety *fuck*!" I shriek and spring back against the glass to avoid the sight, but it's too late. I'll never un-see it. Neo is a dark, nude god and *hard* as a dragon. Nothing but strong-packed sinew, flames edging his body, arms corded with muscle, his herculean chest with minute shadow curls for hair, powerful calves, thick, full thighs, and...*oh, Saints!* I gulp. But my chest lurches, hotter than volcanic pudding. No energy to reprimand the Halo—or my thighs subconsciously rubbing together—, I press my spine to the glass, almost wishing I was on the other side.

"Strange words from the Everblood," chortles Neoptolemus as he approaches me, shadows and fire erupting all over him.

"The prophecy says I have pure blood," I breathe a gasp, or maybe a whimper, and skid along the wall, moving away from him. "Not a pure mouth."

His eyes gleam. "An impure mouth I would destroy ten thousand demons to merely lick."

"Ugh..." I force my eyes to close for more reasons than one. "Your creepy, stalkerish sexual advances are far more impure than my cursing!" I exclaim and keep sliding along the wall till I hit the corner. *Dammit.*

"Is there something wrong with my *body*, Elysia?" He uses my words from the dance against me. "This is a rather new one for me."

I bet it is. Women probably rip their bodices at one smolder from him.

Those well-muscled arms hem me in, one on each side of my body to plant on the wall. Oh, my stomach churns, competing with the hellish Halo casting flushed gold dust around my breasts. My inner angel swoons at the sight of his chest—corded with black-diamonded muscles roaming to a flawless Adonis belt—daring me to lower my gaze to *other* regions. It's not as if this is the first time I've seen one. On my 18th birthday after too much venom wine, Verena reluctantly accompanied me to the blood pond on the outskirts of the Rose City—a popular locale for some rarer citizens who desired a more *immersive* experience. I guess we'd come on a good day, too, since there were plenty of *subjects* to study.

A mere second's glance reassures me Neo would win any pissing match.

No doubt he can hear my frenetic riptide of a pulse…and scent my aroused blood. Maybe other such arousals.

An unwitting whimper leaves my throat as his fire and shades play with my flesh, rippling into my hair, teasing the spaces between my legs, and traveling to flirt with my face as if encouraging me to peek. My Halo currents gush from my chest and prod me. I blink one eye open to spy him an inch from my face. Oh, Saints!

He tilts his head like a raptor would, silver smoke eyes daring me. *Don't do it,* I order myself, thighs practically cemented together. A muscle ticks in his cheek. *Don't.* Damn it to hell! I flick my eyes down where they absolutely should not go. And a shower of gold hearts flares from my chest. *You fiendish fruit loop!* I scold the Halo.

Neo laughs, that wild laugh that could embrace me.

"Holy foremothers!" I moan as he leans in and rubs his head against mine. "You need a lesson in personal space."

"You'll have *all* night to teach me, my love."

Oh! I won't last all night. Then, I remember our blood oath and how I don't have to. A thrill surges up my spine. Because I gave myself the perfect checkmate!

Thank the Goddess my reflexes kick in, and the Halo listens. Lurching forward, I project a host of beams from my hands—enough to launch him across the room, so he smashes against the opposite wall, cracking it.

Yes! I thrill, pride rousing my blood to rush like a wild angel. *Take that, Destruction!*

Stunned, he shakes his head. With a dark growl, Neo gets to his feet and charges for me, but it's too late. Black fog overwhelms my mind. I used too much power. My knees crumble.

Neo catches me, and I can't deny the heat plaguing my cheeks at how I'm pressed against his naked chest.

Before I pass out, I giggle, reminding him, "No touchies."

"Saucy wench." He places me on the floor and moves away. Sometime, I will have to ask how he managed to move me after I passed out in his arms in the Chasm.

But for now, everything goes black.

14

"WHAT DOES THE PRINCE DO ALL DAY?"

I WAKE EXACTLY SEVEN HOURS LATER.

On Neo's bed.

At first, I scramble to double-check myself, cupping my forehead in relief because the blood oath stands. I am gloriously *untouched* with not one stitch of my wedding gown disturbed. Not even the gold rope of a garter.

I shift only to sink into the luxurious sheets, gushing a little. It is, by far, the softest and deepest, and most comfortable bed I have ever slumbered in. For the first time in a long time, I register how my sleep was dark and dreamless. Maybe passing out has its advantages?

My hand curves onto a dip. An indent. The pillows on this side betray a body imprint in...where *he* slept last night. *Ugh*, I inhale his leftover aroma of smoky husk and elite cologne. How in the hell does a devil smell so damn good? The Halo prods the boundaries of my chest in a wagging tendril as if doing a victory dance.

No trace of him in the room. Does he intend for me to stay

here all day? I seal my determined lips because I'm not about to wait around for him.

Shaking out my curls, I hurry toward the shadow door with my train making love to the black fog.

To my utter shock, the shade doors ripple and roll away as soon as I touch them. Huh...not a prison after all. At least he's holding his end of the deal.

I don't waste a second before fleeing from the room. The black wraiths only close behind me once the last of my bridal train is free.

I take the penthouse stairs since I don't want to hassle with a possible blood authentication, nor do I care to shove the chapel train into the elevator. Besides, the grand staircase is more aesthetically pleasing.

I almost wait for a photographer to appear to capture my first morning as Destruction's wife.

But there is no one. Not even in the lower-level Commons area. My train graces the halfway point of the staircase even after I reach the floor. As silverware clinks from a room on my right, I beam because I recognize the accompanying voice humming a whimsical tune. Collecting my skirts, I make a beeline for the archway.

Quillion drops his fork as soon as he sees me, rises to a stand, removes his fedora, and opens his mouth. Before he can speak, Neo enters from the other end of the room. I stiffen. Out of the corner of my eye, Quillion notes how my *husband* surmises me with a clenched jaw. Our gazes hold in a stalemate. I ball my hands into fists, lower my brows to mirror his dagger gaze. *Steady, Elysia*...the Halo chants, and I twist one corner of my mouth into a mischievous smirk.

At last, Neo relents, grunts, then yanks out the head chair and sits with a resounding thud. Quillion snaps his head to me, and we share a wicked grin. I almost do my own victory lap since I am the Princess cat who ate the canary Prince.

While I take the adjoining seat to his right, Quillion proceeds to tap his bishop's wrist marker and summons a holographic chart: Elysia on the left, Neo on the right. A low snarl buds in Neo's throat and he snatches a silver butter knife and digs it into the table. Angelically, I beam at the bishop, the Halo responding by offering a sweet, teasing glow around my heart. Quillion winks, expands the chart, and withdraws a digital pen.

Under the heavy-browed and hooded eyes of Neo scrutinizing us from across the room, my grin slinks across my face while I coolly address the Prince, "Did you wake up on the *wrong* side of the bed this morning, husband?"

Quillion tries to stifle his laughter, but it blows through his cheeks as he adds two tally marks to *my* side of the chart. Tapping his wrist to close the program, he proceeds to offer me his fist. I bump it proudly.

"My Father let you keep your tongue. I can rescind that any time," Neo threatens Quillion, who merely leans back in his seat, dismissive, spreads his cloth napkin over his lap, and summons a Court-app digital newspaper. What did he mean by "keep his tongue"? I ache to know more about Quillion's history. His past. For now, I simply bat my eyes at the bishop.

Until...*Seek the Altar, Elysia. And your mother.* The words haunt me, and I purse my lips, remembering the Goddess's other directive: the Prince has a dark secret. I momentarily glimpse his way, almost giving him a mock-sympathetic pouty lip when his forehead scrunches. If he intends to keep me so *busy*, I doubt I'll determine his secret or locate the Altar anytime soon.

Perhaps dealing with Neo is my first priority.

I flinch when he chucks the knife at the bishop, but Quillion doesn't even look away from his paper and snaps his hand up, catching it as if it's routine for him to capture the Prince's flying objects.

Sighing, Quillion crosses one ankle over his opposite knee but side-eyes me. "You married a sore loser." He fingers his ascot.

"It will be a pleasure to teach him some humility." I prop my chin on my hands, elbows on the table, and carry on with the bishop. "Hmm...should I give him a time out?"

"I would be more than happy to put you in a corner, *Princess*," Neo fumes, revealing his glimmering fangs.

"Hmm..." I muse, utterly diabolical as I thrust my chin toward him and sweetly retort, "I'm certain you already tried last night...and failed."

A reverberating rumble of laughter from Quillion. He adds another two check marks under my name. My inner angel shakes her hips on an invisible catwalk.

Neo grunts again and combs his hands through his hair which looks far grayer in this light. He remains silent for the present, and I use the gap to scoot my chair closer to Quillion. He lifts one brow but doesn't move from his seat, only swipes his hand to read the news.

A number of Court O' Ten servants usher out of two adjoining kitchen doors with the food. More food than I've ever seen in my life: maple bacon biscuits and pancakes, hearty fluffed dumplings, tropical fruit chilled soups, smoked salmon, cold meats, Florentine poached eggs, caviar, and I finally lose track. Neo takes his food blood-laced. Something else I notice is how a servant pours me a glass of transparent clear liquid. I inhale. Spicy and rich but with a bitter after-scent. However tempted, I push aside the venom and pour myself a separate glass of water from another pitcher.

Neo grumbles from across the table, "Ask a hireling next

time," he commands and slices into a slow-roasted pork, shaving off a succulent, thick slice that drips blood before shoving it whole into his mouth. He swallows as if he's destroyed part of it to squeeze from his throat. "You're a Princess."

"Yes," I agree without losing my honeyed smile. "A Princess who can tie her own shoes and everything. Imagine that!" After spooning myself some chilled peach soup, I savor a few bites, then wave the spoon toward Quillion, asking, "Anything interesting?"

He chants, eyes scrolling the digital feedback, "Main headlines: New Strain of SIV Evolves to Target Venom, Court O' Sixes Stock Drops After Capitol Fire, Father Institutes New Blood Priestess at Court O' Tens, Underground Steals Four Children From Court O' Sevens Human Blood Farm—" I stiffen in my seat at the propaganda language, and Neo picks up on my body language, "—Court Mordere Carries off Pure Bloods From Court-Appointed Passenger Train...and the latest Court celebrity gossip."

Quillion reaches for a mug of steaming chocolate, but I notice the scarlet liquid mixed with it. Bloody hot chocolate. I understand it's human, but I can't fault the bishop and choose to believe the best of him. After all, thousands of familiars are here by choice and benefit greatly from living in the Tenth Court.

Directing the subject to his last words, I urge, "Oh, please, don't spare me the *Bleeding With the Berberians* drama!" I guffaw, pressing a hand to my chest, forgetting about the ring. I wince when my palm brushes it.

Quillion winks, adding, "Branwyn had to get fang implants after Briella yanked out the originals."

"No!" Incredulous, I sit straight in my seat and slap his arm, denying.

"At Branwyn's twins' birthday party at Fangtasia Land, no less."

"Well," I ease a sigh and lower my eyes to my food, "when you're out for a few days…" I trail off, reflecting on the events of those days. Neo's assault in the Chasm, the blood canal, the prison, the Spirit woods, the Bridal Canyon, and…

Silent, I pick at my maple bacon pancakes because Quillion missed one truly significant headline. He'd deflected quite masterfully with the others and even more beautifully with the Berberians, but it still didn't rid the memory of ashes and cinders—the destruction of my home.

Then, Quillion touches my hand, leaning over to express in a sympathetic voice, "Prince of Destruction Lays Waste to the Rose City: Father Takes Rose Queen Prisoner. Princess Missing."

From across the table, Neo's eyes impale mine, two silver stakes, but for a passing moment, they liquefy with regret, his features shrinking. Oh, hell no, he does *not* get to act miserable. Not for one little speck of a second.

I curl my fingers upon Quillion's hand. "Thank you, Quillion. At least one vampire here can act with a little civility and kindness."

"I would have shown you *much* kindness last night if you hadn't fainted like a distressed damsel," complains Neo.

"Aww, poor wedded but un-bedded demon. Is your hand so terribly sore?"

Blood spurts from Quillion's mouth and he has to pound his chest from the laughter-induced cough. Well, that ruined breakfast. But oh, so worth it with Neo's jaw turning rigid while his eye twitches in fury.

"I'm giving her three for that," Quillion alerts Neo and wipes his ascot before adding three more ticks to my side of the chart.

As soon as Neo clambers to his feet and stalks to my side, I cross my arms over my chest and remain immovable in my seat, neck high as a cliff. My heart drums a rabid beat in my chest from the approach of his hulking shadow, from his shades and flames projecting from his body to cape my figure. Poor Quillion tips his fedora low over his face while I tap my fingers against my diamonded sleeve until Neo's shadow slaughters my body.

He leers at me and commands, "Stand before me, *wife*."

Oh, no, he did *not*.

I besiege Neo's towering darkness with four words. "That's. Not. My. *Name*." My defiance transforms into a live wire flaming every blood cell in my body. "You would do well to take lessons from Quillion in the art of some *manners*. And anger management."

"I assure you, *Elysia*," he corrects himself but grits his teeth, flames teetering on the edge of my chest, "I am managing my anger quite well."

Now, I rise, nearly toppling my chair. My Halo currents ripple from my heart and hunt him as much as his flames stalk me. "Neoptolemus, I am *not* your property," I repeat my words from the ceremony.

"No, you are my *bride*," he hisses through his teeth. "Blood-bound to me."

"And have I broken the oath?" I trap him because we both know I haven't.

"Your blood is denied to me." He captures my throat in a dark satin caress and brushes his hand downward, igniting my whole body with quivering gooseflesh. He pauses on the ring entombed between my cleavage, and my bosom heaves with my swelling breath. *Steady, Elysia...*I chant this time as he finishes, "Would you also deprive me of *one flesh*?"

With full assurance of my Halo, I rise to the occasion and

take his Prince piece with flawless recitation, "'Therefore a man shall leave his *father* and his mother and hold fast to his wife, and they shall become one flesh.'" Then, I proceed to twist his fingers, remove his hand from my inner bosom, and conclude, "There cannot be *three* people in a marriage." An indirect reference to the blood oath he shares with his Father.

Quillion whistles low from his chair and coolly advises the Prince, "You should quit while you're still in the negative, Neo."

Neo regards me for another few seconds and I brace myself for more scathing words, but instead, he rights his robe, shaking it out, and bows his head in a mockery. "So, you want to play dirty, Princess? Two can play at that game."

Perhaps I do have a bit of devil inside me because I offer him a feeble sigh and go so far as to stand on the furthest edge of my tiptoes so I may whisper in his ear, "By the time you catch up, Quillion's chart will have run out of room."

As soon as I squeeze his shoulder in remorse, Neo growls and turns his back to exit the room with flames shooting out to lick at the ends of my gown. A golden hand emerges from my chest so I may give it a high-five. *Good Halo!*

Beside me, Quillion offers me another fist bump. "It's been a long time since someone put him in his place. Or ruffled his scales, so to speak. Keep up the good work, Princess."

"Thank you for everything, Quillion. Would you be willing to give me a Tower tour?"

"Of course!" He twirls his ascot before offering me his arm and wagging his other finger. "But let us get something else for you to wear first."

COURTING DEATH AND DESTRUCTION

"Absolutely ravishing!" Quillion compliments my choice of garb. "I must say, I almost anticipated something more masculine, but I am charmingly bewildered."

I sashay toward him. If I could wear one gown every day, it would be this one! "Well, I believed it would be appropriate. If I am a Princess bride, I might as well dress like one. And I believe I have a decent sense of style."

Cut in a high inverted V in the front to showcase my dark legging-clad stems, the gown's topmost layer is black as a starless night but with two sweeping visible underlayers: the second of deep, rich umber with the fullest bottom layer a light mahogany brown. Along the bodice, gold and silver Court O' Ten fire roses intertwine and curl along the sumptuous off-the-shoulder sleeves of drapery which tighten at my forearms to my wrist.

"Love the peekaboo neckline," Quillion admires, his eyes lingering only a moment.

I smile, glimpsing the thick velvet trimmed in the same mahogany fabric hanging low but not as obscene thanks to the gold and gauzy illusory fabric sweeping to my neck. Similar to a bateau but with a black choker piece to seal the fabric. It serves two purposes. One, it circles my throat to prevent spying eyes from ascertaining any nonexistent Prince marks. And two: it conceals the treacherous ring.

"I approve of your attire as well," I add, voice light and bubbly as I nod to his fresh change, considering his prior blood-spattered clothes. Now, he wears a royal blue brocade vest and jacket lined with multi-colored gemstones with the same Court O' Ten rose and flame symbols. Matching blue breeches with gold buttons and a leather belt to house a simple sheathed fang dagger. I quite appreciate his blood-red ruffled ascot style.

He touches one finger to the ascot and the closed center

seam of his embroidered vest. "We both know I clean up well. Not half as impressive as you, especially given the gold-winged circlet you chose."

I trace a fingertip across the band of gold on my head and lift my chin. "I won't hide who I am."

"An impossible feat. Now, my lady..." Quillion offers me his arm, and I loop mine into his so he may lead me to the nearby elevator situated at the northwest corner of the Commons area.

For the life of me, I can't determine why a civil, kind-hearted man such as Quillion would choose to befriend the Prince of Destruction. Then again, I married that Prince. Self-preservation, I remind myself. Biding my time.

Quillion selects a slower elevator setting and squeezes my hand as we ride to lower Court levels. The one directly below the Prince's penthouse suites and Commons is reserved for vampire elite such as rooks and bishops and their parties when they don't reside in their own Court castles. I incline my head out the windows to behold tourist hotels with limousines driving through gold tree-lined courtyards, vampires and humans strolling along bridges overlooking blood falls, shopping avenues of high-end retail with internationally renowned fashion designers, theaters, clubs, and more. These modernized elite levels progress throughout much of the Tower, but they still echo the Father's gothic aesthetics whether in black iron trees, gargoyles and angels spitting out blood into walkway fountains, or digital fire-rose walls, ceiling backdrops, or gilded into the architecture.

Monorails twist through the air, reminding me of luminescent serpents circling in double helixes until they become thin silver wisps hundreds of levels below me. Thanks to the elevator's slow descent, I detect some vampire thrill-seekers leaping

COURTING DEATH AND DESTRUCTION

off Tower platforms and balconies to conquer the gale-force winds.

Every last sight is *unforgettable*.

"You have but to ask, and the Prince or myself will accompany you wherever you desire. On levels 756-760, there is a marvelous forest and scenic overlooks featuring splendid views of the Court O' Nines castle."

I thank him but shake my head, grief tucked in my heart from the loss of my homeland. Of those sacred redwoods. I squeeze my knees, rose-flamed velvet boots stroking one another. For a moment, my empath eclipses me. Sorrow is a weight I gladly carry. One I'm not unfamiliar with for past reasons. It reminds me of life, of the chronic healing of my soul. It does not mean I am broken, but quite the opposite.

Finally, I swivel my head away from the higher levels. All so beautiful and advanced, it thrills and terrifies me. I clench my fingers, knuckles whitening because the veins of the Tower city pump the costly price of human blood and even silver blood from the Father's slaves, enemies, or unnecessary pawns.

"Perhaps you'd be more interested in one of our expansive libraries," Quillion offers a substitute.

"What does the Prince do all day?" I shrewdly counter, curving my fingers into my gown.

Quillion grins on one side like a fox assessing another fox. "Would you like to see?"

○

Due to my Bride status, a dozen or so knights arrive at our destination down Tower to provide our escort. I'm not unused to security, though Verena's expertise was unmatched. I don't begrudge the knights but instead barely regard them, lithely adopting my role as Princess bride and settling my hand atop the bishop's as he guides me to a set of massive arched doors of gold and silver fused with iron and glowing from silver blood tech. Out of the corner of my eye, Quillion pauses before the blood authentication device and tests my gaze.

"Are you certain you want this, Princess? It can be...intimidating. And not one eye will miss your arrival."

A tingle invades my hands, wisps of gold light erupting. The Halo's urging. Clenching my hands, fortifying my resolve, I give him one firm nod. At least he warned me this time. The bishop beams, pleased by my determination, and presses his finger into the device. The doors propel open.

Similar to last time, he's escorted me to the highest level of what is undoubtedly the most cavernous and cadaverous building I have ever beheld. It must expand five full floor levels of the Tower and boasts the same medieval architecture. An enclosed rotunda of a massive cathedral arena. No, a Court, I conclude from the sprawling stadium seats sloping to the raised outer circle and an inner Court ring. Situated on raised platforms along the inner circle are statues of the Father. Sweeping throughout the back of the cathedral-like stadium, countless pillars form archways—except every last pillar, everything in the room, from the upper window lining to the inner ring, has been molded of the skeletal remains of vampires. A Court of bones and teeth and fangs. I suck in a deep breath and steel myself, remaining in the shadows for a moment.

So...not an urban legend after all. The Prince of Destruction's Court of Bones.

Dazed, I drop my jaw for more reasons than one. This is why Quillion stated not one eye would miss me. While all other vampires fill the arena floor seats, the private viewing box where *I* stand—an open oyster shell of skulls and bones—is the only one that overhangs within line of sight of *his* throne. The same throne of blood rubies from the theater, but this one is erected upon a mammoth pillar of vampire and human skulls woven with silver blood tech. Higher than all, the Prince robes his throne in unconquerable shades and flames with a regal scarlet cape cascading a few hundred feet to the floor below him. No armor, save for the gauntlets on his arms. Only those black robes like labyrinthine shadows and the horned, flaming crown on his head.

A sudden iciness spears my core, breeding a heaviness inside me like a sinking ship. I chant to myself, close my eyes, and rub my lips together to ward off a panic attack. Exhaling my held breath, I take one step on the little staircase descending to lower chairs as well as a raised balcony with only a few dozen feet of distance between it and the Prince's throne.

Deep murmurs ripple through the entire assembly upon my arrival. Immediately, Neo tenses and stands on the small bone platform in front of his throne with its sheer drop-off. His fingers curl into fists, wreathed in flame. Quillion informs me of the Court misconduct I've involuntarily committed. No one—save for the Father—should *ever* be higher than the Prince. And the bone box lies directly opposite Destruction's throne.

If I were anyone else, my skull and bones would already be promised to the pillar housing his throne.

While I finish my descent to the balcony overlook, Neo assesses Quillion, the hoods of his eyes hanging low and grim before his voice barrages the air like drumfire in a feral greeting, "Thank you for accepting my invitation, Bride Spirit." He smoothly saves face and gestures a hand to the audience. "Give my bride the honor she is deserved."

My heart ruptures in thousands of prisms of warmth when

every vampire in the room drops to one knee. With all attention on me, I close my hands over the balcony railing. Neo's eyes ravage mine, kindling deep to my core. Face, neck, and upper chest flushed, I bite my lower lip, squeezing my shoulders together before I incline my head to Quillion, hinting. Neo gives the slightest of nods, comprehending how Quillion has fulfilled another one of his pranks—though I joined him this time.

What sort of relationship do they have that Quillion can take such significant risks on my behalf? If the Prince were to punish him, I don't know how I could cope with losing his friendship.

Once all vampires rise and lower themselves into their seats, I sit in a bone chair on the balcony, inhale deeply, and prepare for my *husband* to do Court.

15

WHO IN ALL TEN COURT REALMS HAVE I MARRIED?

I REMAIN SILENT THE ENTIRE TIME, LISTENING TO THE SETTLING OF accounts, of trade deals, of the proffering of marriages, the requests of human cargo trains and homeless encampments, the delegating of blood bishop duties, the recordings of Court O' Ten farm gains and losses, the induction of blood pawns, and the distribution of armed forces. I observe the supreme, cunning mind, and quicksilver tongue of the Prince who has ensured an extreme lack of Court breaches and futile attacks on his primacy and dominion.

"My Lord Prince," a blood bishop proclaims and approaches the raised platform of the outer circle flanked by the Father statues. "there are rumors of an uprising within our Court O' Sixes mines. I have dispatched spy pawns to confirm the rumors." The Court O' Sixes is the closest realm to the Rose City. Now, all the ghouls make sense.

Neo bares a threatening fang, eyes two predatory blades to sharpen on the bishop at least sixty feet below him. "Do you have anything productive to add or do you gain sexual arousal in the wasting of my existential fractions of seconds that could very well be your last?" He taps a blood ruby, ripping it from its position and caping it in flames until it melts into a red rivulet to drip from his hands. A symbolic gesture of what he can accomplish in one of those "fractions" of a second.

"My Lord Prince," the blood bishop repeats again, but I recognize the trepidation in his voice, "there is an outbreak of Chasm ghouls and even hell hounds plaguing our borders and attacking blood farms. The Six Bishop Province believes this is the reason for the rumored uprising. Despite the actions of our armed forces, we have reaped more losses than gains. We fear the crumbling of an expansive mine sector if the Crown does not take steps to preserve its rightful property."

Oh, he's good, but a tremor betrays the ends of his words. As is his every right to fear, considering my experience with Chasm monsters, though I've never heard of any that had navigated as far as the mountainous regions of the Court O' Sixes. But despite how smooth this bishop is, I grin because the Prince is far better.

"So...you wish *me* to clean up the mess you are too ill-equipped to handle..." Neo assesses, and I can't help but respect his craft. As if sensing my eyes on him, he shifts in his seat, glimpsing at me. My cheeks burn from those eyes pricking mine, but I don't shrink.

Neo has not risen this whole time from his throne, nor does he rise now. However, he does wave a hand to one of his blood masters who shoots out their wings, so he may examine a document stamped with the blood seal of the Court O' Sixes. "It is tax season as you know."

I rub my lips together, wondering what the document holds. After a mere glance, Neo rolls it up and distributes it to the blood master whose wings do not so much as dare to tread above the Prince's feet.

Neo barely regards the bishop when pronouncing, "For the

acts of my service along your borders, I will increase your tax levies by six percent. Be prepared to get your affairs in order and surrender your assets accordingly."

"Thank you, my Lord Prince."

I may not have unlimited knowledge of taxes, but six percent is not as high of a rate as the Prince could have demanded. It's enough to cause the bishop to squirm, but the bellies of his subjects will not go empty during the winter. Disoriented fluttering wings engulf my belly, adrenaline tingling my nerves as I contemplate what I've witnessed. Next to me, Quillion fiddles with his ascot but mostly surfs the web on his wrist hologram. More celebrity gossip pages. I shake my head and roll my eyes but catch a suggestive glint in his pupils. Pretentious bishop.

The next account holder steps onto the platform—accompanied by a teenage girl with long, bountiful curls of streamlined gold. A loose-fitting velvet robe of deep red swallows her petite frame given she can't be more than sixteen. I straighten and grate my nails into the bone armrests on each side of me, scraping and shedding powder. An internal radar goes off in my head.

Human.

"My Lord Prince," the account holder, who bears a crest from the Court O' Twos casts his chin upward to Neo, daring to meet the Prince's eye. Big mistake. Although Neo disguises it well, thanks to our blood oath, I sense the fiery undercurrent radiating beneath his skin at the audacity of this foolish vampire. "I am pawn-master Byron Hale. I come to offer my pure and virgin-blooded winnings from the *Bark vs Bite Battle* as payment to settle my debts against the Crown with the tribute of flesh and blood."

Oh, Goddess!

I suck a sudden breath through my gritted teeth, tensing

visibly, my cheeks smoldering. Quillion covers my hand, but it's too late for me to settle. My empath has shattered the cage to smithereens. Human cargo trains, the homeless encampments, the farms...all a slow poison of awareness I've ingested over my brief twenty two years. And of the televised game pitting vampires against humans with pure bloods as prizes: something I *never* watched. But the spectacle of trading in blood and flesh paraded before my very eyes...

This will not stand. I. Will. *Not*. Allow. It.

"And what makes you believe I would be interested in such a tribute? I already have a harem-full who worships at my feet. And a bride who begs for me every night." Neo's words confirm my prior reflections as he waves off the pawn-master with a chuckle. More laughter reverberates throughout the arena as I pinch my eyes. My spine prickles, but I could care less about the derogatory quip at present.

More tears squeeze from their corners. I am next to her, sharing her pain, her place. My chest lurches when the pawn-master strips the robe from the human's shoulders, baring her before the entire Court to thousands of feasting eyes. My chest lurches, heart catapulting to lodge in my ribcage. Hot tears cloud my vision as I reach for the balcony railing, but Quillion sets a hand on my arm, preventing me from rising.

He shakes his head, a silent warning before whispering, "Do not rise, Elysia. Wait. Watch."

My Halo scalds the inside of my chest, but serpentine shades whorl along my dress. Now, I realize Neo has been observing me for the past few seconds, but the silver blades from earlier have turned to a cool mist. I'm shaking with the need to act. To leap right off this balcony and use my body as a shield.

But a cool undercurrent hums in my blood, lulls my system and caresses the power of the Halo. It's the first time I truly comprehend our bond. Of Neo staying my hand. It is not possessive. It's *protective*. It's the only reason I slowly, reluctantly slip my hand from the balcony railing.

As soon as I do, he stands! Leaps right off the throne in one mighty arc to land directly onto the platform. It cracks beneath his weight. He is a head taller than the pawn-master, two heads taller than the girl, his shadow assailing her as he approaches them while she desperately tries to conceal herself with her abundant hair. Without his shade lullaby calming my blood, I'd be gasping right now.

Quillion squeezes my hand, a small gesture of assurance.

The pawn-master relaxes, hugging his arms, smug as the Prince eyes the naked girl's face and cocks his head to one side, full lips parting into a pleased grin. Fangs primed and ready to mark her for the payment. I breathe fury through my nostrils. Destroyer. Bride-slayer. *Murderer. Oh, foremothers, deliver her!* I whimper, squeezing my eyes so more tears congregate to golden my cheeks. Roots return to me, and I make a desperate sign of a circle along my chest, but my hand knocks against the ring beneath my illusion neckline. An omen my prayers are in vain.

I hold my breath.

Alongside the entire Court, my whole body jerks when Neo charges for the pawn-master, driving him into the empty inner circle in the shadow of the formidable Father. All fall silent, including me when Neo stands tall and brandishes a scythe. No, not one scythe but two scythe blades of black vampire bone—one on each end of a bone rod—mirroring each other like two black crescent moons. Seamless, razor-sharp edges. Unconquerable and indomitable. Breathless, I clutch my chest, eyes expanding as much as my swelling muscles.

In an eyelash flutter of a second, the Prince of Destruction swings those blades in two precise, clean slices. I anchor my eyes on the pawn master, waiting before understanding what Neo has done when the pawn master's wings slide right off his body and tumble to the floor. Parting my lips, I dig my fingers into the fabric of my bateau, the ring a brutal kiss. The vampire's screams infest the air along with the rich scent of silver blood that oozes down the pawn-master's back. The Prince circles him, those bladed, vulture eyes assessing, toying with his prey. His dark shades abound and multiply from his body, drumming with his army-leveling destructive power, but he will only use a fraction of it now.

Once he finishes circling the screaming blood master, Neo stills.

Breath hitching, one hand's nails breaking on the armrest, I freeze, gazing at the pawn-master's clothes burning from Neo's power. The Prince's eyes become dark shrines. When his molten flames stroke all exposed flesh, the pawn-master screams and writhes in agony from the just punishment deepening to his muscles, and organs, and finally his bones. But not one drop of silver blood is wasted. By the time the Prince finishes, nothing remains but a tiny pond of elite blood and the pawn-master's skull and wings. Trophies.

I'm still spearing my other hand's nails into Quillion's palm, scrutinizing the Prince who shakes out his robe, cracks his neck from side to side, and proclaims to the skull, "Your debt is settled."

Not one vampire in the arena dares to breathe.

Neo flicks his eyes to the girl, then wraith-shadows direct to her. I'm ready to buckle when he goes so far as to remove his dark robe! To spread the protective raiment upon her shoulders and close it to preserve her form. *Oh, holy foremothers!* I practically hiss at Quillion and sear Halo fire into his eyes. He shrugs, squeezes my hand again, and feigns innocence, releasing me.

COURTING DEATH AND DESTRUCTION

When I eye Neo again, he gathers the girl into his arms and vaults her to his throne. But...why? Shadows and smoke surround them in a dark bubble. Then, our bond tugs, except it's not in my blood...it's in my mind! A mental noose cinches my consciousness and lures me forward. Accepting, I close my eyes, and tread carefully into his shade-protected bubble where Neo grants me access to the conversation. As if I'm a fly on the wall of the smoke—cocooned in his shades and flames and witnessing how the girl shivers before the bare-chested Prince, clinging to the edges of his robe as he addresses her.

"What's your name?" he inquires.

"Riona," she doesn't hesitate to respond.

Neo's shadow towers over her as he strokes his jaw and repeats her name. His mind is a fortress, not his body or blood. If he can noose me, I can at least sink my bound-Everblood into him. I imagine a slow immersion of my subtle gold tendrils of Halo light seducing his blood, so I may tiptoe through that pumping network of channels until I arrive at his mind. The doorway is lovely, dark, and deep, reminding me of the haunted doors of his bedroom. They part to my Halo touch, but I've only crossed into an outer chamber where Neo still retains control, where he grants me a sample of his secrets. I sense his emotions. His sated rage. What surprises me is the lack of desire, of possession. Instead, empathy, compassion, pity...they all ripple here and more.

Oh, Goddess! Who in all Ten Court Realms have I married?

After contemplating one more moment, Neo proposes, "You have a choice, Riona. I can offer you safe passage out of my Court O' Tens and beyond the Walls. But once you are outside, you take your life into your own hands. You may seek your family—"

"My family is dead," she interrupts, brazen, but the Prince

merely smirks at the royal invasion to his words. "My Lord Prince," she finishes, bowing her chin.

"Be that as it may, it is your choice. Safe passage beyond the walls or you may remain here in my Court. You may choose life as a fang-maid, escort, elite attendant, or I may secure a match as a Courtier."

"Your harem?" She eyes him from beneath bold, dark lashes.

What?!

"If the harem is your desire, I will secure a position for you," Neo agrees. "Is that your final choice?"

"Yes."

I yank myself from the bond as soon as his fangs sink inside her flesh to mark her.

16
"ELYSIA: TWENTY-SEVEN. NEO: ONE."

"You did that on purpose," I accuse Quillion in the elevator bound for the Commons.

Quillion taps the inner elevator ledge and guffaws, "I am certain I don't know what you mean!"

"You expect that will change my mind so easily?" *Cut it out!* I scold the Halo when stardust drifts from my skin to bathe me in its glow. When it only grows, I sigh, relenting. Why should I be ashamed of any of my emotions from Court?

Quillion shakes his head and stops tapping. "I meant no offense, Princess," the bishop apologizes, "I understand how years of inbred hatred can stoke such emotions. I once shared similar ones."

"How?" I plead.

"Another story for another time, Elysia. Suffice to say, as much as Neo is the Prince of Destruction, he is also a master at saving people from it."

I deny it. I can't believe it. Not after everything I've *felt*. My father turning to dust. My homeland in ruins. And those moments when I'd curled myself inside the Bridal Canyon next to Verena. Some things are unforgivable...and irredeemable without chronic penance. I consider how I've sought mine in the Underground. Am I doing penance for my actions here?

After propping my elbow on the ledge, I debate on whether to ask Quillion the question preying on my lips. Thousands of golden lights from the city twinkle past my eyes as the elevator sweeps upward.

"I don't bite," Quillion teases, crossing his leg over the other. "Not in a year at least."

Despite wanting to latch onto those words, I can't help but consider the girl. No more than sixteen. "She could have chosen anything! Why the *harem*?" There is a visible bite to my last word.

Quillion drags a hand through his rich brown waves and tries to explain, "Neo's harem is...well-known. I'm sure you've seen the—"

I hurl him a glare that could melt daggers. Obviously, I've seen the ads, the clips, gossip tabloids. Even if some of the girls act like gold-digging, naïve little brats volunteering to be on the *Harem of Hades*, I've always known there's more to their stories, remembering how the Tenth Court life seduces many. But still...

"The harem is a life of privilege and protection. For most girls, they are escaping lives of brutality or poverty or both. Harem girls are not born and bred in the Court O' Nines and escorted by emissaries at tax season or groomed for the Bridal Path." He crosses his legs and scrutinizes me, but I still pinch my lips, testing him.

"Why does he have to collar them and parade them?" I stab the words, the Halo spitting a freckling of embers.

Quillion rubs his eyes and drags a hand down his face. "It's complicated. Involves blood oaths and Father. But I assure you, Elysia, not one girl wishes to leave Neo's harem."

I lift my shoulders. "Will you take me there?"

Quillion clears his throat, swallows, and tugs at his ascot a little. "Not tonight. The blood moon is rising." He gestures as the elevator finishes its ascent.

Nightfall...so soon. Between the tour and the intense Court proceedings, it feels like it's been mere minutes.

I accept Quillion's hand and climb out of the elevator, but I don't relinquish it quite yet. Already, an ache grows in my chest, some internal force thrashing in my blood. The bond. Because it's night.

"So, the harem is obvious. But what about me? What is my role here?" I ask as Quillion and I wander the room for a few minutes.

"I believe we both know what your role is here, Elysia." Quillion smiles to one side of his mouth, inclining his head to mine.

"You know..." I breathe, confirming, given his reaction to my epic bride aisle walk with the Halo erupting all over my body.

"Naturally."

"For the record, I've always believed the Father's and the Prince's death were a packaged deal for the Everblood."

"Fair enough. I won't begrudge you."

"But...?"

My heart's throbbing grows. It presses on my chest like a heavy paperweight, making it difficult to breathe. I pant, knowing the pain will thicken until I plunge past those shade doors and come face to face with my...*husband*.

Quillion sighs and rubs a slow circle on my hand before he shifts his weight to stand before me. "I don't know what to say as I do not wish to insult your trauma, Princess. All I will share is how the Prince has been my greatest friend for the past fifty years. And though I would never blame you, I would mourn his loss greatly. And if I may be so bold..." His eye twitches, and he tugs at his ascot again.

I huff through my panting, tossing my curls back. "Oh, for heaven's sake, Quillion, nothing you say will change my fondness for you. So, stop walking on eggshells and spit it out!"

"No bride has ever lived long enough to bear the Prince a child. But I am hoping you may be the first."

To be fair, I did ask him to spit it out. I gust a breath and sharpen my eyes on his, seething, "Never! I'd bed you and bear *your* child in a heartbeat, Quillion. Not his."

I pause mid-step since Quillion has stopped in his tracks. Puzzled, I dance back to his side and raise a brow. "What?"

A bemused smirk appears on his face before he confesses, "As beautiful as our diverse offspring would be from such a union, I could never fathom reciprocating such an offer, Princess."

"Oh..." I pause, frown lines etching my mouth.

And then, the light dawns. "Oh! Oh! Oh!" I beam, and Quillion mirrors my smile in a nod as I conclude, "Quillion..." I use his prior hint as a launching pad and take a leap of faith, "What's *his* name?"

"*Was* his name," he corrects with a pleased nod, pats the back of my hand, and finishes our stroll. "My partner, Dominix, my sweet Nix, passed from this world to the next last October. And I was faithful to him for the full 56 years to the day of his death."

"Quillion." I coil my arms around his sturdy frame and press my cheek to his chest. He startles for a moment before he reciprocates, arms winding around me, cheek angling to collapse against the top of my head.

A deeper ache persists inside me. No, Verena and I only shared a brief amount of time compared to Quillion and his partner, but I empathize with his loss. Still, I won't allow my grief to superimpose his. Not when the Goddess guaranteed mine and Verena's paths would cross again, however much I ache for her. Especially not when the bishop strokes my curls, reminding me so much of Dad. His vest smells like chai tea and cigar smoke. Familiar scents from home. Chanting my father's name, I cling to Quillion and shudder.

"Elysia..." Quillion lights his hands on my arms and tucks his chin low so he may peer at me. "Give him hell again. Seriously, he needs more than one night of ass-pounding."

I giggle a little and bite my lower lip, raising my curious brows. "Were you and he...?" I trail off, considering the Prince's reputation which transcends his brides and Harem, of course. Court myths of secret male lovers. Not that polyamory is a bad thing...when it's respectful. How Verena...but I defy that inner ache that would drag my Empath out of hiding.

"No," Quillion responds, abruptly shaking his head. "I met Neo a few years after Dominix. By then, he and I were joined at the hip. Despite the Prince's occasional flirtatious teasing, we bonded over far *different* circumstances. Ones I will share with you sometime."

"Only you could be as patient and kind to deal with the Prince of Destruction."

Quillion places a hand on his chest and bows his head to me. "True, but not to conquer. An honor I hope you will also hold, Elysia. And I fully intend to fill your chart to the brim."

I grin, nodding, steeling myself to those words I desperately needed. But I note a word in his previous statement "also". An honor he hopes I *also* will hold. Someone else has conquered the Prince? And if so, who?

The infuriating blood bond tightens around my chest, constricting my breath, and I croak, "What do I do now?"

"Fang-maids will prepare you." He gestures to the girls emerging from the nearest preparatory room.

Quillion excuses himself while I accompany the fang-maids, wishing I could stay in the Court gown. The cold poker of a bond stabs my heart while the fang-maids undress me, peeling off my leggings before misting me with a spray and wiping me with strips to rid my skin of any Tower grit. The other fang-maids straighten my curls, tame them into submission as he desires *me* to be. Now, my straight ash dark strands flirt with my lower spine. My golden highlights are thin but bright as dancing faeries. I close my eyes, cringing when they apply rose oil to my skin. One maid ushers in with my "night garb".

"Not a chance," I pronounce sharply and cross my arms over my breasts, lips in a stubborn pinch.

The head fang-maid swings the diamond and ruby bejeweled bustier and matching panties with a black lacy overlay and exclaims, incredulous. "It is the cost of the penthouse suite, my lady!"

I shake my head, firm, and wince from the pain in my blood, urging me to go to his room. My lungs shrink, and I gasp for air. "Please..." I reach toward her, breathless, "Take it," I finish. "It's a gift. Do with it what you will."

"My lady! I cannot—"

"I'll trade you for it!" I shriek and gesture to her Court uniform.

"Please, my lady, I will fetch you a robe instead." Flustered, she hurries to a nearby closet and retrieves a silky robe of royal purple. She drapes it over my shoulders, and I double-knot the ties. One more knot. Parted enough to show a hint of my cleavage and the scoffing ring.

My suffering doesn't find reprieve, not even after I arrive at the Prince's bedroom. Like musket balls, the bond wages warfare under my flesh. So, I stagger inside, plunging right through the shadowy door...and into his arms.

"*Elysia*," Neo purrs warm breath across my face and grips my arms, glowering at my robe. All of him is naked again, and I crane my neck up, forcing my eyes to his.

Instead, I smile, disguising my intentions, and plant my hand on his musclebound chest...sinking onto my haloed brand. Without hesitation, I summon my Halo, imagine Verena's power, and charge electricity straight into his chest, stunning him.

Dizzy black clouds swirl in my head. I fall, but Neo's shadows catch me before he hovers over me. "Savage minx," his voice thunders as I pass out on the floor.

At breakfast the next morning, Quillion gives me another two check marks. I squeeze my lips into a sly grin while drinking my orange juice. This time, Quillion catches a candlestick after the Prince hurls it at him. He reads his paper the whole time.

The bishop wipes his bloodied mouth on his napkin and admits to Neo, "I do hope the suspense will last. I'm having a wager with Nita."

Neo snarls.

"Who's Nita?" I wonder at the unfamiliar name, curious brows lifting, heat rousing my blood.

Quillion fetches his bloody teacup, avoiding my question. I survey the Prince and bend my eyes to his, wishing I could do the same to his will, but Neo shakes his head. "No one. Eat your breakfast."

I gorge myself on every bite, almost elated for our next battle in the bedroom.

On the third night, I refuse his next attempt at lingerie: a crystal-studded lacy one-piece that would dip low to my navel. I don the leggings and a baggy sweater I'd arranged prior. Tonight, he hides behind one of the arches. It's the first time he destroys my Halo surge and gets his hands around my waist, tugging me back against his pelvis. In the barest thread of a second, I spin and slam my Halo in a shockwave of glitter dust to crash into him, landing him on his backside.

Roaring my laughter, I double over and pass out as the glitter-robed Prince snarls, "Treacherous Tinkerbell."

When the fourth night comes, he's on the ceiling, hovering in the shadows like a bat. But I prepared my Halo, fusing it into puppeteer strings.

"Bats should be upside down," I warn him before thrusting those strings to bind his neck and yank his head to the floor with a great burst of light. It takes him less than a second to quash, but by then, I'm already falling.

Each time, he catches my head before it can crash. He always conjures a new insult. "Cheeky tramp."

"No *batting* my eyelashes tonight, Neo."

During the day, I spend much of my time with Quillion, following him on his duties throughout the Tenth Court. Most of the time, he performs blood tests on familiars, but his duties also include the occasional marriage ceremony and even last rites for familiars. What has astounded me most is how he arrives in the name of the Prince who gives him his charge and orders, but Quillion blesses every familiar in the name of a pantheon of gods. At the end of each invocation, he includes the Father *and* the Mother Goddess. We finish each day with a tour of a library, so I may comb through texts for any information about the Altar.

"Princess, I know what you seek," Quillion mentions behind me after I've moved on to the next book in my towering stack. One of hundreds of books I've researched at this point. And the fourth library today.

I peruse his deep hickory eyes as he closes the book, then joins me, lowering himself into the opposite chair and folding his hands. "You won't find it in these books."

"You know about—"

"The Altar, yes. I am one of the very few vampires with the intimate knowledge."

I sigh, lowering my chin, defeated. "I can't expect you to share that knowledge with me. You're so close to the Prince."

"Be that as it may, I am not with Father." Quillion fiddles with his ascot, wincing a little, and I remain patient. The stripes I'd witnessed when he was bathing ranged all the way to his neck. I don't ask why, but I suspect they came from the Father. Quillion folds his hands again. "On the Altar was transcribed the Everblood prophecy from some of the earliest vampires who rose to great fame: they were called the Nephilim." Quillion clears his throat while I contemplate the biblical lore footnotes some rumored to be giants while other scholars likened to warriors. "Because they defied Father, the archangels rewarded them with gifts of supernatural power. Their battles with Father and his sons' unchecked debauchery over the nations of men spanned decades, but they knew the Great Flood was coming."

Yes, when Pangea split into various continents and the Father's hellish reign cracked. An earth-shifting climax in history described by countless texts from the Bible to the Qur'an to the Epic of Gilgamesh.

"The Nephilim knew the prophecy would need to be transcribed on some object the Father could not touch," Quillion divulges, eyes leveling to mine.

"The Altar."

He nods. Even if he's more relaxed, a somberness lingers in his gaze, his shoulders weighing heavier.

"It was the first act after the Great Flood. A monument of gratitude, of blessing. No evil could possibly nullify its existence," Quillion points out, closing his hand over mine and leaning forward.

"But how did the Nephilim—" I wonder since the Great Flood was supposed to destroy everything.

"Obviously, Father and his sons survived. And during the course of the Flood, the Nephilim used all their combined power to create one survivor. With his dying breaths and using his own blood, he chiseled the prophecy into the Altar. Father read the prophecy. He could not destroy it, but he did hide it."

"Where?" I curve my fingers around his.

"That I cannot tell you. But the Prince can." His lids grow heavy, eyes gleaming, and I recognize his growing telltale smile.

I roll my eyes because I recognize what he's doing. So, I lean against my chair, arms crossed over my chest, fingers tapping the sides of my arms. "I'm still giving him hell."

"Wouldn't expect anything less."

○

EVERY DAY, I RETURN TO COURT AND SIT IN THE PROCEEDINGS, proving to the Prince I am his true bride, and he will treat me with the respect I demand. The nights bleed and blur. He has an insult every time, but I thwart him each morning at breakfast. One morning, he misses, and I assume it's to keep his agreement to the Court O' Sixes. It's the most tranquil morning Quillion and I spend it discussing fashion and laughing over celebrity gossip.

It's now the tenth night.

Like the first night, I drape my long, white sweater over my camisole. It falls to my thighs, but I don't get the opportunity to tug my leggings on over my panties.

Tonight, *he* comes to *me*.

All the fang-maids scuttle out of the Preparatory.

I scream when Neo traps me against the room's mirror, his icy, black serpents of shades writhing for my attention.

"*Enough*," he proclaims with a growl, destroying my Halo surge with a force that leaves no question whatsoever: he's been holding back. Fear gushes through me at his power invading my body and voyaging into my mind through our bond.

In the next moment, he wraith-shadows me to his bedroom and shoves me onto the bed. Scrambling against the massive headboard, I summon anything I can think of for my Halo. The Prince obliterates...Every. Single. Spark. Snickering, Neo begins removing his robes. Slowly...inviting me to watch.

"You promised me a battle, Elysia, and you have delivered. Now, you are *boring* me."

Heart convulsing, body in tremors, I'm in no frame of mind to listen. Or to initiate a conversation. All of me wants to escape even if the blood oath will punish me outside his door.

Halo! I cry, but my chest dims. *No! I need you!* I lock my knees, wrench my sweater past my thighs, and search the room for a weapon. Upon him removing his inner robe, I hasten off the bed and lunge for the fire poker, aiming it for his chest.

Rolling his eyes, Neo huffs, seizes the iron, and cracks it like it's no more than a twig. He approaches, closing in on me. "Really, Elysia, are you quite finished with these games?" He scoffs as I roll onto the bed to use it as a springboard so I may barrel for the door.

As soon as I crash into it, a destructive shade bombards me with enough force, I fall hard to my side, knowing a large bruise already forms. Neo's shadow fills my vision, but I don't spy beyond his dark, meaty calves. Instead, I rush to my feet, tear toward the door again, plunging my arms right through. Thorns of fire and ice assail the back of my neck while the cold vapors besiege my body until I'm screaming as I drive myself forward. Painful tears fly from my eyes like tiny shards of glittery glass.

I get one finger through, but the dark energy senses me as a threat. Trapped in its all-encompassing web, it rises—a dark shade horse ready to strike. It will be more than a bruise when I finally land, probably against a window.

Right as the energy barrages me and launches me across the room, Neo catches me. Still, I fight him, quaking, almost catatonic, prepared to implode. Halo sparks flare from my heart and hands, burning thin strips of skin off Neo's flesh. In one solid moment, his eyes glaze over from my desperate assault. Powerless to stop him, he seizes my shoulders and thrusts me onto the bed, so I'm pinned beneath him.

"You're going to hurt yourself," he says with a low growl. "Just **stop**!" His fingers dig into my wrists.

"It's *not* a game!" I cry, my voice cracking, pleading. *It's me...my body, my heart, my soul*, I want to say. "*I am not a game.*" Shaking, struggling for air, hypersensitive to the piercing of fangs, my trauma from three years ago haunts me, plagues me when he holds me still.

Neo gathers my arms, bears them above my head, then nudges his hips against mine. I close my eyes, shifting my face into the jeweled coverlet of his bed where the honed black diamonds slice my skin. My Halo grows colder from the shades bridling my chest. I recite a verse for comfort, "hide me in the shadow of your wings," I force out the frenzied words from a childhood spent seeking the saints in our city's cathedral, taking strength from them even if I haven't darkened the sacred doors in years.

"Elysia," he interrupts darkly.

"From the wicked who are out to destroy me, from my mortal enemies who surround me."

"Elysia." Firmer this time—the edge of a deadly blade.

I swallow and refuse to open my eyes, continuing, "They close up their callous hearts, and their mouths speak with arrogance."

"*Elysia...*" his voice softens to a lull. That time in the prison. The same voice...dragging out each syllable of my name. Silk-swaddled scythes. Like silver raven wings, his hair drapes onto my cheek. "Look at me."

Heaving a few deep breaths, I muster my courage, turn my chin, and slowly open my eyes. He releases one of my arms so he may brush his knuckles across my cheek. Trembling, I lose myself in his winter storm eyes—such a contrast to the rest of his dark princehood. Bolder and more beauteous than ever. And his smoky aroma, that rich cologne enamors my nostrils. I choke a whimper when my stomach somersaults and stardust careens off my flesh. Fire and ice cloy my legs from where he's planted himself. Damn his ferocious, incarnate beauty.

I blink back frantic tears, narrow my eyes, and screw my lips into a fervent glower because I'll *never* forget my father's screams when Neo destroyed him. I'll *never* forget my homeland burning from the work of his hands. And despite the assurance of how I'll see Verena again, I'll absolutely *never* forget holding the corpse of my protector, my best friend, my girlfriend in his canyon.

After an eternity with those knuckles poised on my cheek, brushing away all my tears, Neo proclaims, deep and lulling, "I said to *sleep* with me, Elysia. Not to fuck me."

Oh, Saints!

The Halo sticks out its gold tongue again...*you knew all along*! I exclaim, convinced it's some infernal hellfire device sent to torment me.

Belting out a long train of curses, I clamber out from under him, and he lets me with a breathy chuckle.

"Quite the potty mouth indeed," he observes while I curl my knees to my chest and tip my forehead to my knee pads. "Breathe, Elysia," he directs, and I heave gasps.

Chaotic emotions well up inside me. Some rage for how he let this charade go for several days. Some for myself for not remembering the fine print of all vampire deals: the devil's in the details. Share his bed. Nothing more. Nothing less.

"Why?" I finally lift my head from my knees to face him, keeping my eyes north of his nude equator.

"Elysia: twenty-seven. Neo: one." He shrugs. "Wanted to know how long you'd keep it up for." He smiles, salutes me, then places his hands on his knees, and my eyes follow before swinging back to his as he continues, "It was rather impressive. Don't blame me for your filthy mind. And eyes..." he chuckles, cocks his head to mine, and winks knowingly. "Did you truly believe I would violate the purest being on earth?"

Voice hoarse, I swallow hard and respond, "I-I don't know what to believe..." I bite my lower lip, reflect on the Court proceedings. He'd never punished another vampire as he'd done that first day. No more flesh trading was permitted. I remember how he'd removed his robe and wrapped it around the girl.

I also remember how he had me in his prison for hours. How he didn't raise his hand to me. How he didn't bite me when he had every opportunity. The Halo releases a single tiny heart, but I scowl, shoving the power. The Goddess said he has a dark secret.

No, Elysia, I chastise myself. *This is all deception. He's playing some long game to break you. Break him first. He knows where the Altar is.*

I sift my fingers through my hair and sniffle, my eyes accusatory, jeering, "You could have told me."

"Where's the fun in that?"

"Manipulative prick tick."

"Sassy siren."

"Will you put some clothes on for heaven's sake?"

A deep throaty chuckle. "Oh, wouldn't they be blest by the sight of me?" Neo quips, but before I can interject, he adds, lifting a hand, "I've spent centuries tailoring myself to whatever mold my Father deigns. I am his youngest and his only son now. I am his destructive champion, always conforming myself to his desires, always performing his bidding to set the course of his desired history." I take a deep breath, tugging at my sweater ends as he continues, dropping his hands to his sides, sighing, "My brother's death changed everything. Ever since, I've had to take on more and *be* more. But this is *my* room." He gestures, and some of his shadows leap from the floor and curl along his arms in flirtatious whorls. His voice transforms into something so lovely, dark, and deep, "This is my sanctum."

I lick my lips and lower my head, processing. Yes, my parents protected and guided me, but my mother also trained me at an early age, hoping to chisel me into her warrior. I ultimately forged my own path in the Underground...even if it led me home every time. The Rose City was where I could drop my guard. No, not the Rose City. My secret underground lair. Naked in the dark many times with and without Verena.

"If it suits your *purer* sensibilities..." Neoptolemus masks his pelvic region in shades, forming a dark twisting armor. "And if it brings you any comfort, it's the one time in all my centuries where I have *not* felt safe in my own domain with my bride. Where I've had to remain in more control than ever."

"Because I am a threat…?" I muse, treading onto dangerous territory.

"You are my greatest threat," he acknowledges, voice deepening.

I almost ask *and what else?* Because there is something else, but I doubt he would share with me.

"And the only bride who did not desire me," he chortles arrogantly, eyes of glittery frost as if he's just donned some mask that alludes to what he shared while massaging me: closer in age than I believe.

Licking my lips, I nod and cast my eyes low. "I'm sorry for your brother."

Neo eyes me and reaches behind to pull the coverlet. "Don't be. He was, in your words, a manipulative prick tick."

Once I curl my legs into his bed, grateful for the spaciousness as it can easily hold multiple bodies, I slide onto the very edge and cocoon myself in the sheets. His bed smells like smoke, vetiver, and incense. Still, I place a mountain of pillows all along my back. Behind me, Neo smirks and shakes his head.

"I assure you that is quite unnecessary," he grunts and climbs into the bed after me.

"Agree to disagree." I add another pillow. And another.

Neo remains on his side. I can live with that. I don't have to enjoy it.

"Neo?" I mutter even if I can't see him beyond my pillow fortress.

"Hmm…?"

"I still hate this."

"You brokered the deal," he doesn't hesitate to point out.

"I know." I will hold my end, to the cost. One of his warm

flames crackles against the wall above my head. I spring up, squealing, "Am I going to get burned in my sleep?"

"No." His voice edges with annoyance. "Go to sleep."

As I settle my quaking body, resting my head onto the deep pillows devouring me, Neo utters, "I'm sorry for your father." Thankfully, no shadows curl against me.

A silent tear rolls down my cheek. Too numb and exhausted, I simply tell him, "We're not there yet."

Devilish, I pause and chew on my inner cheek. I whisper to the Halo, questing. Oh, thank the foremothers! He deserves it after all he did. "But Neo?"

"Hmm?" He cranes his neck in time to meet my gold shower drowning him and soaking his side of the bed.

Giggling uncontrollably as the darkness swells, I open my mouth to pronounce, "Twenty-*eight!*"

17
"YOU THINK I CAN BE BOUGHT WITH A FEW PETTY, MIND-BLOWING, SEXUAL FAVORS?"

It's the first morning I wake to him...or rather his knuckles with their slow drag across my cheek. I rub my naked legs together and trail my hand underneath the blanket along my body, double-checking I'm still clothed in last night's sweater... and my bikini panties. I sigh, relieved.

At least he's fully clothed, well mostly, considering his stalwart chest practically eclipses my vision from where he sits enthroned above me, back to the bedframe. His black robes open to exhibit that indomitable powerhouse of ridged muscle. If I angle my face a little, my nose will brush my halo-flesh brand.

My skin tingles beneath those knuckles, goosebumps forming. So, I slowly lean away from him, away from his hand which he drops to his side as I gather the blankets higher.

"I thought I might accompany you to breakfast this morning," proposes Neo, flexing his fingers as I scoot further away until I discover, to my utter dismay, I've run out of bed.

"Ow! Shit," I mutter when my rump thuds on the floor. But I'd swear his shades cushioned my fall.

Neo chuckles before his shadows collect my whole body into their embrace. At first, I struggle until determining they aren't devouring me. Instead, they transfer me to the bed, higher so I'm below his eye level, those pupils exploring every inch of me.

"That's how you did it, isn't it?" I confront him while the shadows dissipate. I narrow my eyes, certain one forms a mouth to blow me a kiss.

The Prince reaches out as if to cup my cheek, but when I flinch, he pauses, curves his fingers, and drops his hand to the bed. Well, that's something, and I'll take it.

Neo's eyes remind me of silver carousels riding mine, confirming, "Yes, Elysia." When I lean my head against the bedframe and rub my lips together, contemplating, he urges, "You may ask me anything. I don't bite," he teases since he literally cannot bite me.

"Can you feel what *they* feel?"

He blows a sigh through his nostrils. "No, much to my chagrin. I control them. I manipulate them. Sometimes, they act according to my subconscious desires. But that is their extent."

My vision coasts to his hand where his fingers twitch, one inch of fabric away from mine—how much he longs to touch me. A stroke of pride lifts my shoulders when I glide my hand away. He can suffer.

"I must extend my gratitude." Neo's next words take me by surprise.

"For what?"

"For your presence at Court."

Cynical, I curl one corner of my mouth in a sneer. "Right."

"Your presence is soothing even if Quillion was a damn devil to expose you to such scrutiny so quickly upon your induction into my Court."

I cross my arms over my chest and snort, "Induction aka. mandatory *matrimony*." When he doesn't thwart my statement but continues his silent appraisal, I tap my finger against my arm before sagging my shoulders to acquiesce, "You're welcome."

"Was that so hard?" He leans over, kisses my cheek, then shadows out of the bed on the opposite side.

The kiss was light as a vapor, but I still press my fingers to my skin and flush all the same. My Halo flushes inside me, too, parading my chest with a hint of rosy gold dust. Neo isn't what I expected. Some things, yes, but last night was a turning point. Or at the very least...a beginning to a turning point.

"Why did you do it?" I refer to the girl in Court.

He shakes out his robes with a stony stoicism, brows knotting over his eyes, so cowled, they beckon shadows. "He deserved it. She did not."

"And I'm supposed to believe you only punish those who "deserve it"?" I test him from beneath low-hanging lashes.

"I don't expect you to believe a word I say."

Immediately, I climb out of the bed and make my way toward him, slowly. "Then, prove it," I dare the Prince, grasping onto one of the pillared bedposts, unashamed to nudge the air with my hips. Enough of a tease with my legs utterly bare below my sweater's hem.

It takes him less than a moment to shadow to my side, his cool shades tempting the pathways of my chest, mingling with warm flames. "What do you propose?"

I curl my hand toward him, playing the long game. "Another blood oath."

Neo dips his head lower, breath hovering across my face, fragrance of blood-laced wine. "Your desire?"

"An oath of truth. No lies."

"Not enough for you to seal your stamp onto my flesh?" He grasps my hand and presses it to his ruined chest.

My eyes burn, and I curve my nails into the center of that circle brand. "It will *never* be enough!"

Neo's hand roams the arm of my sweater, lower to my waist, strengthening in his pursuit, counteracting my fury. I don't stop him.

I don't stop myself. "You laid waste to my city."

He bunches the sweater and I snarl, jutting my chin to challenge his roaming hand. "You destroyed my *home*!"

His brazen hand touches my bare hip, finger hooking under the line of my panties. Hissing, I thrust my neck so high to further my claim. "You killed my father who was as good and honorable as Quillion."

While his other hand sweeps to my back to wrench me closer, and his finger tugs at the fabric line, I shatter his throne. "And you stood by as your Father razed my mother, a Queen, to her own personal hell before you tried to do the same to me."

Neo removes his hand so he may imprison my jaw. "And it was *I* who destroyed the demons attacking you. It was *I* who agreed to your blood oath which betrays my very Father, my blood."

I roll my eyes and huff, jerking my chin away, but his grip is iron. "Don't expect me to give you a gold star and wipe your slate clean. Especially when we know your long game is solely to get in my pants."

"Your intoxicating but whip-smart mouth has all the answers now, does it?" Neo eases that line lower till my full hip is exposed. Tapping my hip, he cocks his head and adds with a wry grin, "But you are right on the last part. And if you weren't so sexually repressed, you'd learn how far the spawn of Satan will go to worship an angel."

Now, I reclaim my jaw and use that smart mouth to bite his

hand. He startles and releases his grip on my bottoms. "Worship this." I flip him off, then stab a finger in his face, halting him before he can sweep in with another attempt. "You think I can be bought with a few petty, mind-blowing, sexual favors?" I slide the line of my panties back.

He grins, and a muscle throbs in his cheek. Damn. I do my ultimate best not to squirm beneath his heady smolder that burns nearly every last bridge to my toes. My core overheats again, and my Halo practically sings.

"Trust me, Elysia, I'd blow away a hell of a lot more than your mind," he assures me, moving in, but I step back, raising my defiant hands, lips parting in a warning. Pausing, he groans and drags both hands through his hair, shoving the silvery strands into a devilishly seductive man bun before dropping his palms to his sides and asking through clenched teeth, "What price will ever be enough, *Princess*?"

I cross my arms and jut out one deadly hip. "Your honest and solemn word would be a suitable down payment."

As soon as I finish speaking, Neo drags his fang across his palm. Not a line but a gash so his silver blood falls in a steady, trickling stream. Sighing, I approach, lifting my hand to his fang. He seizes my wrist, lowers his fang to prick my skin in a tender slit—enough for one or two drops of blood. Right before he crashes our palms together, Neo pauses, eyes carousing to mine to propose, "Like calls for like?"

"What motivation would I ever have to lie?" is my too-swift response. The Altar. The Underground. My smile spreads as I close my hand onto his because nothing about this oath *requires* me to answer.

Once our blood intermingles, I shudder from the familiar quickening in my veins, that cataclysmic power. Considering Neo winces, eyes pinching as if pained, I wonder if perhaps my

Halo-laced pure blood cause him as much agony as his destruction carves its path through my circulatory system.

Once the stinging subsides, Neo collapses his fingers into mine and tows me forward to lull above my mouth, "One question today, Elysia. Make it count." He tempts my eyes with his silver storm.

The Altar, the voice in my mind reminds me. I can't take the risk yet. Not when he's as cunning as me and knows there's no mandate to answer. It could shut him down until he'd blast the drawbridge to smithereens. Too soon. And there is something else I want more. Screw destiny! I can save the world tomorrow.

So, I fold my fingers to unite with his and ask, "Where's my mother, you supercilious ass?"

Neo's eyes visibly harden, pupils dilating as if formed of black ice. At first, I believe he's going to refuse to answer. Shut his bewitching mouth for once, and as appealing as such a notion is, he did yield *one* question.

"I cannot *tell* you—" Neo utters and I attempt to pull my hand away, but he strengthens his grip and finishes, "—but I will *show* you." My heart leaps in my chest, emitting glowing currents to dance off my skin...until Neo warns, voice lowering to a dangerous bass, "But you must hold onto me and do *not* let go. Even after we've arrived, you cannot let go. Not for one moment, Elysia. Do you understand?"

"Where is she?" I tremble, suspecting.

When his hands enclose my waist, and he lifts me, I'm almost breathless. He raises me so high, my head's barest edge surpasses his. My curls fall along his cheeks.

"You will always be higher than me, Elysia," he whispers against my mouth.

Oh, Saints! With my hands stationed on his upper chest,

Neo's smolder returns, and his fingers press down on my hips, urging. He robs all my breath. Flames inject right into my center. Beyond aroused, my Halo glitters off my skin. I bite down on my lower lip, swallow a crusty lump in my throat, and battle the heat hammering between my thighs. Capitulating, I twist my arms around his neck and bend my legs. He anchors his other hand under my knees beneath his robe. I'm pressed against his smoldering sunset, so why am I still shivering?

Despite the honeymoon hold, how his substantial arms tighten around my waist, he does not carry me over the threshold. No, he leads me to the door of bones and skulls and sweeps his hand in the air. The door bends to his will and opens to the Chasm.

18

"YOU WANT ME TO TOUCH YOU?"

"Close your eyes," Neo directs me upon approaching the edge of the stone walkway to the sheer drop-off.

"Don't you have Court?" I remember, snapping my head toward his shade door.

"Court can wait." I swing my gaze back to him, lifting my surprised brows. "Good for those sycophants to learn a little patience and that their Prince does not abide by their schedule. And you come *first*." Oh, heavens! I shove down more Halo stars...and rose-flushed stardust. "Now, close your eyes."

I do more. I bury my face into his shoulder, into the crushed velvet of his robes. Neo's shadows shroud me in a protective mantle, though I get the idea it's far more for my assurance. He touches his lips to my hair. I take one deep breath before his wings slash through his robe and mutilate the air with such force, even his shadow mantle fractures when I'm rocked against it.

I open one eye and freeze, awed. *Not possible!* Even the day in the woods, he'd held back his true wings? The paradox of the silver face and dark side of the moon. Monstrous and ethereal, Neo's black and silver wings were created for battle, no for *war*—all wars throughout all time. Not only do these vampire wings bear a network of silver veins, but they swarm with the blood of humans. As if a dual life force pumps through him, granting him undefeatable power. Though I'm currently motionless, I'm still overcome with the wings' energy—a siren call injecting down to my Halo. It strains. It aches. It practically weeps!

Sliding my hands further around his neck, I don't dare lift a finger to them, but I do flex my Halo. Focus my attention on those wings. Almost causing me to lurch, its golden light branches out as a glowing tether to creep, feather-like, toward those wings. So close...Neo's veins throb in his neck. The only sign of tension right before he leaps from the platform.

Those wings vault in a sharp upward spin, so we free-fall for hundreds of feet straight into the heart of the Chasm! My scream fades to a yelp after I bite my tongue and draw blood. Unashamed of how I must force my face onto his neck, I strive to slow my breath. His spicy incense scent seduces me...and something else. Deep water...like a rain shower.

After the free-fall seems to last for minutes, Neo drives his wings out to strike the air. Again, I scream when the wind rages, burrow my nails into his robes as inertia charges us in a backward swooping arc. Barely a moment goes by before he propels us forward. The most adrenaline I've experienced in a given three seconds.

Not even his power can nullify the Chasm darkness, how my Halo lures the monsters crouching in the shadows. Peeking, I shudder, squeezing my eyes, tears shimmering at the sight of thousands of them in the cavernous waste. We are closer than ever to the entrance of the recesses of the Underworld where the fabric of reality is finer and darker than sackcloth—where all the restless demons of the deep scramble. Mere hundreds may make it through the Chasm chinks to taunt the living world.

Neo flicks his head to them, growling under his breath. His simple action causes the monsters to retreat, but they still hunt the Halo-trail, my pure blood scent.

I tremble.

Neo leans in and murmurs in my ear, "Does my down payment buy me anything?" he hints, sliding his hand to the base of my spine, fingers inching lower.

I purse my lips and pause, surprising myself when I don't shut him down, but I comprehend why. We're in the Chasm. My empath has utterly dissolved the cage. Despair, grief, sin, and suffering swell around my heart, tiptoeing closer to the Halo. All the darkness preys on me, threatening to undo me with memories of my trauma, trauma I hold so close. Neo's hand dips lower, tempting me when it slips beneath the ends of my sweater to slide onto my naked waist...and lower, teetering on the edge of my ass.

Sudden ice, talons of wind, stab at us. Neo plummets, yanking me to reality. Deeper and deeper into the Chasm. I breathe desperate gasps against his neck because I smell decay and rot and ruin. Memories stalk me.

I can't take it anymore and claw my nails into Neo's neck, nodding softly, granting his hand consent to roam. Anything is better than this.

Though he jerks us into a pause, the Prince continues pumping those wings in a hover. "Did you just nod?"

"Yes," I whisper to his neck.

"You want me to touch you?" He seeks me, nose brushing my cheek, his waves mingling with my curls, but I can't bring myself to look.

All my skin turns cold, hairs pricking. Especially my legs

which are a naked, light gold in this darkness. So, I muster another nod and tremble.

"Where?"

I shake my head, somehow gasp out, "I don't care." And I really don't.

After a long pause, Neo rushes forward again, but his hand voyages...higher! To nestle at the back of my neck. He hums low in my ear, explaining, "No, Elysia. Our first time won't be in the Chasm. The first time I touch you, you will be safe, fully awake, and lucid. Because I wish for you to feel *everything*. How your moans will be like angel music to my ears."

Oh, Saints! *His words, his words, his words!* They become a live wire igniting my nervous system, lighting every synapse in the reward center of my mind to trigger a flame that flushes my whole body. But mostly nestles between my thighs. It's a level of respect I hadn't expected from him even if his words are still suggestive...and possessive.

He lands hard, rocking the ground beneath me. When I open my eyes, it's to the edge of a precipice to fathomless pits below. Slowly, Neo's hands slip from my body, releasing me to the ground, but he doesn't neglect to remind me, "Don't forget what I said." *Don't let go.*

Exhaling a ghostly puff of breath, I shiver and place one shoulder against him, and tow my sweater sleeves over my hands. In one supreme sweep, Neo removes his robe and covers me with it. Like he did with the Court girl. Except, his hands linger at my waist, and he slowly pivots me, so I'm facing the yawning mouth of a cavern, back to his lower chest.

"This is where my mother is?" I wonder, more ghost breaths fleeing.

"I cannot tell you. It is forbidden." I glance back to find him wincing as if it requires great energy to bring me here.

Coupled with his, my hand trembles as we embark deeper

into the cavern. A disturbing warm draught of air teases my body, but I register this warmth is not good. It grows, bedeviling my nostrils with a sulfuric after-scent as we progress down a small path flanked by cavernous walls. My bare feet brush past black grit and pebbles, and I touch a wall when the ground shakes to some eruption. Cold sweat flares on the back of my neck, and I pause to slow my breath, to touch my chest where my Halo could claw out of my flesh. Then, Neo raises my hand to his mouth and kisses my palm, my wrist atop his horned crown.

Silencing my quaking emotions, I continue walking and ask, "He's not here, right?" A dumb question.

Neo shakes his head and flanks my left side, his behemoth shadow draping over me. Shades canvas his bare chest to form a dark vest. "Only his power."

"How far do we have to go?"

"Not far. Less if we hasten our pace."

"Can't you shadow?" I wonder.

"No." His mouth sets into a grim line. "Father's power is too much for me to shadow here. He would recognize my shadow path and I would hear about it later."

"But when he returns, he will smell me—"

"I'm destroying your scent, Elysia."

I snap my eyes to his. "What?"

"He will not even be aware of your presence." Neo squeezes my hand in assurance.

"Did you destroy my scent in the woods?" I whisper, reflecting on my ruined home.

"Yes."

"So, he can recognize me, Reyna's daughter, the Princess of the Rose City, but not the—"

"Everblood, correct. To him, your blood does not smell of purity. It is certainly memorable, but not the pure siren call it is to all others. Unfortunately, your dramatic martyr-like net of emotions makes it more difficult to destroy."

I roll my eyes and quicken my pace, only to slam into a corner wall, groaning out, "I'm not a martyr."

He chuckles, tugs me closer to his side, knuckles on his opposite hand reaching out to stroke my cheek. "No? Then, what are you, Princess?"

I shake off the feathery sensation titillating my spine when he touches me. "A dreamer."

He drops his fingers and smiles in agreement. "Yes, your blood never smells purer than when you are fueled by your greatest dream. Apart from one other time..."

"Are you going to tell me?"

He shakes his head, simpering, puffing air through his nose. "Not yet."

Following him closer because he knows the route through this labyrinthine cavern, I chew on the inside of my cheek and debate before my curiosity gets the better of me. "What does it smell like to you?"

Neo deadpans, shifting his body in front of me so he may tilt his head and respond, "Like a starlight host weeping on a sea of crystals. Of the first snowfall crowning a field of ice lilies. Of that sacred place on earth where the moon and stars rise to conquer the sun."

I can't help but tug one corner of my mouth into a slight grin. "How long were you practicing that?"

He winks. "Since the pre-nuptial wedding massage. I'd considered incorporating the words into my vows."

"You should have. They would have been more aesthetically pleasing."

Somehow, his laughter helps. So dark and deep and... lovely, it prompts my shoulders to sink, enabling my empath to return to her cage so I may strengthen my heart.

COURTING DEATH AND DESTRUCTION

I stare at my bare feet, at the ends of his robes that guard each side of me along with his shadows and flames wisping along my legs: dark, whispering allies—as much a part of Neo as my Halo is a part of me.

As the path shifts, beginning a steep ascent, and Neo helps me climb, I finally summon the nerve to question, "Would you have bitten me in the woods?"

A solemn pause. Followed by a sigh. "Must I answer?"

"You just did..." I tread on the confirmation I want to know most. Yes, he professed it before, but now, we have an oath of truth..."Why did you agree to the blood oath when I vowed to destroy you? Why not hand me to your Father?" I consider the irony since I vowed to deliver him from death. However, my quest still burns in my chest. Whatever courtesy he has shown me is still no excuse for what he has done. All the dead brides. My father. Verena. My mother. My home.

I owe him nothing.

"Other than to get in your pants?" Neo diverts, but my eyes hold his, unblinking. Sighing, Neo drags one hand through his hair and acquiesces, "Would you believe I took a leap of faith?"

I don't know, I almost say but sigh because we've arrived at the peak, and there's no more time to reflect. So, I suck in a deep breath. Before me, a sheer drop leads to a small canyon of great, black spire rocks that erupt with lava and lightning. When the entire canyon shakes, I almost lose my balance, but Neo's hand stabilizes me. Taking my hand, he gestures upward.

I gasp. In the canyon's center, about five hundred feet beyond my head is a tiny island prison formed of vampire bones, teeth, and fangs, cocooned by coffins. None of this should be enough to hold my mother, especially with the surrounding lava and lightning which could ignite her elemental core. Through the coffin gap and between the overlapping skeletal vampire remains, I recognize my mother's sleeping form...and all the *cables* stabbing into her spine.

Almost ready to leap right off the precipice, I plead with Neo, "Please?" No wings.

Immediately, his arms embrace me, and I grasp his neck, leaning into the rocking of his body. Three seconds later, he thunders onto the base of the prison. I plunge into its center, grab the bone cage with one hand, and stare down at my mother. Chains yoke her hands while an open-backed purple shift hangs from her shoulders. Attached to her entire spine are those cables that extend in a spiderweb pattern to the coffins. Puckered black lines branch out from her vertebrae in some evil network eclipsing her fair skin.

"Mom..." I whimper.

She immediately flicks her head to attention, her curls ravaging her royal eyes; they well with tears. "Elysia..." she utters, her whole body sagging with the weight of relief. And then, she snarls, gets to her feet, shakes the cables, and roars at the vampire holding my hand. As if prompted by her actions, a sound rushes above my head. Something pumps through those cables, causing her to crash to her knees and cringe, locking her teeth in pain.

I glance at Neo for an explanation. He extends his left hand and unlatches one of the coffins so I may view the inside. Flight triggered, I startle from the sight of the Fallen, those macabre demons with their bloodied eyes and damned souls. Halo light breeds along my chest, bursting forth in little beams, but Neo steps in front of the coffin. He takes my scalding heat which defeats his shadows and attacks his chest. His muscles bulge for a few moments as he endures my righteous Goddess fire. I choke on a ragged breath.

"Fallen blood," he growls, closes the coffin, then relaxes to my light ebbing. I may have a limited knowledge of the

Chasm's species, but I do know Fallen blood has the ability to nullify powers. With such an intense dose feeding her cables and for a human such as my mother, it's undoubtedly equal to Neo's destructive power.

Out of the corner of my eye, Mom observes us, studying, perceiving. She breathes out a sigh, "Now, it all makes sense."

I clutch the bone cage and ask, "What do you mean?"

She hangs her head, then jerks her chin to Neo. "I saw a vision of him taking you into the Chasm. And then, my vision became nothing but destruction. It's why I told you to run and hide."

"I'm...*fine*," I muster the words, offering her some small boon, some shaft of hope.

Her eyes zero in on Neo's silver hair at my neck, and I wonder if she's using a lesser power to determine what it's attached to. As if confirming, she gnashes her teeth at him. "What have you done, you degenerate diablo?"

He can't help but smirk at me on one side of his mouth as if to say "like mother, like daughter" before I explain, "I made a deal with him, Mom. I'm his...bride."

"No! *No*, Elysia!" she cries, curving her hand into the dirt beneath her and chucking it at a bone. "This isn't your destiny."

I lean closer through the gap and explain, "I *am* the Everblood, Mom," I declare even though I struggle through the words. "And I'm *safe*."

"I assure you, Elysia is more than able to handle herself," Neo advocates for me.

"Silence, you brute!" Mom commands him, slipping into her regal posture. Always a Queen even when she's brought to her knees. "You don't even deserve to speak her name."

To my utter amazement, Neo bows his head but still maintains a firm hold on my hand. The canyon thunders again, and

Neo's eyes darken as he surveys the area, jaw turning rigid while I speak to my mother.

"Mom, where is *it*?" I hint to her, focusing on the Altar.

"Hidden," she coolly responds, assessing Neo. I eye him, too, and despite the tapering of his brows, he focuses on the canyon.

With a sudden arching of her back, Mom screams, shrill as a banshee. All her silver veins strike like a flint, granting her an adrenaline burst of energy. Enough to give me *her* mind. Safe and secret from Neo.

The Altar is bound to him. The Father may sense it or summon it at any time. And whenever he returns to Court, it's the first thing he looks upon: the reflection of his greatest fear. I knot my brows, puzzled.

"Elysia..." Neo summons me, tightening his grip on my arm. "We must go now. He's returning."

"Can't you destroy them?" I hint to the Fallen, recalling the Spirit Woods, chest expanding. "Set her free?"

Mouth curving into a sharp glower, Neo shakes his head.

Mom defies me as much as he does. "No, Lyssi. You must go now. This is my burden...to keep you safe."

"Mom..." I moan even as Neo collects me into his arms, preparing to charge away. How can I leave her again? How can I leave her here? How can I run away?

"I love you, Elysia." *I love you*, Dad had said. No, I refuse to believe this will be the last time.

"Stay alive," I plead. "I'll come back for you. I'm getting stronger. I'm safe. I'm whole."

No tears fall from Mom's cheeks unlike mine. No, she can't betray such emotion, not when the Father is coming. Her strength confounds me. As Neo cords an arm upon my waist, Mom snarls at him, "If you lift a finger in harm to my daughter,

Neoptolemus, not even hell itself will hide you from my wrath!"

Neo's silver storm eyes coast to my mother, posture tensing as he straightens like a dark tower but bows his hand to my back, prepared to carry me again. "I vow to you, Queen Reyna Rose, Lady Phoenix of the Rose City, no harm will befall the Halo-bearer from my hand."

When he jumps, I grip his neck and thrust my face into his chest, eyes peeking open once to witness my mother fortifying herself, her love for me fueling her endurance, her protection. A holy, all-consuming rage breaches my chest, but if I unleash it, it would burn Neo who's still bearing me.

With vampiric speed, he tears us out of the caves and back into the desolation of the Chasm. Flames stoked in my chest, battling to get out, I stare at him as he releases his wings in one furious second and shoots upward, fiercer and faster than our descent. His last words to my mother chime in my ears more sacred than cathedral bells. And...I remember my wedding vows:

I vow to be your shield, I vow to save you from danger.

Even if it's *my* danger, I abide by my vow. Somehow, I redirect the undeniable Halo fire coursing within me. Instead of my chest, it streamlines into my hair, attaching to my golden highlights and teasing out into the Chasm in pure kite tails to tempt the ghouls, the demons. I can't deny my growing smile when those demons get too close only for the kite tails to burn them. They scurry into the shadows.

"They run from you now," Neo coos next to my ear, and I rake my nails into his skin when he thrusts higher.

"Thank you..." I express and bury my face in his neck again, scenting the silver blood trickling in his veins beneath my nose. And for the first time, I willingly touch my lips to his neck and glory in how he shudders.

19
"IT'S A PORTAL, ISN'T IT? TO YOUR BROTHER'S TOWER?"

WHEN NEO LANDS ON THE STONE WALKWAY LEADING TO THE BONE door, I beg him, "What's he doing to her?"

"He's savoring," Neo responds, caressing my hair ends. "We are immortal, so he has no reason to rush. Every now and then, he'll withdraw the cables and they'll enjoy a good go at each other. It's why the Chasm rumbles so much and why more sulfuric ash has been erupting."

"And how long will that last?"

"He could drag it out for months or years. He'll probably treat himself to a battle between the three of us for Hallowtide. My Father plays the long game," he notes with a measure of disgust.

I don't know whether to wince or grin at the thought of my mother going toe-to-toe with Neo. But everything he's said...at least it's *something*. I remember my unbroken mother, wishing I could gird myself in her volcanic strength. She will always rise from the ashes. But I must focus on my mission. What had she said? The Altar is *bound* to him. And it's the first thing he looks upon when he returns to the Court O' Tens. So, it's something he *returns* to.

Neo deposits me safely in his bedroom, glances outside, and pronounces a piqued, "Damn..."

I peer through the windows. Outside, my Halo-light has grown to a veritable network of tributaries: trails of golden breadcrumbs leading straight to the Court O' Tens. Neo closes the door with a huff while I shuffle my gritty feet, smiling at the shadows pirouetting along my calves, nudging my toes for attention.

Neo drags his hand through his silver waves and drops a frustrated hand to his side. "I'll have to thin out the population before Court."

"Population?"

I sit on the floor and cast off his robe to curl my hand into the shadows, marveling at how they awaken to my touch and frolic with my fingers. Like little kissing shade minnows.

"Your light will attract the ghouls and more Fallen and devil knows what else. What on earth are you doing?" He kneels before me, and I resist the urge to tell him how much I love when he's on his knees.

Summoning my Halo into my hand, I will it into golden whorls to play with the shadows. "I think..." I chance a glance at Neo beneath my full lashes and finish, "...we're becoming *friends*."

He blinks, eyes transforming to soft silver mist. "You didn't need to do it. I could have taken it."

He's referring to how I shielded him. While the shadows tease my bare legs, I shiver, wondering if Neo controls them.

"I vowed to protect you from danger, didn't I?" I giggle when the shadows partner with his flames to peek under my sweater. I clench it over my thighs.

Neo plants his hand on the floor next to my legs. All the

shadows scuttle away, exposing the floor for the first time. Oh...it's obsidian but riddled with glittering specks like pockets of starlight. And then, Neo's breath drifts onto my cheek. When I crane my neck, I'm eye level with him. *Oh, Saints!*

My cheeks burn as I squeeze my shoulders and wonder, "We're *safe*. Are you going to cash in on your down payment? I'd say you've...earned it." I reflect on his willingness to manipulate his blood oath with his Father by showing me my mother, by protecting me from the Chasm monsters and even his Father. Most of all, he didn't touch me when he could have. My Halo warms my chest at the thought of the Prince's touch.

Neo cocks his head to me and pinches his eyes, honing them to silver daggers. "What is Ezer Kenegdo?"

Squeezing my shoulders, I work my hardest not to squirm under his gaze, but it doesn't stop the blush from swarming my cheeks. "Seriously? You're centuries older. How do you not know what Ezer Kenegdo is?"

He taps the side of his head. "Destroyed memories if you recall. Besides, can you forgive me for not understanding your Goddess truth when the Father of Lies' own son raised me?"

I purse my lips, realizing how Neo's shadows have used the diversion to sneak under my sweater. Devilish little baby shades.

"Ezer Kenegdo was the identity given to Eve after her creation. Everything in my vow is who she is." I still, then squeeze my thighs together when the shadows and flames embark into my navel, migrating upward. They chill me before his flames warm my flesh. Tingles blossom wherever they roam. "She was created to be Adam's equal counterpart."

"As a helpmate."

I hiss through my teeth at the patriarchal term, and the shadows pause right beneath my breasts. "As a *strong* helper," I correct, noting his pupils dilate as he focuses on my words. "Ezer, in the ancient Hebrew, was a *militant* term."

"As a soldier to a general?" he questions.

I shake my head and inhale a sharp, swift gasp when those naughty shadows cavort with my chest. My cheeks overheat. "Not a subordinate. More of a warrioress to a general. History talks of an ancient warrior who refused to go into battle without his prophetess judge. It was common for judges to go into battle, to wield a sword against the enemy. When you use your power to protect me, to help me, Neo, do you become a mere soldier?" The flames and shades collar my neck.

"Well-illustrated, apart from one significant flaw."

I lift my chin. "What?"

"I do not come from Adam's seed." He rises, collecting his shades.

At first, I consider asking him more about his history, seeking a kernel of truth. Was he born from a demoness's womb? Other than his devil ancestor, Neo's background is a mystery.

It's not the right time to ask, but I still rise, rub my sweater sleeve, then stand tall and proclaim, "Regardless, I made a vow. I can be nothing less to my...*husband*."

"I'll escort you to breakfast, then I must thin out the population," Neo states matter of factly. "I took the liberty of ordering an Infinity Wardrobe," he informs me, jerking his head to the opposite side of the room where it rests. I recognize the term, though I never could have conceived of viewing one, much less owning it. "You may choose whatever room you desire in my—*our* suite."

"That one." I point to the room on the left, the multi-level rotunda with no windows and empty walls.

Neo pauses, hesitating, a shadow crossing his face. "My other rooms have furnishings, windows, and overlooks."

I shake my head and point again. "That one." I love blank slates. So much potential for my creativity.

He sighs, relenting. "Your desire."

I smile when he uses his shadows to transport the wardrobe to the uppermost level I request and direct its location against the far-left wall. Rushing up the winding staircases, I seriously can't wait to throw open those wardrobe doors.

Right before I do, I lean over the balcony railing from the third level and call out, "Neo!"

He pauses in the doorway, about to take his leave, and glances up at me.

"Always higher than you, right?" I tease with a cunning grin. Then, I swing from side to side and belt out a jubilant, "Thank you!"

Neo parts his lips as if he's going to say something snarky, but then he simply shakes his head, chuckles, and mutters a "you're welcome" before exiting the room.

My greedy hands swing the doors open to mirrors humming with silver blood tech and outfitted with thousands of clothing options it can form on command. No more fang maids, Goddess be praised!

I tap the mirror and open the *Court Covet Fashion* app, selecting bride options until I settle on one. The wardrobe directs me in a feminine voice to shed my clothes, and I practically rip my sweater to shreds. Thankfully, the wardrobe first scans my body and determines I need a misting to rid myself of all the grit and ash from the Chasm.

"That tickles," I giggle at the spray of water until it circles the base drain.

It takes the wardrobe all of a minute to form every thread of the royal purple gown, a rival to the last one. After the tech summons an array of products for my hair to eliminate frizz and transform my curls into rippled waves, I select another winged circlet for my head. A drawer pops out with my choice. Thrilled, I place it on my head, so it dazzles on my gold-lined ashy hair, and then, I check myself in the mirror. In more ways than one.

What the hell am I doing? It hasn't even been a month since Neo destroyed my home. A subtle voice reminds me he'd formed a new blood oath. No lies. But surely, the Prince of Destruction can manipulate the blood oath. Could this all be Neoptolemus' long game? Am *I* a game to him?

Dread laces its poison into my heart. I lean against the far wall for support, a foreign shuddering there like shadows shifting. Colder than crypts. My hand sinks *into* the wall! What the devil? I stretch it further. The fluctuating shades beckon me, courting me. My Halo glows, projects, hearkening to the shades' call, longing to shine, to dance with...

"*Death!*" whispers the shade.

Neo's hand lands hard on my wrist, twisting and wrenching it out of the shadow wall. His eyes are cold steel, mouth grim and curving down, reminding me of a dragon.

"What was that?" I glance back.

He winces and crushes his lips together, silent as a grave. Our blood oath glares an omen: *tell me the truth*. Without releasing me, he practically drags me into his arms and shadows me out of the room and the suite. In the hallway and descending the staircase to the Commons, those shadows, icy tongues slither along my skin. Nothing my Halo light desired more than to plunge right through *that* wall, that portal.

"Neo..." I pursue again, midway down the grand staircase. "What was it?"

He still hasn't relinquished my wrist. His possessive fingers burrow into my skin, reddening my flesh while he speaks through gritted teeth, "Not even I pass through that passage anymore, Elysia. Not in ninety-five years." He might as well have electrified me with the date.

"It's a portal, isn't it? To your brother's tower?" I challenge him, but Neo winds my arm through his and finishes our descent. "Does it go through your Father's tower, too?"

"My Father does not know of the passage. Something only us brothers created. Father cannot access your room or disturb you."

Not what I'd asked. I don't tell him the real reason for my interest. Even if it doesn't allow access to the Father's room, maybe... maybe he's concealed the Altar there. It would make sense. Hide your greatest fear in the best location of all: the Prince of Death's Tower. Goddess only knows what haunts that place. My quest fuels a conflagration in my heart. All that matters is reading the prophecy on the Altar, learning how to destroy the Father, and saving my mother. The Prince is a stepping stone to my true calling. Foremothers forgive me for getting distracted! No more.

Poor Quillion. He's pacing all over the Commons, ascot sagging from however many times he's pulled at it. He picks at the gold rose threads on his vest.

"Princess!" Quillion rushes to my side and kisses my cheeks before piercing his eyes at the Prince. "I was getting worried. You're an hour late to breakfast!"

"I'm fine, Quillion."

"Careful," warns Neo, releasing me to his friend and shoving past the other vampire, clearly still perturbed by my discovery of his brotherly portal. "She bites," he refers to our earlier encounter right before our honesty blood oath.

Quillion grins when I clutch his hands and smirk. "Twenty-*eight* for me." I wonder how many would be added if he knew about our little trip to the Chasm. Not that I would share.

"Give the devil his due and add my just marker," Neo says behind us. Quillion's jaw practically crashes to the floor, and I wonder if he'll tackle Neo when the Prince continues, "Should have seen how wet she got for me."

I set my hands on my waist and thrust out one prominent hip, correcting, "Funny. I thought you went to bed thoroughly soaked, wanton, and flush."

The Prince growls, and I wink at Quillion, informing him of my Halo shower power last night. Preening and cackling, he produces his tally, granting me thirty check marks. Even if Neoptolemus got his due for the Chasm, he'd still be nowhere near catching up.

"Keep going," Quillion advises and gestures toward the breakfast hall, offering me his arm, which I accept. "I'm beating Nita."

Neo snarls as we pass him.

"Who's Nita?" I ask again and incline my head to the Prince whose posture tightens, a vein quivering in his neck.

"No one," he responds evenly and repeats in a round-about way, "enjoy your breakfast. I must deal with the Chasm chaos. I look forward to you at Court, Elysia."

I don't even get a chance to respond before he shadows away, leaving nothing but a few singe marks on the carpet. Sighing, I shake my head at my husband's returned incivility.

As we usher into the hall, Quillion mentions, "I didn't get the opportunity to fawn over your garb! Let me have another gander at you." He examines me and directs me into a slow twirl. "Insta-love!"

"I thought so, too," I remark on the deep amethyst gown with its high V-neck collar. It teases the edges of my throat before sweeping into a full illusion bodice. The bodice ends at my hips and fits snugly with a subtle mermaid-effect, then gushes into a waterfall of sensual amaranthine skirts, trimmed in lithe ruffles.

"That slit a few inches beyond your knees, such a tease, Princess!" he remarks on the curtain ruffles open to present the offering of my long legs. "And your bodice, hot damn!"

"I'm glad you're impressed." I trace the transparent bodice with tiny amethyst gems stitched into the fabric. Tenth Court designs of roses and flames curl in V-descents above and below the thin, velvet bra for modesty. "My husband didn't even acknowledge."

"Oh, trust me, he noticed. His pupils dilated every time he glanced at you." Quillion pulls out my chair and rushes into his a little too quickly, summoning his wrist program for the celebrity gossip news app.

"Quillion..." I scoot my chair closer and prop my face into my hands, cupping it puppy-dog style. I swear he blushes and clears his throat, averting his eyes. Oh, he's so adorable. I decide to have a little fun and scoot closer while surrendering my hand to his knee.

"What are you doing, Elysia?"

Oh, his beautiful warm skin pales, eyes widening as I slide my teasing hand on his leg toward his inner thigh, prompting him to lean so far against his chair, his stomach might flatten against it.

"Who's Nita?" I press him, pausing on his pants as every vein in his body gleams silver. Something that has *never* happened since we met.

He coughs, eyes darting to each side of the room. "Princess, the servants will arrive at any time."

"Well, then..." I devilishly pop out of my seat until I'm full on straddling him while sliding my arms around his neck. "I suppose there will be some very interesting celebrity gossip in the papers tomorrow. I can only *imagine* the headline:

Prince's New Bride Caught in Steamy Love Affair With *Gay Bishop!*"

"Elysia!" he wheezes, his hands rigid on the sides of the chair, and I have to barricade a dam against my evil laughter.

"After all..." I curve my pelvis to his, "you did mention how beautiful our offspring would be, right?"

"Okay, okay, I'll spill!" He thrusts me off his lap, positioning me in my chair before tugging at his ascot and using it to wipe the sweat on his brow. "Now, you stay there and be a good siren Princess."

I toss my wild curls back with a laugh and cross my arms over my chest, tapping my capped short sleeves. "So, you *do* like my blood?"

He shrugs, tying his ascot again. "Guilty as charged. But the moment you tumbled into my bath and mentioned you had unfinished business with the Prince, nothing else mattered except getting you straight to Neo." His sweet syrupy eyes warm all over me. "You reminded me so much of her. Especially when you continued your descent and had the gumption to dance with the Prince."

"Back to *her*," I laser in on his statement, not allowing him to deflect.

Quillion snorts because of his failure but finally drags a hand down his face, groaning, "He's going to throw me into the Chasm for this."

"I'll take full responsibility."

"Can I get that in blood?"

"Do you one better. You let me decorate your wings sometime, and I won't say one word to the Prince about this *Nita*."

"Decorate my—I beg your pardon!" He guffaws, fiddling with his ascot.

"I'll make them so pretty, please?" I give him the puppy dog pose and bat my lashes.

"Not one word to Neo."

I make the motion of zipping my lips, then lean forward, eager.

Finally, Quillion loosens a sigh and murmurs, "Nita is a dear friend of mine and the Queen of a little island of nothing but bitten vampires and their human familiars. An island Father is not privy to."

"And why did the Prince react the way he did? Why doesn't he want anyone to know?"

"Because..." Quillion drops his hands to the table and concludes, "She's his sister."

I'M SO LOST IN MY THOUGHTS, OVERWHELMED BY THE POSSIBILITIES. Never knowing the Prince of Destruction had a sister. Too distracted on my way into Court, I don't even realize the bone box is not vacant until I've slid into the seat next to none other than the Father of Vampires!

20
"IT SEEMS MY NEW BRIDE IS A LITTLE JEALOUS!"

SHIT, SHIT, SHIT! WHAT DO I DO? NEO'S NOT EVEN HERE YET!

At first, I harness my breathing to slow my heartbeat while sliding a hand along the armrest of my chair. Raising myself high, I act like a picture-perfect bride. But if the Father can sense my heartbeat slowing when it's only natural for it to quicken in response to the supreme creator, will he get suspicious? To my utter astonishment, the Father doesn't even give me a cursory glance. Are the Prince's brides of that little concern to him? No, he can't scent my purity, and my mother did everything in her power to conceal my image, but my lips still part in utter shock.

My Halo combusts inside my chest with the desire to bite and claw past my ribcage to strangle him. Somehow, I lock it away in my treasure chest of a heart.

The Father leans forward, elbows on his knees, fingers steepling as if eager for something. Out of the corner of my eye, a sinister grin slinks across his corpse-pale face. I thread my brows low, confused because he can't possibly be this interested in his gaggle of children swarming the arena seats. Or the endless line of account holders waiting to be settled.

I'm one second too late. Goosebumps explode on my skin when Neo torpedoes down from the domed ceiling and lands in a thundering flawless crouch on the very apex of his throne with hundreds of flames catapulting from his omnipotent wings! My instant reaction mirrors the Court that jumps. And quakes. No robe but a cape of pure silver—woven with glimmering gold roses that twist, bend, and bow from blood-tech. From head to toe, he's arrayed in a full, seamless armored suit of thousands of sharpened diamonds. They overlap one another and prick the air like invincible talons. The diamonds still ooze of black blood from his recent Towers' cleansing: thinning out the population.

Oh, foremothers! Neo perches on his throne, eyes drifting over the Court in a predatory once-over to claw straight into the minds of a thousand. His destruction power is a torrent of shade energy, surging through the arena in an impregnable warning that reminds me of a dragon rumbling and spitting embers and smoke with one bejeweled eye open and alert.

I grip the armrest so hard, my nails crack.

The Father does not shift his focus to me. Not once. But his grin grows as he assesses his son and fondly sighs, "My beautiful war hammer."

Neo flicks his raptor eyes to the bone box, but he already knew I was here. Because the only reason I didn't succumb to a wild tremble is due to his shadow friends soothing the back of my neck beneath my hair where the Father cannot see. I close my eyes and purse my lips, swallowing hard.

Those shadows congregate behind my hair and fix to my brain stem. *Steady, Elysia,* he whispers in my mind. I open my eyes. Oh, I didn't know he could do that. His voice is deeper. Like a shadow stalking my thoughts.

Neo nods at his Father. A mere welcoming nod, for the Father's time will not be wasted. Not even by his son. The Father is here to watch. Not converse. After a sepulchral amount of time, the Prince sinks onto his throne and summons the Court pawn for a generalized introductory report and a summary of the most significant events. Somehow, I manage to square my shoulders, raising my neck bride high.

I flinch when the Father peels the collar on my neck to bare my unmarked throat.

"Oh, what delicious game is my son playing now?" he croons, his voice lilting almost to a soprano, prompting my blood to curdle. "Inviting you to Court, a lovely taunt indeed."

One shade ripples on my chest, stemming the Halo from bursting. Instead, I face my greatest earthly enemy. Because I can play the long game, too. Instead, I bow my head and lick my lips, submissive. A pretty Princely vessel.

Three fingers slip under my chin, tilting it, so I may stare into the eyes of hellish darkness. Of perma-flames of crimson sealed in the Father's pupils which swell as he studies me, angling his head as if discerning...not yet suspecting.

"What is your name, child?"

Neo's shade pricks my neck, and I wish I could tell him, *Not necessary*. Immediately, they travel lower as if...as if they'd *heard* me.

"Lys, Lys Spirit," I utter with my lower lip trembling. No doubt he's already heard rumors that Neo caught the infamous smuggler.

"I do enjoy toying with Neo's brides..." he leans in as if to kiss me, brutal and monstrous, and my Halo longs to burn his fangs.

My empath shrinks into her fetal position, cowering while I rigidify all my muscles. Again, Neo's shadows plunge ice into my spine to counteract my flames. Balancing me. Protecting me. I close my eyes, darkness creeping closer to my heart, a familiar pain.

The Father opens his mouth to bare his fangs. I freeze when he sweeps his tongue along my neck. One flick before he wrenches away, cackles, and taps my nose. "But not till after they're bitten, my dear." He pats my cheek, and I nearly melt into a gold puddle on the floor. "Soon, little bride."

Flight kicks in. I want to stand. I want to gather my ruffled skirts and skitter away like the coward I am instead of suffering through this. My Halo practically liquefies. Somehow, I force myself to sit through the Court proceedings while Neo's shadows post along my back—frigid gatekeepers. Every now and then, his eyes roam to mine.

And then, the Steward from the Rosa Nix Court approaches the raised platform. The only official human court of the Father's world. Not officiated into his Court O' Nines since it's too far north and populated solely by humans. Rolling chuckles resound throughout the Court while countless knights crouch and bare their fangs, wagging their tongues in a silent predatory reminder of how the Rosa Nix Court only exists because they are the Father's puppets. More than anything, I want to stand and grip the balcony railing, imparting any courage I can to the human Steward. But Neo's steadfast shadows anchor me. Thankfully, the Father hasn't acknowledged me since his initial warning.

"My Lord Prince, your High Destructiveness," the Steward announces with a swooping removal of his cap, bowing.

The entire Court breaks out in laughter. Neo chortles but leans to one side, clearly bored with the Steward who might as well be a wingless/toothless bat to him. A heaviness settles in my heart. Too far north. The only way these people can survive is to curry favor with the Father. I can't help but empathize with the Steward who clamps his mouth shut and waits for the rolling tide of laughter to finish.

Finally, Neo waves a hand and permits him to continue.

"My Lord Prince, the snows came earlier to our lands this year and ruined our harvest. To recoup the loss of our coin, we have increased our pure-blood stock on top of our required reaping in the hopes of—"

"You plead to hope?" Neo interrupts in a bloodthirsty voice, tipping his head low and causing the Steward to cow, to kneel before him.

My brows lower, my lips thinning into a seamless line. At my back, Neo's shades deepen, and I want to smother the fiendish things.

"Destruction allows for no hope," continues the Prince without rising. Only tapping his finger like a war drum. Next to me, the Father tips his impressed mouth onto the edge of his steepled fingers as his son finishes, "Destruction takes his due in coin, in flesh and blood, in skin and teeth and bone. And the occasional *tongue*." He chortles, giving birth to another barrage of laughter.

I'm going to be sick. Bile swirls in my stomach.

"My Lord Prince..." the Steward is bold enough to plead. "Surely there is some other boon I can bestow upon your eminence."

The tapping stops, and Neo squints at the Steward, and a sigh eases from his mouth. "You have two daughters, do you not?"

A deep rumble in the Father's throat. "There's my scurrilous son."

No, Neo, no! I scream through our bond. Responding, the Prince's shades slither along my waist and corkscrew even lower. Damn prick tick.

"Please, my Lord Prince, they are my only children. And one

is engaged to your Court O' Eights' Rook—" The Steward doesn't get a chance to finish. Not when my *husband's* shades grip the human like a giant anaconda, squeezing his throat so there's nothing but a rasp, and lifts him off the ground till the Steward is below Neo's throne. My breath turns to a cyclone, a Father-fucking tsunami.

Still, the Prince does not rise. A message to display to the Court how unworthy of his time the Steward is.

What happened to the Prince who reduced the pawn to a silver blood pulp for trading in flesh and dehumanizing a human girl before your Court? I challenge, believing our blood bond must afford him some inkling of my thoughts, of my emotions. His only response is to thrust those shades in deeper, so my hips slam against my seat. That fucker. The Steward only wants what's best for his girls.

"I was only going to claim one of your daughters," Neo addresses the Steward and bares a lengthy fang. "But for your impudence, I will seize both for my harem. They will make fine new additions for my *Hades* show, won't they?"

Upon him flinging the Steward to the platform, the Court explodes into riotous laughter. Two soprano screams cause me to flinch. The Steward drops to his knees, bowing before the Prince in a silent plea for mercy. Ferocity flares my nostrils as the knights carry out the Prince's orders. A current of light furrows from my chest, only for Neo's flames to smother it. No, the Father can't recognize the Everblood, but can he recognize my Halo?

Another scream from those girls as knights force them to the platform to bid their father a last farewell. More flames flicker, sparking like angry fireflies, but Neo destroys each one.

The Father climbs onto the balcony and charges toward the raised platform, cackling maniacally. All the knights scatter to make way for him. The girls, barely older than sixteen, cling to each other and cower on their knees. The petite one, the youngest, she is the bolder because she rears her head. More flames erupt from my chest, becoming tethers to extend beyond Neo's shades. They prepare to soar straight down, lasso the girls, and carry them to safety.

The Father's hulking shadow swallows the trembling teenagers. His cannon fire voice booms, "Let us inspect these little humans. I do enjoy the show and desire for a decent season after all." He bends at the waist and grips one's hair before tearing at her clothes. She screams loud enough to fill the whole arena, louder than the chuckling of the audience.

Destruction! For the Goddess' sake, stop this! For my *sake!*

The shades become an army to assault me. But then, every last one plummets to the ground, pooling at my feet to offer my Halo some relief. And then...his voice—lovely and dark and deep—steals into every corner of my mind.

Stand, Elysia! Stand NOW!

I rise to my feet in one Father-fucking monarchial move.

Neo obliterates my encroaching Halo light at the exact same time. And the entire Court stills, all laughter choked, including the Father.

Disturbed by the interruption of his entertainment, he cranes his neck in the direction of the Court where every eye in the arena rivets on me. Because Neo is still sitting there on his throne, fist pounding on the blood rubies—a gesture of an order. I am *higher* than the Prince. Higher than the Father!

When I lower my head for an inkling of a moment, he sweeps inside again, a brush of dark dragon wings. *You are a Princess,* he purrs a growling reminder. *My equal in every respect. You will always be* higher *than me, Elysia. You are the Halo-Bearer, the Everblood. You are* Ezer Kenegdo!

The last testimonial is lightning rippling through my body.

I step forward onto the platform of a balcony, curl my

fingers around the railing, and raise my head like the Everblood Princess I am.

Unfounded silence smothers the arena, so one could hear a thread drop. All wondering if the Prince will charge for me and slaughter me where I stand. Part of me wonders it, too...until one of Neo's shades rushes into my hair.

Never!

Oh, Saints! He would *never* destroy me.

Finally, Neo clenches both armrests, stands, spreads his black diamond-girded arms to the assembly, and unleashes a mighty torrent of laughter. He performs the spectacle as the Father crouches, springing to the throne to join him as Neo bellows, "It seems my new bride is a little *jealous*!"

The following laughter is so deafening, it nearly causes my ears to bleed. Not one mouth laughs when Neo waves a hand to the knights and pronounces, "Remove the girls to my harem. Let us continue with these proceedings, and I will excuse my *bride,* so she may ready herself for my arrival." I play the long game. What I want to do is bristle, but instead, I blow Neo a kiss as he clicks his teeth. "Tsk, tsk, tsk, the honeymoon phase. You won't have to wait too long, my little smuggler Lys."

Pretentious bastard.

Thank you, my lady.

You're welcome, I say, though I swear the Father's eyes mark me for a target. If I'm going to be in his presence again, it will take far more than Neo's shades to keep the Halo at bay.

21
"OH, THE GAMES WE WILL PLAY WITH YOU, EVERBLOOD!"

Outside the Court, Quillion waits for me, prepared to escort me to Neo's suite.

"Did you see?" I ask the bishop, setting my teeth.

Nodding, Quillion loops my arm through his and pats my knuckles. "I don't interact with Father when he's at Court, but I monitored the occurrence. Rest assured, Elysia, Neo is very good at his ruse when Father is here. He has to be."

"Why?" I demand as we climb into the elevator.

Quillion sighs and shakes his head. "It's complicated. It's—"

"A secret?" I finish, remembering the words of the Goddess haunting me, challenging me.

Quillion blinks, but it's all the confirmation I require. A secret he's not able to share.

"And the secret of his brother's tower?" I press, tempting fate. The Father built the Tenth Court towers shortly before his oldest son's death.

The elevator stops, and Quillion shakes his head, accompanying me down the hall to Neo's suite. "Trust me, Princess, there is nothing in that tower that would interest you. After Father's son was killed, he went on such a rampage. He created hundreds of ghouls overnight and locked them in the tower." I shiver, considering the Father ripping out fangs and sealing their throats, so vampires waste away, so their venom stores rot. "Into it, he channeled such fury of power, only the blackest of souls can enter. Much like the Spirit Woods, it became a Chasm portal," explains Quillion as we arrive at the shadow door.

A Chasm portal. That is why such death whispered to me, called to me. But why hasn't Neo embarked into it since? Shouldn't he thin out the population there, too? One thing I am certain of thanks to my Underground work: black venom from ghouls is a blood deterrent with the capacity to nullify my blood for twenty-four hours. And possibly...my Halo. A worthy counter toxin when injected into my bloodstream, but it won't numb me.

"Princess..." Quillion touches my hand before I enter the suite. "Please, save for the Prince and one other, I've felt Father's unchecked torture. But I trust you will not put yourself in danger even if it may help with your situation."

He suspects my motivation. But it's more than controlling my emotions and keeping the Halo at bay. More than knowing the passage could lead to the Father's tower, to the Altar. When the Father opened his mouth, when his fangs leaned in, when his tongue danced across my flesh...all I could do was freeze as I did three years ago. All I ever do is freeze and run. Even when I courted Neo at the festival, I still shut down in the Chasm thanks to that predatory darkness stalking my heart. Like spiritual serpents. I'll never be free of it, and the Halo knows.

So, maybe it's time to stop running from darkness. I can't

face it yet or own my scars, but by the Goddess, I'll court death tonight.

And capture a ghoul as a bonus.

○

OUTFITTED IN AN ARMORED BODICE WITH A HIGH COLLAR, LITHE, LONG gauntlets for my arms, leather leggings, and boots, I'm ready for the passage.

Can I get the black venom in time? I barely have an hour till nightfall. More than anything, I need this. I need this for *me*. My thoughts are too dangerous. Too dark and deep with nothing lovely. Only monsters hunting my flesh. So, I will hunt them instead.

Securing my curls into a low, firm bun, I gird my thighs in leather belts with multiple stakes—the only weapons allotted to me in this Infinity Wardrobe. I suppose I have Neo to thank, considering stakes can't harm him.

Finally, I press my palms to the walls, seeking, seeking, seeking. Hardly two seconds pass before those death shades creep toward me. Bolder, they wisp into my ear, whispering of doom and demise. The blackest of souls. *What?*

I knit my brows low, sink my hands into the passage. The shades manacle my wrists like dark chains, and I jerk back from the sudden sensation like icicles dragging along my spine. Somehow, I step forward, arms venturing first, then my legs, and finally, I dive into a parade of pitch blackness.

Thick and swelling, it's colder than mist, and I use touch to discern my way. Solid floor still rests beneath my feet. On each side of me are walls, but deathly shades waltz with my hands. Spreading my fingers and praying to the Goddess I don't drown in this all-devouring eclipse, I move forward. More whispers of death.

"*Princess...*" they skulk threats into my ears the more I walk. "*Come to me. So sweet. So sweet. That's right, pretty, pretty Princess.*"

Run and hide, Elysia, chants an internal voice.

I don't look back. The shades snake up to my chest. Triggered, my Halo flares to life, biting at their audacity.

"*Oh, sweet, sweet, sweet!!*" The shadows whisper to my Halo flares. "*Everblood!*" they conclude, hissing poison into my mind. "*Keep going, Halo-bearer. Tonight, I court your soul! You cannot fight me. No, pretty, pretty Princess, you cannot.*"

Something reverberates in my chest. Though my Halo causes the shades to scatter, to scurry, somehow, my heart understands the last part is not a lie. It's not a threat. It's a promise.

"Wh-who are you?" I whisper in the darkness, fearing the shade voice which bursts an ice storm to the back of my neck, suspecting the worst. The Father channeled far more than his power into the tower.

The voice does not respond, and my hands crash against a door. No knob, but it swings open to my touch. Darkness does not greet me. I step onto a stone walkway, connected to another. Similar to Neo's that stretches over the Chasm, these have no railings, no fencing. A network of stone platforms branches out to every level and zigzags for miles below to form an enclosed mega-Tower. No buildings. No homes. Endless doors of uninhabited rooms. But not empty and devoid. One wrong move and I will fall to a crushing death.

"*Yes...Death,*" it purrs in my ear. "*Welcome to my home, Everblood.*"

The hairs on every inch of my body prickle. That voice's identity: the Prince of Death, Neo's older brother! This is where his spirit, his energy resides! Why wouldn't Neo want to come here? Why has he avoided his brother at all costs? Guilt? My thoughts turn into a million pinballs.

"*Everblood...*" the Prince of Death's spirit shades coil all around me in shadow finery. "*How is my abominable brother?*"

I work to block out the distracting voice invading my mind. Because on every level and even leaping along the stone platforms are masses of ghouls.

I only need one.

I grip two stakes. And wait. Already, they form droves, driven by their bloodlust. Capture one, drag it through the passage into Neo's room. Do not move away from the door.

But the voice coos in my ear again, "*He's a player, Princess. Oh, how my brother loves to play! Oh, the games we would play!*"

I work to dismiss the Spirit of Death as the ghouls screech and claw against one another. Bodies knocking into each other, their blindness confounds them.

"Hurry, you filthy bastards," I say through gritted teeth.

"*Oh, the games we will play with* you, *Everblood!*"

My blood boils from the predatory threat. "Never," I hiss at the spirit shades and focus on the ghouls. Ignorant beasts keep battering the stone walkways. It would be amusing if I didn't have a dead Prince's spirit craving my attention.

A cackle breeds but not Neo's dark and sensual laughter. This Prince's chuckle is like falling through ice. I close my eyes, wishing I could rid my mind of its polluted voice, threatening its lies.

"*Oh. Everblood! Don't you know? Don't you understand?*" It hums, it fucking sings to me. "*I would never hurt you. My brother may enjoy your presence, but he is playing a game, sweet star. For you are my salvation! Your blood, your flesh, your Halo. The key to my return!*"

Frost forms in my blood, chilling me. It's not true. It's not true! I shake my head, violent, battling the infection of shades plaguing my veins.

"*Truth,*" it confirms, its shades draping over my chest, suffusing my Halo light. "*Simply ask him, sweet angel. Ask him.*"

Our honesty oath.

The flapping of wings summons me. A ghoul teeters close, its naked skull visible. On one knee, I crouch and raise my hand, preparing. I have killed ghouls in the Underground, in training. This one is no different.

"*No light for you. Only Death and Destruction.*" The Prince shadows around my neck. "*Pretty, pretty Princess. Pretty blood. Pretty salvation. Soon, my brother will set me free!*"

"No!" I scream and plunge my stake into the ghoul's heart, seizing its wing and dragging its carcass to the passage as dozens more swarm near me.

His icy cackle again. More shadows nest upon me. "*His greatest game. Oh, the games we will play.*"

"Stop!" I cry, fierce tears hurling from my eyes as my muscles strain from the ghoul's weight. Somehow, I drag it into the portal. Still, the spirit pursues me.

"*You think the Prince of Destruction can love? If you give me your blood, I will be your greatest lover, Everblood. Court me tonight. You are not Destruction's equal. You are his pawn.*"

"Shut the fuck up!" I scream and grip onto the ghoul's other wing even if it means dropping a stake. "I'm higher than him. I'm higher than *you*!"

"*Game!*" it reinforces.

I am not my mother. But I still adopt her spirit and use her words against the Prince of Death as I get closer and closer to Destruction's door. "I will *never* lose my value! And you will never get my blood. So, you can just go and fuck yourself!" I reach the doorway.

"*Soon!*"

With one great snarl, I project my Halo light in a bursting beam to sear the shades and cause them to retreat through their doorway. Then, I practically kick the ghoul into Neo's suite and dive inside, rolling into a crouch.

Behind me, the portal closes, forming a wall once more. No shades stalk me. No Death spirit hunts me. Adrenaline speeds like vampire wings in my system, but I am safe. I glance at the ghoul with my stake embedded in its heart. It twitches before its head falls to the side, tongue lolling out against its cheek.

Disgusted, I curl my lip back. I will so be taking a bath tonight.

22
"DROP THAT CAT THIS INSTANT, NEO!"

REJUVENATED, I SINK UNDER THE STEAMY BATH WATER BENEATH THREE layers of rose petals.

Draining the ghoul's venom canal was the most disgusting thing I've ever done. After I scoured the suite, I'd managed to locate the perfect weapon, so I could slice the top half of the skull clean off. Then, I had to painstakingly dig my stake into the ghoul's eye, cut the damn ball out, and carve away the flesh until I'd unearthed the venom sac. One final poke, a rapid drain through the eye socket, and now, I am the boastful owner of a jar of black venom.

Proud of myself for not retching, I sing song underneath the water for a moment and emerge to Neo standing directly over me. Still garbed head to toe in his fused black diamond suit and crimson cape, his expression mirrors those adamantine stones.

"Hi, honey, you're home!" I chirp without rising beyond my neck. "Good, you can take out the trash." I jerk my head toward the stinking, festering, oozing ghoul I'd managed to drag down the winding staircase with its skull bobbing the whole way on the steps. Even if I've still got some sour grapes from Court earlier and my literal brush with Death, there is no way in hell Neo will ruin my victory.

"I know what you did," he seethes, eyes icy and brutalizing while I wrinkle my nose and drag my hands through my soaked curls and close my eyes. "*Elysia...*"

Something in the way his tone changes, in how it deepens leads me to wink one eye open. *Oh, Saints!* Neo is half an inch from my face. Pupils dilated. Fucking eyeliner.

When he lifts his hand, still bound by the black diamonded gauntlet, I twist my face to the right, so his thumb narrowly misses my cheek.

Sighing, Neo drops his hand and pronounces, "What my Father did to those girls, to *you* in Court was wrong. And if I'd had the power to stop him, I would have."

"Right...because it's all about you." I sneer, wrinkling my nose.

"I didn't mean it that way," he snarls, rubbing his eyes.

I soften. "How are they?"

He sighs, nodding. "I oversaw their transition myself. They are fine. The oldest was only too thrilled to escape her arranged marriage."

"Right because an arranged harem girl is so much better."

"It is." He deadpans. And I catch myself nearly leaning in, my heart pausing a beat, remembering our honesty oath. And I...I believe him.

"Sometime, I promise I will bring you to meet them, Elysia. But first, I could sense what you felt in those moments," he diverts the subject back to me, or rather back to *us*. "I've never shared a blood bond with any of my brides, but I still recognize the symptoms. You've been bitten before, haven't you?"

Deflecting, I raise one knee out of the water, angle it to the side, and slide some rose petals along my skin to my visible thigh. It does the trick. His eye trails my every motion.

"It was forbidden." Shadows deepen upon his hooded eyes as he grants me a few inches of space. "Why didn't you listen to me?"

I shrug and extend the rest of my leg into the water, then move forward, curving my spine so I may caress the rose petals along my lower calf. "I thought black venom would help in Court when I lose control. Maybe a heads-up next time. Elysia," I lower my voice to a mocking low pitch, "my vengeful dead brother's ghost hangs out in that tower." I don't mention anything about our conversation. *Ask him*, the ghost still tempts me.

Neo cups my cheek. Immobilized, I still because all the bathwater seems to lose its heat. His gauntlet bites cold diamonds to my skin...until his flames warm my flesh.

"You never should feel the need to conceal your scent," he denies. "What happened was not your fault. Nor your responsibility to ensure your protection."

A Halo spark bursts through the water, popping against his cheek and causing him to flinch. A similar heated sting in my voice. "I can protect myself."

I raise a defiant hand closest to him to seek more petals, but Neo seizes my arm instead...lightly tugs. Sensing a possible threat, my Halo skewers the water in jagged, crystalline light beams, prepared to launch. Though my spine is curved, the water ripples dangerously low, ready to expose the side swell of my breast if Neo pulls one more time. I fold my other arm around that breast, affording myself some measure of coverage.

Instead, Neo bends my arm at the elbow so he may press his mouth to his horned mark, his eyes softening to a silvery lullaby. "I would never bite you without your consent. And I meant what I said to you *before* our truth vow. I would never violate you."

He drops my wrist, surrendering me to the water. I have no choice but to believe him, but I'm not quite ready to cut him much slack tonight. Especially after he's implied I've been violated which I have not. At least...not like *that*. Prick tick.

"No, just stretch boundaries as far as they can go," I point out, wrapping my hands around the backs of my legs and tugging my knees to my chest, baring more of my back.

Sniggering, Neo releases his hair from its confining bun. "And we both know you've put me in my place every time."

I smirk to one side, lift my hand above the water, and point to the floor, teasing, "Sit, stay, good dragon." With my arms tight to cradle the sides of my body, I curl my spine until my chest presses to my upper legs.

"*Elysia...*" Neo murmurs, easing my name out one blessed letter at a time, breathing it like a prayer. He brushes his gauntleted knuckles across my shoulder blade. I tremble, sensing a familiar warm flutter between my thighs despite his icy touch. The Prince examines my body language, studies my eyes, my boundaries loosening, and eases those knuckles in a slow drag along my spine while leaning in to ask, "Do you mind my exploration? My testing of boundaries?"

"You're seriously asking me this *now*?" I guffaw, considering all the day's events.

"I may be a pretentious bastard, but I'm still an honest one. If you desire, we may instead discuss all my infinite transgressions, my sins against you. I am more than willing to engage in any penance you deem worthy, my love."

"Ugh..." I groan and tip my head because his shades whisper a truth caress in my mind. He's serious. And it's about more than getting in my pants even if that's still obvious. But I war with myself. The Halo—a Goddess promise that I will never be alone—whispers the reminder of his dark secret.

Though I cage my sides more, I prop my chin on my knees and rub my lips together. Neo offered me something...credible, something *trustworthy* though he didn't have to. A promise never to bite me without my consent...or violate me. Nor did he castigate me over entering his brother's tower. No, he was far more concerned than anything.

Biting my lower lip, I close my eyes and tilt my head so my wet curls spill to one side of my shoulder. Neo lets me process and doesn't interrupt, though his knuckles don't exactly stop. The heat between my thighs grows to a throb, mirroring the thickening tension between us. But that knavish voice nags me. A specter in my mind tempting me: *He's playing a game. So, ask him.*

"No," I decide, confirming the treasonous truth glowing all over my body. "As long as it doesn't go too far, I don't mind you testing your boundaries or *exploring*."

"Do you *want*?" Neo tests further, the black diamonds traveling down the edge of my arm where it greets my body's side outline.

Ripples of light flow from my chest, breaking through the skin between my arms and my sides to greet his knuckles, causing the diamonds to sparkle. Chuckling, Neo opens his palm as if to welcome my Halo ripples that choose not to harm.

"Are we becoming friends?" He jokes, and I smile until he closes his palm.

Narrowing my eyes, I transform the ripples into deadly little snakes to bite at his diamonds, melting them to reveal the sturdy, calloused fingers beneath.

"As long as you don't hurt them...or cage them," I point out with a soft smile, my cheek still warm to my leg, and consider the time in Court when he told me to stand. When he urged me to be Ezer and told me I would always be higher.

"And my penance?"

"We're not there yet. That will take time. But you're off to a decent start."

Leaning in, Neo rubs his cool lips to my shoulder and gazes at me, his hooded eyes of sensual moonlight. Heat swarms my core. Oh, Saints! Shafts of light shoot out from...between my legs...from deep inside me! Of course, they are not lost on Neo who chuckles and touches his ruined gauntlet to stroke my hair. "I'll take that as a yes. You *want*."

"Open to wanting," I correct.

The Prince simpers and picks a few rose petals out of my hair. "Of course."

"Back in the Chasm..." I enter into forbidden territory and dive a little deeper. "Why didn't you touch me then? It has to be beyond my sweet "angelic moans"."

Neo takes a rose petal and brushes it down my neck and along my shoulder blade. Damn. I have to clench my eyes while the water warms. Those light shafts grow until the whole bath glows as if I'm inside a smoldering topaz. Being touched this way...it's not familiar. Ever since I was bitten three years ago, Verena's jumpstart is all I've managed to accept...and a kiss or two. This...this is new, and I can't even hide how much I long for more thanks to the Halo.

"Those heavenly moans will be worth waiting for. But I wasn't about to take advantage of your darkness. Not even to provide you with a distraction from some suffering. Not how I operate."

"Even in your harem?" I lash out and the water grows cold. When I glance down, all the beams are gone. At least I can still kill the mood.

Neo's petal journey pauses midway down my back and he

sighs. "Trust me, Elysia, my harem does not suffer. Except for the times *between* my visits." He flings the petal into the water and grunts, rising and cracking his neck from side to side.

Known territory. And I hack right through all his harem bullshit, straight to the source. "And your *former* brides?"

Neo tenses. His gaze is practically a snarl. "Don't ask me, Elysia. I cannot give you what you want to hear."

"Another forbidden door, Neo?" I thrust my neck high with a snort. "All a *game* to you, Destruction?" I dig the knife in.

He turns and releases his cape to the floor in a pool of cloth blood. "Like the games you play, Princess?"

"I am not *playing*."

Deadly flames flicker from my chest, aiming for his back. Bound to my ignited emotions, I don't stop the weapons. Striking their target, they burn the diamond armor in one great swoop, melting them down his skin. Burning metallic liquid. Every muscle in Neo's back turns alpha aggressive from the pain, and he tears off the front set of armor, chucking it to the ground—hard enough for the diamonds to shatter into black glittering smithereens on the floor.

Wearing nothing but his gauntlets on his upper half, Neo rolls his shoulders and stalks toward the ghoul corpse, bends at his waist, and hauls the rotting flesh over his shoulder before crossing the floor to the bone door. The shadows part like the Red Sea, quaking before their master. Instead, they sneak along the sides of the bath, seeking me for comfort. I twirl my finger around a shade tendril.

"Hush little baby shade," I whisper, cooing to it.

Neo opens the door, and a black, fiery creature darts in, scurrying between his legs. "What the devil? Ugh!" The Prince's subtle growl fades to a groan.

"What is *that*?"

I eye the feline creature—no bigger than the Prince's boot.

Its long black tail whips back and forth with tassel-like ends of fire. Marveling, I hunch over the side of the tub, careful to keep my chest below line of sight, and eye the devilish little beast with its tiny, crescent moon-shaped horns jutting out of its head, talons no bigger than my pinky tip, and oversized ears with their insides pricking fire. It opens its mouth and hiccups. A tiny flaming spark pops from its throat. I giggle and stretch out my hand.

"It's a hellcat," Neo mutters. "A baby. And a runt. Must have missed it when I thinned out the population."

The hellcat pounces on Neo's shadows and flames, jaws snapping, playing with the undulating shades. So adorable! Just a slight amount of fluff on its thick, furry hide hanging tight over its prodding ribcage. Half-starved.

"Aww..." My heart goes out to the little runt, and my Halo responds, charging out a few flames. The cat flicks its head toward my fire and leaps, mouth open to capture them. *Oh, he likes my Halo light!* When I stretch one hand toward the hellcat, the critter crouches, baring the cutest prick of fangs before he sinks them right into my skin.

"Elysia!" Neo exclaims and drops the ghoul, rushing toward me. Eyes wide, he clutches my hand, turning it over, scrutinizing the wound.

Rolling my eyes because it's barely a prick and he reacts as if my hand's been chopped off, I smile as he soothes his shades around the wound and kisses my skin.

Then, I grin at the runt batting at the shadows. "Little spitfire." Huh...

Growling, Neo reaches down and grabs the little bugger by the scruff, so it yowls, talons scratching the Prince's arm. "Back to the Chasm with you."

"Drop that cat this instant, Neo!" I proclaim in a loud voice, then command the shadows. "Shades, on me, now!"

Instantly, all of Neo's shades gather into a protective, dark cloak to mask my skin when I rise from the bath. I don't know which reaction is sweeter: Neo's jaw dropping, his lips parting, or those pupils of his constricting to tiny dots.

"Traitors," he bellows to his shades while I climb out of the bath and steal across the floor toward him. Neo's shadows billow in dark, blanketed swathes descending from my neck to my knees.

The runt hiccups more flames, but I leap over them and reach Neo's side, lighting a hand on his arm, and insisting, "We're keeping him."

When the hellcat yowls and stabs its horns at the Prince's hand, he pronounces a very grim, "**No**."

"I *want* the cat, Neoptolemus," I drag out every syllable of his name.

He eyes the creature as if it's some parasite. "It will claw the furniture."

I lift one brow. "Are you saying you can't handle a little *destruction*?"

"And what are we supposed to feed it?"

When the hellcat runt stabs its fangs into Neo's palm, he drops the little guy. It hisses before skittering toward the ghoul, promptly sinking its jaws into the decaying flesh.

I grin from ear to ear and point a finger at my husband. "We're keeping him. This is not a discussion."

Neo snatches my waist and yanks me to his body in one split second. Oh, Saints! I'm crushed to him. Even though his shadows shudder but obey my word to stay, his skin still overlaps mine, his fortress of a chest prods my breasts. Ripped and hot as a kiln. Does *he* feel *me* beneath his shadows? All my Halo beams ignite inside my center.

"You believe you can command the Prince of Destruction in his own bedroom, Elysia?" He purrs the challenge just above my mouth, eyes skirting to my lower regions and how the shafts of light play with his pelvic shadows.

I don't balk but tiptoe my finger along his bicep that tenses and sweetly beam. "Sit, stay, good dragon."

"You want the runt, Princess. What do I get out of it?"

I toss my head back, groaning a little, "What do you want, Neo?"

"You...supping with me every evening for seven days. In *whatever* I select for you to wear." He threads his brows in a dance, hinting at lust and danger.

I glance over his shoulder at my little spitfire gnawing on a ghoul's finger, its personal chew toy, before ripping it right off. My heart aches to keep him. Oh damn, he'll be worth it!

"But no touchies," I clarify with a subtle tap to his left pectoral which bulges to my finger.

"No touchies *under* the measly pittances of lingerie I'll have you wear," he pushes on my boundary line.

Another glance at Spitfire. Too late, I've named him. "Deal."

One clean thread of blood in my palm and a gash for Neo. Crash, rub together for good measure, and that mandatory tingle echoes the bond uniting our words, our thoughts, our promises, and our blood.

"And by the way," Neo doesn't release my hand yet and slides his palm around my bare waist to finish, "since the little mongrel is already here, your first night of seven starts now."

23

"WELL, AREN'T YOU JUST FIFTY SHADES OF ELYSIA?

"I FORGOT TO ASK, MY LOVE, DID YOU ENJOY USING MY *WEAPON* earlier?" Neo hums in my ear, pulling out the dining chair for me. It's the first time I've really seen another part of his suite.

"This is mortifying, Neo," I sit, remarking on his chosen ensemble for me this evening. "I'm a fallen angel, not a Victoria's Secret angel." I roll my eyes.

Gold filigree sweeps down from a collar-like band around my neck. From there, the armor curves along my collarbone and winds along my back and sides, sweeping to my waist where one solid gold band halters my skin. The armor forms sharp inverted crests that cinch tight under my breasts and curl around the lower cups. I've never had so much of my breasts exposed.

His silver ring rests right between my cleavage: a seductive star.

As Spitfire claws at Neo's sumptuous robes, I lean over and pat the top of my hellcat's head. Yes, it was worth it. Especially when the runt leans into my palm and lets me scratch his ears instead of nipping me.

"Nothing about you is mortifying..." hints Neo, scooting my chair in. His bare chest warms my shoulder as he lowers his head to kiss my cheek, eyes journeying across the transparent ruffles barely skirting beyond my upper thighs. It's impossible to avoid the attention of his monumental member moving beneath his breeches.

I rub my thigh-high stockinged legs together. Trimmed by three gold bands at the top, bottom, and center of my legs. More stardust kindles on my skin, and I sigh internally and acquiesce to the Halo, *Yes, it's the most beautiful lingerie I've worn. Still not my thing.*

"Besides..." Neo takes his position on my right, and the realization of how he's placed me at the head is not lost on me. I observe as he lays out his cloth napkin on his lap and raises a glass of blood champagne to me in a mock toast, declaring, "I believe I have determined your problem. Other than all your pent-up sexual passions for me—" Neo raises a finger when I roll my eyes, delaying any response, then sips his champagne before continuing, "—you have no sense of *balance*."

"Excuse me?"

Neo smirks. "You care too much."

I sample a bite of the steak tartare, practically baptizing it in raw egg first. "Is that supposed to offend me?"

"You care *too* much," he repeats, waving his fork toward me. "Love too much. You fight too much." Neo lifts a kettle chip, pivoting it from side to side while eyeing me at an angle. "Your Halo surges, what would happen if you harnessed your power and conducted it instead of releasing it in one all-consuming burst?"

I frown. "Is this a trick to get me to stop blasting you at night?" When Neo doesn't so much as blink, I set my fork down and retort, "I have never half-measured anything in my life. I've spent so much time escaping or hiding." I reflect on my past, of my childhood surrounded by vampires and in my mother's shadow. Not the only human but the human with the purest blood and a Princess. Of course, there were threats. "When I was a little girl, a bitten vampire breached our borders and targeted me while I played in my backyard. Even though I didn't possess the full Halo power, it still glowed enough to nearly blind the vampire, and then...it severed his spine."

Neo surveys me, maintaining a cautious distance. I can't help the faint smile curling on my lips. Out of the corner of my eye, Spitfire stretches his paws on the edge of my seat, claws extending. My Halo quickens, and I shower him with tiny sparks he thrills at licking up. Spitfire bats at the long white swathes of transparent fabric bound to the gold plates at my back.

"I always knew I was different. Beyond being a half-blood. I'd still glow occasionally. And hiccup stars when I'd steal venom." I go on, lost in my childhood memory as my runt curls around my feet.

"Did he bite you?"

"No." I shake my head. "My mother trained me for years after. But I never truly accepted the device." Apart from when I used it to pull pranks on vampires...like Verena.

"No, you found a different calling, didn't you?" Neo questions, turning his shoulder toward me, the loose fold of his robe exposing the brand circle on his chest. I admire his promise never to destroy it. Neo chucks a bit of his tartare at Spitfire, who hisses but devours the plump morsel.

"Good boy." I reward him with another.

"You used that precious power in the Underground for a time, didn't you, Elysia?" he probes.

Sighing, I deflect to my earlier memories. How I'd wandered beyond the Rose City borders at fifteen and discovered the human blood farm. At first, I'd simply talked to the families, to the children most of all. I'd bring them gifts, food, clothes, but it wasn't enough. Every time overseers herded them during the day, some star died in my chest.

"Hmm..." he muses as I lick my lips and pause to drink my champagne. He must scent my avoidance a mile away. Of how I refuse to share the night my Halo went dark. "What is that aged quote, "for perfect love drives out fear"?"

I clamp my mouth shut, but Neo stands from his chair, approaches me from the side, bends at the waist, and breathes a deep inhale of my curls. I can't shield my mind from that first memory, and his shades creep through our bond.

"There were reports of a glowing girl luring overseers from the farms so children could escape. Show me, Elysia," Neo tempts me, whispering his shade power into my mind.

I show him a few others. Far better than the night of my eighteenth birthday.

Neo chuckles and drones, sarcastic. "So sweet. The Everblood and her savior complex."

Glaring, I snap my hand to strike him, but Neo seizes my wrist, hauling me out of the chair, and growls, thrusting me back. "Do better, Princess. Harness your power."

"Don't call me a savior," I warn, bosom heaving as I size him up, sensing my power rising. "I'm the furthest thing." *Noralice*, I mentally cry the name, the name I clung to on my darkest night to survive. Pain surges at the back of my neck. Halo fire rampages within me, begging for release. As soon as I drive it forward in a defiant blast, Neo smashes it down with his destruction.

"*Too* much! Forge it into a weapon," orders Neo, prompting me again.

"Tell me about your brides." I lash out with a host of sparks.

Neo nullifies them with his shadows, with one crafty wink. "Weapon. Again."

"Your brides," I press, seething.

Neo smiles dragon-like, showing a full set of teeth and fangs, a contrast of pearl flash white to his dark skin. He clutches the ring at my cleavage, his hand brushing my breast swell, fingering it while my eyes burn against his, and…another heat lurches in my belly. Slick tick.

"I'll tell you what, Elysia. If you can find a way in your beautiful heart to bring me to my knees again, then I will tell you about my brides. But…" he wags the ring back and forth and taps my nose with it, "…no passing out. And no Halo bursts. Forge it into a weapon to use over and over. Like this." He retrieves a small-handled curved scythe and sets it in my palm. His little *weapon* I'd found in the wardrobe and used earlier.

Drawing a finger across the weapon, Neo declares, "Hand-hammered and tensioned. Keen edge. Beautifully balanced. For a baby blade." He sniffs and shrugs, folding his hands behind his back.

I weigh the blade, tracing my finger along the handle and edge, finishing at the point to prick the tip of my finger and draw a droplet of blood. "Does this count?"

"I'm going to tell you a little secret, my love." Neo paces around me. "Your light was never more difficult to destroy than today in Court. So, tell me what you were feeling."

A master processor of my emotions, it doesn't take me long to spit out, "Injustice. Righteous wrath." *Empathy,* I don't say aloud, fearing Neo may have already detected. If he does, he doesn't show it.

"Good. Hone those emotions. Perhaps I can be of service." He slides his hand along my navel, triggering my Halo. Except now, it burns brighter, closer, *deeper*.

"Knives aren't really my thing."

I toss the blade into the air, spin before his hand coasts to my cleavage. Sensing the heat breeding beneath my skin, my Halo ignites. Before he can close the distance behind me, I'm going to prove I'm not here for his entertainment. He thinks he can dress me up, play trainer, and I'll behave? I'm going to bring that exploring prick of a tick to his knees.

Brimming with Halo light, I whirl around. The white lingerie swathes swing in the air behind me as I harness my Halo, cord it into multiple thick and full whips, and strike! Neo's eyes roll to their ceilings as I spiral the snakish whips around his ankles and upend him flat on his back with a crashing thud.

Less than a moment later, I crouch, straddle him, and weave my Halo whips around his wrists to jerk his arms above his head. Triumphant, I grin at how he tilts his head till his chin touches his neck, brows lifting in surprise. While Spitfire bats at Neo's lustrous waves, I put my full weight down on his chest, breasts plumping while I ignore the heat pooling in my core, and lower my head to his, my curls dripping over his neck.

"Gotcha," I whisper and nip his ear.

Smelling burning flesh, I glimpse his wrists which smoke from my Halo whipcords. And then, Neo's whole body goes taut, rigid. *Oh, hell*...too late to move.

In one fell swoop, Neo overthrows my body, reversing our positions, though he barely hovers so as not to restrict my breath. Nor does he remove the whips. One cock of his head... One muscle throbs in his cheek...his pupils dilate. Oh, Saints! Halo light festoons out of my core and waltzes with his shadows. And...something *damp* weeps between my thighs.

"Never take your eyes off your target, my love," he advises, head bowing until his brow presses to mine. My whole body rises to meet him, and he chuckles. "Well, aren't you just Fifty Shades of Elysia? That gorgeous neck of yours. It was created for fangisms," he coos, and I bite my lower lip, flushing under his shadow. Is he going to kiss me? Warning bells clamor in my mind, but I can't get beyond that Halo garland parading out of my center. Until Neo winces and murmurs close to my mouth, "Elysia..."

"Mmm?"

"As much as I admire you *whipping* me into shape, can you get these off my wrists before they burn clear through to my bone?"

Oh! I gasp in the same moment when he rises off of me, then jerk my hand to the side, freeing him from the starry whips and reclaiming them into my heart. We say nothing as he flexes his hand. Concentrating on fusing his shades around his wrists to heal the burnt flesh, his veins almost stab through his dark neck. Holy shit! My Halo burned through to his muscles. Awed by its power, I rub a hand up and down my bare arm.

Eyes following my revelatory expression, Neo steps toward me and sifts a hand into my curls, and I find myself biting my lower lip. "You should be proud." I tiptoe my concerned fingers along his wrists, along the puckered flesh beneath his shades. He inhales to my touch, flexing his forearm, and leans down to murmur, "You could never hurt me, Elysia."

As his lips rub my lower lip in the barest of kisses, I close my eyes and two voices echo in my head. *You must only bestow your kiss on the one who is worthy.* On the opposite side of a cruel coin, Death battles for territory. *Ask him!*

When Neo opens his mouth over my bottom lip, I smother both voices and cave my hips to him. His hard length prods my thigh through his breeches at my navel, given his superior height.

I jump at the sudden bitter cold invading the suite. It creeps like a reaper to lick my spine and raises the hairs on the back of my neck. Neo growls, breaking from me, and turns to greet the third party. All his posture changes. As if he's *bracing* for destruction instead of owning it.

"Father," the Prince utters, bowing his head to my antithesis as he steals into the dining room. Spitfire scrambles under the table with a threatened yowl.

"I'll be spending the next few weeks undertaking a reaping of the Court O' Tens' farms," the Father announces, brows tapering, carnal crimson pupils dilating upon me. "Selecting able stock," he adds and drifts past his son, approaching, assessing, judging. His nostrils flare, *scenting* me. I flinch when he thrusts my face from side to side, inspecting. "Little Lys Spirit. Our infamous smuggler. A worthy prize." My stomach churns a whirlwind.

Again, Neo's shades, now hairline phantoms, caress the back of my neck. *Steady, Elysia.* The Halo whips ease out of my chest. Now, I know they are invisible to the Father, but Neo still destroys them. His shadows beckon to me. *Bow, Elysia.*

The Father cocks his head, the corners of his mouth curving low when I don't move.

No.

Neo's shadows bite my neck. *Bow!*

Higher than you. Higher than him!

Neo's shadows attack my ankles, jerking hard so I have no choice but to crash to my knees. Righteous Halo light seizes inside my chest, stabbing out in one instant. Wholly unaware of my whips, the Father chuckles, eyes stationing on me. Neo's shadows hack my whips in half, suffocating their power. Incensed, I swallow my rage, but it manifests in my screwed-down mouth.

The Father pats my head, snickering and craning his neck

at Neo and turning his back to me. "In no way does she smell as lovely as some of your others, so I am expecting *exceptional* skills as a bed flesh-mate," he expresses to his son.

"I'm savoring this one, Father."

I survey them under my thick lashes, how the Father drapes his knuckles along Neo's cheek. "Breaking her *spirit*, my beautiful boy?" He quips and leans in to kiss his son on the mouth, light as the prick of a horn. Then pats his cheek. "Carry on. But remember our little bargain." What bargain? What secret does Neo carry?

"As always, Father."

"After the weekend, you are exempt from Court for the next couple weeks while I reap. Enjoy your time with your bride and your fresh harem girls. I'll have some regional Court O' Nines duties for you, but it's been too long since Daddy reminded his miserable spawn who's truly sovereign over them."

I shudder down to my core.

Once more, the Father flicks his eyes on me, dilates the pricks to swirling blood pools, then shifts to Neo, patting his back. "Enjoy your little game, son."

As soon as the Father's bitter presence is gone from the suite, Neo's shades release me while his arms reach for me. But I rise to take my sanity and dignity and shove him hard with a warning Halo pulse.

"Don't you fucking touch me!"

His eyes are pained, but his lips seal in determination. He drops his hands to his sides, shoulders sinking in defeat. Spitfire scurries from under the table, hissing at Neo before following me into the inner suite bedroom. A holy fire simmers inside me, chastising. Such a damn fool. Cowed by a few overheated butterflies between my stupid thighs. Now, I clench them tight and make my way toward the window.

"Shades, on me!" I summon them, so they instantly mantle

my whole body from neck to toe.

Though the blood moon glares at me, I plant a hand against the window, discerning my reflection in the reddened glass. I find so much of my father in my reflection. After seeing the Father and Neo together, all the emotions from that horrific day well up inside me, curdling my blood with the horror.

Neo's warm flames lurk toward me, trimming his shades, daring to enter their barrier. I tense when the Prince cups my arms and leans his stalwart chest against my back. "Don't, Elysia. Please..." his voice cracks from his plea, and his mouth descends to my hair. "Don't raise your walls again."

"You keep destroying them, *Neoptolemus*, and I'll keep building them." *Ask him,* the Death Prince's voice licks my mind. I don't have to ask. His Father confirmed it. Two can play at that game. So much for penance.

A low snarl skulks in his throat. "Have it your way. But I'm cashing in on the *other* part of our deal tonight."

"Which one?" I've made multiple deals with him, it's little wonder I lost my focus. It reinforces my need to track down the Altar.

"I bought you a present." He jerks his head toward the little corner table. The one where two decanters always sit for a quick fix: one of blood and one of venom-spiced wine. In front of them is a gold-lacquered package with a diamond-trimmed ribbon. A lashing in my chest—a persistent tug and ache. Damn solemn blood oath.

I stomp toward the table and tear into the gold paper, not bothering to savor. Pausing, I trace my fingers along the eye-watering camera—elite silver-blood tech which may produce 4D images immediately...extremely expensive. While I weigh it in my hands, Neo approaches the bed and sweeps away his robe, and undoes the belt at his breeches.

"I can pause if you'd care to grab a mop to wipe up your incessant drool when we're done," he mocks, but his lips pinch in a seamless line.

I glower. "Before or after I use it to mop the floor with you?"

Neo grumbles something about "smart mouth" and "ten thousand demons", then jerks off his breeches, taking residence on the bed, elbow propped on the bejeweled coverlet, palm holding the back of his head.

"I expect *professional* quality, Princess."

A muscle ticks in his cheek while his eyes narrow upon me. In one moment, all the shades abandon me, slithering away from my body. Pretentious bastard. When I glance at him next, I bite the inside of my bottom lip because he's iron, he's rigid, his shaft thick and full and appetent.

"Prick tick." I snap the camera, getting a few shots before mentally adding, *big, moronic dick.*

I heard that. His shades nudge the message in my ear.

A few more shots and I set the camera down on the table while he opens his arms to me. "Come now, wife. Time for *sleep.*"

Tonight, I'll use lightning. For Verena and for my own damned boundaries and foolery to believe any of this was real. Nothing more than his sick, twisted game. After tossing back the coverlet, I wait for him to sink in beside me, throw him my best angel-with-a-dirty-face glare, and scream, "You and your daddy issues can go to hell!"

A bolt of Halo lightning blazes from my hands and strikes him dead center of his chest, whipping him with such a force, it spiderwebs fractures to vein into the room. The bed's base legs break and slam six inches to the floor. I pass out before he can make a cheap shot.

24
"OH, SHE'S PERFECT, QUILLION. WE LIKE..."

Unsurprised by Neo's absence in the morning, I nod to my lightninged handiwork on the wall on the opposite side of the bed along with all the cracks in every window reminding me of a leaf's veins. Looks as though I caused a few bones from his door to tumble. Doesn't seem particularly safe since he's supposed to *protect* me at night. Why hasn't he repaired anything?

All the shadows shoot away as soon as I climb out of the bed, leaving nothing but that cold obsidian starry floor. "Yeah, you'd better run."

Something growls softly from the corner of the bed. Uh oh. "Spitfire..."

I kneel and hold out my fingers to the hellcat. He hisses, baring his fangs, tongue pricking the air. That's fair, I shrug. But as soon as I break out the Halo crackles and twirl them into a little nest on the floor, Spitfire launches right for them and pounces, licking them. I create a bundle for him because it'll keep him busy for a while.

Eager to rid myself of last night's lingerie, I hasten into my room to the top floor and open the Infinity Wardrobe to select today's gown. Simply because I have a mission to complete doesn't mean I can't reap some small reward. Nor will I ever miss a breakfast with Quillion since I'm convinced he's the most loveable vampire on the planet. And I relish his brows soaring from my garb.

Today, I go for something with a demure neckline. A trim off the shoulders, long sleeves hugging my arms to the wrists, and a form-fitting gown that sweeps out at my knees and swishes in a mermaid silhouette to the floor. It conceals my slippered feet. Not to be upstaged at any time today, I've selected sable black with diamonds exhibiting the Court rose designs along the entire bodice. Sweeping from the sides of my hips, sumptuous attachments remind me of a waterfall of full and sensual fabric waves—rippling black on one side and silver on the other.

Confident with my winged circlet and smoky eye makeup with nude brown lip, I descend the stairs, puzzled when Quillion isn't waiting in the Commons. I overhear the conversation from the breakfast hall. But it's not Neo's voice but rather a lilting soprano's.

I don't quite catch what she says, but when Quillion responds, I freeze, "No matter how your tigress eyes pounce on me, Kitty, it's never going to happen. And it's not you, baby, it's *me*."

From the main Commons table, the soprano voice growls, feral. "Damn it to hell, Quill, if you weren't such a rigid *seven* on your Kinsey Scale, we could have a fucking good time. Emphasis on the *fucking*."

"You know I don't fuck, Kitty."

"Oh, you old, flouncy fossil. I'll convert you yet!"

I grin because I like this Kitty, whoever she is. When I step toward the breakfast hall, I overhear Kitty gush, "Oh, my fucking gawd!"

"I know, right?" Quillion echoes as I round the corner of the hall. There he is sipping his blood, but this time, it's from an antique teacup. As usual, he rises from his chair, presses his ascot, and extends his hand to mine.

And sitting at the head of the table is quite possibly the most beautiful vampire I've seen in my life! I recognize her the moment I lay eyes on her. I almost want to shrink to her ethereal beauty—how she reminds me so much of...*him*. Opalescent hair but far longer than his, it spills to her waist in a rippling cascade. Flawless satiny dark skin to match Neo's. Eyes of pure silver song. Her exalted cheekbones are thrones in and of themselves, accentuating the majesty of her long horns curling from her head like twisting dark sides of crescent moons. Oh, I must contain my drool because she is undoubtedly Neo's sister!

"Careful..." Nita warns me, drinking from her teacup, dark mouth stained in rich blood as she appraises me beneath long, seductive lashes. "Your eyes may melt if you continue to stare at me that way." Her voice is rich and smoky.

I lick my lips and form an Elysia response, "If eyes are windows to the soul, then consider me a peeping Thomasina."

Nita snaps her head to Quillion, blinks once. I side-eye him because his lips ease into a smooth, knowing grin.

Nita rises from the table with the grace of a queen jungle cat. Like the Everblood I am, I match her moonlight eyes with mine but take note of her seamless, deep royal purple gown that hugs her serpentine curves. Bejeweled with silver blood tech echoing constellations of stars, the gown's high slit on her right-hand side exhibits more of her sexy skin. Her high neck overlay shrug seals around her body, meandering to her hips but allows the gown to twinkle all over her bust and downward.

I can't help but smirk to one side as she closes the distance between us. Invasion of space runs in the family, but I don't mind Nita's. Not. One. Little. Bit. Hell, I almost lean in, lips parted to pant. The gleam in her eyes reminds me of a lioness! If I wasn't married to her brother, our dialogue would go far beyond flirtatious idioms. At least mine would.

One upper lip curls to threaten a fang, and she urges, "Peeping Thomasina? Is that the best you can do? My Creator Queen slides in to take your Princess pawn." She poises her claws under my chin.

Oh, heavens! She's a Creator like her Father? And *my* mother? And she knows I'm a Princess? I don't give myself away even if my heartbeat does along with my glitter Halo dust wafting off my skin.

"Incurable stalker?" I attempt again.

She opens her mouth a little wider, eyes descending to my neck. She wouldn't really, would she? No, I catch the hint of playfulness curving one corner of her mouth as she drags one claw along my throat. Testing me. Playing a little game, but I don't mind her games.

"Personal poltergeist," I conclude, my brows dancing up and down.

Nita's grin is savage but sexy. "Oh, she's perfect, Quillion. We *like*..."

He nods and returns to his seat. "The feeling is mutual."

"It's an honor to meet you, Nita," I say and offer her a sweet curtsy, biting the inside of my lower lip, unashamed of my burning face when she presses her lips to each of my cheeks. A hint of steam curls when her icy mouth meets the warmth of my cheek.

"Amanita," she grants her full name. "I was named for the Destroying Angel."

I arch a brow and quip, "You were named for fungus?" I stifle my giggle with my hand.

Incredulous, Nita's eyes hook Quillion's, but he shrugs, sipping at his teacup while Nita declares, "Oh, I will make her pay for that. Now..." she flares her nostrils, scenting me, "for once in all my years, it's an equal honor for me."

Quillion sniffs next to us, feigning a whimper. "Nice to see where I rate."

She waves him off, and I observe the rings on her fingers. Not jewels or gems but fangs. Oh! I can imagine her ripping the fangs right from some abuser's mouth right before disemboweling him.

"You're a *pleasure*, Quillion, as always even if Kitty won't stop her fruitless pursuit of you. *Elysia* is a splendorous honor."

I peer around the room, but there's no one other than the three of us. No Court servants bustling in the adjoining kitchens either.

"Take a turn with me, Elysia, while we wait for breakfast..." Nita offers her arm, the velvet shrug sleeves a second intimate skin.

Despite how this vampire could suck me dry in less than three seconds, I sidle next to her and loop my arm around hers. The sensual folds of my gown nudge against her one leg bared by the slit.

"Enjoy your reading, Quill," she expresses.

He offers a two-fingered salute and returns to his celebrity gossip.

At any moment, I anticipate another vampire to sweep right in and invade our casual stroll about the Commons.

"Looking for someone?" Nita smiles at me, sly as a raptor as I match her stride. Well, almost.

"I heard Kitty before I came in," I mention, practically fawning over the name. "Is she—"

"You just missed her," explains Nita, tightening her grasp on me. "But I'd prefer you all to myself for the present," she dictates and leads me toward the Commons' elevator, blood-authenticates it, and climbs in first without letting go of my arm. She seats me next to her. I glance at Quillion, who's sipping tea and reading, and Nita squeezes my hand. "Quillion can amuse himself for a time."

"Even if Kitty comes back?" I tease.

"You don't have to worry about that." She closes the elevator door, but something is lost on me, judging by her knowing grin. So familiar.

For a moment, I consider how I'm in a golden cage alone with the most powerful vampiress in the world. As if she senses my budding nerves, Nita squeezes my hand and assures me, "Not to worry, angel eyes. It's a perfectly human response. But I am not about to let anything happen to the young woman who has captured my big brother."

"Oh, I thoroughly trussed him last night." I preen, straightening against the elevator and reflecting on my Halo whips.

"Tsk, tsk, tsk, you shouldn't say such things. Kitty will sniff it from a mile away and come. And I cannot be responsible for her actions 100% of the time. So, please don't take offense if she decides to hit on you. *Most* of the time, she abides by a 'look, but don't touch' policy."

I smirk as I consider this Kitty. Maybe she could give Neo a run for his money.

"Will I meet Kitty later?" I wonder, face falling a little.

Out of the corner of my eye, Nita dons a knowing smirk. "Probably. Especially since I'll need your help with my brother."

"What do you mean?" I tense.

"You will be my secret *angel* weapon, Elysia."

I startle when she lights on the word 'angel'. With a sudden intake of breath, I inquire, "How much do you know, Nita?"

A sound caught halfway between a low growl and a chuckle germinates in Nita's throat as the elevator lurches to a stop. "I know *everything*."

I shiver but don't get the chance to address her because she opens the elevator door to a long skyway that curves around the tower in a semi-circle.

There is so much I wish to ask her, but I must tread carefully. Infinite power abounds beneath her skin...with a host of secrets locked in her mind.

Nita leads us to another elevator on the opposite side of the immense arc of a skyway, though this one is formed of iron and not gold. Part of me wonders why she doesn't simply wraith-shadow us wherever she desires, but I imagine she's building the suspense. And I'm marinating in it all. I don't even guffaw when the elevator plummets several levels in seconds.

"He said you never cow," she alerts me from the opposite bench, shadows toying with her face...or maybe she's toying with them?

"Excuse me?"

"You don't cow before the Prince of Destruction. Not even on the day of your wedding. Or your honeymoon," she mentions. "Or any nights following. And you *refused* to kneel before our forebearer." Her teeth set on edge at the last line.

I do not turn away from her, but I do tense, hunching over a little, nails digging into the iron seat below me. "Why should I? He said it himself: I. Am. Higher."

Nita deadpans. "Not higher than me, angel eyes. Today, you will bow before *me*!"

All I can manage is a wild grin to tempt this grand succubus. *Oh, I don't think so.*

Incensed by my silence, which is outright defiance, Nita flares her nostrils, lips curling to reveal a full mouth of razor-sharp fangs. Oh, Mom would love her! She's practically Mom's evil twin. I still don't flinch and earn a hint of a growl from Nita's throat.

Finally, the elevator stops. Except there is no hallway but a single door comprised of unyielding and mellifluous swirling silver blood. Some sort of advanced tech. And the door only swings open to her hand.

"Welcome to my sanctum." Nita steps off the elevator and through the doorway, beckoning me, pausing as if waiting for me to change my mind.

Instead, I am bold enough to touch her hand—no more than a feather wisp, but she reacts as though I've sparked her. I flutter my lashes, almost blowing her a kiss.

She closes the door behind me to nothing but darkness as thick as Neo's robes. Her icy breath lurks behind me, the familiar click of her fangs, the snap of her teeth. I grin.

"*Elysia...*" she hums. "My brother *never* sends a distress call. And he *never* asks for my help. He knows better. So, what makes *you* so special?"

Nita turns on me, fangs poised, but I brandish my Halo light. After last night, it's effortless to form my golden whips. I twirl them on each side of my body like fiery jump ropes, beaming a delirious smile.

"Do you need a moment to pray?" I laugh and crack one whip. Sparks shower the air, flickering off one full wall of piked skulls!

"Oh, you wicked, little seraph," Nita comments, steps away from me, and waves a hand.

At once, hundreds of candles and torches flame to life to betray the aged dungeon of walls formed of nothing but skulls and bones. I swear, if there is one last thing I will ever do in this world: I will introduce Mom to Nita.

She leads me deeper into the dungeon. Suspended cages swing to her presence as if a warning to me. Piles of ash drift from inside them—strands of hair, more teeth.

"Are you certain *you* don't need a moment to pray?" Nita wonders when I pause.

I bite my lower lip, debating, but oh, it's too much fun! So, I tuck my hands under my chin, childish, and echo sweetly in the dungeon, "Only if I can say one for you."

She groans and rubs her eyes, retracting her fangs. "Prophetic child indeed!" I resist the urge to giggle.

After leading me down two flights of railing-less iron staircases, we arrive at the threshold of a great lake with fog looming over its surface like undulating phantasms. As soon as Nita takes one step closer to the water, and the fog rises in a feral crouch, hissing at her, I comprehend: they *are* phantasms. They are lost spirits. She narrows her eyes upon the expanse, and every last vapor of spirit fog quakes and pitches into the water.

Instead of shaking, I kneel on the threshold and hover over the water, peering at my reflection, at my gold-ringed eyes. Beneath that water, their forms remind me of will o' the wisps. Ghostly…no deathly! One strikes my hand, taking the form of a serpent sinking its fangs in. I flinch, biting my lower lip, scrutinizing, concluding. Not just lost souls but damned souls: vampires and Chasm monsters.

"My army," Nita proclaims above me, and I sit, focusing on her. "For the final war with my punishing procreator." Her mouth eases into a savage smile. "Sometimes, the best secrets are hidden in plain sight. Neo's power hides them well."

Nita stretches her hand to me, and I accept, allowing her to lift me, but she proceeds to seize the back of my neck and thrusts me toward the water. My gasp perishes in my throat.

"*Listen*, Elysia..." Her voice reminds me of Death's. "I would normally have flown you into the middle of the lake for a trial by *water*, so to speak. But since you bested me twice already, this shall suffice." With a mad undertone of Destruction. Nita is the culmination of the Father's children. Not one or the other, she is *both*!

"Thank you?" I don't cow before her. I don't shake. But I do shiver.

"That sounded like a question," her voice preys in my ear.

"Thank you."

"Hmm...we shall see how *grateful* you can be." Now, I remember she used the term "we" back in the Commons. A will o' the wisp breaks the surface, daring to peep its head above the water, but with one quick gnash of Nita's teeth, the lost eel-shaped spirit flees. With her hand anchored on the back of my neck, a foreign soprano voice chirps, "Perhaps we may use whips on you!"

Wait! I recall my eavesdropping moment outside the breakfast hall. It's the *same* voice! Kitty's voice! What. The. Fuck?! I don't dare look behind me. I simply heave a few breaths, eyeing the shifting souls as they collect like beggars to a pope's blessing.

Nita squeezes my neck, nails extending into claws. "I'm going to ask you some *questions*, Elysia, and if I don't like your answers, you're going into the water. Bride or no bride."

"That's fair," I breathe out, focusing on those souls and not on her nails digging in. I love all these emotions budding within me. The exhilaration of these moments. Adrenaline bullets up my spine, igniting my Halo, but I advise it to stay down...even if I am in danger.

She cackles and inquires, "Is my brother on his best behavior?" This is a test.

"Depends," I tell her, considering his actions last night.

"Hmm…I do not appreciate one-word ambiguity."

I dare to buck, to crane my neck so I may face her. Those eyes become silver whips, marking me, flush with red pupils. I am not ashamed to fling myself against the iron stairs, but I still do not cower. No, Kitty is not here, though I distinctly heard her voice. Regardless, without backing down, I hold those eyes. I desire to know as much about this singular woman in Neo's life. This woman who plays with me. A lioness toying with…a Princess.

So, using the stairs for leverage, I envision my Halo forming little rings, tiny circlets. Projecting them from my fingers, I launch them in two blinding mini whirlwinds to carousel along her horns.

Eyes catapulting to their ceilings, Nita tips her chin down, head tilting in sultry allowance. "Oh, you naughty little angel. Very well, Elysia. You win this round."

"I thought I'd won three," I point out.

She snarls, "Don't push your luck."

I smile and refrain from my urge to sweep my hand in a mocking bow and instead swing from the staircase toward her, my gleeful hips gliding from side to side. I almost ask Nita about Kitty, but I'd rather earn her trust first. So, I confess, "It *depends* on whether the Father's around."

Nita rolls her eyes, her silver beam hair mimicking. "You won that round fair and square. You didn't owe me anything. But since you've betrayed your hand, I will capitulate: yes, Neo fulfills a role for that bane of our existence. But rest assured, it is merely a role. Yes, his Court O' Tens is our beautiful love child while I hold the bastard daughter of an island."

"Island?" I lift a brow as she turns to the lake and cracks her neck from side to side, bones popping.

"After everything, Neo gifted it to me. My floating realm of bitten vampires and humans beyond my sire's reach. You must come and visit me sometime." She threads those brows, and I detect Neo in that mischief.

"If I make it out of here alive," I banter.

Nita lifts a finger and taps her nose. "Good, you're catching on. Now, I am far more interested in what role he plays with you and how you play with him."

Death's voice returns. *You are a game!*

I drift my gaze across her, across her glittery velvet night of a gown, of her shimmering dark skin, and her eyes that remind me of *scythes*. **Soul**-hammered and tensioned. Diamond edges. Beautifully *and* precariously balanced. A matriarchy blade. But I am not weaponless. I sigh deeply and lean into my Halo, slowly guiding it out of my chest in fine filaments, desiring to gift her with something.

"I hadn't realized we were playing roles," I tell her and use my hands to weave the filaments into a form, hoping to offer her a worthy symbol. Somehow, a lioness doesn't do her justice, but my mother is a phoenix. What is Nita?

"Have you shared with my brother about your two-for-one Father and Prince *packaged deal*?" Her eyes skyrocket into silver fury, nostrils flaring like a...like a *dragon*.

I vow to be your Ezer Kenegdo, my Halo sings a hushing lullaby. Retribution gnaws on me a moment later, nauseating my stomach.

Because...I remember my homeland in ashes, my father dead from the Prince of Destruction's hand, and Verena in the Bridal Canyon. And how Neo raised me higher than him before attacking me and driving me to my *knees*. All of it is my internal lake of writhing, dark souls...quaking before my inner Goddess throne.

"I-I haven't made my choice." It's a grim offering.

Nita does not answer, but her eyes have roved to my filaments. I consider a dragon and loom my power into the image of that powerful beast.

"**NO!!!**"

Nita screams louder than a banshee! My heart slams against my chest, and I nearly tumble over the edge. Countless gold threads scatter into shooting stars that rocket into the water.

When I recover, I spin my head to face her, to question my astonishment, but there's nothing but open air and the lake. Where is—

Oh, Goddess! Nita is on the floor! Curled into the fetal position while her arms clutch her knees tight to her chest, head tucked into the gap between them. She whimpers, "Don't send us back, please. Don't take us back!"

What? Perplexed, I kneel and hover a hand along her quivering body, too careful. I will *not* touch her because I recognize she's in the eye of the hurricane of her trauma. Triggered by my dragon symbol I'd hoped would be a gift. No, it was her curse. Instead, I give her my Halo to warm her, to hopefully make amends, but the glow I encase her body in does nothing to soothe her.

"Nita...?"

She whimpers, "He won't hurt us anymore. Neo protects us. Not a monster. No more monsters..." She snaps her head to me—her eyes transformed from moonlit silver to the color of a shimmering indigo seascape. "*We* are the monster now."

That is *not* Nita. It's not Kitty either. But she weeps, face to me—her tears staining the stone, becoming a trickling river to feed the ghost spirits lapping her trauma. I desire her trauma. I desire her pain, for if the Prince of Destruction must call for this horned little sister, this *Queen* for help, then it must be the most beauteous suffering in the whole world! A pain I have no right to but pain she shares with me regardless.

Instead, I give her my heart. "I made a vow to him. I vowed to be his Ezer Kenegdo…"

The. Queen. Does. Not. Look. Up.

I pour out golden treasure from my Haloed heart. Something lovely, dark, and deep. "I vowed to be his Ezer, his strong rescuer, and warrior princess of light."

The. Queen. Goes. Still.

"I vowed to be the power that will carry his burdens." I remember the time in the Court with the screams of the two girls. How he could not have spared them without me.

The. Queen. Uncurls. Herself.

On my knees before her, I repeat my wedding vows and cast fine wires to festoon her horns and shower her back in a waterfall of gold. "I vowed to be his shield. I vowed to save him from danger. And I vowed…to deliver him from **Death**!"

No! Those Death shades roar in my head.

Oh, yes! I confirm, sensing the exultation, this dark, glorious *secret*. My Goddess beams launch throughout the cadaverous dungeon and send every last damned spirit diving to the deepest pits of the lake.

Because **Nita** is Neo's dark secret. She is why he never embarked through that portal. Why he wanted to protect me. He doesn't love his twin. He *fears* his twin. He *hates* his twin!

Neo loves Nita. And Nita, Neo.

"Oh, do the whips again, do the whips again!" Nita's whole posture changes…to something resembling more of a *pouncing tigress.*

Neo's sister. And something? No, someONES!

Like a Halo flower bud, the knowledge blooms in my heart. Petals opening, layers unveiling…so lovely, dark, and *deepest*.

Right then, I know. Somehow, in the deepest corner of my being, all the pieces—however I may not understand them—connect. So, I form her symbol. I spin my filaments into a beast *mightier* than the dragon. *Mightier* than the phoenix. Her *monster* of Death and Destruction…and Rebirth! Cut off one head, and two more will grow from a fresh, bleeding wound. In her case, a multitude of wounds, and I can't imagine how many rebirthed souls she carries within her. Perhaps hundreds of souls.

A Father-fucking Hydra!

A soul appears…emerging right out of Nita's chest to appear before me…a mirage…an echo! The echo of *Kitty*. So different from Nita, Kitty has fair skin, dark, silky hair with pronounced bangs, doll-like cheeks, a pert nose, and playful eyes. Nita remains in the background—royal silver eyes blinking. Below the echo mirage, she waits, observing Kitty's soul with a soft smile, quiet and waiting as…the *host*.

Pursing my lips, I lower my head, and whisper to the host, "Nita…" In a breath prayer, I chant her name. I *seek* beyond Kitty. "Is Nita still there?" I *knock* on those windows to her soul. "Nita?"

Kitty sighs and puckers her nose before she spins and flees back into Nita's chest. Then, Nita's whole expression shifts. Her *posture* shifts. I examine her body language. The way every diamonded vertebra in her spine hardens, rolling back as if she's mounting an unchallenged throne! *This* is Nita.

And I lose all my breath because she bows. To me.

25

"IN THE BEDROOM, HE BELONGS ENTIRELY TO YOU. PROSTRATE AS A SERVANT."

A MERE LOWERING OF HER HEAD, BUT A BOW, NONETHELESS. *Holy foremothers, she's bowing to me!*

Nita's lustrous horns pierce the air an inch from my face. I clasp my hands at my chest, whimpering a little, tears glistening in the corners of my eyes because somehow, I know, I know, I *know* this will be the *only* time. "Congratulations, Elysia." Nita sweeps her

hand toward me and lifts her head. "And thank you, sweet angel. I've been waiting for you for nearly 84 years now. Please don't make me do the granny Rose voice," she teases the old *Titanic* film reference.

Overwhelmed with emotion, my voice cracks as I proclaim her name, "Nita!"

"Now, don't you fuss, sweet Ezer." She raises me, weaving one arm around me and guiding me up the iron stairs. A gold butterfly flutters out of my chest. Nita catches it, blows it a little kiss, and sends it on its way.

A high lilt I'm not quite certain I've ever heard invades my voice. "My mother is going to love you so much!" I squeal and reach the top of the stairs where I do a little twirl while Nita hoists her gown to follow.

"I have not had the pleasure of meeting the Rose Queen, though I have longed to challenge her as she is not too much older than myself."

A shaft of light pierces the dungeon from my chest. An incandescent beam. A ray of hope. Before I open my mouth to ask, Nita's already predicted and responds, "No, Elysia. I am sorry. I cannot free your mother. Yes, I am a Creator, but my power works on everything and everybody...save for that, that—"

"Old Scratch spawn?" I offer.

"Good one! I'll have to remember that." Nita escorts me to the elevator. "And what of you, Elysia?" she challenges before opening her silver blood door. "You say your mother would love me. But I wish to know your first impressions."

I chew on my lower lip, eyes sinking to the floor.

"Oh dear, do I want to know?" Nita hisses through her fangs. "Disappointed, darling? Think you me I have a host of demons in my flesh? Well, I carry pieces of them...and many others." When I sigh, cheeks reddening while even my Halo blushes, Nita laughs, "Goodness, sweet! You're not disappointed. You're *jealous*."

I shift my weight. "I should be used to queens by now."

"Pish." Nita plays with my curls, though I'm not entirely sure if it's because she wants to view my neck or not. "We will make a queen out of you yet."

I muster my courage to ask, "Who was crying on the floor?"

Nita inhales and taps a finger on her brow. "Briony. She feels that dark pit of my life more than any other. She is the alter who remembers my dark dungeon days most...when Father would send monsters to battle me, to torment me."

Though I yearn to know more about those days and how Neo relates, I tug my lips into a smile. "And Kitty?"

Nita flutters a hand, and the silver-blood door opens to welcome us into the elevator. "A hypersexualized alter. Emphasis on the *hyper*."

"I can't wait to get to know her!" I climb into the elevator and slide into the seat, swishing my gown folds.

Nita eases onto her seat, back high and regal. Her eyes still have not lost their scythe edge, but she doesn't wield them against me anymore. "You may regret that, my dear."

She may only look a few years older than me, but I understand she's much older. Her words are more befitting of an older sister, bordering on maternal. I imagine, unlike Neo, she has never destroyed any memories. I imagine she keeps him in line and not the other way around. This time, Nita sets the elevator to a slower ascent for which I'm grateful.

I shake my head. "Hoping she can give me a few tips." For the first time, I am actually...*restless*. An inner cauldron stirs inside me. Oh, heavens!

"Oh no, I've seen that expression." Nita grins knowingly. "Kitty's the same when she finds fresh meat." All of a sudden, Nita dips her head low and seductively. Or rather Kitty, not Nita as I'm beginning to detect the differences in their expressions and the subtle shifting one moment prior. A flirty tigress, Kitty cups one hand to the side of her face, and whispers in that same lilt, "Sex is the sweetest of ice creams with sprinkles, fudge, whipped cream, and the ripest of cherries dripping its juice. And we don't even mind the nuts!"

I cover my giggle with my hand.

Nita returns, posturing to an arrowed back. "I warned you."

"How often do they come out in their mirage forms?" I wonder.

"Not often. Sometimes if they are extremely scared or quite gleeful," she hints and makes a little kissing noise with her mouth. "Or meeting someone for the first time."

I bury my face in my hands. "This is all so new to me."

"Could have fooled me, love," Nita grumbles and rolls her eyes. "I have never in all my life lost a bet to that baby llama in rainbow pajamas. And ascot." I laugh, considering Quillion.

A few more golden butterflies unleash at the thought of my battles in the bedroom with Neo. "My parents raised me on the *progressive* side."

Nita nods, curling a hand in the air. "As it should be."

"But when your mother is the Rose Queen, you don't get many opportunities beyond lots and *lots* of reading." Well, and...an underground lair, but that was sacred and sensual for me and Verena.

"The most important thing to remember, love, is that you command his throne above all. In the bedroom, he belongs entirely to you. Prostrate as a servant."

I reflect on the image of Neo on his knees begging for forgiveness for the previous night. His prostrate self is what I desire most. And more sensual touching, courting me.

"You and Kitty may swap notes later. But me first. Neo shared some intimate details. Of the *exploratory* nature, a rose bath, a hellcat, and his lingerie choices."

I'm certain I turn so red, my cheeks catch fire.

Nita preens. "Not to worry, sweet girl. My brother has exquisite taste."

Gold dust drifts off my skin when I consider what else he might have me wear tonight. Until I remind myself of my true calling. Nita is a Creator. And if she loathes the Father as much as I do...

"I caught that stray thought, Elysia." Nita crosses one leg over the other, concealing the slit side. "After everything we've shared today and considering all our hopes rest on your sweet head, I am going to bestow upon you a boon of *foresight*." My heart stops every last flutter. Listens. Nita's chin soars, her horns like her sovereign, dark crown when she utters, "You will not have much longer to wait for the Altar. And it is much closer than you believe."

Golden bows shoot from my chest to fill the elevator with a flawless, shimmering rainbow. My hands fly to my exuberant mouth and giggle, "I have the best idea!"

○

"ADORABLE PLAGUES!" QUILLION DUBS US AS I FINISH MY CREATION with Nita perched high like a bat in the domed ceiling. A super bat with a crown of horns. Silent and dark and concealed in shadows.

Neo will be here any minute. I'll betray myself if I can't rein in all the stardust blossoming on my skin. Thankfully, my gown and sinuous cape folds conceal all the exhilarated golden heat between my legs. All the tightening anticipation in my core at the thought of seeing *him* when I've bonded so much with his sister.

"You look so pretty, Quill." I giggle too much thanks to Nita's other brilliant idea which I am thoroughly enjoying: venom-laced wine. All my skin tingles! I get a hint of pink paint on my lower lip. "Now, you'll have to stay this way for an hour or so while your wings dry. Scroll through the feeds. Oooh, since you can't move, maybe I should call Kitty."

"Don't tempt her," Nita pronounces above our heads. "I've been looking forward to this for months."

Shades shift into the room, betraying *his* presence. First, they peck at the ends of my gown as if pleading forgiveness for the other night. Oh, he should. *Prostrate...as a servant*, Nita had mentioned, but I can't imagine such a thing. At least...not right now.

Neo finally embarks into the Commons from the accompanying skyway but stops in his tracks when he beholds Quillion splayed out on the Commons floor with his *rainbow*-painted wings fanned out like a glorious fairy. And me...with pink paint and venom wine on my jubilant lips.

"What the hell is going on?" Neo threads his brows low and eyes the bishop. "Are you all right, Quill?"

"Just dandy." The vampire fingers his ruffled ascot. "I find the rainbow wings compliment my ascot. I may add them to my repertoire. Thank you, Elysia."

We share a smile, and I chirp, "You're welcome. You are perfectly fancy."

Neo stalks toward me while I squeeze my shoulders, all innocent. I hiccup, and a few butterflies festoon from my mouth and flutter right for him. Warmth infuses me like a thousand teabags. Neo raises a brow, bats at the butterflies as Spitfire would—aww!—gaze centering on me and noting the change in my...ahem constitution.

"Adorable plagues," is all Quillion mentions before Neo closes the distance between us.

Oh, not quite there. I take one step back, and Neo stares down at me, puzzled because my chin sinks to the floor. But I tilt my neck to the side and peer at him beneath sultry lashes. Now, I understand why Nita wanted me to lead him to this specific point of the room.

"Oh, hell..." Neo proclaims, eyes vaulting to their ceilings, realizing it a second too late.

Not just sneaking up on him. Neo is Nita's *throne*! Deja vu strikes when I consider the last time in Court when Neo swooped down from the dome as Nita does now. Except, she doesn't vulture perch. No, she's a hydra goddess winding her leg around his throat and knocking him to the floor. Dominating him.

Oh, Saints! If I ever get wings, if I ever get wings, if I *ever get wings!*

"Nita?" He sighs, deadpanning with his little sister's eyes, only flicking away once to anchor on...me. Expectant? No. Hopeful? No. I grin. *Desperate.*

The vampire presses her body deeper onto Neo's chest and leans in. Not sultry at all but a flawless blend of intimate and dangerous. "Neo..."

"Nita...alters?" Is he holding his breath?

"We *like!*" She murmurs in his ear and gives it a little warning nip. "We *love!* Do. Not. Fuck. Up."

And Neo sighs! A visible sigh. Oh, Saints! He was desperate for Nita's approval. More damp Halo dust breeds between my thighs. All my insides prepare to overheat...and ooze.

Uncurling herself from her brother's chest, Nita waltzes over to me and bumps her hip to mine. "Beautiful performance, angel eyes!"

"Hey, I had to sit here and get all painted," Quillion interjects.

I bound right over to him and kneel to kiss his cheek. "And you are an adorable plague, Quill," I revel.

He offers me his hand so I may kiss it. "Charmed."

Neo's shades whisper along my skin, prodding through the bond, requesting access. It completely shut down after I lightninged him. I spring back to my feet to face him and nod my acceptance. More gold flowers bud on my arms when he fingers a few of my pink-tinged curls. It takes all my strength to tear my eyes from his.

Uh oh. I'd recognize Kitty's body language from a mile away. But I decide *not* to tell Neo about her tigress ready to pounce, bedroom eyes solely for my husband. My cheeks flush with envy, though I'm not entirely sure why, considering Nita is still the host, and the alter identity of Kitty has momentarily overtaken her body. Another new one.

Kitty moves at lightning speed, pouncing palm poised for his iron-hard ass, but Neo snatches her wrist, leans over to sweetly kiss her cheek, then gives her a tender poke in the chest to thrust her away. She pouts.

"Kit!" Nita returns, shifting to the side, hands on her hips as she scolds her alter, carrying some mental communication—similar to me and my empath but oh, so much more powerful. My empath isn't real, just someone imaginary to help me process, unlike Nita's very real spirit entities. "I swear to the Father, do I have to put a collar on you and lock you in the dungeon again?"

I bite my tongue to prevent my laughter from escaping.

Kitty returns, swinging in, eyes glinting with mischief as she waltzes about the circle. "Only if you promise to do that whipped cream and handcuffs thing again." She blows her Host a kiss and taps Quillion's forehead. He barely acknowledges her and turns the digital page on a trashy novel.

"Hush. No boudoir backdoor talk," Nita returns to chastise her, crossing her arms over her chest.

Neo elbows me from the side, summoning my attention with a wry smile. "Nita will have the occasional fling with Kitty. With Tourmaline's blessing."

"Who's Tourmaline?" I flick my eyes between them.

Nita simpers. "My first alter, my internal systems helper. And my *wife*." I perceive the importance even if I don't have the history.

Neo braces a chin to his fist, his eyes all silver swaddle blankets for his little sister. "They've agreed to a one-Kitty open marriage. Of the masturbatory kind."

Didn't need clarification, Neo.

"How on earth...?" My morbid mind can't help but dissect—

"Oh! She's so adorable," Kitty exclaims, flaring her nostrils. "Are you sure we can't bring her to Valhalla with us?" Is that what Nita calls her floating island? So fitting.

The two of them argue for a moment, and Neo lowers himself to my ear, raising the hairs on the back of my neck as he explains for my *exploratory* thoughts, "Wings."

I jerk my head to him, eyes rocketing wide open, gold rings nearly short-circuiting. Before I combust, I slow-lean away from him and bite my lower lip. Oh, Saints! Would he ever...with *his*?

My cheeks burn as he coddles my thoughts through our bond. *Far more uses besides flying and painting.* He taps each of his arms, grinning at me like a hellcat. A golden glow steeps all of me, but thankfully my plush gown folds do a decent job of hiding it. If only I could stop the shuddering between my legs.

Nita straightens to her throne posture and bristles. "For the last time, Kit, best behavior." She side-eyes me, explaining, "The three of us are hearts over parts, of course, but Kitty is our strongest heart. And she loves any and all parts. It was an awkward journey when she began flirting with Neo, but we came to an agreement." Nita rubs the bridge of her nose while avoiding Neo's gaze. "You must understand, Kitty is the sweetest and most social of us. But she only knows how to process life through the filters of love and sexuality. So, Kitty gets to flirt with Neo on the understanding that he will *never* reciprocate and that I allow it...*under protest*. But no touching aside from her one ass-slapping attempt which she knows Neo will always thwart."

I beam, first at her—then at him.

Nita crouches, transferring back to Kitty to stick out her

tongue. "You can't possibly expect me to be on my best behavior all the time." Kitty shakes her hair back and forth—a silver pendulum. "Quill is one thing. He's a solid ten but gay as abandon." Quill nods with a wave of his hand, consenting while recording the lot of us. "Neo shatters all the sexy beast charts. And Elysia..." she peers at me, bobbing her brows.

I giggle, covering my mouth. "I'm as *purple* as they come, Kitty, so you can steal a kiss from me anytime you want. But that's all I can promise."

And quick and lithe as a silver fox, Nita returns with her brutal Queen eyes. "Remember, Kit, Neo's *thoroughly* taken now. Check the mark." Nita taps my brand over his chest and compliments me, "Halo Queen indeed."

"Well, I—"

Nita gives me her iciest stare, brandishing her finger like a deadly scythe. "Elysia, Father be damned, if you trigger Briony, I will have you on your knees so fucking fast, you'll have scars on those starry caps forever."

"All right," I sigh, relenting with a two-finger salute. "But only because you curse the Father. Hail, Hydra!"

Nita turns her pointed nose at her brother, sharpening those scythe eyes. "Neo, if you fuck this up, you won't even have kneecaps anymore."

And oh, Saints! Neo bows *at the waist*! "Yes, my Lady Queen." After a pause, "I played Rose to her photographer Jack last night," Neo utters to Quillion.

The bishop rubs his eyes, murmuring, "My poor sweet Princess".

"Yes, I also brought her to her *knees*."

I slow-turn a smoldering stare. Oh, no, he didn't! That fucker did *not*! Volcanic heat ignites retribution to swirl lava in my Father-fucking core.

"Sexy devil..." Kitty wags her shoulder, index finger tipping to her tongue in a wet hiss. As if rewarding him one point.

I twist my whole body to him, stab out my dangerous hips, and rise to break his throne. *Kneel, demon servant!* "What a gorgeous sight you were on your back, wrists and ankles bound from my punishing Halo and me straddling you and ready to ride you until your cock damn well fell off!"

Quillion doubles over, choking, and sputtering and smearing his paint while Kitty struts right to me and practically twerks against my pelvis, swirling her arm in the air, and singing my praises, "Bow before this angel goddess! Ow! Ow! We're not worthy!"

Neo bows to me. All. The. Way. To. His. Fucking. Hips!

Nita winks at me from the side. "I'll allow that."

She wraith-shadows, and a cold draught invades the backs of my legs. Oh, the humanity, I groan as Kitty peeks under the ends of my gown. Oh, Saints! And releases golden Halo streams right from between my legs.

"Oh, she's positively dripping liquid gold down here!" Kitty thrills.

Oh, the mortification! Neo throws his head back, laughing while I bury my flushed face in my hands. That deep, dark laughter I want to wrap myself in. And someday, I swear he will share his eyeliner secret with me. Thank heaven for venom wine! I hiccup more stars.

Right after Kitty cackles and holds her sides, Nita postures and touches my curls near my burning face and reminds me, "Don't forget. He's *your* servant in the bedroom. If ever you're not satisfied, my sweet angel, you send him to me, and I'll whip him into shape."

I touch my chest and unleash one Halo whip. A sneak peek. "No thanks."

"That's my girl."

"Oh, Neo!" I gush and sweep into his room. *Our* room. And spin and spin, spreading my arms and arching my neck while his shadows swish to my gown.

Spitfire charges for me, tongue lolling out of the side of his mouth. I laugh, scratch him behind his ears, and then placate him with another bundle of Halo flames, sending him chasing them into the corner of the room. Then, I catch the Prince staring at me. Winter mist. And I beam, voice softening and deepening when I draw out his name, reflecting on its meaning for a moment. "*Neo*...she's so—"

"I know."

"I *love*—"

"Me, too." And

then, he's there. Arms around my waist, moving with me in a slow dance.

I slide my arms around his neck and swing back and forth, curls straying. "Thank you for your *distress* signal! You can play damsel anytime."

"Elysia..."

Oh, wait! I still don't have my apology yet...for *everything*. But I don't want to tell him. He needs to earn it. So, I glide my hands from his neck and down to his chest, bare between the curtained sides of his robes. As always. I tap my mark, offering a little hint. Halo Queen. I will totally keep that.

"She's the key, isn't she? The key to everything?" I hint.

"I wear a mask, Elysia," begins Neo, knuckles brushing my curls. "Trust me when I say I hate wearing it, but I must regardless. And it's not my place to share why. I am bound by a blood oath. Nita is the only one who understands who I am behind the mask. Quillion's the only one who's ever peered behind it. And you..." he envelopes my hand and with his other, slow-drapes his knuckles across my cheek, finishing with a seductive purr, "...are where the mask doesn't exist." I treasure the words while he kisses my hand until he adds, "Though to be fair, you've really burned it off." He gestures to my charred cracks in the room.

I wince, considering my last-night lightning strike, but Neo coils a hand around my neck and deepens his eyes against mine as I part my lips and inquire, "So, what I'm seeing are the scraps of the mask that are still branded to your face?" I lean into the analogy, I lean into him, my hand on his mark, *my* mark.

With his hand soft at my neck, Neo uses his thumb to persuade my chin to rise. "The vampire of my past. A role I still must play. But *you* make me feel as though I can remove the mask and say to hell with it all! And you're the only one who can destroy it completely."

I dip my chin lower, smiling at the dual joke. And then, I'm lifting my eyes to his, trapped in that silvery web. "Neo, when you are not bound to your Father, the Court is your domain. And you rule it well," I strengthen him, fingers tracing the Halo brand. "On my first day in Court, I hadn't known what to expect. But how you conducted yourself with the Court O' Sixes bishop and with Riona...that was all *you*. Not your Father. If he wasn't in the—"

Neo clutches the hand at his chest and presses my palm down. Hard. "I would never desire to rule my Court without you. I would erect another throne beside mine."

Oh, Saints! My Halo glows, curling star patterns all along my arms. Neo's shadows twirl around them in a creeping caress.

"If he doesn't exist..." I ease out the sigh.

"My throne. My scythes. My realms. My heart..." Neo presses down on the tips of my fingers, muscles flexing beneath, "They would all be yours to command."

Halo stars spin all around me as if daring his shadows to chase.

Then, that nagging little voice in my head. That nagging little voice caped in Death shadows. *This is his game. He wants to be king over his Father. Twin kings. When he gets what he desires from you, he will throw you away as he did all the others. Ask him.*

But I won't listen. I *won't* listen. I won't *listen*.

"And now, my lady..." Neo coaxes my chin with two fingers, winter mist from his eyes nearly drifting to speckle frost onto my cheeks, "what dost thou require of me?"

Oh, Saints!

Remember, he is your servant. You command him in the bedroom. He will worship at your feet.

So, I channel my inner queen and remember our blood oath. "What you desire for me to wear tonight will be what *I* desire to wear."

Accepting, Neo nods and combs through my voracious curls, voice dropping to a low octave, "May I ask a boon of my lady?"

"Go on."

"May I remove her gown tonight?"

The Halo practically bakes my nether regions upon his words and launches golden whirlpools in my belly. I imagine once he does remove my gown, he will find nothing but a scarlet, star-swooning light.

Neo destroys my embarrassment. "Always higher than me, Elysia."

Strong and sovereign, I nod and ease my back to him, slowly. *Breathe.* But my lungs constrict more when Neo scatters my curls over my shoulder and onto my chest so he may access the buttons on my gown. First, he unhooks the folds at my waist and casts them to the floor in a cascade of velvet. Breasts infused with a heaving heat, I incline my head over my shoulder and observe my husband moving for the buttons of my gown. My skin still tingles thanks to his cool shades and the venom-laced wine, and when he pops the very last button, all of me burns. I almost rip the very gown to shreds.

Neo glides the dress down the curves of my shoulders, kissing each one, until the gown pools at my feet. I step out of it.

Breath bursting, I slowly twist around, grateful he doesn't invade my space. His eyes soak me in silver pools. The first thing he does is drape my curls over my shoulders to display my pale pink rose chemise—empire cut and trimmed with lace all over the bodice. His silver ring dangles between my cleavage.

"This is what you love?" Neo wonders, eyes worshipping my entire form through the transparent chemise, and oh, Saints!—he etches his knuckles along the swell of my breast. They crawl all the way down. My nipples pucker.

I lick my lips and close my eyes as those knuckles continue their path to my other breast. "Well, in different colors." Halo heat wrangles with my core as I approach him, flushing my cheeks.

"Brings out the gold in your curls," Neo admires, moving his hand and flexing his fingers. Walking away.

Wait, what? What the fuck? Where's my kneeling prostrate Prince? I want to scream for Nita.

"Come to dinner, Elysia," Neo beckons to our private supper hall.

Defiant, I cross my arms over my chest. "I'm not hungry." I nearly stomp my foot.

"Yes, that is apparent." He tips his head toward the liquid

gold ripples escaping from the bottom of my chemise. And walks into the other room? Oh, that bedeviling fucker! No, he did not!

I march right past the archway, almost bumping into him. I stomp on his robe, jerking him back by the shoulders. Sighing, Neo cranes his neck back and releases the robe, so it bathes my feet before he moves toward the head of the table. I race past him and cut him off, hand touching the chair at the same time his does. He steels his eyes. I burn mine. We vie for dominance.

"No, Elysia." He shakes his head.

"Why. The. *Fuck*. Not?"

"Because I meant what I said in the Chasm. The first time I touch you, you will be safe, fully awake, and *lucid*. Eat dinner. Sober up." He rubs his thumb, smearing away some pink paint from earlier.

I shove his arms away and turn, flipping him off, my Halo light properly dimming. "Pretentious bastard."

He sighs, mutters, "Ten thousand demons. How about a little deal? No blood oath." I pinch my eyes from the opposite side of the table. "You may order dinner tonight. Whatever you desire."

Is that so, Neo? You think I'm just an angel dancing on the head of a pin?

Neo's lip corners tug, slithering serpentine as he counters, *Only fools rush in where angels fear to tread.*

I check him with my dinner order. The ring at my chest burns as I sample bites of each of my selections.

Neo grunts and raises his blood wine glass to me from the other end of the table. "Well played, Princess."

"Mmm..." I roll through my list one bite at a time. "Maca fruit salad to increase libido." I fold my lips slowly and sensually over the spoon with a preening pride.

"Tribulus terrestris aka bindii to boost *your* testosterone,

Neo." I clean my fork and raise my cup to drink my, "Red ginseng and fenugreek." My smile is radiant from that little something I'd added to his nightly blood-cap to, "treat poor sexual function and increase sexual arousal," I tease darkly, reveling heat budding inside my chest. The Halo seems to enjoy my teasing.

Swirling my cup, I ogle him under heady lashes. Then, I crack a pistachio seed shell and pop the seed in my mouth. "Did you know pistachios help increase blood flow for firmer *erections*?" I bait him, licking my lips. "Surely such an accomplished Prince with a harem would know that!"

Add saffron and chilies-laced chocolate truffles, oysters on the half shell complete with gold pearls, chocolate-dipped strawberries, and for the checkmate: Devil's food cake. By now, I've fully sobered up. Halo *liquid* circling the drain. Not fast enough.

Neo wags a finger, a knowing glint in his eyes. "I wasn't lying when I told my Father I am savoring you."

I press my lips into a glower and set my teacup down hard enough to fracture it. "Sure know how to kill the mood, Neo."

He downs his wine glass, flexes his muscles, and then cocks his head to me. "Oh, all right. Fine, Elysia. Have it your way." He slides out of his chair, undoes his belt, and drops his pants in one fell swoop to exhibit his amassed, rigid calves, redwood-thick thighs eagerly flexing their muscles, and his massive vamp-shaft quivering as if surrounded by a halo of joy! He approaches. My pulse thunders to life!

"Holy fuckety fuck, Neo!" I practically fall out of my chair and scurry away to the opposite side of the table. Halo hearts pitter-patter out of my chest, evaporating from the sight of Neo's gargantuan cock.

"Are you satisfied it's working *perfectly*?" Neo plants his hands on the table, hunching over. He eyes me with a lascivious, predatory grin.

Skin flushing heat around my neck, I suck in a deep breath and stab a finger at him. "Now, you just stay over there on that side of the table and be a good dragon," I chastise him, but my gold-ringed eyes overheat and short-circuit. And my sex begins to drip like a weeping angel!

Neo touches one deliberate finger to the table.

I raise mine like a scepter. "Don't you even think about it!"

With a feral grin, Neo destroys the table until there's nothing but ash, then stalks toward me, member aimed like a wagging sword. His silver eyes are wolfish and ready to plunder.

My eyes practically double in size! Traitorous flutters multiply in my stomach. That tiny ticking muscle in his cheek—the winding down of a clock. History repeats itself when I tip my hand by flicking my eyes down. Neo's massive length throbs. Fire rages in my core! And I *know* Neo can scent my arousal.

"Shit!" I whirl away—whole body tingling. Scampering into the suite, I head right for my room so I can hide my blazing cheeks in the Infinity Wardrobe under a mountain of fabric.

Spitfire beelines in front of me. I dodge out of the way. Treasonous fiend! Neo corners me at the bathtub, and I back up, hitting the ledge. Wince. It's always something. Neo invades my space, and I plant my hands on the ledge behind me and lean back as he closes in. I can't tell whether I'm gasping or gushing. Oh, Saints!

"I've really gotta talk to Nita about that whole prostrate servant thing," I default and snarl, snapping my teeth to bite him.

He dips his head, eyes of festering flames. "I am no one's servant. But if you want me, angel, you got me."

"Don't call me that," I warn him, leaning further away, wrinkling my nose. The heat in my belly doesn't stop whirling. The liquid gold inside me, chronically oozing. But there's no way in hell I'll let him get the upper hand. Or any other extremity for that matter.

When he blinks, I glance up at him. Then, I glance *down* at him. His length nudges my inner thigh through my chemise. Ugh, why did I just arch my neck and thrust out my chest? I excuse it as the Halo...and my subconscious. We both know I want him. Not that I'll ever admit it.

"You've got the weight of the world on your shoulders. Little wonder you're so tense..." he coos.

I cringe when my lower spine mashes against the faucet. He's deliberately doing this so he can get a better view of my neck and beyond...obvious when his eyes rove lower before his pupils blush with bloodlust and he adds, "Quick romp in the sheets would do you wonders. Play a little seven minutes in heaven, kissing notwithstanding of course?"

I thrust out my jaw and scoff, "How about a round of Kiss. My. Ass?"

"I'd prefer to suck it." His brows prance as he continues, "Then spank it..." he croons and taps his nose to mine. My bare feet scramble with the tiled floor while he continues, "...then undoubtedly suck it again...along with every inch of you."

"Screw you!" I hiss and eye the warm blood bath. The ends of my curls dip in it. My breasts grow heavy, nipples pebbling to betray myself.

Neo fixes his hands on either side of my body and tempts me, "How about now?" He cocks a grin. Damn it all to hell: fresh Halo-light blooms from my core, branching out and flirting with the shadows along Neo's thighs. Stupid hormones.

"Bite me!" I finish in a cunning dare, sporting a triumphant grin, holding onto the sense of pride as I lift my chin.

He winces.

"Aww, that hits *below* the belt," I chuckle and deadpan, thrilling. I don't mention how I never *ever* want him to bite me.

Still, Neo chuckles and touches my cheek, knuckles brushing my curls out of the way. "I can do this all night," he invites me, cock twitching. My limbs tremble. A warm shudder ripples along my spine.

I slip, and my hands lash out when I begin to fall. Neo catches me, shocker! But he doesn't raise me yet. Instead, he hovers me right above the blood till the liquid swallows an inch of my curls. Damn. Did harem girls donate to fill his bath?

"Neo!" I grip his shoulders and demand, "Lift me up, now!"

His warm flames at my waist travel past my chemise to my flesh. *Pompous bastard!* My legs slightly part in a subtle offering.

"So long as you're caught between a rock and a hard place—" Neo cunningly chortles, bending his head to mine, and I press my other hand to his chest, "—tell me the truth just for the devil of it." His grin spreads.

"Are you going to ask a question or just spew Daddy's one-liners all night?" I taunt. Flames from his chest twist and spiral upon my fingers, casting warmth along my knuckles, palm, and wrist. They tingle. He flexes, hard as horns beneath me. I whimper. *Fuuuuck.*

"Touchy touchy...hot and cold, why is that, Elysia?" He pinches his lips before tilting his head, so it brushes mine at an angle. "How long's it been, darling?"

"None of your fucking business," I hiss again.

"For my own edification, sate my curiosity."

I jut out my jaw. "What do I get out of it?"

"Clever girl." His fingers caress my lower spine as he debates, "Hmm…a new deal then. One week without any harem girls."

"Two."

"Will you be supplementing then?" he hints, hand rubbing lower.

"Ugh…what do *you* think?" I snap. My curls splatter blood droplets like tiny rubies into the air.

He primes his full lips and weighs his options. "Perhaps I'll accept your challenge anyway. Worth it to learn about your sexual history."

"And no more public innuendos regarding my sex life," I add and burn daggers in his eyes. "Say whatever you want to me in private—"

"Promise?"

"—*not* public," I solidify.

"Our breakfast verbal spar still holds? I do enjoy watching Quill blush."

"If your goal is your own public humiliation…" I preen and consider how many times I've won and cringe when his fingers trench onto the skin of my hip.

"Deal."

Neo sets me on my feet and launches me into a twirl before capturing the front of my neck and dipping his face so low, his mouth touches my upper lip. A lightning spark of a mouth rub, casting the scent of ginseng fragrance on my face. I don't register my lips part until I've dragged my tongue around them.

"Now, spill," he commands, releasing me.

With a deep sigh, I roll my shoulders and shake off the close encounter, wishing I could deny the heat, those flames swelling in my blood. I hug my arms, blow a few flustered breaths to get a hold of myself. Then, I gesture for him to follow me to the corner table where the decanter of venom-laced wine rests. I'm so going to need a drink for this.

"Elysia." Neo moves to stop me, but I throw him one keen glare like a throwing star, warning him not to interfere. Relenting, he removes his hand from the bottle. "*Spicy...*" Neo muses when I tip a full glass and swallow it all in two gulps. "Is your past so licentious, Princess? After all, I already know you're confident in your own body."

I glower, spine hardening from the implication. "As if my physical confidence has anything whatsoever to do with my sexual history?" Even if it wasn't hyper-sexual or anything, I won't share my lair with him. Instead, I opt for my inner goddess. "Did you know ancient cultures associated sexually independent women with strength and confidence?"

Neo blinks. "Elysia..." he chides me as if reminding me of his age.

"A sovereign unto herself," I prevaricate and pour another glass, chuck it down. Okay. More than one. Liquid courage. "Her own lover," I finish.

Neo sets his hand on the decanter before I can grab it again, scoots it to the opposite edge of the table, and slides his body in front of mine. A soft playful smile on his face. Shadows contort all along my skin, nestling into my curls. I study the floor because I assume he's assessing the meaning behind my evasive language. This whole conversation is pointless, but I'm bracing myself because I'm never going to hear the end of it!

"Elysia." Neo settles two lithe fingers beneath my chin and coaxes my face to his. "Are you a virgin?"

I roll my eyes and jerk my face away, grimacing. "Because my sexual history can be reduced to a patriarchal construct such as *purity*". I make air quotes for deliberate effect.

He says nothing. But one corner of his mouth crooks. I

glower and give him the finger, but to my utter shock, he fetches the decanter and hands it to me. This time, I don't hesitate to drink from the bottle, gushing from the rich spiciness stinging my throat and warming my insides. Numbing. My Halo has multiplied into thousands of miniature babies jittering inside me—aww my tiny, celestial parasites. I hiccup a glittery trail.

The first time I hiccupped a star was with Verena.

Neo's shadows continue teasing my skin, and he cocks his head to the side, observing me with that suggestive smile.

Gripping the lip and pointing my index finger at him, I scold with a slight slur, rambling, "Don't you dare believe that just because I haven't had "penetrative sex" that it somehow defines my worth or perception. Or allows for the justification of elevated or de-elevated social and romantic reception." Imaginary fucking social construct. I grind my teeth, nostrils flaring.

"So, you've never—"

The room spins a little as I shriek, "My identity and worth are not dictated by whether or not I've had a dick in me, Neo!"

He's there, steadying me and scooping me into his arms. I clutch the decanter to my chest as if it's a life preserver. And moan, "Stupid fucking patriarchy believing dicks are so important, they change who a human being is," I slur every word in a pout as he tucks me into the bed, cocoons me in the blankets, brushes aside my curls, and kisses my brow.

"And it's not like I've had no experience," I mutter. "Fingers, toys in my...sex, don't laugh!" I warn him when he smirks at the antiquated term. "Call me old fashioned, outdated, I don't care. I like it." Sometimes, I say 'pussy' or 'cunt', but at least it's better than 'well' or 'heat'. My eyes roll back, and I turn onto my side as he climbs in next to me.

"For the record..." I half-sigh and half-slur the words, "I like your dick just fine." I don't admit that I love it. "But like I told Kitty, I'm as *purple* as they come."

"Ahh..." he says knowingly, purring his warm breath along the back of my neck. "I've had some male lovers in my past. No grooms though. Solely female brides." Interesting. Not like I believed he'd object, considering Nita. Or Quillion. He's not disappointed. "Did you have a—"

"Yes," I cut him off, my voice cracking. Tears sting my eyes as my rage splinters to grief. An ache lances my throat. "And it wasn't like that. It was but more than that. She was *special*." At the worst time of my life, I needed Verena. I still need her. In my heart, I believe our paths *will* cross. And she'll be my thrice-a-year affair, one I trust my main partner will bless.

"Elysia..." Neo pauses on the opposite side of the bed and kisses my teardrop. My Halo tempts its way out of my chest to couple to his fortress of a chest because he senses my sorrow, my grief. "It was her, wasn't it? The one in the canyon. The one with the power of lightning?"

I whimper and curl into him more.

Sighing, Neo kisses my brow and declares, "You won't believe this. You have no reason to, but I am sorry, my love."

"Did she suffer?" I dare to ask.

He shakes his head. "No. My Father abhorred her. A half-blood with such power and one he couldn't control. He ordered me to destroy her. And according to blood magic, I..." he winces, his breathing growing heavier as he reveals, "cannot...*refuse* my Father's direct commands."

My eyes shoot to his like a laser beam. It's not *the* secret, but it's a secret all the same. As close as he's ever taken me. Judging by how he had to force the words, revealing it alone must have caused him great pain.

"She fought to the bitter end, but Father was going to

torture her. So, I shut down her heart but refused to destroy her mind and body as he desired."

A sob escapes my throat. Nodding but not thanking him, not forgiving him yet, I swallow the remaining splash of wine, drop the decanter to the floor, then crane my neck to him. Thanks to the venom and alcohol levels, Neo is a blur of dark shadows and hair of silk moonbeams.

"Mmm..." I murmur and stretch my hand toward him. "you'll let me braid that mane someday, Neo." I giggle and hiccup, giggle again. "Oh, I'm a *light*weight." Emphasis on my light.

He lets out an airy chuckle and props his head on his elbow. "Another deal, another day, my untouched Elysia."

"Ugh, you prick, I said no dick. Never said I was untouched."

He taps my nose. "I meant other than me."

"Because it's always about *you*, Neo," I drawl, annoyed. But the venom wine chases away any hint of emotions, of memories from *that* night.

"Sleep."

I close my eyes. For the first time ever, it's venomous black fog lulling me to sleep.

26

"I'LL LOOK FORWARD TO SITTING NEXT TO YOUR BRIDE AND WATCHING COURT TODAY."

IN THE MORNING, I WAKE TO GOLDEN LIGHT FESTOONING ME. AND A cold, hard body pressed to my back.

Split-second trigger. My hurricane eye of trauma. A hurricane of a hundred invisible bite marks. And *I scream, I scream, I scream!*

Neo rockets to his knees, fumbling with the blankets. Panic spikes, shooting adrenaline into my veins. I scream again, scrabbling with the coverlet and throwing them over my head in a vain effort to cocoon myself and drown in an ocean of black, creating whatever lair I possibly can. *Safe, safe, safe...need to be safe.*

"Elysia!" Neo yells, his hands seeking me through the layers. "What the hell?"

Yes, hell. *My* hell.

Screams and sobs rack my body. Shards of pain convulse the back of my neck. In my head. In my chest. All the non-venomous black serpents stalking my heart have united. They're *squeezing, squeezing, squeezing*. And sucking. But not breaking.

I. Won't. Ever. Break.

I can't get out. I can't find my Halo light. So, I go *in*! Dig in deep into myself like a tick the same as that night. Neo's shades and flames inject themselves in my blanket tomb and surround me, swallowing my shaking body. Warming me. Stilling me. I dry heave and tremble. Sobs quaver throughout my body. I'm all curled in an Elysia-shaped ball shivering from goosebumps, every last one bearing bite-memories.

Shuddering in the depths, I lament and whimper, "*Noralice*."

His deep purring voice hovers above my head. "Who's Noralice?"

"She's mine," I say but not to Neo. "You can't take her." No one can take her from me. No one will steal her from me. I shake my head. It doesn't sound like my voice. It's Empath Elysia. I can't even remember the cage, can't imagine it. Instead, I bow to my dark empath, granting her equal power until we unite, knotted and twisted together because I never fully fade.

The Father's cold force sweeps into the room. I cower under the blankets, but Neo rises to greet his Father without exposing me. I knit myself into a tighter ball, wishing I could fade right now.

"Father..." he addresses Satan's son. Can imagine him lowering his head. Can imagine his Father patting his cheek.

"A perfect morning, son. My reaping did not take as long as I'd believed. I should have expected thus. Fine stock during a fine year during a fine tax." His voice looms closer to the bed, and I wish I could curve myself into the spaces between worlds, imagine this is the portal. I'd rather face Death than this trauma pit.

Neo's body was pressed to mine—his breath drifted across the back of *my* neck!

"I'm glad it was a successful reap," expresses Neo, and I resist the urge to choke.

"I've already delivered them to my quarters. Best to build it till night. All their delicious *fear*!"

Fear...I latch onto that statement. Trade fear for anger. Trade it for wrath and retribution. But I don't have any bargaining power. Any stock of such emotion has crashed.

"Yes, Father," Neo states through gritted teeth.

"Not having second thoughts about our little deal, are we, my boy?" the Father hints after judging his tone.

"Never, Father."

My empath stutters as vicious predators of questions gnaw on my thoughts. What deal? What are they talking about? Suspicion preys on me, needles into my mind because this role Neo plays, the mask he wears, and his love for Nita are all part of this *deal*.

"I believe I've been more than generous," the Father states, his voice a venomous vapor above me. Through the bejeweled coverlet, it drifts across my skin with a desire to pillage my flesh.

"You have." Neo responds through clenched teeth.

"Perhaps I'll have to remind you of my generosity. It's been quite some time since I reaped from your harem, has it not?"

What? No! I should protest. I should retrieve my Halo whips, drive them around the Father's neck, and strangle him now. Instead, I huddle into myself more because I can't force my body to form any other shape.

"Father, I apologize for my tone. Please forgive me." *Neo*...I wince, pinching my eyes because that is not the voice of my Prince. Not the voice of the overseer of the Court O' Nines.

Stay down, Elysia, he directs me.

I clamp my hands over my mouth, try not to breathe, but it doesn't matter. The Father scents me all the same.

"Or perhaps..." the Father of all vampires rips the blankets off the bed, baring me before his eye. "This little Spirit will do. Bed flesh indeed." The Father brushes his knuckles across my bare shoulder, and I tremble from his crawling touch. The ultimate black serpent prowling my heart, hunting my blood, seeking my flesh. In nothing but my chemise from last night, I feel more naked than ever. I bury my head, so my curls fall to eclipse my face from his eye.

Neo's voice wafts over me. "You may have any girl in my harem, Father," he offers. *No, Neo. Please don't.* I can't muster anything beyond a couple protesting whimpers through our bond.

"You know our bargain, my boy. I tire of your *savoring*. Unless perhaps you have found something special in this one?" There's a dark undertone as he drags his finger down the curve of my shoulder, breath aroused. My empath unleashes a primal scream inside my mind from the splintering spasms in my chest. All I want is to claw at my cheeks, at my hair, my throat.

"She is a bride. Like hundreds before her."

"Hmm..." I quiver when he plants one sadistic thumb on my cheek, rubbing away curls, slow to expose. The Father observes me, tilting his head and inhaling deeper. I don't mask my tears, grateful he doesn't remark on their gold...likely doesn't see. "You've never allowed yourself to be upstaged in Court...unless it's by me, of course."

"And as you can see for yourself, Lys has been *reprimanded*. Did I mention how she actually came to me at the tax festival for the first time unaccompanied and without escort or sponsor to offer herself to the Bridal Path?" A low, seductive hum in Neo's throat.

A wicked cackle explodes from the Father, and I flinch, tightening my arms around my legs as he turns and slaps his son on the shoulder. "No wonder you're savoring, boy! I doubt you've had any other so entranced. Apart from one perhaps."

Neo winces. "I opted for flesh over blood this time," my husband sniggers. "On her knees, she begs for me like a prostrate servant each night."

Neo, I moan through the bond.

A role, my love. My mask.

A game, his brother's voice echoes in my consciousness.

"Besides, do you honestly believe I could betray our blood oath...for *this*?" Neo rolls his eyes before thrusting the blankets over my form.

The Father sighs. "I should never have doubted you, my beautiful Warhammer. You are all I have left in the world. I'll look forward to sitting next to your bride and watching Court today. And tonight, I will enjoy the sweet blood-fruits of my reaping."

Please, Neo, don't make me go to Court.

You are where the mask does not exist, he reminds me, shades soothing my body.

"But I vow to you, my boy, we will find that accursed Everblood and restore Thanatos if it's the last thing we do." Thanatos...his brother, the Prince of Death. Ice crystals grow in my veins, a snowsquall in my blood as the Father continues, "His spirit has been far more restless. Plaguing my dreams. Taunting me of the Everblood."

I clamp my hands over my mouth to cage my breath. I send a maze of Halo light to my throat to confuse the screams longing to rise. Oh no!

Oh yes, Thanatos whispers.

"I'm growing rather *impatient*." The Father's last word hints of a threat. "Reyna would not have surrendered herself without reason. Why ninety-five years? Since she slaughtered Thanatos, why make a deal with me for *ninety-five* years, to grant me the world without her interference in my plans? Why not one hundred? Beyond her hidden, little Princess, she is protecting the Everblood. Perhaps I shall ask her in less than *pleasurable* ways than we've thus far enjoyed."

Dread rattles my stomach. I did this. The moment I went into the tower to get the black venom. From the moment Thanatos whispered his spirit poison into my mind.

"But first, enjoy the blood-fruits of your spoils, Father," encourages Neo, voice wandering away while their footsteps move to the shade doors. "They will help with your impatience."

"Quite right, son. I simply wish they lasted longer," he sighs, voice further, and I ache for him to depart. "None can survive my appetite. Perhaps your Lys will offer more stamina by the time you are finished with her. I'm waiting, my boy."

Neo! I wail, a bitter taste in my mouth, but I can't hope to swallow.

The Father's icy presence disappears from the room. As soon as Neo's familiar footsteps, garbed in shades, approach the bed, I throw the blankets back, get to my knees on the bed, and confront him, "Why, Neo, why?!"

"Elysia—"

"It's not enough for you to use them, you have to surrender them to *him* before you destroy them altogether?" I press my lips into a thin line.

A shadow crosses Neo's face, his silver veins humming a warning. "I'll do what it takes to protect you. And..."

And Nita, I wander into forbidden territory.

Neo cannot tell me, but I read between the lines, especially given how thick as blood they are.

"And the lives of those girls are the price? The lives of thousands of others?"

"Yes!" He grips my face. His silver flame eyes stoke mine,

trailblazing a path to my heart until my fickle muscle is ready to skyrocket out of my chest. "You are worth *any* price! I vowed to protect you when you fainted, but when you brought me to my knees that day in the woods, when you walked down that aisle and looked me in the eye the whole time and refused to bow, when you proclaimed your Ezer, when you stood higher in Court, when you courted this heart of Destruction, I vowed I would slay ten thousand demons. And now—" those flames impale my gold rings to the wall! "—I will damn my soul itself so long as you live to see another morning. And your purpose fulfilled!"

Hot tears leach from my eyes, stagger down my cheeks as Neo lowers his head to kiss my brow as he did on our wedding night.

"Neo." I pull away with a moan, but his iron vice hands refuse to offer me escape. "I made another vow, remember?" He gathers me into his arms, close to his chest where there is no heartbeat...my lips press to my brand. "I vowed to be your *last* bride. That the Bridal Canyon would claim no more bodies."

"That's an impossible vow, Elysia." His damning words reverberate into my body. "Trust me, I've tried."

Now, I unleash my Halo light in the form of deadly throwing stars, direct them with my hands, sending them flying. They all strike his chest, searing his skin and flesh but not the muscle or bone. Neo doubles over, not quite kneeling, but he growls to the cauterizing force while I ball my hands into fists above him—my words a scythe to cut him. "How many have you destroyed for *him*? How many weigh on your soul from that Canyon? Can you even remember?"

Neo seizes my wrists, pins me to the bed, and thrusts them on each side of my head, fuming maddening breath through his nostrils, through his cheeks. Shades breed on Neo's skin, birthing heated flames to swell all around me. Just like a...*dragon.*

His brows sink lower than the Chasm because I know he *heard* that word. He *saw* the Halo-filamented image in my head—the one I'd conjured in Nita's dungeon. The Dragon: a title gifted from the Father. Of the role he still plays. The mask he wears. And her trauma-trigger.

Gritting my teeth, I spit the weaponized words, "You say you wear a mask. Prove it!" Neo's eyes dart between mine as I challenge, "Set them free! I can get them to the Underground."

A moment's pause. Neo blinks. Swallows. Then releases me with a little push, getting up, and turning to proclaim, "I can't."

"Then, Thanatos was right!" I hurl my secret at him, and Neo's every back muscle turns taut and rigid. "It's all been a game. *I* am a game!" Pain still gashes my neck. The invisible serpents lurk closer, so I summon the anger again, driving it homeward. "You're not wearing a mask, Neo," I cry, battling tears. "It's just your fucking dragon face!"

Without turning, Neo cracks his neck and commands, "Get dressed, Bride Lys Spirit. I'll be taking you to Court now."

○

IT'S CLEAR HE WON'T LET ME OUT OF HIS SIGHT. NO PRIVACY EVEN IN my personal suite. I emerge from the Infinity Wardrobe decked to the *Nines*—in a scarlet and black off-the-shoulders, low-cut heart neckline, mermaid-silhouette dress cherishing every curve. Great rippling ruffles flow from the hooked cape attachments. My gold-tinsel curls ripple long and voracious down my shoulders and topped with a winged diadem to conceal the vial of black venom.

I pray to every foremother in heaven for this to work. Because if he refuses to set those reaped girls free, then I will!

Unsurprised by his black diamonded battle gear, I follow him to the shadow door and step outside. Before I move, Neo grips my elbow, hard. Confused because he doesn't take me into his arms and wraith-shadow me to the bone box, I pause and survey him. Instead, he directs me to the staircase down to the Commons. No.

"Don't, Neo," I warn him, but his eyes transform to brutal Destruction. Like his dragon. His warm flames nip at my body. Before I can protest, the Prince shadows the two of us to the Commons where Quillion and Nita wait.

One moment's pause for Nita to behold him in all his battle gear paraded in shadow and flame. A perfect Warhammer of a warrior. Her brows shoot up. She's returning to the Dragon, her trigger. I recognize the symptom—the way her eyes shift, ready to fade to an alter.

Why are you doing this? I cry through our bond.

I summon my Halo, but Neo's flames and shades attack me, suffusing my light within an instant. Now, Briony weeps in the background.

The Prince shadows me right out of the Commons and into the bone box beside his Father before leaping from the balcony railing directly onto his throne landing.

"Sit, stay, and be a good bride," Neo purrs before the arena, causing a roar of laughter throughout the audience. A jab at my previous time when I surpassed him and his Father who chuckles next to me before taking my hand and kissing all my fingertips.

"Mmm...lovely bed flesh," the Father coos, his breath reeking of blood drunkenness.

I sink deep inside, cage the Halo light so I don't betray myself.

Though Neo's shades gather around me, they do not soothe me. Possessive, they besiege my flesh, reminding me of wrath and war. A double war when the Father sinks his fingers onto my thigh and palms me through my skintight gown. His eyes glitter like blood rubies to the sight of his son who looks upon several knights as they thrust a rook onto the raised platform.

The Father sniggers. "According to my Court O' Nines laws, when a rook is thrice-late in his payments, Destruction takes his wings."

Oh, foremothers. I breathe heavier, sensing my Halo lurching. I tiptoe against the door of the bond, sense a veil of shades and flames between us. Asking, seeking, knocking. But Neo slams the bond between us, sealing it shut, charges right into the rook, and unleashes his double-scythes.

It's now or never.

Another prod of those Father fingers. Two single scythe-strikes. The rook's wings tumble to the floor. Doubling over, I pretend to be the weak, submissive bride they desire. I cover my mouth, feigning a cry, and swallow the black venom because too much induces insta-vomiting.

With the raging rook screams in the background, I wince and throw my head to the side, retching right onto the Father's boots. I grin for the barest of seconds as he charges to his feet and shoves me away, seething.

"Ugh! You are dismissed, child. Get out of my sight!" He jerks a thumb to the box door.

Gladly! With my faux shame trailing me, I flee the box and make a beeline for the elevator that will lead me right to Neo's bedroom because Thanatos loves his games; the Prince of Death would not have agreed to a secret portal door to his brother's suite without having another for his own Father.

The Father will claim no more girls tonight!

27
"NO BLOOD DO I REQUIRE. ONLY ONE STRAND OF YOUR HAIR."

I BRING NO STAKES.

Clothed in nothing but one of my chemises so the undiluted, untarnished power of my Halo may do its work, I slowly sink into the portal. Jesula, the Underground schism leader, is waiting outside the tower at the location I told her. And Nita is with her to transport the girls to safety. She touched me, injecting a mental tether into my mind, affording her the ability to read my thoughts and hone in on my senses when the time comes to get the girls out.

Thanatos has already sensed my arrival. No sooner do I step inside the portal than pretentious smoke and shadows waft around me, filling my nostrils, reeking of decay and blood. Heart more turbulent than an ocean storm, I inhale deeply through my nose, waiting for his voice.

"*Pretty, pretty Princess...*" he sings.

Undaunted by the shades and vapors, I pin my upper lip to my lower, march onward to approach his Tower, and finally speak his name, "**Thanatos.**"

"*Ahh, my name is a sweet angel refrain from your mouth. Lovely, dark, and deep!*"

"Get out of my head!" I seethe and touch his door.

His evil smoke coils around my arms—a serpentine bracelet. "*Oh, but you desire me there, sweet Everblood. For, how will you ever learn the entrance to my secret door?*"

I pause, stilling. Spin my head to each side as his shades prod my ears. "*Yes, it coos inside my head. You suspected. You are here to save Father's pretties. You cannot save them in time through that door. Father will come soon. So, at what cost, pretty, pretty Princess?*"

"Where is the door?" I refuse to mentally speak to him. Refuse to grant him that acknowledgement of power.

"*I will show you...for a price.*"

"You will *not* have my blood!" I shake my head, fingers curling, ready to embark into Thanatos' Tower, but I linger in the portal.

"*I would* never *ask the Everblood for such a glorious boon.*" His smoke slithers around my chest, coiling in and out of my strands to circle Neo's ring. "*No blood do I require. Only one strand of your hair.*"

Without delay, I pluck a strand of my gold highlights and allow it to tumble into his shades. Why should I care if he claims a mere memento strand? A poor price compared to helping these captives.

"*One thing more. Grant to me that memory, sweet angel.*"

"What memory?" I pant, invisible hair ice tickling my spine with the suspicion, with the fear...

"*You know which one. The one where your heart was darkest, sweet star.*" The shades rear, forming the image of a foreboding, robed vampire, mouth open, fangs prepared to pierce the moment I agree.

My heart falters. All the trauma serpents around it deepen,

squeezing. This is my trauma. **Mine**. Admonishing tears encroach into my ducts, but I try in vain to dam them, knowing I can't possibly plug those channels.

"*I feel it,* Elysia," he sighs my name as if savoring the emotion, the depth of its gravity. "*So lovely, dark, and deep. The night you wrestled with me! Oh, how I hunted you that night...*"

The dam breaks. No, it shatters. I hang my head, press it to his Tower door, and murmur a breath prayer. Far more of a sigh of a futile prayer because I've dealt with Destruction. And now, I will deal with Death. Goddess forgive me, I cannot allow another corpse to plague that canyon. Not while this Halo still chooses me as its fallen angel can I ever hope to forsake this calling. Come hell and high water...or Death and Destruction.

At what cost indeed! Thanatos' will have the deepest and most sacred part of me where no others have. Not my mother. Not Verena. Not...Neo.

"*I long to behold it from your eyes, sweet Elysia. Show me your greatest darkness, and I will show you the way!*"

I turn. I kneel. I kneel before the Prince of Death. His shades wrap around me, embalming me to preserve my form, infusing me with black ice—so familiar. Poised serpent fangs ready to strike.

Toxic, traitorous words on the tip of my tongue, I permit one tear, one single tear to roll down my cheek before I swipe at the rest. Thanatos' shade kisses that cheek but does not claim the tear. Squaring my shoulders, I screw my brows low and command, "Take it and be damned!"

Those fangs sink into my flesh, into my blood, into my soul.

At first, that trauma-born torment terrorizes the back of my neck until powerful ice bursts into my spine, lacing into my nervous system and obliterating the pain at the back of my neck.

What. The. Fuck?! Bewildered, I slam my eyes shut, finding

myself leaning into the icy quietude in my spine, understanding this...this is Death's power. Even as he claims my trauma, my pain, he's robbing me of the symptoms. As if he's inoculating me, immunizing me, *curing* me. Fucking impossible! I lick my lips, arch my back to that chill traveling to my brain stem, and cage a gasp because I can't show how much I don't ever want to live without this...serendipitous serenity.

Now, Thanatos' darkness penetrates, pierces with omniscient force. All I know is that he cuts deep—to all that is *my* lovely and dark.

"*Ahh...*" Thanatos samples. Thanatos drinks. Thanatos *savors*. And departs from my heart with one word I'd repeated in my mind throughout that longest night: *Noralice.*

Thanatos shows me the way. Another hidden path at a diagonal to my right—one I'd never have found without him. Closer and closer to the Father's Tower, closer to the Chasm, he leads me, whispering his venom, his poison the whole time.

"*So, now you must know how Destruction plays. Did you ask, little angel?*"

I lie. "No."

Naked in the dark with nothing but his smoke and shades girding me, I stretch my arms and feel along. His serpent fangs nip at my hands.

"*Centuries bound to our Triumvirate cannot be destroyed. Not by a mere horned little vampire girl. Not even by the Everblood. Destruction will always destroy for the Father! You will learn, sweet Elysia.*"

"Your brother's lusty idioms are heaven compared to your fucking monologues!"

His deep cackle reminds me of the Father before he shows me the door. "*Go and claim your pound of flesh, Princess. You have earned it. And I will grant you a boon. I will protect you!*"

"Protect me from what?" I whisper and touch the doorknob, turning it, and slowly opening…

To the Fallen!

In the inner Father's chamber, they surround a treasure trove of innocent girls. Only two young women and the rest are *girls*! Nine in all. Some are hardly more than children! Most shake, huddled so close to each other. Some passed out from fear of the macabre, wizened monsters with their three-foot long black claws of sinister needles. The Fallen slowly twist their fire-ridden eyes upon me, fresh blood like scarlet rivers falling to their heartless chest cavities and shrunken ribcages.

My Halo heart burns. Its energy glides across my skin in flaming embers.

The Fallen shift their heads to my presence.

One brave little girl dares to lift her eyes and open her mouth. "Are you an angel?" She prays.

My Halo blazes!

"I don't need your protection!" I scream to Death.

And cast out the demon Prince with one shockwave burst of light that shakes me down to my core. Slamming my hands to my chest, I withdraw several whips, and strike the Fallen eyes deep into their damned souls. Every last one writhes before me. With thousands of golden prisms purling in my chest, I grow my Halo-light. Beaming incandescent, it coruscates until the room transforms into one glowing orb.

Waking, the girls stand, clasping each other's hands. And with starlight shafts radiating from every strand of my hair, every pore of my skin, every opening of my body, I chant my light, I chant my sacred, I chant my heart: *Noralice!*

Gasping with the Halo still scintillating stardust upon my skin, I stare at the floor where the Fallen have…fallen! Nothing but cadaverous twigs and a tiny pool of red blood. Hope flutters in my chest but remembering not to drop my guard, I swallow back-to-back gulps and turn my eyes to the girls.

"Come with me now, princesses!" I command the quaking girls in the voice of my foremothers. "It's time to go home," I repeat the words I've said to all the children I've smuggled.

They flock to me.

This will take time. Only one at a time. Tonight, the Halo will project my inherited phasing ability. A common vampire power. It humbles me to know I could not do this without Nita. Coupled with her tether, we are a force to be reckoned with.

I touch the one closest to me and pray to the Goddess for a nine-fold blessing. *May the Mother shine her favor!* No time to waste, I hone the emotions into a powerful weapon. Righteous wrath. Injustice. *Empathy.* Unlike me, these girls will fly!

As soon as I feel the tug of that tether like a jolt to my nerve endings, I phase the first girl. She disappears, relocated to Jesula at the lookout point where Neo first escorted me in the coach. Nita maintains her mental tether upon me, reassuring me the girl made it. It takes the breath right out of me! But I don't stop. I don't stop for anything. Not even to pray over their souls.

By the time I reach the sixth, I can barely breathe. A thick sheen of gold liquid bathes my brow. Still, their soul eyes look to me for hope, and I touch the sixth one's head, sparking the Halo, surging it, shaping it to a keen edge. A grace of fury...of sin and suffering. She phases, joining her friends. Crashing to my knees, I replay Nita's earlier message in my head:

"Once *he catches you, Elysia, nothing will be able to save you.*"

Once.

And this is why. I send the seventh girl away. My throat constricts, my lungs tighten from the effort it takes to flare my Halo. I've saved the littlest ones for last. The smallest are the simplest. I can't stop now.

That deathly shade prowls into my mind, *"He is coming, sweet Everblood!"*

My heartbeat is like a thousand war-hammers punishing my inferior eardrums. Taking one deep, avenging angel breath, I transport the eighth child to the Underground. One more.

But history repeats itself. No, *my* history!

A strong hand grips my wrist before I touch the last child. Tears blot my vision. But I don't need my vision clear to know it's the Father.

I unleash one savage scream before passing out in my antithesis' arms.

28

I WILL LEAVE THE COURT O' TENS. I WILL NEVER RETURN

When I jerk awake, I'm still in the Father's inner chamber... lying on his bed. His hands on my chest! The ultimate Creator. Other than Nita and my mother, he can wake me. All my muscles tense. Veins strain against my skin.

"Welcome back to the land of the dead, *Elysia Rose*," he greets me, knuckles slowly skimming down my cheek. I lean away, contempt tightening my chest. "To think my son baited me with the Everblood, but all this time, it was Reyna's spoiled little girl come to try and liberate her weak mother! And any other human chattel she could. I should have known my son would have captured you when he left your city to hunt you down. He always captures his prey."

No, he still can't recognize me. But I don't have time for relief to flood my chest from his belief that I am merely a hybrid Princess.

I spin my head, searching for the girl; she huddles in the corner of the room just as I'd huddled inside the blankets this morning. Always one. I couldn't save one. I forbid my heart from sinking low, trade any grief, any torment for the purity of wrath.

"Oh, he will join us soon." The Father misconstrues my gestures as looking for Neo and leans in to murmur in my ear, "Little wonder he's been *savoring* you."

Exhausted, belly already roiling with nausea, no better than cornered prey, I lash out with my tongue, "Get the fuck away from me!" I shove hard on him, but the Father wrenches my hands and binds them with thick chains, fastens them to his iron bed, and hovers low over me. My heart staggers, chest caving in. "Like your mother, I will break your spirit."

"No!" I scream. Gold tears sting the corners of my eyes as my darkest memory threatens to drag me under again.

Thanatos hums along in my mind. *Pretty, pretty Princess. I shall protect you.*

And then, shades...lovely, dark, and deep and *not* vaporous form a protective net around me. I almost pass out again when Neo shadows into the inner chamber, appearing on the other side of the bed, marking his Father and his position over me.

"Father...you have no claim over her yet," Neo states in a deep and foreboding voice while studying me, eyes of velvet-wrapped silver flame. I close my eyes, my head downcast before him. *Yet.*

"She stole from me!" the Father screams like a petulant child and opens his mouth, fangs gleaming while scrutinizing my neck for a blood feast.

Neo's shadows eclipse my throat. "My *bride*," echoes Neo, approaching the bedside, hooded eyes caped in unfathomable shadows.

The Father growls and rises—bound by some blood law writ into his very cell matter. His pupils dilate to demonic hellish flames when he announces, chilling me to my Halo core. "Out of all brides, why this one? Not just once bitten. She is *one hundred-bitten*, beyond shy. I can see her marks, son."

No, no, no! My scream flagellates my throat but can't find the release of air.

"*Mine!*" Neo echoes.

"Very well! This little Princess wishes to dance with Destruction? Let's show her what he can do!"

Dismounting from the bed, the Father turns and approaches the little girl tucked into the corner of the room, facing the wall, praying she can become part of it. Pain and panic engulf my body in tremors as her screams fill the air, her little legs kicking.

"Leave her alone!" I scream, clenching my muscles, struggling against the chains, thrashing my weakened body, battling with all my soul's strength. Neo's shades attempt to soothe me, but I won't let them!

The Father chucks the girl to the floor at the Prince's feet as if she's no more than a rag doll. "Destroy her, son. Show your bride what happens to those who try to run from the Court O' Tens."

Neo steps toward the child.

NO!

I don't just ask, seek, and knock. I use my Halo and shatter the damned door to our bond and unleash my holy wrath. I go deeper than ever. So deep, I'm standing before a canyon under a dusky sky. Neo's innermost core. Like a spirit room. On the opposite side is a fortress with a drawbridge—a raised drawbridge. The fortress of Neo's mind. I must scream to make my voice heard beyond that canyon.

NEO! I scream.

I show him Ezer inside our bond. My warrioress of light. Naked before him and robed in nothing but my Halo, I approach the edge of the canyon—a yawning pitch black gap between us. My hands weaponless. My mind stripped before the Prince of Destruction.

Your name means "new warrior". But I call you Neo. Because you are a new *creation! You are* my *husband. Just as Nita became new. Rebirthed. Please, Neo, do not destroy the child. If there is anyone you must destroy, let it be me. Destroy me!*

A still quietude. The fortress is a tomb. Not so much as a shiver shakes that drawbridge. Desolate, I arch my neck when Thanatos' voice hunts my mind.

Destruction will always *destroy for Father.*

The Father grips my jaw and head and forces me to focus on Neoptolemus who becomes nothing more than a dim shade behind the film of my tears...

My mask, is all he says before the Dragon Prince of Destruction touches the girl. And...reduces her to ash as he did my father.

I scream, I scream, I scream!

○

He carries my quivering form to his bed. No longer our bed. It will *never* be our bed.

Not even little Spitfire can help me crawl out of my shell tonight—the lair of my mind, of my heart, of my soul. Back-to-back anxiety attacks shudder my body. Tonight, my empath doesn't simply unite with me: she's eclipsed me. Instead, I've crawled into her cage—crushed under the weight of my grief.

Spitfire nudges my chest. He seeks my Haloed sparks, flickers of flames, but I have none to give. Nothing but numbing ash on my skin from remembering my homeland in embers. Nothing but the little pile of soul dust on the floor of the Father's room where the girl once stood. A little light snuffed out.

Tonight, I wade deep in the memory of Noralice—her darkness consuming me for the first time in years. She makes it her bed. Last time, my heart damn-near broke, but I'd managed to transform the pain into armor. Shattered armor now. If I stay, I won't survive this time.

Neoptolemus tries to stroke my hair, but I recoil, curling into the fetal position, whimpering. Refusing to come out. Not even his shades seek me. All this time, it was a game. Thanatos was right. I tuck my chin low to my chest, feeling colder. Buried under layers of thundering snow from the grief numbing my blood.

Sweet, little angel. I will protect you from Destruction. Simply grant me your blood! I'll ask for nothing more than a drop.

No, I moan inside my mind because I'll never court Death again. I already gave him too much. And lost so much more.

He plays his games, but he will destroy you, love. Run and hide, little Elysia!

Get out of my head! I cry and somehow muster the vulnerability to add...*Please.*

Nothing but silence. When I open my eyes, all that greets me is Neoptolemus' suite with its pirouetting shades of dark fog that still creep so lovely, dark, and deep. But there is nothing lovely about the Prince of Destruction. It was all a dream. He uses Amanita as nothing more than an excuse, some balm to soothe the sins of his black soul.

What will the Father do now? Will he go to my mother and tell her how her precious Princess resides in his Court O' Tens? I can't, I *won't* let him use me as a pawn against her.

Spitfire pounces on me from behind, hot tongue scratch-licking at my cheek as if goading me for flames. He's at least twice his size now. I remember when he arrived...from the door.

"You climbed the Tower, didn't you?" I wonder to the hellcat, scratching his ears while licking my lips.

It's not the first time I will have escaped his prison. All I know is I can't stay here or sleep in his bed anymore. Tonight, I will break the damned blood oath.

I will leave the Court O' Tens. I will *never* return.

I dare to open the bone door. I dare to step onto the walkway to face that dark expanse with its ever-streaming ash, wildfires, and deep booming thunder. Chasm voices haunt me, mocking me with my past sins, with my failures. I'll never stop running from them.

Nothing but an open expanse on each side, I remain close to the Tower foundation and ease one naked foot onto an iron gargoyle, identifying a firm groove. This high, sharp gusts of wind flog my back, but I grip onto the spire-like architecture. And descend.

My Halo flickers—a spark. Pursing my lips, I do not accept it yet because I couldn't save her. My mother could have. My mother could have saved them all. The Goddess was wrong. She chose the wrong Rose.

Millions of souls wail for salvation, vying with the growls of Chasm monsters, prickling my spine like thorns. I can't give them salvation. I can't save anyone because I'm not a savior. And I wasn't strong enough to be the warrior the Goddess needs.

Descending, I grasp more handholds from buttresses to gargoyles to arched windows. My nails crack and bleed, skin chafes. On more than one occasion, I have to pause on a landing to catch my breath.

I lose my footing, sliding with a shriek before my hand clamps onto an iron rung protruding from the Tower, suspended thousands of feet in the air. Sharp iron rips my chemise, draws my blood. Tonight, I will suffer and bleed with the lost souls and their spine-chilling wails.

All my muscles ache. I tremble, arms shaking, ready to let go. Again, my Halo sparks, and I accept, forming a rope. It still takes me an hour to climb down from this height, but I finally arrive at the ground, bending at my knees. Now, Neo's Tower is a dark shadow scar of my past. Another to add to my hundred-bitten collection.

I was a damned fool to believe I could court Destruction!

So, I run. With tears hot as acid on my cheeks, I run from him, from the Father, from Nita, from Quillion, from the entire damned Court O' Tens! My muscles *weep*. Everything feels like death and murder. Sin and *suffering*. Instead of cursing my human limbs, I bless them. Because I am still alive. I've survived. And I will free my mother another way.

When I stumble and crash to the ground, a splitting pain racks my side. Groaning, I get to my knees, prepared to launch into a run again and head for the Underground.

Until multiple foreign growls echo behind me.

When I turn, my adrenaline nosedives while all my nerves shatter from defeat. There's no point in running now. No flight left. I hang my head, remembering what the Court O' Sixes bishop had said: more Chasm monsters every day.

I sink to my knees before a full pack of the mighty hounds of hell!

Skeletal faces of bone armor as hard as vampires. Horns corkscrew at least two feet into the air. Mouths open to betray canine teeth and incisors as long as talons. Sniffing, they approach, scenting my pure blood. Their thick, massive bodies must be at least five times my size. There's no point in fighting. Due punishment for my failure. I was not strong enough to conquer Destruction, and I made a deal with Death. Tonight, they have come to devour me and drag me right into the Chasm. A fitting fate.

May I feel it one more time? I plead to the Goddess, chest expanding, heart daring to hope.

The hounds crouch, collective.

One Halo flicker. One tiny orb I cup in my hands like a precious, twinkling soul. "Forgive me..." I breathe the prayer.

Then heave the longest and last breath I'll ever take.

The hounds charge.

Clothed in destructive flames and robed in shadows, invincible wings unleashed, *he* appears, smashing into three charging hell hounds. My heart melts as he positions himself before me. Like a *shield*!

My warrior. *My* Warhammer.

I gasp before the Prince of Destruction who sets his teeth, targets the hell hounds with dilated pupils, and growls, "*Mine!*"

Not once does he turn his gaze to mine. Eyes pinned on the hellhounds. One split-second. Then, all the bones in his body shift until he is on all fours, muscles expanding and swarming. I flinch, I shrink, I claw at my throat, at my arms, at my chest—eyes rocketing wide. Unblinking, shell-shocked, I watch every speck of flesh thickening to an armor of black diamonded scales—*oh, Saints*! Claws as long as his keen bone daggers. And horns. Glorious horns of constellations-arrayed night—as long and beautiful as twisted bone scythes! Omnipotent silver and black wings thrusting out and spreading until all of him is a Warhammer of a Dragon—a *real* Dragon—beating his wings into a mighty whirlwind around me.

The Dragon Prince of Destruction! Not just a title. Not just an urban myth. The *last* Dragon.

On my knees, I behold him, his eyes as steadfast as a silver sea as they glimpse at me, only to transform to flames when facing the hell hounds.

His growl is so thunderous, it rocks me to the ground, and I roll and roll out of the way while he addresses the hounds which I hear through the bond:

Give Cerberus my best!

They attack!

Neo roars a conflagration that instantly destroys two hounds and singes my skin from my position behind him. My heart lurches when the pack closes in as one body and strikes. Their armored, flaming jaws target his diamond hide, teeth tunneling. My Prince, my Neo, my *husband* swipes multiple with his scythe-like talons to prevent them from even getting close to me. His Dragon mouth rips into one, smothering the hound's bay. Like it's nothing more than roadkill, he flings the creature from side to side and spews flaming blood. Embers land on my head. I hold my arms around my chest, hold myself together. All my nerve endings scream, my every thought willing him on. He throws the beast so far, it must land right in the Chasm.

Still, more descend, and I wince and clamp my hands over my mouth as the rest of the pack targets Neo's wings, taking away his ability to fly. My pulse thunders faster than the speed of light as Neo stabs his horns, impaling one. But the remaining pack members mount him—teeth hacking at the diamond armor of his chest and goring into his heart.

Neo stumbles, spewing fire.

No! My lungs slam together. Tremors rupture through my body, but I don't dare scream.

Roaring, he snaps his jaws on one hound. Even as the rest deal him pain, he sinks his teeth into the other's throat, growling at the remaining three atop him. Neo falls while the hounds of death continue tearing at his flesh where they've stripped his armor. Mouths feasting on his carnage, the hounds torment him while he digs his talons into the ground, struggling.

I vow to be your shield. I vow to save you from danger. I remember my Ezer.

So, I rise!

Somehow, I embrace a raw surge of adrenaline and unleash the full force of my Halo in mighty flames of retributive light to skewer the hounds, stop their mouths, silence their growls, and shatter them into nothing more than blinding ash!

Lightning jolts me to movement. I hurl my body forward and fall onto my bleeding Dragon Prince, my hand centering the circle brand upon his chest. His silver blood floods the ground all around me.

He doesn't move. Breathing shallow, growing longer and slower.

When I move my hand one centimeter down, something like flaming jewels scalds me, and I shriek. But instead of wrenching away, I sink my hands through the blood, through the shredded muscle intensifying heat until my fingers freeze as I unearth...*stone.*

Holy foremothers! I discover the altar. It's the Father-fucking *Altar*!

Hidden. The Prince can tell you. What the Father looks upon first when he returns to Court. His greatest fear...

One layer beneath his diamond armor, the Altar is writ—inscribed into the Dragon's very chest all around his frozen heart! Yes, frozen. Stone that does not beat. No wonder my stake had no effect.

I cast Halo heat along the remainder of his armor, melting and peeling it away until I behold every glorious chunk of it. Its prophecy unites to my Halo, forming an indissoluble bond that transcribes itself upon my mind so I may access it whenever I please. What I sought all this time...

"Neo," I whisper in the darkness as my Halo wanes to a budding flicker.

His breath is heavy, strained...fading. No. Please! Horror thickens in my chest. For one moment, one single moment, I flick my eyes behind me. Because I owe him nothing after all he has done. Because I could break my vow and walk away from him with the Altar sealed onto my heart and my mission like a glorious sunrise.

But I would *never* forgive myself!

And I will *not* break my vow.

So, I mount him, fold my hands across my chest, and *I pray*. Then, I shift until I'm face to face with my mark. In the lightest of touches, I brush my lips across the Halo-brand. I give him the healing kiss of my heart. I plead, I petition the foremothers that it doesn't break the Goddess' warning...or our blood oath.

Gazing at his beautiful face, at the black diamond scales and the almighty horns, I proclaim the truth upon my Dragon warrior, "You are a new creation. You are *my* husband. Mine! My *new*!"

It doesn't seem possible, but my Halo strengthens as if it senses my bridal oath wrought with righteous fire into my very soul. Pure Halo beams—my final *Scheherazade* crescendo—surge in golden waves like rays of blinding sunlight. They strike Neo's chest and pierce deep to his core, triggering and jumpstarting and renewing what was frozen and granting him my healing light to restore all his muscle, sinew, flesh, and armored scales.

Halo spent, all my energy snuffed, my chest turns dim and cold, though the Halo undercurrent lingers. My pulse slows from exhaustion. But I feel *everything*.

Neo's dragon body collapses in on itself, leaving nothing

but a nude Prince underneath me. And Princess. My chemise is no more. Burnt to cinders. All my flesh hums, thrumming with the tingling aftermath of my Halo as if thousands of twinkling butterflies flutter their wings one layer below my skin.

Somehow, I find my breath but do not open my eyes. First, I sense. I *touch*.

Beneath my hands...a murmur. No, a beat! For the first time in his birth, no, his *rebirth*, the Prince of Destruction bears a beating heart! One created by my hand, by *my* Halo.

He breathes. I open my eyes to find the silver mist of his. Oh, Saints, my heartbeat stumbles, skipping multiple beats.

Neo gazes at me and grins, touching my face before his eyes drift downward in a cursory once-over. And then, his lips pull into a pretentious grin, and he asks, "Is it my birthday?"

"Neo!" I gasp right before my adrenaline crashes.

I pass out into his arms.

29
"YOU CAN RIDE ME WHENEVER YOU DESIRE, MY LOVE."

I WAKE TO NEO ON HIS KNEES BEFORE ME.

Head bowed to the ground—one arm anchored on his chest. All his shades and flames twist whorls around his nude body, shrouding his privates. Still as a statue as if he's been there all night watching me as I slept.

Spitfire is curled on the bed behind me, basking in the subconscious glow of my Halo, looking pretty sated. My hand scrambles to my chest, and I breathe relief through my nostrils because it's warm, kindled. And stardust slowly drifts along my arms.

Thank you, I whisper to the Halo because it hasn't abandoned me. It healed Neo. *I* healed Neo. I may be a vessel, but it was still my choice.

The Halo responds by offering me a shower of gold hearts to crown my head and gush down the sides of my face. I giggle, shaking glitter from my curls to tumble onto the bed. Then, I bite my lower lip and flick my eyes to my Dragon Prince.

"Neo?" I breathe, rising so the bejeweled coverlet falls to reveal another chemise clothing my body. My flesh bereft of any blood or injuries from last night. He used his shades to heal me again, to dress me. That was...sweet.

He does not lift his head, but when I narrow my eyes to discern how his palm weighs hard on his chest, I understand. Has the Prince of Destruction ever felt a heartbeat?

No, not in nearly a century, he responds, puzzling me. *And never like this.*

Easing out of the bed, I lower myself to the floor to mirror him, but Neo reaches out with his other arm, halting me before I can. He wags his finger, and I smile softly at our "higher than you" secret. Neo raises his head. Oh, Saints! Silent tears like black diamonds fall on his cheeks.

His voice doesn't even crack when he proclaims, "All my heart is yours, Elysia Rose."

Still, I slide down, curl inside his lap, and urge my hands toward his. He eases aside his palm, permitting mine to slip under so I may touch the steady beat. It's slower, humming with silver blood. A re-born vampire heart.

And every last speck of it is, *"Mine,"* I claim, heat radiating through my body and especially between my thighs as I curve my fingertips onto the circled brand.

My eyes lose themselves in his. Neo straightens, raising his head to capture my brow with his mouth in an intimate kiss. Closing my eyes, I lean into his kiss and the next one he presses to my cheek and the other to my neck, his supple lips like frosted velvet upon my skin. Fresh Halo light laces around his neck, urging him closer as my body responds more than ever, as my thigh muscles clench with desire.

Ask him, Thanatos' voice haunts me.

I tense, pulling away because whatever else has happened between us, I can't forget how he destroyed that innocent, little girl. I can't forget the Bridal Canyon, how I was neck-deep in corpses. Even if he can't defy the Father, I can't forget how Neo is still Neoptolemus, the Prince of Destruction.

As if sensing my inner battle, he eases away and looks down, nodding. "Yes, Elysia, you brought me to my knees. I promised to tell you, and I will. Tonight, I am surrendering my mask to you. Do with it what you will."

Rooted where I am with my legs curved in his lap, his flaming shades caping his lower regions, and his stalwart thighs bearing my weight, I tip my head against his shoulder. And listen. Cobwebs of shades billow around us, restricting my vision, silencing everything else. At the backdoor of my mind, his force stabs me. A painful nest of memories pierces my mind, shaking our very bond as he reveals the past.

Within the shades of Neo's memory, the Father roars upon emerging from the dungeon, Nita's dungeon, and arriving to greet his prized son. His only son now.

"That fucking little succubus still refuses to bow! Willful, stubborn teenager."

Silent, Neo regards his Father. How deeply Thanatos' death affected him. How enraged he was that he could not take his immediate revenge, but Reyna's offer tempted him beyond refusal. Other than destroying the Everblood, the opportunity to remake the world was always Father's ultimate goal.

Now, their unsurpassed Court O' Nines with the Tenth Court of Tri-Mega-Towers is the fulfillment of that dream. A meaningless dream without Thanatos...for both of them. Because the Triumvirate is broken.

"How many demons have you sent to torment her?" Neo *wonders, considering the Creator byproduct of his Father's nationwide razing of a thousand women.*

Ever since the Father had learned he was cursed to never recognize the Everblood, his one true destruction, nor could he fathom her powers, he'd embarked on a trial by fire of chronic rape. He required a strong surrogate to birth a new child. Determined to bring another son into the world to fulfill the Triumvirate so they could stand as an unbreakable cord to Father's future bane.

Only one woman had carried a babe long enough to birth her.

A *daughter, not a son.*

"I lost count after she destroyed number 9,076. I have but one last resort."

After years of failures of corpses dumped into the Canyon beyond their Iron Walls, Father finally had another child. And a Creator. Neo had confirmed her power when she was a toddler, though Nita's greatest power was the territory of souls...like Thanatos. Father charged Neo with her training, hoping to hone her into the powerful weapon of Death that he'd lost.

But *Nita enjoyed* playing *more than anything.*

And playing most with the souls who were left behind because Neo didn't even know they haunted him until Nita arrived.

Neo tugs on an invisible shadow tether, unraveling it so it multiplies and feeds me wondrous images of brother and sister! I grin, I gush at the sight of Nita's younger self as she frolics behind Neo, shifting her hips from side to side, bumping into him a few times. Curious...she doesn't have horns in these memories.

Neo sweeps his hand to the battlefield, urging his fifteen-year-old sister, "Training, Nita."

"Her name was..." Nita muses, twirling the soul on the tip of her finger, making the glowing wisp visible for her brother as she concludes, "Kitty. I like her. She was feisty. Oh!" pouts Nita, caressing the shimmering orb to her chest. "You destroyed her, brother."

"We have to resume your training."

Ignoring him, Nita tilts her head and collects Kitty's vitality, her essence, and her memories. "Why did you destroy her? She was so much fun!"

Neo sighs, dragging a hand through his silver hair. "I haven't taken a bride since Thanatos' death, Nita. There's a reason for that." He considers his frozen heart, his only peace along with this little vampiress coquette who has become his shadow.

"I know, silly dragon. But still..."

"Kitty was sweet and flirty and very childish. I didn't mind her flirting with my subjects everywhere we went or even her pranks. I treated her well as I treated all others. But as soon as Father was on the receiving end of one of those pranks and learned about her flirting, he ordered me to destroy her. Now...back to training." He winces, not wanting to delve deeper into the memories of his brides and how his Father commanded him to destroy every last one. How he was powerless to do anything but fulfill the order according to their blood laws.

Nita blows away the wisp, but she won't truly leave the Tenth Court, and Neo knows she will add her to her personal collection. He would rather not consider the hundreds of brides in his centuries' long history and how his little sister has captured so many of those souls, how much she plays with them as much as she plays with him.

"Nita!" Neo yells, spine tightening following her drowning his flames for the hundredth time.

"Gotcha!" Nita parades a proud and savage child's grin before leaping onto Neo's shoulders, legs coiling around his neck, pretending he's her personal throne.

"You must take your training seriously!"

"You're too serious, Neo."

"Do not call me that, Amanita." The Prince pushes his little sister off his back, and she double flips and lands into a crouch of flawless precision and grace, her wintry hair whipping like a cathedral bell.

Neo chooses a different tactic. Father expects a Princess of Death. If Nita cannot mold herself into that role, then Father will determine another use for her. The second potentiality shouldn't cause the Prince of Destruction to shudder, but it does. Time is running out. He's spent years on the training fields with Nita, but whether turning scythes into flowers or his shades and flames into fireflies and fairies, Neo fears the worst: Nita cannot be Death.

Another memory, and my smile from my sister-in-law's past only grows.

Nita faces the portal, cocking her head to the side. "Curious..." she muses, planting a hand to the cold wall. It bites her. "Naughty, big brother," she scolds the Death spirit while Neo observes behind her. Nita turns to Neo, jerking a finger to the wall. "He wants you, Neo."

Neo shakes his head. He will never darken the doors of that portal again. The day they lost Thanatos was the day Neo's heart stopped beating. For the first time in all his miserable centuries, Neo did not feel his Death. His Destruction memories didn't plague him anymore. No battle smoke. No clashing of shields. No cannon fire to haunt his dreams. No shattering of armor.

But neither was his heart dead. It was merely frozen.

For years, he'd tried to jumpstart it from partaking in pleasures of blood and flesh to acting as Father's personal executioner. No, the only time he felt anything was with...Nita. All he'd felt with Thanatos was the omen of Death. Neo knew Father prized his eldest son. Over the years, he'd worked like hell to surpass his twin's shadow. But to no avail...until Reyna killed Thanatos.

Then, he became invaluable.

Nita must become invaluable, too.

"Go," Neo urges her to enter the portal. "Learn from Death. He will teach you." His eyes crease in concern, but he tries hard not to show it.

Nita cups her brother's cheek, reassuring him, "He has never met this saucy wench!"

Neo remains on the other side for one full hour, pacing, apprehension gnawing on him. Until Nita emerges. No, until Death practically vomits her out of the portal, shades sealing it shut behind him.

Neo's eyes bulge as Nita barrels toward the portal, smashing against it. "What?" He questions, stunned.

"Come back here, you coward and face me like the damn Reaper you claim to be!" She shakes her fist at the wall, then positions her fingers, curling and ready to destroy it if necessary. "Can't handle a little soul battle, can you?"

Shaking his head—incredulous at the spitfire teenager before him—Neo hauls Nita into his arms, hurling his sister over his shoulder while she protests.

"Prince of Death indeed!" she scoffs with Neo carting her out of the suite. "He's the Prince of Pathetic Pep Talks! How did he kill people?" She tumbles her head over and jabs Neo's side. "Talked their heads right off?"

Laughing, Neo puts Nita on the floor outside his shadow door. Still, his shades curl around her, longing for her presence. A byproduct of his subconscious. He smiles while his little sister kneels to play with his shades. It's the first time he's felt anything remotely resembling warmth in his frozen heart.

Neo considers the little girl swinging her hips from side to side. His thoughts war with one another. Since her toddling years, this girl has trailed him around the Tenth Court, capturing the ghost souls of his brides and carrying their flying wisps like a bouquet of balloons. This little girl who plays hide and seek in the mega-tower so he must search for her for a solid week at times.

Nita is Neo's ultimate shadow. The echo of his soul.

Tasked by the Father to study her older brother, Nita has watched him carry out Father's raids and executions. Duties as the Prince of Destruction. She's never cowered or run. The only one who does not fear his Destruction. No, Nita's admiration for Neo has only grown. He's hoped all that time and study would have penetrated, especially considering how much she loves Neo unleashing his

Dragon. Nothing but loathing for the Father and his Court proceedings, but Neo...

"Neo!" Nita summons him later on the training field, dancing into his inner circle. "Carry me today!"

"Nita..." Neo puffs out a groan, hinting of his predictable capitulation. He's never managed to deny her.

Nita clasps her hands at her chest, beseeching with liquid mirror eyes—carbon copies of his. Something she'd gifted herself with her unlimited power along with the silver waves, mimicking her big brother from an early age, though she'd inherited her exquisite, sculpted features from their Father and dark skin from her mother.

"I'll give you a piece of treasure for your hoard," she teases, hinting about the black diamonds she will create for him.

Neo sighs, throwing down his scythes and driving out his horns. Immediately, Nita grips those twisting black horns and uses them as leverage to haul herself onto his back. Leaning low to her brother's ear, Nita urges him, "Onward!"

Not one of Neo's brides has ever ridden his Dragon. Unable to ever refuse Nita, Neo shifts his form into the Dragon so she may ride...

Neo's face falls, his back muscles clenching, jaw hardening. I don't tear my eyes from his, cheek nestled into his strong shoulder. Bating my breath, I palm his chest, fingers trained on the brand. One violent shudder, and he welcomes me into the darkest memory of his life.

Neo *is Father's last resort.*

Father leads him to the dungeon where the stubborn sixteen-year-old swims in the Soul Lake. Countless spirits flock around her as if she is their shepherdess, their salvation. Neo cocks his head, admiring his little sister's fortitude. Nothing but smiles for Neo as always. Whatever Father did to her, she healed herself relatively quickly. And due to all her hundreds of battles, she has claimed her own horns, grown them from her soul-victories.

"Ready for a rematch, Father?" Nita taunts him. "After all, you must be so proud of yourself since it takes no skill involved to best me when my powers cannot touch you. Send me any demon or weapon you desire. I'm ready. Neo can stand there, look all dark and sexy, and watch the show!"

Sinister, Father grins and examines his son out of the corner of his eye. "She believes you are here as a viewer, Neo. Let us redefine your role for her."

It's the first time in all his years of knowing her that Nita's eyes fly wide open. Death could not terrify her. Only Destruction.

Father preys his eyes on his daughter and with his brows threading low and dangerous, he commands his son, "Destroy her until she bows."

Neo regards Nita, hands dropping to his sides in surrender because he cannot refuse his Father's direct command. His entire body responds from the blood-summoning force—irresistible, omniscient, a commanding abomination. He winces when Nita shrinks, his mind staggering from the punishing weight of this.

"Neo! No..." Nita's voice cracks, fear fissuring into her whole body.

Neo removes his robe.

It's the first and only time he prays for forgiveness from heaven, wishing an angel would fly in and save him from this hell. Or at the very least...smite him where he stands. With no power to do anything but surrender to Father, Neo thrusts out his horns, spreads his wings, and becomes diamond armor, talons and claws, hot belly, and throat roaring fire.

Though Nita dives under the water, it takes Neo but one crouch. He sinks to pluck the vampire from the lake, claws trenching into her back, and battering her body against the dungeon sides, breaking bones. Nita screams. To Neo, it's a lethal scythe piercing deep right through his armor. With their Father cackling in the background, Neo brands his sister with his searing flames. She tears at her hair, the hair she grew from childhood—the same luster and shape of his—her screams wild and ravenous.

Several bones broken, Nita curls on the ledge where she's landed. Neo hovers, wings beating violent wind around her. His bond with his Father is a towering force inside him, pressuring him to continue. But Neo pauses when Nita shakes...and cries! He's never seen Nita cry. Father has trapped her here for months, launching thousands of Chasm monsters to inflict pain on her. Whole gangs of them. A few broken bones would never cause Nita to give in.

Puffing, Neo lowers his voice to a bass rumble, "Nita?"

She shakes her head, curling more. Soaked silver strands eclipse much of her dark face, but he can make out thick, delicate eyelashes. When she opens her mouth to utter, "Please don't hurt us."

That is absolutely not Nita.

Her body shifts, transforms into something more befitting of a tigress. On all fours, with her bones healing from her supreme Creator power, the little vampiress raises one hand, curling it into a paw-like state with a rippling "meow".

"Sexy beast dragon," she proclaims, swinging her hips from side to side. "You wouldn't destroy us before we've had a threesome, would you?" She proceeds to curl her hands to her face in a pout.

Neo huffs at the foreign voice invading his little sister's. Foreign and familiar. A ghost from his past. Now, he knows why Father could not break her spirit. No demons could triumph against her. Only Neo. But something deep within Nita still loves him. Despite his outrageous attack, despite him placating their Father, Nita will not fight him. She'd rather shatter her own soul than fight back.

Since her childhood, she's collected those bride souls. Now, they have bound to the broken pieces of her soul, protecting her.

The knowledge spears Neo deep to his bone. No deeper. It penetrates past that Altar and cracks his stone heart. A hairline, threadbare crack. But it's enough.

Neo transforms into his Princely self, clothed in shades, to face the new entity.

"Kitty," Neo determines, recognizing the soul. No, only the echo of her soul. A different version, an altered version—a new creation extension of Nita. Kitty was simply her inspiration.

Kitty kisses the air, eyes raking over his Prince form. "Care to see more? They would all *love to meet you,* Neo. *Even the beastly ones."*

Neo raises his brows, understanding...inspired by more than his brides. The monsters, too. And Nita is far more *monstrous than Neo could ever be.*

Impatient and frustrated, Father arrives to behold more of Nita's soul alters rising to the surface. The forms are far more an illusion, misty at the edges, mimicking a mirage. Father leers down at her as she reclaims all her alter identities and finally reverts to the Host.

"Hide and seek, Neo." Nita winks.

"Destroy her mind!" Father rails, the order as powerful as his dragon itself.

"You will never find me this time, brother!" She smiles as Neo approaches, balls of shadows and flames in his palms.

When she curls again as if folding in on herself, burrowing beneath all those alters, Neo chooses her. If there is one last thing he will ever do with his damned existence, he will protect Nita. All of her.

For the first time since his birth, for the first time in all his centuries, Neo stares his Father down, and challenges him, risking death itself. "What do you most desire, Father?" His jaw hardens as his Father slowly swings his head in Neo's direction.

Father's eyes dilate on his son. "Destroy her mind."

Neo winces, his veins warring, his soul sundering as he battles Father's blood supremacy. For one fleeting moment, he reflects on his sister...on all her alters. He remembers her legs around his neck, knocking him to the ground. He remembers her little shadow haunting him for years. He remembers her riding on his back and walloping cheers, spreading her arms to the night sky. The only reason his worthless existence holds any meaning is because of Nita. And now, whoever else is inside of her.

So, Neo pits his own blood against his origin, knowing he cannot ultimately dominate. But he can become a shield and offer a substitute path. He can negotiate.

"You hate the Court, Father. I will take it from you."

Father's eyes narrow...a sudden pause as he listens to his son's proposal.

"You may have all the world and the Chasm instead," offers Neo, his eyes of silver lower thrones, tempting his very blood and seed.

"For the price of—"

"Nita," Neo contracts, tilting his head, eyes and muscles primed and steeled. "From this moment on, no harm will befall her from your hand or any other you may send."

"I want your brides and harem, too." Father sneers.

"I haven't taken any brides since Thanatos, Father. Nor harem."

"You will now. In fact, we will raise the stakes to a harem show because I'll enjoy watching you when I'm off in my playground. We will call it the "Harem of Hades"," Father leers at his son, twisting the blade in deeper. "You will entice brides to you and determine if any are the Everblood. If any are pure-blooded, you will give them to me once your honeymoon period is over. After you bite them of course to determine if they are such. And once I'm finished with them, if they're still alive, you will destroy them. Your Bridal Path as it were."

"For the price of Nita, I agree," Neo capitulates.

"And I may lay claim to any in your harem any time I choose."

"Give me Nita!!!" demands Neo with a growl.

"Take the little babe, damn you!"

Yes, damn him. Neo would damn his very soul if it meant Nita would live. He and Father forge a new blood oath. Father and son bond, it will never be reversed unless...the Everblood. If such a girl exists. For now, he will keep Nita from Court. As long as it will keep her safe, Neo will hide her from his damned self.

And pray the Everblood exists.

The visions fade, and Neo wrenches me to reality until I'm staring dead on into his silver mist eyes with him uttering, "Now, you know."

Shifting my weight, I ease my leg around his waist, do the same with the other until I'm straddling him. Controlling the flush from my naked nether regions, I coil my arms around his neck and press my forehead to his. "You did it for her. You did it *all* for her."

Neo nods.

"And the Bridal Canyon..."

"Father doesn't always reap them. But when he does, I destroy their minds, so they feel nothing but joy," Neo confesses, lowering his head to my bare shoulder, lips rubbing its curve, then the chemise strap. Tingles feather all over my skin. "It was the least of boons I could offer. And I've always imparted the swiftest death without fully destroying their forms."

I breathe a steady inhale and consider the girl in the Father's room. How I still blame myself for not having the strength to save the last one. It's a heavy lament, but I have a deeper, more personal weight I wish to contend with him. So, I bite my lip and hold my breath to strengthen myself when he kisses my other shoulder, mouth roaming to my throat.

"And my father?"

At first, I believe Neo won't meet my eyes, but he does. He doesn't hide his guilt. Wrapping his arms around my waist, settling his fingers low, he expresses, "I am bound by blood to obey my Father's command. He wanted me to torture him before your mother...or you. I ensured he had no pain. But forgive me for being a damn devil to you that day."

I stab a finger at his face, forcing the issue, "And the night in the Chasm."

Neo smiles and agrees, "Yes, and for imprisoning you. I never could have predicted you would come to me, to my Court. I had never met my match, and you came with such retribution and Goddess light, I feared you would destroy me as you vowed. And if you destroyed me, Elysia..."

"The Father would take Amanita." I sigh and touch my head to his shoulder, understanding and...opening my heart to forgiveness.

"I couldn't allow that to happen. Even if it meant acting like a damned bastard and scaring you. I swear it was never my intention to kill you or hurt you or *trigger* you. But I swore to Nita never to share what happened in that dungeon. And...my mind and stone heart still held traces of the demon of Destruction of my past when Thanatos was still alive. Now, I will only use Destruction to protect you. You..."

His fingers move from my waist to my front where the chemise edges expose my naked thighs. Slowly, he presses his fingers to my flesh, staining their tips with damp Halo-dust. Given how I'm straddling his lap, I'm aware of how close my center is to his naked member. How I've already felt it growing to nudge my thigh. I take one deep breath, battling the urge to arch when Neo's fingers tap dangerously close to my sex, and he finishes, "...are my future," he annunciates every word. I ooze gold.

"So..." I lean in until my forehead bumps his, pushing my lips together, eager, "can I see them?"

Neo chuckles before he stabs his Dragon horns into the air. They twist and curl from his head—frozen glittering serpents of pure obsidian. I grip those horns. "Why don't you show them all the time?"

He shrugs. "They're Nita's thing. Shades and flames and wings are mine. You'll notice she doesn't show off her wings like I do. They're beautiful but heavy. I've carried mine far longer."

Practically fondling those horns, I tease wickedly, "I am fire! I am De—" I almost lose myself but quickly make the correction, "—Destruction!"

As quickly as he unleashed them, Neo retracts them, but I pop the question, "Now that I have a pet Dragon, do I get a ride sometime?"

Snickering, Neo touches the edges where my pelvic bones meet the soft inner flesh, wets his fingers, and purrs low, "You can ride me whenever you desire, my love."

Core tightening, all my inner muscles spasm.

His vamp-shaft throbs beneath my lap, and I jerk from the brush of that monstrous member along my thigh.

"I guess I walked right into that, didn't I?"

His grin is far more wicked than mine. Neo nudges his hardness along my sex. I freeze as he rubs all the way to the tip, causing me to suck in a shrill gasp through my teeth. "Oh, you naughty Dragon. You and your big, moronic dick." I can't control my rising whimper of desire and arch my neck as he yanks away. When I peer down, I champion my inner warrioress for soaking his crown in liquid gold. My fingers curl, twitching, but I resist the urge to take him in my hand.

"You think I have a big head now, my love. You should see my Dragon's," he hints in a husky low tone, fondling my thigh flesh.

I thrust my chest to his, my breasts heavy and aching. But I hiss and somehow manage to control myself.

"We should tell Nita," I say, but the shade doors part

behind us, a rush of wind from her figure sweeping inside the room.

"No need, the Queen has arrived. Oh!" She stops in her tracks, gazing at us.

Nita's posture shifts into a familiar tigress. I beam at Kitty, who fawns over the sight of my naked husband and me—clothed in nothing but my chemise where my nipples practically stab through the fabric. "I've had so many wet dreams of this moment!"

Laughter surges out of me, and I get to my feet, casting gold dust into the air. Neo gathers his shades around him into a thick suit as tight as his armor.

"Way to go, Halo girl!" she joys and does a little pirouette, rubbing her body against my back.

Nita returns and squares her shoulders, striding further away from her brother so she can hopefully put some distance between him and her alter. "Kitty, behave."

Kitty's mist figure flees Nita's chest and springs onto the open bed and splays out, arms spreading. "So, this is where the magic happens." Flicking her head to me, she inquires, "Is he as earth shattering as everyone says he is on the *Harem of Hades* and throughout the Court O' Nines? Come on, spare no details about his Dragon dick!"

"Um, uh..." I shrug sweetly, heat raging upon my neck and flushing my cheeks.

Kitty smacks the bedframe even if her hand scatters into mist particles. "Oh, come on, seriously! You still haven't—"

"Nita..." my voice cracks into a plea. "Help!" I gulp.

Next to me, Nita postures and balls her hands into fists. "Kitty, he is *my* brother!"

"*Mine*," I solidify, brows practically doing a proud salsa while Nita turns on me with a deadly, possessive glare. Her horns themselves pierce the air close to me as if primed for my tongue.

Kitty—her mind still on sex and not hinting my claim—puts her hands on her hips and adds, "What did Nita tell you? Prostrate servant."

I smirk at Neo from the side who makes the sign of a halo, ushers to my side, and kneels before me, head falling low to the ground. Oh damn, his back is so damn...sexy.

Nita returns and wraith-shadows to us, silver harp eyes studying her brother. "What the fuck happened?" She demands, eyes flicking to me for an explanation.

I fold my hands, one on top of the other, and tuck them under my chin to gloriously announce, "I captured a Dragon."

"What?" Nita threads her brows low, gaze darting between us.

I beam at her. With gold hearts glowing beyond my chest, I squeal a little, "The Princess fell in love with the Dragon!"

"And she gave me a new heart," echoes Neo, smiling in gratitude. Once he raises his head, Nita slams her hand to his chest and glories in the miraculous beat.

I touch my fingers to my Halo brand and stake my claim again, overshadowing her, "Mine."

Nita sweeps me into her arms and embraces me so tightly, my lungs protest. She kisses the side of my head, and scarlet-swooning adoration erupts in my chest when she announces, "That's our sweet Ezer. We forever *love*, Elysia Rose."

"I guess we should tell Quillion," I wheeze.

"He's waiting in the breakfast hall. Reading as usual." Nita wrinkles her nose before Kitty adds the chuckling jab, "Flouncy old fossil."

"He'll definitely run out of room on my side of the chart for this!" I beam, tossing my curls back.

Neo suddenly snatches my waist and kisses my wrist while

cementing, "You shattered the chart, my love." Shifting his eyes to Nita, he declares, "I have somewhere I need to take my bride. Tell Quillion my apologies for missing breakfast." She nods.

Confused, I lift a brow. Where could he possibly take me now? Judging by the way Nita blinks before she imparts a soft smile while Neo gathers his robe, I assume she knows exactly where her brother is taking me.

After draping his robe over his shoulders, Neo tugs my body to himself and sweeps me into the honeymoon hold, approaching the bone door. As he commands it to open, Neo murmurs low in my ear, "I have a gift for you."

I thrill when he launches his wings, leaps from the walkway, and soars into the air.

30
THEY ARE DREAMS AND SECOND CHANCES AND RECLAMATION

As soon as he flies beyond the Iron Walls to the far west, I recognize where he's taking me. Tender magic from the suite broken, I remember the little girl, the pile of ash, and bury my head into his neck, wishing I could escape into the familiar scent of smoke and vetiver cologne and deep water. A paradox like everything about him...and us.

"Trust me," Neo breathes close to my ear, dark ice girded in silk, but I don't open my eyes.

This place, these woods and the Bridal Canyon closing in remind me of the Chasm. Shadows of lament stalk me, familiar serpents squeezing. An updraft of wind causes my stomach to pitch, and I peek to survey Neo flying in a direct line over the Canyon of fallen brides.

"Trust me," he repeats, no more than a featherlight whisper.

Pressing my mouth to his neck where his silver veins hum, I hold my breath as Neo circles the furthest reaches of the Canyon until he tenses, bracing for something. When he strikes the air with his wings and sweeps us into a blindingly swift descending arc, I shriek and trench my nails into his skin.

Dark walls close around us, caping us in shadows lit only by his flames mating with my Halo currents. On each side of us are inner canyon walls: a hidden gap in the cliff faces like a secret path, but where does it lead?

"I shared a portal with my brother, but this is mine and Nita's secret," says Neo as he flies us through the labyrinthine path skirting the boundary of the Iron Walls built into the canyon rock faces. Beyond the Walls are the Father's ash-topped mountains. Neo's secret path is a tiny canyon in and of itself—more of a slit of a canyon. It descends lower and deeper, narrowing until the rock faces dare to brush the edges of his wings. They lead to an overhang protecting a black tunnel in the ground. Still, Neo does not slow, and my hands instinctively seize his robe, fearing we will crash.

"Trust me," Neo issues the third plea, then swings back for one second, wings propelling us before they close around my body.

He dives right into that black pit! I lose my scream somewhere between the darkness of the pit and his wings.

Once inside, Neo lands, the force of his body storming the rocky ground and rumbling through my chest. I'm convinced I have no nails left.

"You can let go now, Elysia," he informs me, but I don't let go.

Clothed in only my chemise, I shiver from the drop in temperature, from the darkness veiling us until Neo's flames ignite my skin. Roused by those flames, the Halo couples to them until my star-fire flames twist around his Dragon ones. I summon my courage to untether myself from his body.

Compared to him, I am a glowing orb in the pitch black. "Where are we?" I whisper.

"My special place. Come with me," Neo beckons, offering me his hand, voice deeper and more solemn than ever.

Silence is a necessary reverence. I trust as he leads me further into this tunnel with only his flames and my dim, glowing skin to light the way. From the side, I peer at him. His eyes are still soft silver mist, but even the hoods around them seem heavier—eyeliner grayer, reminding me of secretive fog—weighed down by the past. Neo bows his head, and the sound of gushing water fills my ears. Before I take another step, he closes his hands around my waist, preventing me. When he waves a hand to project his flames, they reveal a little cliff. If I'd continued walking, I'd have walked right off the edge. I lean against him, lighting my hand on his arm in a gesture of gratitude. His smile is faint.

Neo shoots his flames into the air, gathering and circling them higher to form a fiery chandelier to bathe the area in a dazzling glow. I gasp, tears breaking surface, heart lurching till I nearly tumble. It's the most beautiful place I've ever seen in my life. This is Neo's secret place. Neo's secret *lair* underneath the Bridal Canyon.

All along the sides of the rock face, great, dark trees grow to greet the ceiling of crystalline stalactites—branches sprouting and veining onto the shimmering rocky walls. Most enthralling are the thin silvery waterfalls gushing from the center of their earthy bodies like the cascades of bridal trains...and flowing in tributaries to congregate into a massive pool. An underground grotto.

Smoke. And deep water.

With eyes wide and glowing, I feel my knees weaken from this place, its beauty, but a host of questions swarm about my mind. Why bring me here?

Something splashes in the pool. What? Before I can question, Neo cups my waist and lifts me into the air, winging us closer to the grotto pool and setting me on the earth closest to it. Gray moss grows all around it to form an organic, soft bed.

Another splash triggers my curiosity. He simply smiles and gestures to the pool. So, while clasping my trembling hands in front of me, I slowly approach the pool of rippling glass. There is my reflection of cacophonous curls spilling down my back, my gold skin glistening through my chemise, gold ringing my brown eyes, and Neo's wedding ring—an iridescent but simple treasure at my chest. Another splash cracks the surface out of the corner of my eye.

I kneel. Planting my hands on the soft moss, I hover above the grotto pool. When I lean over, Neo's ring dangles and skims the surface.

The entire pool erupts! Luminous, the water brightens, flares, and shines in a blinding starry, spirit-filled light. So bright, I must close my eyes. Until finally, starlight dims.

I blink my eyes open to a soft glittery body of water. It brims with what reminds me of moving, silvery dragon's scales. Similar to the damned souls of Nita's dungeon lake, except these are far wispier with countless silvery, transparent ends pulsating through the water like quivering tendrils. And they all congregate to me.

My Halo breeds, easing out of my chest in soft, undulating currents as if to encourage me. Hand lingering over the water, I part my lips and gasp. I marvel at how the wispy souls form a spirit chain, curl around my hand, and burst gooseflesh on my skin. Unlike Nita's slain demons, these souls do not bite. No, these spirit wisps circle my skin, sighing prayers, petitioning for healing. There must be...

"Hundreds," Neo echoes behind me, but I don't face him yet. Too swept in the pearly wisps tickling their way on my arms.

More unite in their haste to envelope me, but it's not

enough for them. Or for my heart ready to unleash wings and fly out of my chest!

Without another moment, I slide into the water and tread in the deep pool, sucking breaths because the water is cold, but it hardly matters with my Halo radiating around me. All the souls crowd my skin and twirl with my Halo currents mirroring them, becoming gold wisps. I sink beneath the surface until they submerge me and welcome me in an underwater dance.

They whisper to me. A different symphony of stories, of lives snuffed like candle wick flame doused by a storm.

They are dreams and second chances and reclamation.

They are *hope*!

The Souls of the Lost Brides.

"How?!" is my first gasping question while facing Neo who kneels on the mossy bank, then extends a hand to help me out.

"Nita." He smiles, and I laugh because I should have known! While I comb my hands over my hair and wring out my curls, Neo explains, "After I made the deal with Father, I made one with Nita. She and the alters could not bear the weight of knowing the cost for her soul was the loss of thousands of others. So, I destroyed my Brides' memories so their souls would not feel their trauma."

Halo light buds between my legs, curling beyond my soaked chemise, spiraling around my thighs and downward.

"I destroyed their hearts but not their bodies, though I left them in the Bridal Canyon, so Father would believe it's a dumping ground and not a preservation temple."

My golden light flourishes, uncontrollable to the emotion welling inside me, expanding my chest, prompting tears of beauty and power.

His voice deepens to a black velvet lullaby, "Nita captured

and redirected them here because if there is one thing I can never destroy, it's a soul."

"Neo," I gush, clasping my hands in front of me, "Please, is *she* here? Is Verena here?" Is this where our paths cross? Hope swells inside me.

Neo lowers his head, crushing that hope. "No, Nita could not capture Verena's soul. Quick as lightning, her energy could not be harnessed. Nor your father's. But her pure energy is not gone, Elysia. Only transferred to the Soul Plane. Unfortunately, my territories are only the mind and the body. Not the soul."

The Soul Plane. I breathe, wondering if I could ever have the power to travel there, to claim a soul. "Wait, does that mean your brother, the Prince of Death..." I trail off, fearing the worst for Verena's soul, for my father's.

Neo's shoulders sink, eyes falling. "I cannot say. Some souls...they roam Limbo. Verena's soul was powerful. I have no doubt she could have escaped my brother. But there's more." Puzzled, I taper my brows as Neo retrieves something from inside his robe. A small velvet pouch. He unties the gold thread and bids me to peek inside.

I wince, harnessing a moan, remembering the little girl in the Father's tower. "Ash."

Neo touches his fingertips to my cheek, brushing aside the tears. "The reaped girls...this is why I re-routed us through the Commons. So Nita could see. Triggering Bryony is the worst part, but we agreed to this in our deal. She had to know. She had to be ready to capture their souls in case I didn't make it in time to...save them."

"What?" I whisper, shivering at a slight chill prickling my spine.

"After Court, I went to the Chasm, Elysia," Neo explains, lowering his head, fingers coasting along my arms, along the water droplets glistening with rich light. "Blood oath or no, I tried to free your mother. I knew if Father were to lose his reap, his wrath would be unleashed on her. Her liberation would be enough of a diversion to draw him away so I could free them."

He shakes his head with a chuckle. "I should have known from the moment you vomited all over Father's boots that you were planning something."

"You came back..." My voice cracks with emotion, and I purse my lips, considering how I passed out in the Father's arms. Our bond must have summoned Neo to protect me. Again, the chill on my back gnaws on me, but I shudder it away. And resist the urge to chastise myself for my lack of belief in him. But there was absolutely no reason for me to trust him. And I have no regrets. No regrets when it led us to this moment!

"Yes. Your words were my greatest hope. Neo..." he trails off, referring to my proclamation in the Tower. New. *My* new. "And your screams, my greatest torture. But her lost, little soul found its way here thanks to Nita." With golden streams for tears, I touch my wedding ring and whimper my gratitude. "And Elysia?" Neo purrs.

Those fingers, which cradled my cheek all this time, curve under my chin to coax my eyes while his other hand closes mine over the pouch. "I may be a destroyer first, but I still carry my Father's blood. Nita may create apart from Father. And *I* may restore whatever I have destroyed..."

Oh, Saints!

"*Neo! Neo! Neo!*" I nearly scream at the same time he dips one finger into the ash and restores the body of the little girl until she's curled in my arms. All of me bolsters with elation, with astonished hope. I cover my mouth with the tips of my fingers, but I can't contain my awe-soaked sobs, my brimming tears. Her heart does not beat, but she's here! It's her body. An empty vessel. Devoid of a soul. But she's *here*!

"But where—?" When the chill invades my back again, I shake my head, laughing at Neo's knowing grin.

"She followed you out of the water."

At once, I reach behind me, scrabbling for the soul but can't quite grab her. Instead, I jut my shoulder forward and gesture to Neo, desperate and pleading for help. He pauses, brows threading low. Shakes his head, shame darkening the shadows around his eyes. Now, I touch my fingers to his cheek, then guide his hand beyond my shoulder to seek her.

"Ask her," I murmur with a soft smile. *Seek...knock on the door of her soul.*

Inhaling long and deep, flames dimming, Neo glides his hands along my back to the mischievous, little soul. He does not breathe, chest motionless and still. Those fingers tiptoe closer to her soul threads dangling down my back, and I angle my neck. Neo winces, pausing when her soul quivers and slides lower, but I whisper to her, praying she hears me, "He. Is. New..."

Her soul dares to tread on the fingertips of the Prince of Destruction and skims over his hand. I study my husband. Study the tenderness of his palms, of his fingers curled, soft in protection. Hands bearing scars of a Warhammer of a warrior. But he has proven he uses his power to protect. And when he must use it to destroy, it is not him but the blood force of the Father inside him.

My heart shudders from his pupils dilating to infinity black pools, focusing on nothing but the little girl he'd destroyed while bearing her closer to me. I pause while she hovers like a twirling silver jewel before accepting her into my palms. With a smile teasing the corner of my mouth, I nod for Neo, petitioning his help.

"Open her eyes for me, *husband*."

Magnified by my declaration, Neo's eyes flick to mine while his silver-blooded veins kindle beneath his beautiful, dark skin. Without hesitating, Neo eases her lids back so I may embed the soul through the windows which open only to my hand. Closing my eyes, my Halo bursting, I weave it deep into the fabric of her being.

I remember the Goddess' words: *You hold the power to heal deep within you. To restore souls...*

With those billions of constellation particles teetering on the edge of my skin, ready to dazzle her flesh and engulf her blood with the divine trademark, I touch my lips to the girl's and murmur my greatest breath prayer where I shine brightest:

"*Noralice!*"

Overflowing warmth—a lifeforce I sample when my Halo awakens and releases—flows free into the little girl. Writ into her cell matter, into the double helix of her substance, into the fabric of her identity. Blessed by the kiss of the Goddess, of the angels, the little girl's heart beats. She stirs, lashes fluttering, eyes opening.

The first one she sees is Neo, but the first thing she does is—

Oh, Saints! She hugs him!

While he embraces her, Neo sinks deep into my mind to proclaim, *I vow to you, Elysia, on Hallowtide when the fabric of reality is thinner, I will personally cross into the Soul Plane and bring Verena's soul back for you to restore. Then...your father's.*

Hallow Tide...I consider their Halloween Court festival just a few short months away. I ease a deep sigh, gratified by Neo's promise, the gravity of his vow.

Undone from the emotion, from the utter soul energy I've

expended on this night, I start to pass out to the sight of her kissing Neo's cheek. With the barest thread of consciousness left, I slip into the bond and proclaim to Neo:

I want to tell you about Noralice!

31
FOR ONE NIGHT, I DO NOT WANT TO BE THE WARRIOR. OR THE HEALER. TONIGHT, I WANT TO HEAL. MYSELF

It still takes months. Every night, Neo flies us to the grotto where we restore one girl. Sometimes, I use my Underground connections to get them to safety. Other times, Nita transports them to her island sanctum. Neo also brings me to visit my mother again. Even if it aches each time, she says it brings her strength. Each time, she trusts Neo a little more...as do I.

All these weeks, the Father preoccupies his time in the Chasm where he's building an army of monsters for the Centennial Eclipse according to Neo. To war with...*me*.

At night, I still pile a fortress of pillows between Neo and me. Our training continues, but I unleash a great surge of power into the suite at night...or drink venom to fall asleep. Old patterns are difficult to break.

Other nights, our conversations drift into the wee hours of the morning. For Verena and me, trust was automatic. Won with fire and lightning and...blood. With Neo, it's a process. I've shared nothing about my bargain with Thanatos who still haunts my dreams...and my spine with a hailstorm of tranquil ice to stem any panic attacks.

Tonight, the night before Hallowtide, Neo and I are closer than ever following another soul restored. Tonight, I vowed I would share Noralice. The first time I will share my trauma—though Verena witnessed the evidence transcribed all over my flesh the morning I returned home.

Shadows abound around the floor where I lie with him kneeling before me. His shades caress my naked gold legs, playing with my Halo curlicues. I say nothing first because serpents close in again, squeezing. I've never told another soul the full story. Tears burn the back of my throat.

Until Thanatos. When his fangs sunk deep into my heart, he claimed my deepest darkness. My *Noralice.*

I cry, I sob, I whimper, curling into myself again, returning to that trauma state, its familiar pain exploding on the back of my neck.

"Noralice is why you can't fall asleep at night, isn't she?"

Despite how much silk and velvet Neo pours into his voice, it doesn't matter. Those words trigger me.

I knit my brows low, a lethal venom in my voice. "What the hell did you say to me?"

Neo shakes his head and cups my cheeks. "No, Elysia, don't. Please! Don't make another excuse. Don't pick a fight with me so you may use your Halo and pass out. Do not run from me!" Inside those words is his mask. His Destruction pushing and probing, battling me.

Yes, I could storm the Halo, pass out, and escape. But I battle him in the bedroom because I need to know he can bleed. I need to know he can share my hurt, my grief, my sin and suffering as I've shared his.

"Maybe if you could stop acting like a manipulative horn-dog." I bait him.

"Stop that." Neo touches my wrists, and stares his silver flame eyes onto mine. "You disguise it behind your wit, your feminine wiles, your sharp tongue, but it's there under the surface. You can't fall asleep naturally. You can't wake with me next to you. Who is *Noralice*?"

I chuck my head down, fury fuming through my nostrils. He has no right to this. More pain flares on my neck, dark serpents needling their fangs into my brain stem. Neo seizes me while I crumble. Lightning-quick, my pulse races as I adopt the fetal position, tuck my head into my knees, and screech long and shrill. I hyperventilate inside the eye of a panic attack hurricane.

"Elysia…" His words become a dark blur when he lets me drop.

"*They were babies!*" I scream, lashing out bursts of light.

He grits his teeth around a multitude of growls, enduring my wrath which burns his flesh.

Until I look up. Through tears, I see him, his pain. Chest throbbing, I flow soft, starry healing beams to restore him until the quivers fade, until his wincing ends.

The moment he's still is when I collapse against him. At first, he flinches, startled by my sudden caving. My first true surrender of every non-venomous serpent gloating and threatening to squeeze my heartstrings, every soul wound…

A storm ransacks my body. And I shake and shake and shake, kicking wild and offensive. At any moment, I'll release all my Halo power in an almighty surge. It's so tempting to shut down, to sleep.

I'm feeling a multitude of my emotions from that night.

Instead, Neo's strong arms merge around my body, fierce and foundational. Not trapping but *securing*. When he binds his legs around my lower half to stop my chronic kicks, I shake inside of him. His body becomes my bulwark. My dark fortress. Tremors fade to trembling tears.

But I want *more*.

I nudge my hips, and he releases one powerful leg. Hopeful, I curve my knees into my chest, facing him in a fetal position. Neo grunts, but he rocks his body to a sitting position and folds his arms around my shaking self until I'm curled into an Elysia-shaped ball in his lap. Hard and strong, he holds me through the shudders. The side of my head brushes his chest, my lips near the Halo brand.

Now, I close my eyes, feel him. My breath slows while my heart palpitations fade. A sudden force rumbles inside him. It jars me to my bones, but I don't need to open my eyes. All the air around me grows cold from his massive vampire wings draping around me, those pinions great enough to shroud my body. Cocooned by the light and dark side of the moon.

He doesn't say a word. Neo's hand grips the back of my neck, anchoring me, bearing me in place while the other berths around the base of my spine. His flames blossom there, warm tassels to prevent my flesh from numbing. A tourniquet to preserve my blood flow.

Yes! I sink into him, almost breathless.

It's enough to stem the instinct of Flight. It's enough for me to stay. But I'm not ready to shine.

After what feels like hours with my ear pressed to his heart-murmuring chest, I finally stir and open my eyes to his dilated pupils: two twilight orbs fixed on me. Waiting.

Then, Thanatos whispers to me—strengthened by the bond from his bite—conjuring those images of my burning homeland. Of my father reduced to ash. Of my mother's capture. Of thousands of bridal scraps in the Canyon, including Verena.

He coos, *Once you show him your darkness, sweet angel, he will destroy you. He can't love a fallen angel. He'll give you to Father. You gave* me *your greatest darkness. Now, you will become* my light.

I freeze when Neo's fingertips embrace my chin, luring me to tilt my neck.

"*Elysia...*" he murmurs, then his fangs glint from his parted lips. So deep inside my abyss, I flinch from the trigger. Except, Neo tears his fang across his palm, bleeding silver. He offers me his hand. "I grant you my solemn blood oath: you may trust me with your secrets, with the curse inside of you."

He lowers his chin until his forehead presses to mine, eyes of silver keys...but they don't unlock. Instead, they *ask*. They *seek*. They *knock*.

I hold my breath as he finishes his vow, the vow he should have proclaimed on our wedding night, "I grant you my solemn blood oath: I will touch your past tonight and return it in full tomorrow. I grant you my solemn blood oath to understand your darkness."

Understand...not love. A deep, shuddering sigh of utter relief, of surrender releases from my mouth. And I touch my fingertips to the edge of his palm, hovering above his trickling blood. The greatest form of love is the ability to *understand*.

Neo whispers, feather-light, across my mouth, "For tonight, I grant you my solemn blood oath to be your Ezer."

My hand sinks. *Oh, Saints, yes!*

The serpents disappear, vanish like dust from forgotten bones. Deliverance from death. Tonight, he will provide support, foundation. Tonight, Neo is *my* shield.

I can shed my cross. For one night, I do not want to be the warrior. Or the healer. Tonight, I want to *heal*. Myself.

This is why the Goddess has thrust us together. Neo has shown me his darkness—a darkness of which I can *empathize*.

In the darkest and most paradoxical twist of fate, the heavens transcribed Neo and I as two dying stars side-by-side. Cosmic bodies of *extremely* intense gravity. Unstable gravitational forces. Not quite black holes because we aren't dead yet. Perhaps the only way we can burn bright again is...together.

Now, I will show him the deepest of my darkness. And I will...*shine!* For myself.

So, I dance with Death and scream at Thanatos. *It is* my *light! Now, I am taking it back!*

I take a leap of faith into Neo's silver keys and open the door. "Nora and Alice."

No! Thanatos snarls.

I give Neo their names. Two names I'd repeated ten thousand times in one night until they'd become one. "Twin babies. Three months old."

My chin trembles as Thanatos slinks further and further out of my mind and into the portal and leaves me alone with... my husband.

It shouldn't be possible, but Neo deepens his wings, tightening them more. All the way around me now, they protect me. A safe, dark haven. A black cocoon. *I am safe*, I remind myself, easing into him.

Tonight, I will not show him the memory. Tonight, I own my trauma. I will proclaim it.

And...I deserve to *feel*. "I *want* you to touch me, Neo," I invite him for the first, the truest, the realest time.

Neo sighs and nods, eyes not fleeing mine. "If I cross a boundary, simply say the word *Noralice*, and I will stop."

"Noralice," I confirm.

Neo's hand glides along my chemise and stations on my chest, above my rapid beating heart. More tears blot my eyes and trickle down my cheeks like starry trails.

"It was my first year capturing for the Underground," I

begin. A sigh staggers from my mouth when his knuckles skim the line of my throat and descend. Not once do his eyes retreat. Fixed. Intent. "I'd grown so used to being successful. I was on a high from my previous time. Four children, four glorious children!" I laugh and sob, shivering as one fingertip trims my neckline. The corners of his lips tease into a smile.

"On that night, I hit the blood farm furthest from our tunnel. I knew it was a risk, but I was foolish and stubborn and—"

I gasp when Neo rubs his mouth to the edge of mine. Not a full kiss. A half kiss. I wince from the painful vibration inside me. But his lips are dark grace—soft and strong and black as his wings. A half-kiss to swallow my shame, my guilt.

"*Elysia*..." he centers me and eases one strap down the curve of my shoulder, exposing the upper flesh of my breast.

I eye him as he lowers his lips to that curve and kisses my naked skin. I still do not use the safe word. No shadows. No flames. Tonight is all about *me*.

"I took two babies." He kisses down my arm, eyes curving to their ceilings so he may still gaze at me, but his mouth forsakes the fallen strap. "I gave them a sedative. And I ran..." I swallow and arch my neck when he closes his eyes and kisses my throat twice while inhaling my scent.

"There was...a surprise fire hunt that night."

Tears flow from my eyes. I cram them shut, remembering the stench of the burning fires. The vampire revelry since fire hunts are about pomp and grandeur. Several bone-fires before the great open sea of a field that was my shortest route to the Underground. "They'd blocked it. I-I didn't know. Goddess forgive me, I didn't know. Vampires on fire hunts..."

His fingers on my arm tighten because he understands how they starve themselves for weeks. Full wanton thirst.

"I tried to go around, but it took longer. I-I made it halfway and then...o-one," I jam the balls of my hands down on my eyes. A haunting trauma of coos and cries. "Alice woke."

Neo still says nothing. He kisses my tears, his mouth of frost nipping at my cheeks. I whimper. I moan, nestling my curling hand at the base of my throat. "I tried to hide, but she kept crying, and the Halo was glowing. I had no more sedative. They were closing in, Neo, I—"

I wail and lean back, spine hitting his wing. The silver veins inside it awaken to my touch, pulsing their strong network. Every muscle clenches in his membrane, but he doesn't move. His expression is unreadable. But those wings bear my weight. For the first time since I learned of the Halo, for the first time in all my years, the light flows *inside* of me. It swells, warming me as if I am wading inside a pool of sunbeams.

"Lose one or lose both," I gasp, sensing the inpouring of healing, of love channeling into my skin.

Neo studies me, but his fingers close over my hand still curved around my throat. He lowers it to my side.

Accepting, I part my lips and sob a well of emotion and continue, "I could still save Nora. But I couldn't let them take Alice alive. What they would do..." My hands fly to my mouth, stifling gasps. My light pirouettes along my skin, but my chin quivers, my jaw muscles spasm in distress. "I ended her cries, Neo. I suffocated her. I kill—"

He jerks my hands down. Another half kiss. On the other side of my mouth this time, cutting off the last word. *Destroying it!*

I love the brief bursts of pain in the back of my neck. They remind me of my inner lies. Why I'm not a savior. Why the Halo shut down. *Mercy killing.* Is there such a thing? *It was your only choice.* There were a thousand other choices. *You were only eighteen.* That's no excuse. *You prayed for her soul. You kissed her.* It doesn't matter. She died...by my hand.

"After she stopped crying, they were only inches away. Only one way left to save Nora. I threw Alice." I threw her so high, wishing she would grow wings, wishing she would fly straight for heaven. I may as well have tossed a sacred star. I'd begged the foremothers to welcome her before she could hit the ground. Her body cracked and thudded all the same, her infant cries forever ended. "It distracted the vampires long enough for me to get across the field..."

I bite my lower lip when Neo ushers the other strap down my shoulder curve, printing his fingers there. No safe word. Full credence. He pauses as my breath hitches, but his eyes still do not travel lower. The silver keys stay, seeking and understanding. My Ezer. Light beams frolic with my curls.

"The Underground waited on the other side in the ruins." I nod frantically, pursing my lips and breathing furiously through my nostrils, deadpanning with him as Neo traces the lowered neckline, dipping between my cleavage to thumb the swell of my breasts. Oh, Saints! Golden light breathes from inside my chest to exhale across my skin. "I got Nora to them." Coruscating currents swirl around his fingers. "But the vampires were still hunting. They were going to find the tunnel. So...I gave them another target. Oh, Goddess!"

I rake my nails against his wing's wall, clawing to the touch of his hand as he brushes his knuckles across my breast. It's the first time I've been touched...like this. He pauses, brows screwing low, knowing...*understanding*, but his eyes deepen against mine because I still give no safe word. My light comes in flames now, heating every inch of me. Beyond physical, this intimacy is emotional, psychological, and spiritual. He absorbs my darkness. I internalize my light.

"They ripped..." I take the nightgown strap in my hand and

tug, snapping it. Neo stares at my face, eyes never sinking when I tear at my chemise. My battle. He doesn't lift a finger. My whole skin turns luminous. The chemise scraps fall away like burning embers until I am as naked as the dawn before him. A glowing candle in the lantern of his wings.

"They bit..." I urge his hand to my neck, but I slip mine beneath his. For one moment, his eyes narrow to slits, his shoulders and neck tightening, but he controls it, discarding his anger so he may take my pain. "Only their fangs. Nothing else," I point out. My blood was the goal. Not my flesh.

His hand nearly swallows mine, but he allows me to lead, to guide. Warming, I glide my fingers across my throat, sprinkle a few around my collarbone, tap one or two on my upper chest because I have memorized the fang-map. Rub my hand over each breast, travel lower, roaming across the panes of my stomach down to my hips. Trembling, I open myself a little, tilting my body so his arm may cradle my back. When I continue with his hand over mine, when I touch my most intimate spaces, his body rumbles. Flames crackle. Shadows summoned. Staring fixedly. Jaw hard. Mouth pressed into one vicious line. A snarl longing to unleash. But he quells his destructive fury.

"One hundred times bitten." All the way down to my toes. "A fang-rape. But not a penetrative one." It didn't matter that their dicks stayed in their pants or how they didn't touch me. Their fangs were enough.

My body has transformed into one lustrous orb.

Shaking and shuddering, I burrow my head between my knees, squeeze them till the caps press into the sides of my skull. When I regain my breath and raise my head, all I detect are fragments of Neo's face thanks to my siege of curls veiling my eyes. The silver of his eyes has turned to war smoke.

But I am a star.

No, I am a constellation. A galaxy. Naked and glittering. I've gifted him my supernova.

Now, I wait. I position myself before him, lean against his chest...and wait.

It's the first time his eyes lower to my skin. Not in lust. They squint in confusion. "Where are your marks only my Father could see?"

I wait to erupt. Sunbeams ready to split. My spirit on an effervescent high. I joy at the simplism of the question. At his eyes rising to mine when I announce, *"No venom."* Full-body torture because without venom, there is no numbing, nor paralysis. Held down by the sheer force of their fangs stabbing my flesh.

Neo cements his lips together to cage the roar, but I detect it in his throat regardless. And in his iron jaw locking. His nostrils flare. Every muscle is diamond-hard. His scales protrude through his flesh. I touch his fortress of a chest, almost jerking from the pounding heartbeat that is all mine. If he could, I imagine he'd hunt them all down and take their wings. His lips part with need, seeking.

"When I came to, one vampire still lay behind me. Blood drunk. Passed out. It's why I screamed the morning I woke with you next to me. I'm so—"

He destroys my apology with a kiss to my brow.

I kneel on his legs, so we are chest to chest. Light against dark. Wedding ring to halo brand. Princess to Dragon. Angel to demon. *Wife to husband.* I touch his face, cherishing his acceptance, treasuring his belief. I nod for his next question.

"All night, Elysia," he treads, pupils contracting to winter storms. "After they were safe, why didn't you use your power? To escape?"

I open my mouth with a multitude of excuses. How I'd frozen

with fear. How the torture was so chronic, I'd passed out from the pain. How I'd prayed my hardest ever for the Halo to come, to destroy the vampires. Nothing but darkness. I pause because the answer is much simpler. So, I wrap my legs around his hips, my core like a fire-blossom unfolding to him, and I confess, "For Alice."

Neo's hands unite at my back, and he raises me in one powerful sweep before pressing his mouth to each edge of mine. Half kisses all the way around, lower lip rubbing the top edge of mine. His wings curl around me again. I feel their bones and packed sinew. The serpent pain crawls out of my heart, out of my chest. Neo devours it all. Carries me to bed. Lays me down. And trims diaphanous shades and warm flames around my glowing nakedness.

I carried her home, Neo. I carried her little corpse home!

He prepares to wander to the other side of the bed, but I grip his hand at the last second and shake my head. His eyes soften, yet waver. I don't let go. So, he settles in behind me, cocooning us, curling his wings away. Shaking my head, I twist around. Tonight, I want to sleep facing him.

"I want to wear your wings." I beam, gesturing to them.

Neo licks his lips, raising his jaw, ready to resist. I want their mantle on me all night. After his posture goes unbelievably rigid, his corded muscle along his arms and chest all bulging as if waging warfare, Neo finally relents and folds his wings around me to overlap my back, behind my legs and curling under my feet. Cuddled within them, I swaddle them around my naked form. Neo weaves his arms around my waist. Tomorrow, I will wake with him next to me.

At peace for the first time since I arrived at Court, I close my eyes and smile when Neo brushes the curls from my face, tucking them behind my ear.

"I don't take babies anymore, but come hell and high

water, nothing will keep me from the Underground, from smuggling. I'm a very good runner, Neo."

After a few moments of silence, he kisses my cheek and offers the mere reminder, "Ten thousand demons, Elysia."

I sigh and curl, tucking myself into his wings for the night and respond, "I love you, Neo."

"I love you, Ezer."

Ezer...I remember my mission and the Altar upon his Dragon chest. Circling my finger around the brand, I plead with him, "Will you transcribe it for me? I'm sure your words will be sweet refrains to my ears," I tease. A damp glow buds between my thighs, my appetite beyond whetted from the emotion of tonight as I reference the prophecy on his stone Altar chest. Deep emotions, the healing ones. And physical touch. Together, they are my love language.

Neo cants his head low to me, silver mist eyes questing upon my body before his lips open to speak inside my mind.

Here is writ the prophecy of the Halo-Bearer, the Everblood, who will bring the Father of Vampires' end:
Begotten of sacrifice and unconditional love
Her Spirit will be sent from heaven above
Her purity of blood is Father-forbidden
In realms of Death, she will be hidden
With the Halo of blessing inside her heart
The Everblood must find the Grail split apart
With the Angels' kiss upon her lips
On the blood moon's Centennial Eclipse
Of six broken pieces the Courts have forgotten
The Grail can restore the world that is Fallen
The Halo-Bearer's bond is the key
She will seal the Chasm and the Father for eternity.

I sigh from the weight of it and lace my hands around

Neo's powerhouse of a frame, my dark, stalwart bulwark until it feels like we are one flesh.

"Wonderful. Only need six pieces of an ancient artifact the whole world has forgotten." I peer at him, at those winter mist eyes. As full and swollen as our wedding night.

Neo's shades travel my glowing chest to dance around my wedding ring. In the silver and black moon of our cocoon, he breathes against my mouth, "You're already wearing one."

With my solar eclipse of a Halo erupting, with my warrioress of light naked before him, I lift my head to kiss his mouth because I have to believe he is worthy!

But before my lips can crash against his, Neo moves so they capture his chin. "No…" he purrs low—a subtle, silky growl as he brushes his knuckles across my cheek and down to touch the ring, the first piece of the Grail. "I will *never* be worthy, Elysia. My soul will never be worthy of you. My heart is yours regardless. But do not pit your light against my darkness. The Halo will break."

I whimper. I moan. I weep with righteous need to kiss him, to take him into my heart tonight. So close…teetering at the doorway of one flesh. Neo shakes his head, continues, "My soul is too damned. Centuries with Thanatos cannot be redeemed. You may have my flesh if you desire. My mind, my blood, my bond. Even my Dragon. Everything but my soul."

"Neo…I will settle for nothing less than *all* of you." *I want everything*, I whisper inside our bond and kiss every part of his face, every part but his lips, though I tread dangerously close.

As if sensing I will cross his boundary, Neo proclaims, "*Thanatos*." His eyes hook mine in a dead stalemate; it's *his* safe word.

Before Flight can trigger, Neo pits himself on top of me, wings still cocooning us. My body instinctively rises. "What are you doing?" I whisper, welcoming the blushing stardust wandering my entire body.

"Tonight is for *you*."

Slowly and deeply, Neo presses his lips to my neck, pausing, then printing them to a space direct to the right. Oh, Saints! He kisses the bite marks! Traveling my fang-map, Neo rubs his lips across each invisible wound, reminding me tonight is for my healing and *feeling*. Not for him. Breath quickening, I cry out in a long moan when those lips open to my breast, to one peaked rosebud—a brush of a kiss. Velvet-light and not sinking. I need more!

He pursues my trauma while my heart heals. With every caress of his lips, I reclaim. Mouth stroking the soft panes of my stomach, lowering to my thighs. Bowing prostrate before me. I gulp from his tender lips granting each thigh a sacred kiss. Liquid gold drips right out of me.

I plead for him to continue, gripping the sinew of his wings, aching for more. The doorway of one flesh unlocking and opening a crack...

Neo deadpans. A muscle throbs in his cheek. Oh, Saints!

All of me quavers with pleasure when he dives to part my thighs like they're heaven's gates. Neo worships at *my* altar. His tongue spreads my fire-blossom folds to taste me before he circles, halo-like, around the golden nub. He trains all his centuries of mastery upon it while his tender fingers rub along my wet folds until I throw my head back and moan as he'd predicted, clenching every muscle in my body.

An otherworldly scream rips from my lungs as lightning corkscrews up my spine and splashes my face with hot bursts of constellations. Star showers of ecstasy explode from the elated Halo in my chest, showering the room with a rainfall of glitter to lavish our bodies. Not a jumpstart, this is unlike anything I've ever experienced.

My whole being trembles as Neo finishes the fang-map, my legs quivering, my sex gasping and gushing a golden tide. Chest heaving, I cup my forehead and stare down at him in awe. "What in holy fuck was that?!"

Grinning, Neo ascends to kiss my brow. "We both know very well what *that* was, my love."

32

WRESTLE WITH ME AGAIN, SWEET ANGEL!

"Your gown is positively wicked," Nita compliments me as I study my reflection in the Infinity Wardrobe and the gown which doubles as a form-fitting black suit studded with black diamonds. The neckline plunges a few inches past my bust but doesn't quite reach my navel.

Nita's posture shifts to Kitty who nips my ear and purrs, "So damn yummy." I roll my eyes with a little laugh as she adds, "Remind me again, are we being invited to an orgy? Please say yes!"

Nita squares her shoulders, clarifying, "I will not be participating in any orgies, Kitty. You know Tourmaline and I frown on such a thing."

Kitty sighs with full pouty lips and informs me, "Respect sucks."

"But if you're a Creator," I prompt Nita, curious, "can you create a body for Kitty?"

"Yes, but Kitty is still an alter," explains Nita. "Bound to my soul and mind. On a rare occasion, I will form her a body for our lovemaking, but only in the Soul Plane could she possibly mate with another. Still, her mist form may roam tonight."

Kitty cups a hand to one side of her face and hints, "I love scaring all the humans."

"You like *flirting* with all the humans," Nita clarifies.

Smiling, I turn to the mirror. At my thighs, the black suit shifts colors to diagonal-patterned and alternating black and scarlet stripes to mirror the sleeves hugging my arms. My favorite parts are the full, blood red sinuous ruffles attached to the suit at my shoulders that flow down the sides of my body. The matching velvet red and black boots are also cunning.

"I'm still uncertain about these *imposters*..." Nita remarks on the faux horns curling from my head, a glittering black to mimic Neo's.

I spin around, my cake ruffles twirling behind me, and reach for her hands. "No horns could ever be as glorious as yours, Nita." I gesture to her scimitar horns of polished obsidian. "I thought it would be fun to dress like him tonight." I touch the V-shaped choker at my neck that showcases my wedding ring.

Nita raises one brow, eyes narrowing in discernment. "There's something different about you."

I bite my lower lip and she circles, assessing. Squeezing my shoulders together is a natural reaction along with my flushing. Not to mention the gold butterflies curling from my heart. Traitors. I almost believe Kitty will emerge, but Nita remains and taps the side of her nose to pronounce, "Prostrate servant."

Kitty lifts her arms to the sides and gushes to the ceiling, "Oh, Elysia, did you drip with nectar of the Goddess last night?"

I can't help but beam at the thought of last night...and cover my mouth with my fingertips to stifle a giggle. And from the thought of this morning when I woke with him next to me.

No, healing is never won in a single night, but the invisible serpents feel further away. It had helped to face him. I still can't imagine him sleeping behind me, waking to his mouth on my neck, but his dark beauteous face...yes.

After breakfast, Nita had promptly kidnapped me for a full day of beauty treatments and preparation for Hallowtide.

"Isn't it ironic how the Tenth Court celebrates a religious festival?" I wonder.

"I'd wager that's the whole point." Nita curls her hand in the air. "Not only due to my origin's sick and twisted humor. But you mortals have always sought to tempt and mock the monsters of the night. Tonight is simply when we engage in the mockery." She heaves a deep sigh before posturing, side-eyeing Kitty whose echo form peruses the costume options in the Infinity Wardrobe. "On this night, more Chasm monsters will rise than any other. Blood cake and other related offerings have already been spread out along the Chasm boundary. And my brother will need all his strength in case of an attack. Especially when the souls of the dead may test the fabric of our world as it's thinnest on this night."

Yes, the Soul Plane. This is the night we will seek Verena's soul. Once we bring her soul back together, he will restore her body. Of course, she'll laugh at me for falling for the Prince of Destruction, but she'll still be my thrice-yearly fling. Or perhaps more because maybe I'm not as traditional as I'd always believed. Neo would never fault me either, considering his sister and her relationships. Or how he's taken an occasional male lover as he'd shared with me recently.

As long as he weds brides and takes harem girls to seek the Everblood, his Father could care less about any of Neo's other proclivities. We still haven't worked out my vowing to be his last bride yet.

Another thought haunts me. If Thanatos' spirit can breach that fabric, will he come to me? Will I battle him tonight?

"Speaking of souls...how's the little girl?" I divert from my thoughts and eye her ravishing gown: a royal blue skin-tight mermaid silhouette, fanning out at the base with matching satin gloves.

After collecting Kitty into herself for the time being, Nita fingers her low-hanging black fur shawl adorning her shoulders and neckline while answering, "She is safe. Along with the others you restored who chose my island and not the Underground. I'll keep the child at Valhalla until she's older or until our origin is dead. Perhaps that time will be sooner given how far you've already come in the past few months."

It's difficult to imagine it's been such a short time, given how much has happened. I purse my lips, considering how little Neo and I know of one another's pasts but have somehow managed to bare our souls to one another. Sometimes, I wonder if it's all a dream, if I'll wake in my lair. Or in his prison. I center myself with one touch of Neo's wedding ring. Still, the chill lingering on the wall next to the Infinity Wardrobe lurks closer to me.

"Nita..." I take a deep breath while she adjusts her black belt clasped at one hip with a glimmering black pearl. The belt descends in an arc beyond her other hip. "Neo shared his memories. He shared one with you and...Thanatos."

She stiffens. At first, her back muscles ripple, and I wonder if I've triggered Briony, but Nita steels herself, turns, and faces the wall. She promptly snarls at the portal and slams her gloved hand against it, rocking it with her power. "You boorish bastard! You so much as breathe one sick and twisted shade at my angel, and so help me, I will climb in there and show you a *real* brush with death!"

One shade dares to stalk her, smoking around her wrist. I

grin as she stabs one threatening finger into the portal right before thrusting it out. She sneers and mutters, "I'll show you the valley of the shadow of death, smoke-bag." Nita loops her arm in mine and leads us out of the suite. "A pity he has so much power tonight as he controls the Soul Plane."

"Wait...what?"

"Neo didn't mention? You must understand what Prince of Death means. Neo is Destruction. Thanatos is Death," she reveals as we continue down the hall. "While his entity may rest in that Tower, his true soul resides in the Soul Plane. Thanks to your mother, his mere physical form does not traverse the world. But the souls of the dead still lie in his care. Or at least whichever ones the laws of heaven and earth grant to him."

"What about him and Neo? They had centuries together. And I'm supposed to believe he just moved on?" He could not have destroyed *all* their memories of one another. Certainly not his knowledge of their past.

Nita pats my hand while I slide my other down the staircase banister. "Of course not. They were thick as thieves, you see. Twin jewels in the Father's crown, and he unleashed them on the world. Oh, the trouble the boys caused. Neo preferred war. He loved impressing his older brother and giving him souls. And Thanatos...he played the *long* game."

I shudder, remembering his voice all too well. "Meaning?"

"Death by a million soul cuts." We arrive at the halfway point where Nita pauses. "When I met him, he loved to brag about his exploits from Neo's wars and all the souls he collected." She pats the back of my hand knowingly again. "Neo fueled wars around the globe. Thanatos reaped the soul profits." She grits her teeth, and if her horns could lengthen and sharpen to compete with Neo's scythes, I imagine they would. "Why do you ask?"

I shrug and excuse, "Just curious about the vampire Neo was before all of this."

Screwing her mouth into a tight line, Nita's eyes turn to silver blades as if she suspects something else. I don't cow beneath her gaze. It still turns my blood to ice at the thought of how Death knew the deepest part of me before Neo.

Wrestle with me again, sweet angel! Thanatos coos to me. Will I ever be rid of him?

Nita's shoulders sink, relenting because she respects how we all have our secrets.

At the base of the staircase, Quillion clears his throat and adjusts his ruby-broached ascot with his gloved hand. I lean closer to him, swinging from side to side in admiration when he imparts a sweeping gesture to his silver blood vest over midnight blue tunic. Armored plates overlap one another in curving patterns to mirror his knee-high ruffled armor boots. Simple matching blue breeches.

Kitty fawns over him. "Look at you, you beautiful, flouncy old fool!" She flicks his extension ponytail. Blue to match his tunic.

I grin as Quillion extends his hand to me and kisses my cheek before bowing at the waist to Nita and proclaiming, "My adorable plagues."

"Perfectly charming, Quill." I imagine Neo has shared with him all recent events...well almost all. "I thought you hated these festivities."

"I always make an exception for Hallowtide. Every Court bishop will be in attendance. Representing all Court O' Nines realms."

"Maybe you'll find a new flame," I suggest but clamp my mouth shut once the shadow crosses his eyes. The most well-dressed and civil vampire I've ever met...and the most bitter-sweet. Hmm...I wish I could introduce Quillion to Uncle Heath.

Tilting his head low, Quillion utters in a heady murmur, "I suggest you consider your new flame instead." He winks.

One second later, *his* shades nudge me, and I spin around.

My jaw nearly hits the floor. From his great cape of gold, splendorous enough to be a groom's train to the regal-tailored long tunic clasped by silver blood tech broaches, my Prince echoes my Halo in every sense of the word. Aww, we opposite match! My eyes roam hungrily to the silver armor girding his legs, sharp and pointed from the knee and gleaming like deadly moonbeams. Part of me wonders if Quillion had recommended the high-collar and ascot. Neo is the only one who can pull off the fanning element while still appearing menacing.

I almost liquefy in envy at the sight of his eyeliner. A vicious pageantry of shimmery gold above the lid. Beneath his lash line, flawless angel wings of iridescent white sweep from the inner corners of his eyes to flick outward at the ends. Keen tapered edges. A perfect mirrored wings below the eye to curve upward without the points uniting. I still haven't mastered this unlawful allure, though he did catch me peeping through his array of silver-blood tech makeup products. I swoon internally because he was late that morning to Court so he could offer me an introductory tutorial.

Neo arrives at the base of the staircase where we stand about six inches apart. Last night's memories return to me, causing my Halo to spit countless butterflies from my chest and a gold glow to blossom on my skin. Limbs lighter than sprites, I almost do a devilish twirl to break the sexual tension thickening between us.

On our side, Kitty—still inside Nita's host—rubs her gloved hands together and squeals, "Oh, it's like watching wet sexual vapors!" She fans herself. "Okay, can I watch just one eeny weeny time, pretty please?"

Before Nita can reprimand her alter, Neo leans over and

kisses Kitty's cheek, causing her to freeze, eyes flying wide as he murmurs in her ear, "We both know it's not eeny weeny, Kit."

I cover my giggle but welcome his hand caressing mine and raising it to his mouth to kiss. What would Mom think of all this! Then, I lower my head, parting my lips as I ache for her. Reading my ache from our bond, Neo combs his hand through my long, ravishing curls and assures me, "I checked on her earlier. She's fine. Father is planning on another battle following the festivities. Once he's finished, I'll take you to her. And we can set about planning her freedom."

I practically melt into a puddle of gold.

33
"I HAVE FOUND MY EVERBLOOD!"

WE MUST CROSS A LAKE OF BLOOD TO ARRIVE AT THE BALL.

My breath stalls. Thousands of scintillating gold lanterns float far above our heads, casting moving starlight onto the blood and along the domed muraled ceiling. Constructed into the very Tower itself are rock faces broken by thin blood-falls to cascade into the lake. Plenty of lower Court vampires and their human familiars swarm around the falls, diving into the lake, swimming in nothing more than Hallowtide masks. Others float in small, intimate canoes, dazzled by the synchronized lantern performance.

Upon our approach, dozens of armored knights bearing bone swords, wings unleashed, form ranks above the blood lake welcome the Prince of Destruction and his company. Not one vampire or human in the gargantuan space moves whether in the lake, on boats, or along the rocks. Do they mean for us to fly? Nita stepping a good few feet to the side is my first hint. With one great thrust, Neo's wings pound the air and nearly strip Quillion's feather piece from his ponytail.

When Neo weaves a hand around my waist, grins down at

me with those familiar pupils dilating, then hoists me into a honeymoon hold, I inhale sharply. Desire swells heat inside me, and I arch my neck in a subtle offering. Touching one hand to his chest and coiling my arm around his neck, I lean in and press my lips to his throat, smiling as his veins hum silver.

Tapping his chest above that heart, I whisper, "Mine," and nip his ear. A single shaft of fresh Halo light bursts from my thighs. Between my gown ruffles and with Neo's power, no one notices. But Neo undoubtedly scents my arousal.

Winging off, the Prince purrs low in my ear, "Perhaps we will rectify that desire of yours later tonight, my bride."

Oh, Saints! Prostrate servant again? Something more? All I contemplate are his wings and more uses beyond flying and painting.

On its opposite side of the lake is where the true Hallowtide Ball awaits. Is the blood real or synthetic? At heart, I will always be an Underground member, wondering if humans have fed this lake, but too much hope radiates in my being.

Thousands gather in a cavernous canyon at the threshold of three monstrous staircases formed of vampire bones fused with gold and flanked by statues of winged lions and angels glowing from silver blood tech and dripping blood from their eyes. Every last face is masked. Only the Prince and his company do not hide. An ocean of bodies sweeps apart to pay homage to the Prince. They instantly descend to their knees. As soon as he lands, the entire canyon convulses.

With Nita on his left arm and me on his right, Neo coasts his eyes across the expanse of thousands of masked faces, insta-commanding their heads to bow, to pit their eyes to the floor. I raise myself higher from a sudden stroke of pride because I have won that Prince in the most grandiose of ways.

Neo's silver boots echo along the staircase like lightning-bound thunder, and my luxurious, blood red ruffles make love with his surpassing groom's train that spills a glittering treasure trail behind us. The staircase ascends to a mammoth arch and beyond...a single tower—open at the apex to display a dais. Upon that dais sit three monstrous thrones of blood rubies, black diamonds, and vampire skulls. Dozens of chandeliers float in mid-air, arranged in a semi-circle around the tower to bathe the thrones in splendorous light.

Once we move beyond the archway, Neo secures one firm arm around my waist, vaults from the bone platform, robbing my breath.. He lands with dangerous precision on the small staircase below the dais. Inertia sends my chest lurching, but Neo kisses the side of my head, and I'm confident he would never drop me. I brush my lips across his cheek.

"If you two would cease your googly eyes for five minutes?" Nita alerts us from behind.

My giggle mimics Neo's rumbling chuckle before he sweeps a hand to the staircase. The center throne is obviously the most supreme. Behind all three thrones is a smaller one. No diamonds or rubies but only vampire bones and fangs. It must be Nita's. Still the Father's blood spawn but a lesser Princess to his crown jewel sons.

Clutching our hands, Neo ascends toward the throne on the right. The one with a horn curling from each crest and caped in shades and flames. On his right side is not a throne but a smaller ornate chair. Reserved for his bride.

Where is he? I wonder regarding the Father's empty center throne as Neo leads me up a small dais to his.

Father enjoys making an entrance for these festivities.

Like Father like son? I tease.

Nita blows frustration through her nostrils, perturbed at her exclusion from the conversation, so she invades. *What of your Hallowtide game, brother?*

I flick my head toward her, one brow quirking.

Neo pauses before his throne, feral lips grinning, silver blade eyes drifting between us. *Father and I raise stakes on special occasions,* he explains to me. *Tonight, I am shattering his with a worthy check!*

As soon as Nita prepares to take her place on the throne behind his, Neo seizes her wrist and does not even permit me to move. *Nita!* He roars within our bonded minds, and then purrs low to me—*Elysia*—rousing gooseflesh. Puzzled, I lower my brows.

Before I can say another word, Neo lowers himself into his throne in one ferocious sweep! Oh, Saints! Nita and I still *stand* before him. Out of the corner of my eye, I note the delicious savage grin on her face. Far more beastly than his. I part my lips in a silent gasp when Neo does not allow us to bow but instead, extends his hands to each of us, and compels us to approach, to turn around, and oh, Saints!—to face the crowd!

We may be on each side of his throne, but Neo has positioned me on his right, his thumb rubbing my knuckles before he eases his hand to my back. *Both of you will* always *be higher than me*, he hums within our shared bond. On impulse, I lift my chin loftier, shoulders squaring.

When I turn my gaze to the ball masses, everyone is on their knees but with mouths open, bewildered and stupefied. This is the *only* time the Prince of Destruction has ever lowered himself and not to simply one but *two* women, and one, a *human!* Well...half human half wingless, fallen whatever angel. Not one speck of gold inside me resents sharing this position with Nita. If anything, her Queenship humbles me.

Placing her hand upon his throne crest to touch a skull infused with blood ruby eyes, Nita raises her lofty chin, her horns stabbing the air to her motion. *We will make you a queen yet, Elysia,* she reminds me.

Neo grins, dipping his head low in a predatory gaze of deadly scythes to prick every dumbfounded eye in the audience. Destruction by a million cuts. Neo opens his mouth, voice booming to proclaim, "Check, Father!"

I can barely keep my breath caged inside my heaving chest. Only Neo's shades soothe me—an adumbral symphony on my skin that reminds me of our dark *Scheherazade* waltz.

Three moments after Neo utters his conquest, the Father rises! Whatever breath that was ready to burst and cast Halo showers all over the canyon is absolutely suffocated, absolutely devastated before the Father rising from the center of the blood lake. Not one drop dares to cleave to him but tumbles to the water like bloody, weeping tears.

It's not his black diamond armor with the fist-sized blood ruby shining like a faux beating heart in his chest that strikes terror into me. It's not his black boned horns, curved scimitars, soaring from his head. It's not his gruesome cape of black hair waving in the air behind him or even his blood-blotted pupils. It's his hand closed into a fist around a chain that he slowly and proudly lifts from the blood lake. A chain fixed to a powerful iron collar shackling a neck belonging to none other than my...

Oh, God, Neo! I scream inside our bond, my knees weak, body ready to crumble. Neo's shades chain me, preventing me from leaping right off the tower. Nita's nostrils flare, silver veins hearkening to life in her neck.

Steady, Elysia!

The Father commands the audience, his children. And raises my unconscious mother, raises the Phoenix Queen from the lake, blood clinging to her naked skin like crimson paint. At once, he hoists her form into his powerful arms and with one hand positioned on her back and the other under her legs, the spawn of Satan thrusts her body above his head and proclaims in a voice as loud as the last trump, "I have found my Everblood!"

Every vampire in the canyon roars their applause—thousands of war drums reverberating into my chest.

The Father lifts his raptor eyes to the thrones. Even from this far, I chill from the force of his malevolent eyes targeting *me*. Promising *me* hell. Because he suspects. Because this is what he has prepared for over the past few months while Neo and I have grown closer.

I close my eyes because Neo throws open the doors of our bond wide for me to eavesdrop when the Father chants to him:

Checkmate.

34

"REMEMBER YOUR OATH, MY SON. AND REMEMBER THE PRICE SHOULD YOU CHOOSE TO BREAK IT..."

Raw dread convulses the back of my throat.

Does he know? Or has my mother convinced him that she is the Everblood to protect me? Willing to make the ultimate sacrifice for me.

All a game, sweet angel, Death hums in my mind. A game...or a trap?

I gaze at my husband, seeking his eyes which are rooted on his Father. What will Neo do? How can he possibly go against him?

Neo curtains the tower with his private shades as soon as the Father arrives on the dais and hurls my mother to the floor with a cunning pronouncement, "Behold, Neoptolemus! The salvation of Thanatos!"

At once, I get to my knees to touch my mother, to shield her, thankful Neo doesn't stop me. Nita curls her lip, an empty threat of a fang when the Father's hand descends to my hair, a predatory promise.

I flinch and grip my mother's shoulders as the Father rubs

the top of my head and he coos, "One drop of blood, one piece of flesh, her tear, her tooth, and a single strand of hair. They are all we need, son."

Through their bond, his voice lowers to a deep octave in a mental reminder to his son. An undercurrent of his demonic spirit—a blood force harking to mine. Of another prophecy. A prophecy of Death! The Father's secret.

Her hair to form the roots
Her tooth to birth his fang fruits
Her tear to wake his eyes
Her flesh to birth his disguise
And her blood to grant Death his life!

Shit, shit, shit! One strand of hair. He took my hair!

My salvation! Thanatos cries in my mind, crystallizing my Haloed heart itself.

You won't get anything else, I deny and lean over to press my brow to my mother's, wishing I could wake her as she has awoken me so many times when I've passed out.

"Mom," I whimper and stare at the slick layer of blood coating her naked skin. I gaze at Nita, desperate. She doesn't even need to nod. She creates a gown of royal purple for my mother, one to mirror her own. "Thank you," I breathe a trembling whisper.

Only now do I realize Neo has not left his throne. His eyes have not once departed from the Father's hand that caresses my curls, though his fingers clench each side of the throne, nails scraping the diamonds and rubies, scattering gem dust to the floor.

"Such sweet bed flesh..." the Father mutters above me—a familiar and lustful lilt—fingers descending to trickle along my jaw. And I cringe, triggered. Throbbing throes stab the back of my neck. My Halo shuts down. Trauma stalks me, promising a hundred new fang bites from the Father. "I will take your bride tonight."

Neo rises. With flames and shades in his wake and shooting out to protect me, the Prince of Destruction thunders his way toward his Father, his pupils dilating, a dominating throne. "I am not finished yet!"

The Father grips my hair and yanks my head to expose my neck. I shriek when he rips Neo's ring from my throat and chucks it at the Prince's feet only for his shades to swallow the precious boon into their protective embrace, vowing a return. I gulp, swallow the urge to cry from the assault as he wrenches me so hard, pain attacks my scalp.

"Finish her now!" growls the Father in an overthrowing command. Hands balled into fists, Nita steps forward, but the Father brandishes one warning finger, reminding her of how her powers do not apply to him. Her upper lip puckers, her razor-sharp fangs extended, but she does not move.

When Neo pauses, it incites the Father's fury. I struggle to swallow my anguish because the Father acknowledges the threshold of deep betrayal from his own blood. And he preys his outraged, lethal eyes upon mine, gnashing his teeth. I muster some battle. A Halo spark, but all the Father does is blink when an ember lands on his cheek. The slightest of pauses. He sensed my spark, but he cannot recognize it. He cannot see *me*!

Neo can.

I see you, Elysia.

Neo does.

The Father digs his fingers into my head, snarls at my throat, and rubs his nose along my jaw to hum in my ear, "You have bedeviled my son, and you will pay the price, pretty little Princess. I will use you as a pawn against your mother until she surrenders every strand, every tooth, every tear, every flesh, and every drop of blood I desire!"

"Father!" Neo protests, triggering a split-second growl from the Creator.

"No," I snarl. I wrestle more, clutch my chest. My Halo forms throwing stars. Deadly but far too slow. Neo hacks away at them, but they keep growing.

"Bite her and give her to me," the Father demands, taps my throat once, twice, three times, beckoning his son. A vein pops in Neo's neck. He swallows, contending with some omniscient force inside of him. Pitting my blood oath against his Father's origin oath. Testing. "Now!"

Neo's eyes pinch as he kneels before me. The Father does not relinquish his hold. When I dare to crane my neck to gape at him, the Father hisses and grips my curls harder. Pain rockets into my skull, and my treasonous throat confesses a tormented moan.

The Father swings one finger down the line of my throat in an authoritative gesture. For a moment, he snaps his head toward Nita to remind Neo, "Remember your oath, my son. And remember the price should you choose to break it. Is one simple, pure bride worth the cost of warring with ten thousand demons?"

Oh, heavens! *Ten thousand demons!* If Neo breaks his blood oath with the Father...oh, Goddess, all this time, he'd said—he'd *vowed*!

"Or perhaps..." The Father's hand descends to my chest, a slow conquest of the flesh above my heart as he finishes, "...she is no simple *pure* bride, nor simple *pure* Princess after all."

Holy foremothers, he knows!

Just as Thanatos hinted: this whole performance has been a game to determine how Neo would react, how I would respond.

A trap. Baiting the Prince of Destruction...and me. When my Halo rears from my chest and bites the Father's hand, he yanks his palm away, snarling at the burn of my star-fire.

"There she is!" he sings to me and seizes my throat before I can scramble away. "I am so disappointed in you, Neoptolemus." He raises his chin to dethrone the Prince. "Wooed by a bit of angel light. Nothing more than a golden fire blossom." I whimper at the memory Satan's spawn has stolen. "You've sacrificed your Warhammer for her. Look at her!" He grips my jaw, forcing my face toward Neo. I clench my teeth, but my eyes soften and warm before my husband. As they had on the night of our wedding, Neo's pupils dilate to the extreme. "She's *tamed* your Dragon. Bite her now and reclaim yourself. Together, we will bring back Death and tonight, she will worship at *our* thrones like the prostrate servant she is!"

Neo, I breathe a prayer into our bond. A petition. A silent will o' the wisp of a soul kiss.

He lingers in that space of the bond. A space so lovely dark and deep where he utters, *You are nobody's servant!*

Neo rises to stand *above* his Father, staking his vampire origin with the silver scythes of his eyes—destruction by a million cuts in that single gaze.

My shoulders practically sink to the floor when Neo proclaims, "Send me your ten thousand and be damned!"

35

"YOU COURTED DESTRUCTION. NOW, SWEET ANGEL, YOU WILL COURT DEATH!"

Oh, Neo...

My quavering heart wants to sink so low, my stomach will swallow it, but it paradoxically longs to explode from my chest at the Prince's profession.

The Father's jaw turns to iron, his eyes to blood diamonds, and his breath to venomous vapors following his son's proclamation. Immediately, he taps his fangs to my neck, his growl triggering my adrenaline, "What have you done to *my* son?"

Before Neo can defend me, I stake my claim, "*Mine!*"

Nostrils flaring, the Father pricks my skin to spill one drop of blood, growls deep, faces Neo, and utters, "So be it!"

Every being in the canyon turns in the direction of the blood lake where waves crest its surface. Where an army forms—a hellish force born and bred from a broken blood oath. A foreboding Chasm curse, every last summoned ten thousandth demon slowly rises from the lake—ghouls, hellhounds, the Fallen, bone-stalkers, widow-demons, blood wyrms and more—pitting their eyes against...the Prince of Destruction. Sweat cleaves to my brow, but ice engulfs my blood at the thought of Neo battling such a force, remembering what one pack of hellhounds did to him.

As the demons ascend into the air from the Father's power, the blood falls from their bodies in crimson rain showers. With every right to fear, all vampire revelers claim their humans and charge into vampire speed to escape the encroaching battle, leaving only Quillion who stands on the platform below the tower.

In the time it takes the Father to form his army, Nita has managed to wake my mother. As soon as she beholds the Father caging me by my throat, her eyes blaze like sacramental suns, but the Father wags his finger in warning and explains, "An oath has been broken, Lady Reyna." His ten thousand demons approach, raging, ready to take on the Prince.

Neo unleashes his double-scythe blades and moves toward me, but the Father does not liberate me, staking his own claim and dragging me back.

Neo! I scream inside our bond.

"Mom!" Desperate, I scream outside and thrust my head, gesturing to him. The memory of the night he slaughtered the hellhounds for me, the night I almost lost him thrashes panic in my veins. "Please! Protect him, Mom. Nita, don't let him die!" I beg even if it means they must let me go. Because nothing in Neo's bargain stated he is required to battle alone.

Elysia, no...let them protect you! Neo growls, his fists braced, longing to seize me from the Father, but the demons encroach.

But it's too late. Nita charges out her ferocious wings and steps to her brother's side to stand with him, to fight with him. And by what otherworldly foresight my mother possesses, she listens to me. She bows her head and sweeps to Neo's other side, igniting her Phoenix fire. Flanked by the two greatest Queens in history, my Prince, my husband prepares to slay ten thousand demons to reclaim all of me from my hair to my teeth to my tears to my flesh to my blood.

I am your Ezer, Neo, I remind him. If I'm going to die, this will be my last offering.

The very moment that Neo transforms into his Dragon is when the Father attacks, arresting my waist and forcing me into his wraith-shadow hold. Too many ghouls, too many Fallen, too many demons attack Nita, my mother, and Neo. Monstrously, possessively, the Dragon roars as the Father carries me away.

Even as the vampire's shadows fold around me, imprisoning me, the Father endows his venomous breath upon my neck, kissing my throat in a threatening promise. "Let me tell you a secret, Elysia...I made another vow long before my blood oath with Neoptolemus. A vow forged in blood, spirit, and Death. I vowed to Thanatos to find that damned Everblood and use her to resurrect him even if it took me one hundred years! Imagine my great pleasure that it will only be *ninety-five*."

The plague of serpents returns, writhing and overlapping and squeezing. The memory of a hundred bites when the Father whispers in my ear, "Come, little angel. You have unfinished business with Death."

The Father chucks me onto a stone platform inside Thanatos' Tower. A whirlwind of breath escapes from my throat. At once, Thanatos' shades cover me, robe me, submerging me into his deep darkness as if I'm falling inside his personal Chasm. The Father remains, waiting for his son to break my spirit, waiting to take everything I am. My throat constricts to those dominating shades.

"*Ahh, sweet angel! Tonight, we will finish what we began. You took a soul. You owe me yours!*"

The words terrify my flesh, my blood, my very bones. That

moment in his tower when I surrendered my hair, my memory of... Noralice.

"*Yes, my little angel. You gave me your darkness. Now, you will dance with Death. You will shine for me.*"

In the midst of the eclipse of his shades, on my knees with hands splayed on the floor, I tremble. The power transference of that memory has damned me to this fate, to Thanatos' hell.

"*And as predicted, Destruction has destroyed you. In keeping his blood oath with you, he has handed you to me on a gold platter.*"

Desperate, I wrestle with the darkness entombing me, battling his voice, battling his venom, warring with the Spirit of Death. Life by a million Goddess kisses, I breathe prayers and summon my Halo. I create throwing stars to pierce Thanatos' darkness with divine light. But not enough to overcome his shadowy tomb.

"*You courted Destruction. Now, sweet angel, you will court Death!*"

His shades waltz with my quaking body, caging my waist. Raising me to a stand, those shades arrest my hand to fold into his. What? The robe of shadows shifts, transforming, becoming...a figure. Not quite solid, not quite shade, but somewhere in between. As if he's dwelling between the fabric of reality and luring me into that between to join him. Strong enough to hold me, powerful enough to command me into a dark dance.

Maddened by his touch, by the onslaught of violent emotion, I narrow my eyes to fix them on the deathly shade orbs. It's as if I'm on the edge of an...*abyss*. One I must cross to reveal the truest version of myself. I war between emotions that threaten to destroy me, each one a thorn: loss, rage, hurt, abandonment, betrayal, guilt...

Now, Death speaks to me. It's the first time his voice reaches my ears and not simply my mind as he leads me into a new dance to rival the *Scheherazade*. "I will claim your heart. I will claim your soul." I gasp, set my teeth, close my eyes to the hand of Death upon my waist, to his breath a seductive reap upon my face. "Sweet, sweet fallen angel without her wings," he woos me, fangs descending, ready to bite. "Your soul is just as black as mine, Elysia..." *Murderer*, he claims.

Elysia...that serpent pain flares in my mind! A golden spark of a hint: *You will call her Elysia, for she will walk the realms of the dead.*

The Halo intensifies.

The one with the most darkness inside his soul must never bite you.

The final serpent squeezes, ready to pierce my heart, ready to break my Halo. All this time, it wasn't Neo. *Never* Neo! Not even the Father. It's *Thanatos*! If he bites me, it will resurrect him. And the Father will reap my Halo.

Am I strong enough to face such darkness?

"No..." Thanatos soothes me with a single brushing kiss upon my throat—a nightmare oath to shiver my very soul. "I missed you last time. From now on, you will shine for me, only me. I will claim you. I own your soul. I will take all your worth, your value. I will take *everything*!"

No. Phoenix fire rebirths within me. As if the heavenly host rises from the ashes as fathomless and blinding as a *million* solar eclipses!

I own my spirit scars, my wounds—my one hundred and *one* bites.

I own my trauma.

It is my greatest weapon in this battle because there is more than one way to be a warrior.

Neo was the battle. Now, I face the war.

Steeling all my muscles, pressing my lips into a seamless line, and with my empath spirit uncaged and free to unite with me, I don't simply accept or welcome or embrace the Halo.

Instead, I surrender to it and gift it *my* power, my identity. Its purest Goddess-born power doesn't simply accept or welcome or embrace me. It stakes me deep into my heart, into my very soul!

It whispers: *You lost Alice. You saved Nora. Together, you and Neo and Nita saved the reaped girl. Your bond is the key!*

In the same moment, the Halo scintillates from my chest in brutal and blazing streams of star-fire. Eyes burning, I stare down the boundless eyes of Thanatos—a supernova gazing into a black hole because I'm no longer dying. Reclaiming my trauma, my heritage, myself, I profess my blessing, "I will *never* lose my value! I am the *Everblood*."

Before Thanatos can bite me, I arch my back and scream my Halo fire like ten thousand and *one* angels to overthrow Thanatos and the Father. It harks from the depths of my soul.

And I herald my truest name of, "Ezer Kenegdo!"

Constellations rupture from my chest, charge into Thanatos and the Father, and drive them back. Glorious beams of golden, blinding light smite and bathe the whole of Death's tower, forcing *them* to their knees until they are prostrate servants howling and wailing and screaming and writhing before me.

In one final burst, everything fades to a dark peace...until it's only my quivering breath and twinkling nerves from the starry aftermath. Thanatos is nothing but cowering shades. The Father is unconscious. All the constellations return to my heart, suffusing my chest with more warmth than ever.

And then...something breaks.

My chest caves in from the agony.

Not my Halo, but something else... A bond un-scribing from my cells. Un-writing itself—blood ink fading. My mouth turns dry from the realization of his destructive darkness fleeing my pure angel light. Blood thrashes in my ears, silencing everything until all that's left is the slowing of the heartbeat inside *his* chest. My heart slams against my rib cage and grows wings with longing to escape, to fly to him.

Fire and ice carve their way into our blood to sever the bond between us.

Because…Neo is dying!

36

"YOU ARE NOT GETTING OFF THAT EASY, YOU SUPERCILIOUS ASS!"

I BARELY REGISTER THE HORDES OF DEMON CARCASSES, THE FESTERING remains, or the monster blood swelling in the lake like black ink. Ash and embers gather in my hair as I rush toward Neo's broken body in the canyon center. By the time I fall over my Prince, my husband, my *Neo*, his heartbeat has begun to wither. Chest ripped apart by a multitude of talons and claws, countless broken bones, a mass army of bruises, and a lonely pool of silver blood christening the ground around him. Ragged wisps of his breath fade.

"Neo, *no*..." I whimper and plead with him, prepare to mount him, to heal him, but something tells me it won't be enough. He's too far gone. His soul is already retreating. Perhaps the only thing left is my kiss.

With the last of his strength, Neo opens those eyes. Those pupils dilate to me before he breathes his last word, "*Thanatos!*"

I throw my head from side to side in a wild protest at his safe word, his final plea for me not to kiss him, not to risk my Halo.

But I won't listen. I won't *listen*. I *won't* listen! To restore souls with my angel kiss to all those who are worthy. The warrioress of light within me confirms it. My heart brimming with righteous indignation and Halo fire confirms it. And the blessing of the Mother Goddess herself.

"You are *not* getting off that easy, you supercilious ass!" I pound my fist on his ruined chest still housing the Altar. "That is *my* fucking heart! Do you hear me, Neo? That is your name! And I am your Ezer. And Saints forgive me, foremothers bless me, and Goddess help me, I will deliver you from death itself!"

I press my mouth to Neo's and open his full lips beneath mine. Cold and soft and supple, lovely, dark, and deep and the most beauteous mouth I could ever imagine kissing.

Infinite constellations, fathomless galaxies of gold dust erupt from my heart. A host of stars dazzles my flesh and envelopes me in a blinding whirlwind of warmth: not a life-force but a soul-force that rockets my spirit into the next world. No, the *in between* world!

My body fades to evanescence while my soul sighs like a breath prayer into this new realm. I unravel into a new form to fit this...Soul Plane. A blissful form. My soul-flesh.

You will call her Elysia, for she will walk the realms of the dead.

The sensation of thousands of feathers tickles my body while shooting stars radiate from my curls. I open my eyes and touch my astral body clothed in a thin sheath of lace—a chemise. My skin has become translucent, luminous gold, echoing of celestial flesh. Here, the windows of my soul are naked. Even my veins are a roadmap of gold—a compliment to Neo's silver network.

The Halo gleams its infinity symbol, pulsing its power inside my chest. Not broken, but my hands fly to my heart when I narrow my eyes to detect...a crack! It's no more than a hairline fissure but a crack all the same.

I glance around. It's like the canyon has turned upside down, masked at its edges by an endless, tremulous haze. The deepest of darkness quivers, spreading like an endless mantle before me. Perhaps it would feel cold if I hadn't transformed into an ember star. I whirl all around, seeking the expanse for him. Where is he? Where is my dragon? With no corpses, no Neo's form beneath mine, no chandeliers or lanterns or candlelight, it feels as though I am the only soul in this darkness.

"Lightning Rod."

Not the only one.

A thrill of lightning prickles my spine at the sound of her beautiful voice!

When I turn, Verena's spirit stands before me, wreathed in amethyst tendrils of lightning. Glorying, I hasten to my girlfriend who wraps her hands around my face, wiping away my gold tears.

"Verena...I can heal you!" I gasp.

"I'm not here so you can heal me, Elysia. I've chosen another calling. Just as you've found yours."

I thread my brows low, puzzled...until she hands me a soul trail—the tail of a kite. Oh, Goddess, it's Neo's soul strands, his spirit breadcrumbs.

"V..." I moan before her.

Her green eyes glitter upon mine, mirthful and strong. "Your spirit is beautiful, Lys. Now, go and claim your Prince. We'll see each other soon. I promise. I haven't forgotten our thrice-yearly bargain."

With those words strengthening me, I kiss her and latch onto those soul strands, wincing and crying in pain because they are hotter than war flames, than embers and ash, than scythes of wrath and dragon ruin: of centuries of stockpiling corpses.

But when I sink my fingers into those strands, they uncover an inner lining. Desperate, I peel away at those outer layers, my eyes widening when I unearth cold, silvery, and silken strands. These are shades and winter mist echoing of vows formed in secret, of deep water and a Soul Pool, of a sister's shadow, of silver keys opening the doorway to love!

Battling the paradox of fire and ice, I braid the spiritual strands, forming them into a three-corded chain, knowing such a chain is not easily broken.

And then, reinforcing my muscles, raising my spine straighter than an arrow, I tug!

For dear *life*, I yank on that tether. Why does Neo feel like Death? My muscles burn from the effort, but I speak a power blessing on the pain, for it means I am more alive. More alive than ever.

"I vow to be your Ezer Kenegdo!" I scream when the tether bites my hands, drawing soul blood to trickle liquid gold to the dark haze below me. "I am your militant helper. Your strong rescuer. And your warrior princess of light!" My Halo vibrates my soul flesh as I stake my claim.

The tether slips. Inches fall before I scramble to grip them again, pitting my soul against his.

"*NEO!*" I scream his true name. *New, new, new!* This is *my* moment of reclaim. "I am the power that has and always will carry your burdens. I am your shield. I have and always will vow to save you from danger. And I vow..."

Glowing tears fall from my eyes. My breath cleaves and heaves. I exhale golden gasps. The Halo barrages in staccato beams—powerful enough to lace into that soul tether, burning my own brand, my unbroken halo deep into the core of his worthy spirit.

Before I finish my proclamation, Thanatos' shadows tangle around my body, whispering of smoke, of fang-rape, of trauma.

He is an equal contender to clamp onto the tether because Death will settle for nothing less than *all* of Destruction!

A dual set of shades drifts around the curves of my body, cherishing the Halo light, soft as if urging me to let go. To spare me this burden. Neo's dark, erotic shades.

"Come hell and high water, Neo, nothing will keep me from holding on!" I chant through tears.

Posturing, clenching my jaw, straining every soul muscle, and ignoring the burning pain in my palms, I do not release the tether. Not even when both brothers take their shape before me. My heart thrums, quickening with golden currents when I see my husband's shadowy form. Lovely, dark, and deep, he bears silver mist eyes and black robes as he did in life.

I swing my head to his right, to...Thanatos. Blink once, twice. Twin souls, they are bonded to one another, their shades fused. Except while Neo's wages are his flames, nothing but frost and ice gird Thanatos' shades. Two sides of the same coin. But I've set my seal upon Neo. As a seal upon my heart, upon my arm. My Ezer.

Thanatos approaches me, cocking his head to me—crowned with strands that are not wild and unbound around his neck as Neo's but rather black, lustrous, and silky and controlled—obedient to Death's every whim. His eyes are nothing more than two combative pupils. Nothing in me can avoid those deathly orbs.

"Let him go, little angel," Thanatos coaxes, his brutal shades shackling my wrist, deceptively tender and urging. "He did vow on your wedding night "till Death do us part"."

My cheeks claim more of my tears to drip and squeeze between the cracks in my clenched fingers to salt my burning palms, stinging me with raw torment. And still, I lay my claim, my soul-blood, my very Halo against him, spreading them out as if on an invisible altar.

Maddened, I shake my head, wrench again on the tether, denying Thanatos his claim. Neo steps toward me, and my heart seizes at his emotions. Regret and guilt and shame of centuries in those eyes...of trauma. His greatest trauma stands at his side. Like his powerful alter.

I stare into that great silver abyss of Neo's eyes, and I ask, I seek, I knock on the windows of his soul. In the depths of my being, I understand just what I need to speak, to vow. "Neo, I grant you my solemn blood oath: you may trust me with your secrets, with the curse inside of you."

By what strength I cannot conceive, I pull harder. Thanatos' shades reinforce, biting into my wrists, and drawing my soul blood, but Neo steps forward.

The. Twin. Bond. Tears.

"I grant you my solemn blood oath I will touch your past tonight and return it in full tomorrow!" Wailing the words, gripping tighter through the agony with golden rivers upon my cheeks, I hold on for dear life.

The. Twin. Bond. Rips.

Neo lowers his chin until his forehead presses to mine, until he takes my hand in his. I inhale my greatest breath and continue my vow, pleading, "I grant you my solemn blood oath to *understand* your darkness."

Whipping my gaze to Thanatos, my eyes burn as I seal my resolution, my claim, my Bridal Vow. Those dark Death eyes narrow upon me, in defiance and awe.

My Halo light drifts around the edges of Neo's form to mirror the shades cocooning mine. In no louder than a whisper, I finish, "I vow to deliver you from Death!"

I write this new altar onto Neo's soul—one that bears an echo of the prophecy:

The Halo-bearer's bond is the key.

I scream, I scream, I scream, "*Our* bond, Neo! Our *bond*!"

"Elysia..." Neo purrs my name and cups my face, scenting every inch of me.

Beacons, pure and unconquerable, radiate from my heart like a thousand lighthouses to guide him home. Some scatter upon Thanatos, who stands at my other side, his Death shadow forging its own conquest.

As soon as Neo kisses me, I close my eyes and shiver, angling my neck in surrender to his taste of fathomless water, of venom wine, of an aphrodisiac dinner that nearly has me buckling. His soul kiss feels like dreams and second chances and reclamation. It feels like *hope*!

The. Twin. Bond. Severs.

The three-corded tether of his soul merges into my heart because I have captured him. So much more powerful, so much better than a dragon. I have captured my Prince, my husband, my Neo. I've captured his soul. Now, he must capture me. He must believe he is worthy.

Not once do Thanatos' eyes depart from us. Not even when I throw my head back and scream, "Bite me, Neo! Take my blood for your life. Bite me now!"

Neo plants one indomitable hand on my chest, unleashes his fangs, and bows his head to my throat. I clutch the hand at my chest. I catch my breath because it's not just Neo sinking his fangs into my soul flesh. It's Thanatos!

The Prince of Death's hand at my neck is a sudden storm, reminding of the night we first wrestled when my soul conquered him, when my heart shined brightest. Now, Thanatos unleashes his newfound power from that memory; he stakes his claim to capture me, to wrap his Reaper around me like a deathly halo.

Destruction and Death, both brothers stake their claims.

And I crumble, I fall to my knees from their force.

You are strong enough! I pray inside my mind. *Higher than them.*

So, I rise. Shoulders driven back, chest thrust out, I reap holy fire because I am not shining for either of them. I court Death and Destruction. And I smile because I *shine* for me.

When I stand, the Halo's light splits into ten thousand stars. Full galaxies explode from my being and drive both brothers to their knees!

For the first time, I don't pass out.

I pass through the 'in between' fabric back to reality.

All that lingers now is the breath of our two dying stars of intense, unstable gravitational forces. And the steadfast beat of a new heart. Neo and I return, burning bright …together.

When I open my eyes, the gaze of a thin ring of silver mist around dilated pupils greets me, cherishing me, treasuring me. Heart practically weeping, I grip Neo's robes and charge for him, kissing him long and hard on the mouth. He raises me by the hips so I am higher than him, so he may change the angle and depth of the kiss to grant himself more of me. I spread my legs around him, ready to tear at my gown here and now until we are one flesh, one heart, and one soul.

For some reason, some bitterness bites the back of my neck beneath my storm of curls. A familiar pain, though I can't fathom why.

"You two should get a room," Quillion announces, causing our lips to part, though Neo's eyes do not forsake mine.

Kitty's familiar lilt squeals, "I'll get them a room! I'll get them a hundred rooms if I can stay and watch!"

I giggle against Neo's mouth before his strong hands seize my waist and bear me into the air, setting me down on the canyon ground. Much of my Halo burned away my gown from earlier. Now, my bare feet lodge into a cold pile of ash…and blood. Instantly, Neo folds his robe around me and warms me with his flames. My Prince of Destruction. My new warrior. My husband.

Together, we face the company.

Quillion resembles nothing of the proper and civil vampire I've always loved, though he does remind me of the first time we met.

Nita approaches us, her familiar obsidian hand sliding to cup each of our cheeks while her other hand unites with ours. Diamond-flecked tears twinkle on her cheeks. My heart warms inside my chest, pirouetting Halo currents when she kisses her brother's cheek and confesses, "Guess you get to keep your kneecaps after all."

I throw my arms around her neck and lean into my sister-in-law and all the beautiful, monstrous and bride souls living inside of her.

"Now, don't you start fussing, sweet Ezer," she echoes, stroking my hair. Except it's not one gold butterfly that escapes. Now, it's a hundred. Nita catches them all, blows them a kiss, and sends them on their way.

Finally, she releases me to my mother. I nearly hold my breath because till now, she's been observing, perceiving, assessing, judging. Her gaze passes over all of us but wavers most between me and Neo. Is she traveling through our shared memories? Has she seen what happened in the Soul Plane? Can she discern each brother's soul mark on the sides of my neck—invisible to the mortal eye?

While I slide my hand into Neo's, Mom opens her mouth to speak, but he stuns her by bowing before her all the way to his hips. "Forgive me, Lady Reyna, but I kneel before none other than your daughter."

I beam, angelic at the perfect thought. Already, liquid gold warms my core. No, an angel would absolutely not have my dirty mind.

I exhale when my mother dips her hand beneath his chin and prompts him to rise. "I forgive you for breaking your vow to me, Neoptolemus." Yes, his vow that no harm would come to me from his hand. Nothing worthy can be achieved in life without harm, without pain, without darkness. Together, Neo and I destroyed our old entities. Our black holes have united to form a burning star of a bond.

"Neo," he corrects with a wink. Countless of my Halo hearts throw themselves at him. I want to roll in that deep, wild laughter while he turns and weaves his hands around my waist, raising me until I practically dance with stars.

Until that dark, icy force invades with the promise of war.

Neo's eyes sharpen. His jaw hardens, back muscles steeling, teeth gritting to his Father flying to the center of the canyon to greet us. No, of course I hadn't killed him in the Tower. Woken from unconsciousness, he's prepared to do battle again. Neo sets me down, positioning me behind him, becoming my shield. I wince because bitter pain infects my scalp. Like shades and...frost.

At once, my mother stands and brandishes her fire and lightning, but the Father raises his hand, staying her, "No need for that tonight, my Lady Reyna. I am merely here to bargain."

"You have nothing to offer!" I cry, moving to stand at Neo's side as his equal. "I captured his soul. His heart is new and it's all *mine*. You cannot take him from me!" I seethe.

The Father chortles, a deep, resonating sound from within his throat. I hate it because of how much it reminds me of Thanatos'. He circles, eyes predatory and dilating upon my form. "Even if one mere *human* girl, however touched by the angels, could stake a triumphant claim on my beautiful Warhammer, it's not his soul in question on this night." The Father snatches my curls as he did earlier, but this time, he tips my head forward and drags a finger to the back of my neck. I shriek as soon as he touches the mark on my flesh—the force of a hundred and *two* fang bites in that brand. And the crack in my Halo.

"Damn it all to hell!" Neo roars before the Father shoves me to him.

"Neo..." I breathe against his chest, petitioning his silvered blade eyes, his soul windows. "Yes, I—that night I went to save the girls, I didn't know the way. Thanatos showed me...for a price."

So lovely, dark, and deep, Thanatos echoes inside my mind. No longer a battle, I can't even hope or dream to wrestle with him. Now, his soul venom is inside me and his mark on my flesh. A brand of shades and frost, of Death.

Neo combs his hand through my hair. "This is my fault," he blames himself. "That night, I should have told you. Give me the mark!" Neo challenges his Father.

"No!" I protest, shaking my head violently and rocking my fist against his chest, to my brand wrought into his flesh. "I didn't go through hell to break your twin bond and free your soul for nothing! We will fight this together. Our love is strong enough. *We* are strong enough!"

"Care to bet on that?" the Father thunders behind me.

"No!" Mom shrieks, but it's too late.

The thunderous sound of *wings* echoes all around the canyon.

Deep and dark and beauteous. That lightning-clad figure, wreathed in holy fire with several wings branching out from her body. All over again, my bones prepare to liquefy to those eyes housing endless galaxies. Everyone in the room plunges to their knees. All except me and the Father, though I still tremble with every ounce of my being. My Halo blossoms on my skin, radiating its echoing light to beseech the Goddess.

"How long will you continue sending mere girls to fulfill

your plan?" The Father challenges the Goddess. When her flaming tendrils branch out from her body, from her hair, even he balks before her. For the first time, I thrill at the sight of the Father of Vampires quaking.

Her heavenly warmth protects me when she responds with a prophetic voice, "My warrior conquered your Dragon."

"She won't conquer his brother," the Father prophesies, fisted hands at his sides, brows tapering low over hooded eyes to appraise me. A chill skitters up my spine "She claimed Destruction. According to the blood oath laws transcribed by my origin, she must now go to Death in his realm. Unless…" the vampire feeds his cold kiss into my skin, haunting me, breeding gooseflesh, "…a new Triumvirate is formed to prove this little mermaid effecter bond with my Dragon are strong enough. My master has played with pawns before. Shall these two be our new ones?"

"Elysia…" the Goddess approaches, those infinite eyes usurping me and forcing me to my knees before her. "If you wish to claim more pieces of the Grail, if you wish to earn your wings, and prove your bond strong enough to defeat the Father, you will walk in realms of the dead. Even with the crack of darkness you've brought into your heart, there is grace. From this moment on, you will have a Scourge of a curse upon your heart but not your soul."

*You will never lose your value…*I echo in my mind, petitioning ten thousand breath prayers to the Goddess, accepting this new darkness, this trial of a Triumvirate, this Scourge.

The Goddess smiles, her warmth spreading, shining into me with the host of heavens. "You will carry healing to all the innocent who suffer from the Scourge. But you will pay the ultimate price of sacrifice to prove your strength."

"You hold great power within you. Only together, the Prince of Death and the Prince of Destruction may unite to bring you to your knees. You will be brought low. Your faith will be shaken. And it will be another who will carry you till you rise into the stars. Nor will you face Death in your next great battle but rather a new Scourge of Destruction."

My eyes fly to hers and my lips part in agony as the multitude of divine eyes impale me with angel fire as if prompting me to lay down this battle, to surrender my Halo. Instead, I trace a circle around my chest in a silent gesture of acceptance. I will carry this new prophecy she transcribes upon my heart: a new altar.

"Only once you defeat this Scourge will you find the next piece the Courts have forgotten." But not my wings. I lower my head, shoulders sinking, but I guess I should have known it wouldn't be that easy. How many more trials? It doesn't matter. I clench my fists, slamming my eyes shut from the smoldering pain of reclaiming Neo's soul tether. I'll take ten thousand trials if necessary.

I am strong enough. We *are strong enough.*

Finally, the Goddess turns to the son of Satan, to the devil spawn and issues the command, "No death shall befall them by your hand or any that you send. Nor may you steal her tooth or anything else. As long as she still lives, she must grant them freely."

The Goddess departs without another word.

The corners of the Father's lips tug into a grandiloquent grin as he tilts his head toward Neo and me and utters, "Come and let us draw a contract for our new Triumvirate."

37
"YOU WILL GIVE US THE WHOLE NIGHT. AS HUSBAND AND WIFE."

A SILENT WARRIOR, NEO STANDS BESIDE MY CHAIR, GRANTING ME THE supremacy to deal with his origin who sits at the other end of the table. The Father folds his hands with that same pompous grin on his sick, sadistic face. I've considered all the Goddess' words, treasured them. Everything I will use to fuel the righteous fire, to forge a new path that will lead me right to the other five Grail pieces. And my wings.

"To prove how generous I am, I will let you go first, little Princess." The Father sweeps his hand in an exalted gesture to me, his face statuesque and spectral in the dim lighting of Neo's suite. We chose to discuss terms at the supper table in the adjoining dining hall.

"I keep his *soul*."

He nods. "As you wish. But I will take his new heart."

I deadpan. Hiss at the invasion of what I'd resurrected, what my Halo bought. The Father does not surrender. And I have no choice. He knows I cannot give up his soul. That vitality, that life force bound to mine—an invisible and indissoluble current of pure energy tethered to the Grail ring around my throat.

Touching Neo's chest, I curve my fingers down onto his chest, onto that beating heart, and stare at him with a mournful plea, *Forgive me, Neo.*

He squeezes my fingers and kisses my wrist horned mark. *You are the only one in the world who can forge a new heart for me again and again, Elysia.*

So, I turn to the Father, steel my shoulders, and nod. "Agreed."

"Please go on, little angel. My ears covet your sweet refrains," he quips, pupils glinting red like fat rubied blood.

"I'm keeping mine and Neo's blood oaths," I solidify, claiming one night in his bed at Court, our honesty oath, and even Spitfire and Neo's lingerie choice.

The Father's grin lurks across his face—a malevolent serpent. "And I will take his mind..." When I open my mouth to protest, the Father raises his finger to clarify, "everything after your wedding night. You will still be his bride. You may keep your wedding and any memories you shared previously. Perhaps I'll even sweeten the deal. Yes, if you manage to create in him a *new* heart, all his memories will immediately return."

I ponder his pompous dare. I will keep that day in the woods, the coach, the prison, *Scheherazade*. And...the wedding. I remember what Neo said to me: *when you brought me to my knees that day in the woods, when you walked down that aisle and looked me in the eye the whole time and refused to bow, when you proclaimed your Ezer...*

He won't remember or understand beyond the wedding, but somehow, the laws of this new Triumvirate will set the order in such a way, none may overthrow them. The knowledge guts me, but as Neo had declared: I will resurrect a new heart, and his memories will return.

Gazing at Neo from my strong lashes, I burn my rings of gold into his silver mist, forging a new promise that asks, seeks, and knocks on the windows of his soul. We need that blood-forged oath. Our bond transcends his mind.

You are strong enough, Neo confirms, eyes of steadfast silver mist, his knuckles slow-dragging across my cheek. *You will bring me back, Elysia.*

I breathe a long, suffering sigh and profess, "Agreed."

"Now comes the matter of allies—"

"Nita!"

The Father grins, countering. "*Reyna.*"

I seethe and rake my nails into the table. "You have the whole damned Chasm, you sick devil-spawn!"

"And you have Death."

I narrow my eyes and open my mouth to debate until a prickling of frost invades the back of my neck. Another bond whispers venomous ice into my flesh and blood. The Father's words are a cursed assurance. Some promise of the vampire my husband will become, a shadow of who he was before...a shadow of a vampire who was closest to Death. It's why I cannot surrender Nita. Neo's touchstone. Even if it means I must relinquish my mother. Because I highly doubt Death will ever be an ally.

I still brandish my finger in my own shadow of a promise. "You may summon her whenever you desire. You may battle her. You may even use her power. But you will not cage her." A cage is the worst torture for my mother. If anything, I will spare her that.

The Father steeples his fingers and bows his head. "Agreed. Choose your next ally."

"Quillion." Naturally.

"And as you stated, I will take the Chasm." The Father touches his brow, proud. "Are we ready to seal the deal?"

"One more thing." I plant my hands on the table and rise higher than him.

The Father remains seated but does not lose his carnivorous grin. "The devil is in the details, darling. Speak!"

"You will bend the laws of nature tonight. You will give us the whole night. *As husband and wife.*"

"Agreed. Now, let us deal in blood."

A fang slice to each of our palms. A new Triumvirate. Before the Father inches his bleeding hand to us, he touches two fingers to my chin, raising my lofty eyes to his and warns me, "Thanatos may summon you whenever he desires, little angel. You will have no choice but to go."

I bristle. "If he tries to summon me on this night, I will elatedly use my powers to burn his tongue and force him to choke on its *ash*!"

Neo grins, wry from the same threatening promise I'd once used on him. She'sthree palms crash together.

After the Father departs, I fall into Neo's arms and weep.

"Why did you ask for one night?" Neo wonders from our place by the bed. He'd carried my shuddering, crying self to the inner suite.

Tears finally spent, Neo now eases his arms from my waist to light them on my hips, and I internally chastise myself for falling apart, for wasting another valuable moment. We still have one night.

Swiping my tears away, I smile and throw my arms around my husband's neck, press my body to his, and project my Halo light in ten thousand butterflies that waltz around us.

Cocking his head with that knowing pretentious smile, Neo lifts one brow and inquires, "Is it my birthday?"

Smirking to one side, I stand on my tiptoes, breasts nudging his chest, and murmur, "Wrong holiday, Neo."

"Oh?" He simpers, eyes canting to mine.

"Tonight..." I trace my tongue across his earlobe, humming a promise, "I'll light up your crown jewels like they're Christmas balls. And I'll turn your big, moronic dick into my shiny gold disco stick."

As soon as my tongue finishes its voyage to the tip of his ear, I grin in triumph from his member awakening, prodding my lower stomach through his robes. Leaning back with my arms united around his neck, I greet Neo's eyes—dilated to their fullness.

"Is that so?" Neo muses, stroking his jaw just before he sweeps me into a honeymoon hold, prompting me to gasp from the sudden shift. Pressing his head to mine, brows waggling, Neo whispers his chilled breath across my face to promise, "I'm going to stake you so deep and hard, my love, your beautiful heart will feel it. And the angels who birthed it."

With my head so light as if swarming with ten thousand luna moths, I stem the yearning whimper in my throat, the pang of desire in my chest, and the craving between my thighs. I nearly laugh at his words since I was the one who staked him the moment I met him. The dampness between my thighs confirms my need for him to reciprocate.

"Where do you wish to go?" Neo tightens his grip around me, muscles as eager as mine.

"Somewhere lovely, dark, and deep..." I sigh the words, tap his brand, and request, "somewhere...*secret*."

Neo grins.

Within minutes, he's shadowed us to the grotto where our only light comes from the silver, silky souls. Deep water. Neo's robe still smells of seductive incense and the aftermath of smoke.

Turning my body to his, I ask him to remove my chemise. All but the Grail ring.

Neo obliges me. Except he does not remove my chemise. Instead, he *destroys* it. One agonizing fabric tendril at a time, careful to turn any embers cold before they touch my skin.

Finally, I am naked in the soul-lights before him. I purse my lips, biting the lower one—my cheeks blushing like the blood moon—but don't lower my head as his eyes sail across my body, dilating and darkening to a deep, craving hunger.

Before he can raise a hand to me, I lift my fingers to his robe, curve it over his shoulders, and slide it off. He destroys his breeches. Winks at me. Tonight, I study him. I touch my hand to his honed chest, the slabbed muscles—and to that mark that is all mine—down to his dragon-hard abdomen and flawless Adonis belt. I trace lower to hold his abundant length—thicker and fuller than ever thanks to our desires, the foundation we share, and the vow that tonight is all we have.

His dragon shaft is nothing short of glorious. A thick and ribbed crown with multiple curves, seamless, converging to the tip. Tiny silver scales riddle all along his massive length. When they flare beneath my touch, I nearly jump, hand twitching away, but Neo meets my eyes with his devilish smile—one sinful but sweet enough to turn me into a gold puddle. Claiming my hand, he directs it back to his cock, to all its ribbed bends and curves.

Leaning closer, the Prince purrs close to my ear, commanding the hairs at the back of my neck to stand on end. "It will be an honor for my cock to be the first to penetrate you, my love."

I press my lips into a smirk. "Toys don't count, do they?" He throbs in my hand, and I look up to find that devilish smile growing into a cocky grin. "Oh, saints!"

"No boy toys here tonight, Elysia," he hums, gripping my hips to bring me closer until a whimper catches in my throat. "Once you go dragon, you never go back."

All of me is flush against him. That's about as romantic as it gets for Neo. But I don't need poetry or romance from him. I wrap my hand around him, close my eyes, and memorize as much as I can. When I take him, it's a guaranteed pain but one I'll claim, one I own as his true and last bride. I revel in my Prince's sharp inhale followed by a low growl. He throbs and twitches when I weave curlicues of Halo warmth all along his erection.

Tremors rupture through his body, and Neo's horns stab the air. I hold back my gasp at his demon form, at those wings growing to form the silver and black ones mirroring the dark side of the moon. The same ones he once wrapped around me on the night I shared everything with him. Raising my eyes to his chest, I explore his scales with my other hand—those tempting black diamonds.

"Elysia..." My name flees his mouth in a long and deep Dragon purr, and I savor the sound, closing my eyes to cherish.

When another tremor rips through his body, I recognize how much he's holding back, how much control he's giving me. So, I arch my neck and beckon him, "Touch me."

I hiss and hold my breath when he cups my breast, fondling my flesh, kindling me all the more. I inhale sharpy as he slowly drapes his knuckles along my breasts as he once had. Halo currents gush forth in a grim bass, mimicking the introductory domineering motif of our song, flowing to wind around him in sensual and tender gold whorls.

Neo rubs his mouth along the line of my jaw, growing my desire, swelling the liquid gold inside me to coat my folds.

Something else throbs beyond my knuckles where I'm still touching, still holding his shaft.

"Neo..." I breathe, nudging the scaled skin all around his cock. When something nudges back, I let out a weak moan in understanding. "Neo!" I gasp.

He brandishes the sexiest crooked smirk I've ever seen. His silver flame eyes ignite every nerve ending in my body as he cups my chin and rubs his lips against mine in a tender kiss. "You're not ready to take both of them, my love. There will be time for that later."

So, dragons really do have *two*. Despite the inferno of my curiosity, he's right. For now...

Our hands, our fingertips, our mouths, our tongues embark on a long and slow exploratory night. Neo discovers my birthmarks and freckles while I trace his horns, peel away his chest scales to touch the Altar inscribed into his chest, and memorize the rhythm of his heartbeat that will be gone tomorrow.

Despite months of slow-burn, I demand everything of him as I'd vowed. I deserve to have my breath stolen. I don't want just his flames. I want his shades, his soulful eyes, his promise of how far a demon will go to worship an angel. Star-fire and destruction will come later.

I lower myself to the ground, presenting myself as a photograph for him to capture. While I touch myself, hands mimicking the fang-mark roadmap, lingering on the liquid gold drenching my thighs, I stare at Neo from beneath sultry lashes and revel in his massive shaft twitching. With that cocky, pretentious grin, Neo tilts his head to the side, dilated pupils smothering the silver mist so he may commit my image to memory. He's photographing me. A snapshot in one night.

"Are you still breathing?" I whisper. Curling one hand, I lay it soft, tangling it into the gray moss that will be our bed.

"You've granted me the breath of life, my love," he quips

sweetly, voice deep and dark and wild and beauteous as he kneels before me, hovering, and studies me. "Now, I'll give you mine."

Oh! His mouth traces the outline of my body, nose caressing every curve and drawing gasps from my throat because every brush of his lips is a euphoric jolt. My body rises with each one, back arching. All my inner muscles clench with hunger and need.

Gradual and intentional, he pauses now and then to rub his lips on my flesh, cherishing my form. Full of thoughts and words and emotion inexpressible, I clutch handfuls of moss, nearly convulsing when he arrives at my neck and kisses his way to my jaw.

Pausing there, he sweeps his eyes to mine—a sea of silver silk—and parts his lips. My head rushes with renegade emotion.

"I will *kiss* you," I proclaim the paradox to our blood oath, touch his stalwart chest, sensing his slow vampire heartbeat.

"And I will *bite* you," he growls.

Staccato Halo ripples thrum from my chest. Damp gold dust trickles down my thighs to bathe the ground.

Panting, I rise to meet his mouth, demanding an entryway. One forbidden for months. He opens and dives in, tongue dueling with mine. But he goes deeper. I moan and curve a hand around his strong neck. Muscles responding to my nails penetrating his skin. He strokes my breasts, palming the soft, heavy flesh that aches for him—and rubs the pads of his thumbs over my hard nipples. I love his taste and the low growl rumbling from his throat. Of his shadows, his monstrous depths.

Neo trails his mouth across my abundant curls, then lower to my neck, fangs tempting its curve. Whisper-gasps flee my mouth while I drive my head into the ground. Close to tears, I shut my eyes and lose myself in every sensation, wanting his fangs, needing his bite. Warm flames dance with my Halo tendrils to tickle my arms. They spread stardust all over my skin. Neo's flames pursue my form and ripple across my breasts and stomach to tantalize my sex, predictive and promising.

A great rush of air suddenly whips all over my face and casts my curls along my cheeks. "Neo!" I cry out, suspecting what has happened from the drop in temperature and the deeper layer of darkness.

"Open your eyes, Elysia."

When I do, Neo is inches from my face. His mighty wings, his *Dragon* ones have driven from his shoulders! Great enough to slam against the grotto sides so the waterfalls wet their edges.

He kisses my brow and says reverently, "Not once in all my centuries have I unleashed my Dragon wings for any bride. You, Elysia, are where the mask does not exist. You are my one true bride."

Certain I'm ready to combust, I press my lips to his. He changes the angle and deepens the kiss. His flames continue their delirious torture—like warm breath prayers across every inch of my skin, but I want his hands. I want his heart. I want his soul branding mine.

As if reading my thoughts, he breaks from my mouth, one hand capturing my breast, scooping it up to claim my pebbled nipple in his mouth. A sob escapes my throat. He circles his tongue around the peaked bud and suckles it into his dragon-hot mouth while his flames stoke my center, my heat. I work so hard not to convulse because I want him inside me first.

Wing edges curling, he holds both sides of my face and utters, "My mind will lose you tomorrow, but tonight, I will take you deep into my heart. And my soul is yours to own."

Lowering my hands to his hips, I part my thighs, inviting. I burn my eyes onto his. "I'll have *everything*, my Prince." I raise my head to whisper against his ear, pressing my mouth there. "Your heart. Your soul. Your horns. Your wings. And I'll have your *Destruction*." I kiss the side of his face and shiver when he drags his mouth down my neck, opening.

"And I'll have your Everblood."

"*Everything*!" I gasp when his fangs etch my skin.

With our souls unbound before one another, Neo buries his fangs inside my throat and stakes his cock deep into me. At first, I wince from the onslaught of pain, the stretching of my flesh, the burning. I clench harder than ever, but I'm so thankful he didn't slide in slowly. I thrust my hips forward to receive him, owning the pain as I'd promised myself. Oh, saints!—he fills every part of my flesh.

Tonight, I bleed. Tonight, I grow. Tonight, I *thrive*.

Tears flow as I helplessly try to clench around him. Moaning, I wrap my legs around his waist, spread my hips, and curve my body against his, craving his touch.

"Now, Neo!" I shriek, lurching.

Understanding, Neo digs his fingers into my spine, then grips the back of my hips, raising me into his arms, bearing me while he stands. My steadfast fortress, my winged haven.

Clenching my fire-blossom core strong and tight around his cock, I whimper when it pulses inside me. I can feel all those ribbed bends, the ridged curves. Neo beats his fierce wings, kindling my longing to fly. I tangle one hand into his moonlight hair—wreathed in flames—while my other grips his back, nails raking into his muscles.

"Don't drop me," I command in a rush of breath.

A hint of a smile, a beguiling shadow crosses Neo's eyes. "Never..." He cups my thigh.

He moves slowly, thrusting deeply into me while that hand

at my thigh curves a cunning finger to work my swollen clit back and forth. His wings time to the motion of his thrusts in perfect synchronization. I love those wings that cocooned me during my deepest trauma.

Moaning, I study that rhythm, time its beat to *Scheherazade*, pitch my hips forward to mirror him, and bow my head to his shoulder. Sweat sheens my brow.

"Look at me, Elysia."

I match my eyes to the Prince of Destruction's.

"Do you need a break?" He wonders, easing out ever so little.

I grip the base of his cock, glorying in how he throbs in my grasp. I shake my head with a smile. "Not till we reach the break of day. My *husband*." Every moment counts tonight.

Chuckling from my well-timed quip, Neo gapes at me in awe, beams from ear to ear with the ends of his fangs coated with my pure blood. He crushes his mouth to mine, hands roaming my back, my hips, across my stomach, and to my breasts. Treating my body, my heart, my very soul like a shooting star he will always catch.

He bears us in the air directly above the Soul Pool.

"Touch me," I whisper. "Kiss me." My breath grows heavier, turning to pants when he caresses my breast. I curl one hand against my throat, close my eyes, and whimper when he lowers his mouth to my breast's swell. He tongues one erect bud, fangs slow-dragging around the nipple. Whirlpools of heat swirl in my belly, between my thighs. Throwing my eyes to the ceiling, I gasp, "Take me higher!" In more ways than one.

Neo brushes his lips across mine and murmurs, "Your wish is my command, my love."

He flies higher, those wings launching air to spiral all around us. Curving back at the hips with him still buried to the hilt inside me, I recline into the wind currents—confident in his control. Dark shades gather all around us, seducing my Halo beams. Still, I trust him. No safe words tonight.

With that same hand anchoring my lower spine, Neo moves inside me again, stirring my arousal like a spiraling flame. I time the thrusts to our song until…he strikes gold! Light explodes from my chest in my climax! Bolts of lightning vault up my spine and rock into the grotto to shower the darkness with streamers of stardust.

"*Neo!*" I scream, clenching around him, almost falling.

He stakes me hard and deep as he vowed—shades and flames penetrating me—but he forces me high. Those silver eyes ignite mine with an everlasting love…and lust. More scales swell from his chest to rub my breasts.

Gripping his neck, I toss my head back and scream to the rapture building all over again, to this supernova storming through my body until I'm riding him as I'd vowed. Neo catches my hair, the back of my head, hand overlapping that cursed sickle brand, and he kisses me, tasting my blissful aftermath. I slam my hand against his chest to the pounding of his heart.

Parting from his mouth, I beam and claim, "*Mine.*"

Even after he's lowered us to earth and his bare feet hit the ground, I clench around him, preventing him from pulling out.

"You are my last bride, Elysia," he professes and kisses me again.

"One night!" I cry and lightly beat his chest with my fist. "Holy foremothers, what the hell was I thinking?" *I could have asked for a week, and he would have given it!*

"Elysia…" Neo soothes me with one kiss to my brow. "We still have all night. And for one hour, you will sleep…with me behind you."

"Half an hour," I bargain, clench around him again with the promise of more.

"Deal." He pulls out.

○

Gold stains the ground all around us. Neo chuckles at the sight before kissing me again.

"How long until morning?" I whisper, on the verge of a breath prayer that we have hours.

The highlight of our night was when he shifted, and I rode his dragon in all my naked glory with the Halo radiating beams and stardust all around me. On a mountaintop above the Tenth Court, bathed in the light of the blood moon, Neo showed me how wings can be used for far more uses than just flying and painting.

"Fifteen minutes or so. I'll need to leave before, Elysia. You know that."

A tear glistens on my cheek, but I purse my lips and keep the tide at bay. Facing him, I thrust my hips toward him, trembling and urging him on again because he almost gave me everything. Except for one thing...

"Destroy me, Neo."

He deadpans. "No."

"I am your *equal*," I remind him. "Your Ezer." My Halo is the only force in the cosmos that can match his Destruction, his dark energy. Grabbing his hips, I tilt my neck so he may have full access to my throat. Hungering, yearning, I insist, "I want your power, Neo. I want the pain..." I bite my lower lip, my whole body relents.

You won't remember. But I want to remember...everything!

The Halo grows from my chest in slow, undulating tendrils, sinking onto his chest and downward, enticing and inviting. I feel his resistance. "You could never hurt me," I whisper, eyes softening from the familiar words as I pull his neck toward me. Neo's eyes become gray, silver smoke.

Curling back his lips, Neo bares his fangs and alerts me, "Venom first."

Whimpering, I close my eyes and nod, accepting the jubilant numbing and a perma-mark on my skin. The venom warms me, rouses my Halo, humming into my veins. I kiss him so he may taste my stardust.

"Hold my horns," he commands in a low Dragon rumble.

Nodding, I close my hands around the black horns and grip them hard. His whole body shudders.

And Neo drives himself into me, unleashing a fraction of his Destruction to shudder into my very core. I scream, but my light beams grow and unite with his shadows and flame as the Halo consumes the brunt of his force.

Tomorrow, he will be gone, but I want to feel his repercussions for as long as I can. I want his destructive energy, that powerhouse that defines his soul, his mind, his body.

Tonight, the earth fractures when he stakes me, stakes a claim to my heart even as he's losing his, but he steadies one hand around my waist, centering me, and whispers in my ear, "My Everblood."

EPILOGUE
"I SEE YOU, MY LOVE."

CONFIDENT IN THE CONTRACT, THE FATHER STEALS AWAY TO HIS INNER *suite, eager to move his pieces. As soon as he enters to discover the shade form standing before him thanks to the power transference once Thanatos bit Elysia in the Soul Plane, the Father acknowledges his son has already set the board.*

Grinning, the Father accepts the strand of hair of a pure-blooded Halo-bearer who will never lose her value. Her hair to form the roots.

"I will put it to good use, my beautiful Reaper. Perhaps...Lux?"

A chuckle...lovely, dark, and deep.

I'D PASSED OUT AFTER OUR DESTRUCTIVE CLIMAX, MY HALO HAD radiating my chest and bathing the whole grotto in my light.

Aching and sore, bleeding but not broken, I muster the strength to get up, fetching the robe he left for me. I cannot access our blood bond. Not that I would thank him since he doesn't remember. Somehow, I'd slip it into his blood like a lullaby of a prayer.

Attributing the lack of that bond to my current state, I simply throw the robe onto my back, fasten it, then curl onto the moss beside the Soul Pool, and whimper-cry her name:

Amanita...

She comes. At first, her hand hovers above my body just as I did for Bryony in the darkness of that dungeon.

"Sweet Ezer..." she whispers and carries me to her floating Valhalla island where I spend a full week grieving and healing. Now, I understand why she never wants to leave. Why it's her secret.

But I need to go.

"He has not been waiting for you, sweet angel," Nita explains, rubbing her hands along my arms as I stare out at the great, misting lake spread out like her own personal mantle upon which rests her castle.

"Why?"

She breathes a deep sigh and kisses the back of my head. "I am your ally, Elysia, but there are some laws that even I am bound to. The Triumvirate is one. And I cannot share certain secrets, however I may wish. But you are free to stay here as long as you desire. Perhaps I can plead you to him first."

"He still remembers you..." I trail off.

"Yes."

It's all she offers. To me, that's all that matters.

Sealing my determined lips, heart resolved, I command, "Take me back to Court, Nita. I am going to capture my husband."

"That's my girl."

We arrive at the Tenth Court Commons at the cusp of nightfall with the blood moon high and blotting the sky with its crimson beams. It's been a solid week since Neo has seen my face. What's happened to him? Why isn't he waiting for me? That familiar ache throbs through my being, the same undeniable homing beacon drawing me to that shadow door.

There's only one way to find out. Nita doesn't ask if I want her to come. My oath. My bond. If I'd wanted her to come, I'd have said so.

Some things never change. Spitfire pounces on me as soon as I enter the room, tail swinging. At least he looks...healthy. Neo has maintained the bargain and given him meaty table scraps, but I can tell by the dim glow in my hellcat's stomach that he's been waiting for me. So, I oblige him with an extra-large pile of Halo flames, shift them into my suite, and close the door behind him.

Neo's shades nip at my bare feet, but far more have gathered around the bed. On the far end, on Neo's side is the large shape of his powerhouse of a body beneath the bejeweled coverlet that betrays his presence. Our blood bond lingers, so why can't I hear him in my mind?

As soon as I peel away the coverlet, I understand why. My scream catches in my throat. I leap back, hands flying to my heart to protect the pure muscle, to cling to the ring as I behold the naked woman sleeping next to *my* husband!

Young and pale and beautiful and silvery as a star. And gloriously scarred, for she wears her trauma on the *outside* of her body. Each one of her scars echoes a hundred fang bites... and *one*. From Neo's recent mark in her throat. Pain converges at the back of my neck. I work harder than ever to contain my urge to convulse.

The girl stirs, but Neo doesn't because he's blood-drunk. Only she opens her eyes to me, shooting wide irises of pure gold. She puts her ruined finger to her lips in a silent hush, then tiptoes multiple fingers along the naked lines of *my* Neo and touches the Halo brand in his flesh. "I am Lux," she whispers. "Neo's very first bride. Father forced him to destroy me, but I crawled all the way out of hell and sought the blessing of the Goddess. She blessed me with immortality and the halo in my heart! And I used it to give Neo a new one!" She taps *my* Halo brand and hints at the foreign beating heart that thrums beneath his chest.

My Halo radiates from mine, ready to rage an inferno!

She presses her hand to her chest above her bountiful breasts and summons an inner glow. A faux halo that reeks of the Father's Creator power.

I blow righteous fury through my nostrils as Lux sing-songs sweet to my ears, "Neo's told me all about you, *Elysia*. And even if I am his first wife and the true Halo-Bearer, even though he is truly all *mine*, I do not mind sharing. We will be sister-brides!"

THOUGH THE BLOOD OATH SCRAWLS A WARNING OMEN TO RETURN TO the bed, I seek out the Father. Rage pumping in my veins. This time, Thanatos does not need to show me the way. No, he's quieter than ever.

I waste no time before charging into the Father's inner suite and lashing out, "What. In. The. Hell?"

The Father cackles from the bed, lodged between multiple naked demonesses. "Hell is right, little angel!"

I swing my hand around one bedpost and sibilate with a crouch, "You think that cheap, imitation, silicone glowing hussy can compete with a *real* Halo-bearer?" I project my Halo in deadly throwing stars that stab every demoness whore and snarl-scream, "Challenge accepted!"

I HAVE NO CHOICE BUT TO RETURN TO THE BED. THE NOTION MAKES ME want to spit flames, but I will not break my vow. No matter how far I've come, the urge of Flight rears her ugly head.

After I crawl into the icy bed, after I spread the sheets over my skin, Neo appears at the back of my neck, his mouth voyaging across my curls, a threatening promise.

"*Elysia...*" he growls my name, sweeping aside my curls, fangs unleashed and ready to bite me. Violence flushes his pupils...a stoked and entirely unexpected hatred.

"Oh, yes! Bite her, Neo," Lux lilts in a starry soprano. "She and I can match at Court!"

I snap! Familiar fight or flight.

Every last ounce of my Halo power bursts from my body in furious flames that burn Lux's silver song hair. I glory in the sound of her scream.

Neo grips my throat while he snarls, but I check him with our blood oath. "No touchies, *husband!*"

Pain thunders into my neck right before I pass out...no! Damn it all to hell, I pass *in!*

The world shifts, turning upside down, welcoming me into its shadowy embrace. Reality is paralyzed before the throne of the Soul Plane. I pass into the blissful sanctum of that tremulous dark haze, adorned in my soul flesh and skin, my soul form of a burning ember star.

Before I can even consider moving from the bed, Thanatos' icy arms surround me—a deep tomb with no opportunity of escape. For I cannot run from Death. His breath is a seductive reap on my neck, a dark Scheherazade symphony when he threateningly promises, "*Elysia*...you will not escape me here. Tonight, you will *sleep* with me behind you."

Sighing in surrender, I close my eyes to his nebulous force. To that hand secured around my waist. To that hand that sweeps away my curls so he may kiss the brand that he transcribed into my flesh when he bit me. I shiver. Tonight, his fangs slow-drag along my throat but only a luring, future promise. No, he won't bite me. He will *savor*.

I crane my neck. My solar eclipse eyes greet Thanatos' black hole orbs in a deadly stalemate. I will not shine for him. He will not release me. Tonight, he has Elysia.

So, I will savor, too. I can't get out. So, I go *in*! Dig in deep like a tick.

I live inside my trauma. He breathes the other powerful twin names against my skin: *Noralice*. I dry heave and tremble. Bolts of panic sear the back of my neck. I'm all curled in an Elysia-shaped ball, shivering from goosebumps, every one bearing the memories of that night.

Until...Thanatos' frost injects into my spine, a prickling lullaby. Chilling me. Stilling me. Freeing me of the pain. Déjà vu from that time in the Tower when he bit me, when I gave him the memory.

I turn to him again, asking about the quietude, how he stemmed my panic attack, "How did you—"

"I *see* you, my love." Thanatos prints his beauteous mouth, a twin echo of Neo's, to the side of my neck. He kisses the site of the very first bite, his frost promising a claim to the rest. "Sleep, Elysia," he whispers his reaping into my heart...

And I fall asleep to his soul—loveliest, darkest, and deepest.

End of...Book One
Keep reading for a sneak peek of book two!
*REMEMBER: Reviews mean the WORLD to authors. If you enjoyed, please support by rating and reviewing on Amazon. It can be one line!
FYI: Please connect with me if this book brought you healing... Share on your Booktok, and I'd love for you to tag me @authoremilybshore!
If you're interested in seeing exclusive art, spicy bonus scenes, ARC access, please consider supporting me on Kindle Vella with your vote aka Top Fave crown. *USA only for now* Or find me on REAM. Connect with me to learn more!
Tempting Death and Destruction is coming to KU/paperback
11/23.
Hunting Death and Destruction is coming to KU/paperback
12/23
Redeeming Death and Destruction is coming to KU/paperback
1/24

WANT TO READ THE ***CROSSOVER*** SERIES? YES, ELYSIA AND NEO AND co. paths will cross with Astraea and Lucifer and co. and *The Sacrifice*, a brand new release trending on KU and a Top 25 release for Dragons.

BRIDE OF LUCIFER ON KU/PAPERBACK

Spicy dystopian fantasy—18+.
Lucifer opens Hell on Earth—a tourist trap on steroids—then hosts Trials to find a new bride.
To end the war between heaven and earth, one sweet but psycho angel assassin must conquer the Bride Trials, survive the wedding, and make it to the honeymoon and kill the Devil...
Unless she falls for him!
THE SACRIFICE: A Dark Dragon Fantasy Romance –

ON KU/ PAPERBACK/ HARDCOVER/ DECORATED EDGES

"Don't you know better than to play with monsters?"
Perhaps I'd rather play with the monsters than kill them. But loving them is suicide by sacrifice. Lucky, I'm not looking for a happily ever after.
I'm looking for a dark and dangerous once upon a time…

ACKNOWLEDGMENTS

For my *Roseblood* books which paved me the way for this book. (Yes, this series is technically a prequel, but I'd prefer everyone read *Courting Death and Destruction* first to see me, my true identity which hadn't surfaced before 2020).

For the books that triggered me so much (no, I'm not sharing, if you know me, you know): you gave me so much angst and righteous anger, I needed to write CDnD, and my heart awoke and bled all over the page. My triggers turned into healing, the courage to come out as bisexual, awareness of my strength, and my first tattoo!

For my first Court, including the ones no longer with me: you were there devouring the chapters as fast as I could write them. I'll never forget all the deep feels and how we made a tiny, intimate, and special community together.

For my second Court, Court O' Crazy: thank you so much for threatening to kidnap and torture me, to crush my legs, or to create a SIM's of me and lock me in a burning room with no doors and no locks if I didn't release this. If you still need to do the last for cathartic reasons, I give you my blessing. Thank you for becoming my sisterhood, for being the best cheerleaders and supporters in every way. I promise if I become an international bestseller, I'm getting a place where we can all meetup and laugh and cry and hug together just like we do in Messenger.

Special thanks to two significant readers: you told me

you read CDnD on a very dark night where you thought about ending it. It melted my heart to learn that my words saved your life and that you found your own inner halo.

For the DID community: I may struggle with dissociation, but you and you alters with your amazing and beautiful stories became the key for this book series, and I never could have finished it without you. To the DID sensitivity readers who fell in love with my Amanita who is truly my favorite character I have ever written. If you have DID and you or you alters ever want someone to talk to, I would be honored to connect with you.

For the Kindle Vella Community: From the moment I contacted KDP, and they told me I was a Kindle Vella bestseller, I was over the moon! Special thanks to this platform, for giving me the opportunity to launch with you in 2021, for those who have voted for me week in and week out to keep me in the Top 25/Top 10/Top 5 for the past two years. To the readers and authors who have supported me and fallen in love with my Vella babies. **You funded:** my husband's cancer surgery/chemo medical bills, hospitalization bills for my blood clots, daycare for our littlest daughter so I could write full time and follow my dream, professional editing, formatting, covers, so many beautiful art pieces, and of course: my caffeine addiction. (*If you're interested in supporting me on Kindle Vella, crowns help most! Connect with me on FB to see some exclusive NSFW UNCENSORED art.)

To my oldest daughter, Emmyleigh: while you can't read this book yet, I've shared special scenes and the storyline with you. I love how you ask about the Princess and the Dragon more than any other book. You've even helped me brainstorm since you are a budding author. And you'll have a mother who will always tell you to keep writing and doing what you love.

To my husband: for that night on the porch and then that night in the garage.

To anyone who is struggling with their identity or with trauma: the major themes of this book are light in the darkness, finding your voice and strength, and embracing your inner halo. Your halo might be cracked, and your wings are broken or gone. But sometimes you need to fall to your knees before you can rise! To learn more of the story behind this book I wrote in three weeks with its sequels back to back but took three years to release, please connect with me on Facebook, "Emily's Vella Verse".

ABOUT THE AUTHOR

Emily used to be the good little church-going girl who snuck peeks of smutty romance books at the store. Now, she proudly writes smut into fantasy and has forsaken the religious cult of her past.

In 2020, Emily found her voice while writing dark fantasy romance. In 2021, she rebranded on Kindle Vella and has been a Vella bestseller for two years. Her writing always features enemies to lovers featuring heroines who don't need a sword to be strong, "touch her and die" monsters and villains, and trauma healing.

An abuse survivor and trained advocate, Emily has worked as an awareness speaker all over Minnesota. Identifying as bisexual and feminist, she loves to showcase sex and kink positivity, trauma-overcoming themes beyond stereotypes, and LGBTQIA+ inclusivity.

When not writing enemies to lovers, Emily is addicted to the Enneagram, rewatching Schitts Creek, cuddling with her kitty, and spending time with her online sisterhood where she can exercise her big empath heart.

Emily lives in Saint Paul with her husband and two daughters. She loves to write at her local coffee shop where all the baristas know she's an author and have memorized her order. Emily is thankful she's far-sighted and can write her spicy scenes in small print while hiding her screen.